PROTECTING DESTINY

C. J. Corbin

ISBN: 1542730066
ISBN-13: 978-1542730068

Cover Design by Scarlett Rugers

Berliner Bear Publishing
BerlinerBearPublishing.com

DEDICATION

To
Nancy...

The foundation has been laid
...so we leave the details to God.

ACKNOWLEDGEMENTS

Tugaim mo chroi duit go deo...

As always, thank you to my sisters from different parents, Nancy, Robin, and Jennifer. Your support and love are what keeps me going.

To my editor, Cassandra Garofalo, you made it fun! Thank you for loving the characters like I do and for understanding me.

Thank you, Scarlett Rugers, you captured my heart in your cover design.

Thank you, Michelle Andrade, for the awesome back cover copy; you nailed the essence of the story.

Thank you to my alpha readers,
Cherlene Walmsley, Robin Walker, Nancy Merola, Cassie Garofalo
Your time and energy were invaluable!

To the San Diego Chapter of the Romance Writers of America, your camaraderie and support always lifts me. And a special thank you to Tameri Etherton for your 30-Minute a Day challenge!

Thank you to my niece Briana for naming Koa. Perfect!

Thank you to Dad and my sister Kim. Your love and belief in me makes this journey worthwhile.

I give my heart to you forever...

ALSO BY C. J. CORBIN

EAGLE'S DESTINY

REVEALING DESTINY

A NOTE TO THE READER

Canyon Lake, California ~ March 2017

My dear reader,

Tugaim mo chroi duit go deo...

The third Destiny book continues an animal conservancy theme and delves into the serious world of dog rescue. I urge you to be involved in your local animal shelters and rescue groups. The slogan, "Adopt, don't shop" is a real one. Both of my Cocker Spaniels are rescues, and they agree, rescues make some of the best pets.

Thank you for choosing this book to read. I write for you. I am an indie author, which means I do not have a big company backing me. While this allows me to make all the important decisions, (which I love because I'm a control freak) it also means I pay for them too. From the cover to the editor. So, my dear reader, if you find a typo or two ... or three ... please forgive me. A group of us combed through the manuscript countless times, and your eye may turn out to be sharper than ours are.

I always love to hear from readers! You can find the latest news and me on my website CJCorbin.com, and while you're there, you can click on my Facebook, Twitter, and Pinterest links.

I hope you enjoy this book, and yes, the fourth one is on the way!

I give my heart to you forever...

C. J.

"You are meant to be here. There are

no coincidences. It's all happening

the way it was meant to be."

Anthony Horowitz

CHAPTER 1

The tires screeched loudly when my foot slammed on the brakes. The idiot in front of me stopped suddenly, and the wet pavement put my Escalade SUV into a slide, and me in a panic. I tugged on the steering wheel to fight the spin and finally came to a halt in the middle of the dark mountain road. The late model black pickup truck with its red taillights glowing in the heavy rainfall paused for only a moment to open the cab door. A small bundle landed on the ground, and the truck sped away.

What the hell? My eyes fell on the little gray pile lying at the edge of the road. What was that? I squinted hard to try to see through the moving windshield wipers.

Shit! An animal!

Quickly turning on the emergency flashers, I leaped out. The rain pelted me hard as I knelt on the ground.

"Oh, sweet baby," I cried aloud.

Lit up by the headlights, a thin dog lay on the road whimpering. Visible all over its body were blood and bite wounds. A million thoughts rushed through my head, but the priority was to find help.

I grabbed the blanket and medical kit from the SUV's cargo area. While the rain pounded away on me, I found a roll of gauze and ripped off a long piece. Fashioning a muzzle around the dog's snout, I tied it lightly. The frightened look in the dog's eyes was apparent as he tried to move away from me.

Petting him, I spoke in soothing tones. "You're going to be okay, little fellow. Let me put you on this soft blanket." Lifting him gently, his shrill cry pierced through the sound of the storm. "I know it hurts," I murmured, "but, this is the only way."

He struggled, cried, and then gave up. I carried him to the car and placed him in the blanket on the front passenger seat. He seemed to understand that moving wasn't smart, but his soft brown eyes never left me. Soaked to the skin, I dripped water everywhere as I sat behind the steering wheel. The engine roared to life, and I pulled over to the side of the road.

Running my hands over my hair to pull it back off my face, I quickly dialed information on the cell phone. The computerized voice spoke over the car's speakers, "City, state, and name?"

"Mintock, California, Mintock Animal Hospital." I frowned at the multiple rings. Why did it take so long for someone to answer?

I loosened the muzzle, and the little dog did not move but watched me warily. He closed one eye when I scratched him behind one perky ear.

"I'll get you some help. Why did that nasty person do this to you?" I whispered, continuing to stroke him.

A bored voice finally answered the phone, "Mintock Animal Clinic."

"Hi, my name is Christina Hoffman. I have an injured dog. He's bleeding and needs medical attention. The guy in the pick-up in front of me threw him out of his truck. The bastard just drove off. Where are you located?"

"I'm sorry ma'am, but we're closing for the weekend. You'll need to take the dog to the emergency clinic down in Ashley. We have an affiliation with them. They'll send a report to Dr. McDermott. Let me give you the address. Do you have a pen?"

"No. You don't understand, this dog is wounded," I said irritably gripping the steering wheel tightly. "Ashley is too far to drive. It's pouring rain. He needs immediate medical attention."

"Ma'am, you don't understand. We do not have a vet here. We are closed now." The young woman's tone of voice challenged my patience.

I articulated my words slowly but kept them under control. I couldn't believe this girl was arguing with me. "Then call Dr. McDermott and get him to come in."

"I can't do that. We are closed. You will need to go to the hospital in Ashley. Do you want the address?"

"No, there's no time to get to the emergency clinic!" Now my patience was gone.

"Ma'am, please stop badgering me. You need to go to Ashley. Now, do you want the address? I'm not going to continue this conversation."

Fine, if she didn't want to talk to me. I pressed the disconnect button. What to do? I was wasting time. I hated going all the way to Ashley. Then a thought hit me. Michael would have the veterinarian's home telephone number. This was a small town. My brother was Mr. Social, and a famous animal conservationist; he would have the number ... I was sure of it.

Michael answered on the first ring. "Christina? Is everything okay?"

I sighed inwardly at my big brother who always worried. "I need the veterinarian's home telephone number."

"Is there something wrong with the dogs?" The alarm in his voice was unmistakable.

"No," I began and explained why I wanted it.

"Carrie at the office should be able to call Dr. McDermott."

This time I sighed aloud. "Look, the receptionist was not helpful at all. I need the phone number. Time is ticking."

I checked the dog, and he was still immobile but alert.

He chuckled softly, "So, you were your typical friendly and not demanding self on the phone?"

"Michael!" I implored.

Hearing the frustration in my voice, he relented, "Okay, here's the number."

I wrote the number down quickly. "Thank you. I'll call you later. I love you."

"I love you too. Now, go take care of the little dog."

I immediately dialed the vet's cell number, and he too answered on the first ring.

"Hello?" His voice was rich with an Irish lilt to it.

"Dr. McDermott," I used my pleasant voice, Michael had been right, I'd get more with honey than vinegar. "This is Christina, Michael Hoffman's sister. We met briefly at his house the night of his fiancé's accident."

"Ahh... yes, Christina. Please call me Kian, what can I do for you?"

Oh, his voice was like melted dark chocolate. "I know your clinic is closed, and I'm so sorry for calling you at home. I had to drag your number out of my brother, but I have an injured dog. I'm up here at the top of the mountain highway, and the person who drove in front of me discarded a small dog out of their truck. I saw it. The pick-up just drove off. I don't know how hurt the little guy is, but he looks battered. He's bleeding. I hate to ask you..."

He interrupted, urgently instructing me, "Get him to the hospital."

"Yes," I said breathlessly. "Please." I let the brake out and began to drive forward. "Ashley is so far. You're so close."

"I'll meet you there. Do you know how to get there?"

He quickly gave me directions, and my foot pressed hard down on the gas pedal.

"You're going to get some help little boy," I said to the dog who was now shivering on the blanket.

Both of us were drenched. Still dripping water, my blouse stuck to my skin. I tried to find a place on him that wasn't bloody. He didn't lift his head again while I stroked the small white patch on his chest.

I pulled into the parking lot of the clinic beside an old and beat-up, fire engine red pickup. Dr. McDermott jumped out of the truck and nodded his head when I pointed to the passenger seat. The pounding rain flooded

3

in when he opened the door.

He quickly assessed the dog and saw the makeshift muzzle, which he re-tied. "Smart," he commented. "I'll carry him in, will you catch the door?"

The doctor was fast. He had him scooped up in his arms before I had the chance to blink. I heard the howling cry of the dog while I ran to hold open the front door of the clinic. He rushed by me and began to shout orders.

"Carrie! Is Luke still here?"

"Yes, doctor. He's in the back." When she saw me, a frown filled her face. "I told her we were closed. I told her she should go to Ashley."

"It makes no never mind. Call Leonard. Get him in here," he called back to her as he disappeared past the swinging doors.

The receptionist glowered at me as she walked back to her desk and picked up the phone. I retrieved my purse from my car, and on my way back inside, I caught a glimpse of my reflection in the door's glass window. My shoulder length blond hair was plastered to my head, and my bra showed through the thin blouse. I looked like something the cat had dragged in.

"Leonard, Dr. Kian said to come in. We have an emergency. I know, but you know how he is. He's not going to turn anyone away." She continued to scowl at me. I felt like smirking at her, but I controlled myself.

Five minutes later, the swinging doors opened, and the doctor appeared carrying my blanket. I remembered him being handsome, but the view of him walking toward me made my breath hitch.

Handing a towel and wet wipes to me, he placed the blanket on the bench. "Thought you'd like to clean off."

Oh, I remembered him. His eyes were dark sapphire pools, and his short cropped, ink-black hair framed his chiseled face. The day-old beard didn't hurt his appearance either. The white coat over his jeans and t-shirt didn't hide his tall, muscular body, and it was clear he spent serious time in a gym.

I nodded mutely accepting the towel from him. "Thank you," I said clearing my throat.

"We've stabilized him, and we will take some x-rays to see the extent of his injuries. He seems to be a tough little dog." His melodic Irish accent made my knees weak. "Carrie will help you complete some paperwork. I'll be back out as soon as possible."

"Thank you, Dr. McDermott, I really appreciate this. I'm sorry to pull you away from your evening," I babbled.

"Not to worry Miss Hoffman, there was only a hockey game on TV tonight." He grinned, "As it happens, we have a fine television in the back." He turned to leave and then twisted back toward me. "And call me

Kian," he said winking.

I tried not to drool as I watched him walk away.

Carrie instantly pulled me back into reality. "He's too young for you."

"I'm sorry what?" She did not just say what I thought she said.

"He doesn't care for older women. Besides, he's used to having them drool all over him," she said flatly.

I stood there and blinked at her. Was I that obvious? I couldn't have been. I had hardly said anything.

The towel smelled clean, and while I dried my face with it, I hoped it had not been recently used to mop up animal mystery fluids. While folding the blanket, I used the time to think of a snappy come back to the young woman who sat expectantly behind the desk. If she said another nasty word to me, I would bitch-slap her into next Tuesday.

Finally, I calmly walked to the reception desk and looked at her with my best *I can crush you to dust* face. "I believe the doctor said that there are some forms to be completed?"

She didn't smile, but no further snarky comments came from her. "Your name and home address."

Hmmm... No please at the end of the sentence? She would not have lasted five minutes at my company.

"For the sake of repeating myself from my phone call, my name is Christina Hoffman. I'm Michael Hoffman's sister. You probably know who he is."

Carrie colored a bit at the mention of my brother's name. Yes, I smiled inwardly. That's right. The one you all salivated over last summer when he moved into town.

"Which address would you like? I have several homes."

She frowned at me, another spark of snarkiness rising in her eyes. Her dull brown eyes matched her boring brown hair. "Where you currently reside," she said with a tinge of impatience and mockery in her voice.

"Well my dear, I'm building a new home in Mintock. I guess you can use my brother's fiancé's home address since I'm staying there during the house construction. You know, he's getting married next weekend."

Carrie looked shocked but managed to hide it. "Oh, he is? He didn't mention it when he was here the other day."

"Oh yes, he has planned a beautiful surprise wedding for Elizabeth in New Orleans. Why don't we use her address?"

She looked down at the computer screen with a glum expression. "I'm sure the new couple will be very happy. When you see Michael, please wish him the best from me."

I didn't plan to remember her name that long. With the paperwork completed, I sat down on the bench to wait. The sounds of a hockey game floated out from the back room as well as different barking dogs. Instead of sitting at a veterinarian's office, I should have been on my way to San Francisco to stay in a cute little bed and breakfast before my flight to New Orleans in the morning. But, what could I do?

I traveled frequently. I had earned my fortune and fame by being a tech savvy internet whiz, which led to my current career as a financial investor in technology-rich companies. This was why I didn't have pets, kids, or anything else that would tie me down.

The front door to the hospital swung open with a hard whoosh, and the small bell attached to the bar across the door clanged when it hit the glass wildly. A large man who had probably seen too many pizzas and beer parties stomped in. His angry, blotchy red face looked like it was ready to explode. He only glanced in my direction and dismissed me immediately, which didn't surprise me considering I looked like a drowned rat.

The man fixed his hostile eyes directly on Carrie and given what I felt about her, I didn't blame him.

"Where is he?" he said between clenched teeth.

However, when I spotted the look of fear in her eyes, I almost raised up from the bench.

"Um, we're closed," she said with a small voice, no longer the arrogant receptionist.

He grunted while he headed for the swinging doors.

"You can't go back there!" she called out with alarm.

The man didn't bother to look back at her as he hit the door so hard it slammed against the wall.

"McDermott! I want my dogs!" His voice didn't belie the fury, which had been on his face.

The swinging door finally closed after it moved back and forth several times, but we could hear the conversation clearly.

"You have abused those dogs. You'll not be getting them back," Kian said in a clear and firm voice.

"They are my property! You will return them to me! You don't know who you are dealing with here," the man shouted.

"I know exactly who you are and what you do. I'm not going to let you abuse these dogs any further."

"Mark my word McDermott, you will return those dogs to me, and you will continue to treat any dog I bring in here. Don't mess with me, you won't like the results!"

The door swung open again just as hard as the first time and the man walked back out to the lobby. He didn't say a word but hit the front entrance open with his fist as he exited. I turned to look as it slowly closed, and he climbed into the same tricked out late model pickup I encountered earlier. This time I saw the license plate clearly, BIG ONE. My blood boiled! Who the hell was he?

Both Carrie and I sat there in silence. I didn't know what to say, and probably for the first time, she didn't either. Finally, the swinging door swished opened, and I looked up expectantly. A man in his forties walked out, with his name *Leonard* emblazoned on his tech coat. He had a smile on his broad dark face and warmth in his cocoa colored eyes.

"Miss Hoffman? Dr. Kian would like to speak to you in his office."

"Oh! Okay!" I stuffed my laptop into my bag and followed him back through a hallway door. I held my bag up against my chest. Although my blouse had dried a little, it was still damp and see-through.

The doctor's office was neat and orderly. His desk was a rich dark mahogany with a large black leather chair behind it. A soccer ball lay on the floor near the trash can under the credenza. On his desk sat a gray rock with the words *Blarney Stone* written in green, and a little leprechaun doll dressed in a t-shirt that said *Kiss Me I'm Irish*. He had a few more Irish souvenirs lying around along with several hockey pucks used as paperweights.

"Have a seat," Leonard said pointing to one of the guest chairs. "The doctor will be right in."

I nodded and thanked him as he left. When I turned to see the rest of the office, I noticed all the small photographs on a corkboard covering the opposite wall. All the photos were of different dogs, and each one had either saved or lost written with a black Sharpie in a neat scrawl on the bottom. Were these all the dogs he had treated? Surely, in a hospital the size of this one, he would have treated more dogs.

"Ahh, I see you've noticed my wall, Miss Hoffman," Kian said when he walked through the door.

I spun around quickly because I hadn't heard him coming in. I forgot to hold my bag against my chest until it was too late. He sat behind his desk with a small grin on his face.

"Please call me Christina. Are they all the dogs you've treated?" I asked pointing to the wall.

His manner turned serious, "In a manner of speaking, yes. They are all the dogs that I've rescued, or attempted to save."

"And the ones that say lost on them..." my voice trailed off.

His sigh was a profound one, "Those were the ones we couldn't protect." A shadow passed across his eyes, but it was there for only a moment. "Now then, let's talk about your little boy."

I sat as he rotated one of his computer monitors toward me and called up the x-rays. "He's a very lucky dog. He doesn't have any internal injuries, but see this," he pointed his pen tip toward the monitor, "there are two small breaks in his forearm." As he pointed to the screen, his sleeve moved up and revealed a small tattoo on his inner wrist. I had to tilt my head to see the shamrock.

Kian had beautiful hands, with long fingers and rounded nails cut close. I thought about what those hands could do and had to smack myself out of the fantasy. He stopped speaking in mid-sentence for a moment, and we both looked at each other. It was as if he read my mind. I almost blushed but controlled myself; after all, I wasn't sixteen any longer.

He cleared his throat. "We have three options," he continued, "we can let it go, and it will eventually heal, although he probably won't use the leg again," he paused.

"No," I replied firmly. "That's not an option."

He smiled, "I'm glad you think so. We could cast it. It would heal, but again he'd have a severe limp the rest of his life. He's a young dog and probably has many years ahead of him," he stopped again.

"And the third option is surgery?"

He nodded, "Aye, it is."

"Would you do the surgery?"

He hesitated before answering. "I could do it. But, I have a good friend at UC Davis who comes up here to help. She'll be glad to pop over here for a few hours. I've already spoken with her."

"And his other injuries? There was so much blood, and I saw several fierce bites."

Kian nodded again, "No doubt he was used for dog baiting."

"Dog baiting? What is that?"

His sigh was heavy and troubled, "There is a dog fighting ring in this area."

"Isn't that illegal?" I interrupted.

"It's a felony, but the clubs still proliferate." His Irish brogue became thicker. "They use strays, dogs from animal shelters or just plain steal them to toughen up their fighting dogs. Your little guy definitely was a stray."

"How can you tell?"

"The pads and nails on his feet are worn down." He pointed to his open palm as if to illustrate. "When an animal has been out on the street for a while you can see the wear. With wound treatment and antibiotics, he should heal well. We must remove his right earflap because it's only hanging on by a hair. It will give him character." Kian smiled warmly. "I'm glad that you insisted on bringing him here. We'll get him cleaned up, stabilize his leg, and do the surgery tomorrow."

"I'm sorry that you have to give up your weekend." I rose to my feet and stuck out my hand, "Thank you again for coming down here tonight, I appreciate it."

He stood and took my hand in both of his. I felt a strange tingling sensation run through me, his hands were warm and soft, yet I could feel the strength in them. My mind shot quickly again to thinking about his hands touching me, in very intimate ways. I almost had to shake my head to rid myself of the thoughts.

He was grinning; even his eyes were smiling. "Thank you, Christina. You're his angel of mercy. Without you, he would not have survived very long." His deep voice had a little purr. "Carrie will have some paperwork for you to sign, to authorize us to do the surgery."

Kian placed one hand on my back as he opened his office door and led me into the large room. That one gesture seemed so intimate to me. I'm sure he didn't think anything of it. For me, however, I could feel heat surging through my body and a sense of giddiness. A sensation I was not accustomed to experiencing. When his hand fell away, I was almost bereft. I missed the warmth.

"Please let me know how he's doing okay? I'm flying to New Orleans tomorrow morning for my brother's wedding, but you can reach me on my cell. I've given the number to your receptionist."

He smiled and took my hand in his again. His handshake was firm but not crushing. He wasn't trying to prove anything. "Don't worry, we'll take good care of your dog, and please give Michael and Elizabeth my best wishes."

I stopped at the table where they had placed the stray. The little gray body lay motionless with closed eyes while he breathed slowly.

"We've given him some pain medication," Leonard said as he glanced up from his paperwork.

Nodding, I petted the small dog's head. He opened his eyes briefly and stared at me. His scruffy tail wagged twice, and then his eyes closed again.

My breath hitched slightly, and I fought back the tears. "Take care little guy."

Kian led me out to the reception area. "I'll say good night to you here, Christina. We still have a bit to do before we lock up tonight."

I smiled, "Thank you again Dr. ..." I paused briefly, "Kian."

"I'll be in touch," he said as he disappeared back behind the swinging doors.

I turned toward the reception desk to find Carrie glaring at me again. What had I done to this hostile young woman?

"The doctor said there were some documents for me to sign."

"Yes." She laid them out in front of me. "They are financial responsibility documents indicating that you will pay for the surgery no matter what the outcome."

"Well of course," I answered tersely.

"I'll need a credit card for the fifty percent deposit."

"Put the entire amount on this." I handed her my black American Express card.

Her eyebrows rose, "The whole three thousand dollars?" she asked with incredulity.

"Yes. Is that okay? I expected it to be more expensive," I said signing the documents.

"Well, Dr. Kian gave you a discount, since the patient is a stray dog and you're taking the financial responsibility." She handed a flyer to me. "This is all about Harry's Hounds, the doctor's dog rescue organization. He works hard at getting corporate and private sponsorship. It helps with the bills to take care of all the strays he rescues. So many of them are injured and need medical help. He donates all of his time, but the drugs and supplies have to be paid."

Carrie surprised me. Her voice became quite animated as she spoke about the rescue group. Her brown eyes sparkled.

"What would have been the usual charge for a surgery of this type?" I asked.

"At least five to six thousand by the time everything is done."

"Wow! A fifty percent discount. Go ahead and put the entire charge on my card."

"Really?" she squeaked with excitement. "Okay!"

She didn't hesitate to run the card through the machine.

"This is very generous of you Miss Hoffman," Carrie said enthusiastically. Where was the young woman who insulted me when I first arrived?

"It looks like it goes to a worthy cause."

"Very much so." She smiled brightly. "I'm sorry for not being more helpful when you called, it's just that Dr. Kian is so kind, and he never turns down anyone who asks. He hardly ever gets any rest."

"You're protective over him."

"Well, kind of," she said, as a rosy blush appeared on her cheeks.

I nodded. Somehow, I understood and appreciated it.

"I've asked Kian to keep me up to date on the dog's progress."

She jumped in, "Oh! We'll do that for sure! Drive carefully. It's still pouring out there."

"Thanks." I stuffed the flyer and the rest of the paperwork into my purse, picked up the blanket from the bench and went out into the rain.

CHAPTER 2

My cell phone rang as I pulled up to the back of Elizabeth's cabin. "Let me call you in a few minutes Michael." I didn't wait for him to answer. I disconnected and made a run for the back porch in the rain.

My brother had installed a timer for the exterior lights on the cabin, and tonight I was glad for them since the neighborhood was without streetlights. With no moon, it was pitch black outside.

The cabin sat at the end of a utility road on the south side of Lake Mintock's shoreline. The town was located about two hours northeast of San Francisco. Michael's house was next door, and my newly constructed home was situated on the other side of his place. He hadn't been a happy camper when he discovered I had purchased the lot next to his. He had grand plans for buying the property himself and expanding his home after his marriage to Elizabeth.

The interior motion detection lights went on automatically when I opened the back door, which was another one of Michael's ideas. He did it mainly to allay Elizabeth's fear of going into the dark cabin, but truthfully, I was grateful for it too.

The small single story cottage had two bedrooms. I felt odd about using Elizabeth's former bedroom even though she offered, so instead, I used the guest room to the right of the kitchen.

Throwing my purse on the bed, I pressed my brother's name on my phone while sitting to kick off my heels. Michael's face and a bare chest filled the tiny screen.

"Hey," he said.

"Are you naked?" I said with disbelief.

He smirked, the area around his light blue eyes crinkling. He panned the camera down to show his pants. "I will be as soon as we get off the phone. Elizabeth's in the bathroom, and I plan on getting it on tonight."

I winced as if in pain. "Stop it! Stop it right now! I don't want to hear about you getting it on, at any time. How is Elizabeth? How is she feeling?"

"She's okay. The morning sickness seems to be going away." His fiancé's four-month pregnancy had put her through all sorts of difficulties.

"How's her ankle?"

Elizabeth recently had a scare after she fell from a tree while she was watching the eagles that lived on Mt. Mintock. The accident resulted in a severe sprain, but we were all thankful she and the baby were not injured more seriously.

"I'm making her wear the boot or, at least she does when she doesn't complain too loudly about it. It still gets sore, so if she can stay off it or wear low heels, all the better," he reported.

"Has she gotten a whiff yet of the wedding you're planning for the two of you next Sunday?"

Several months ago, when Elizabeth discovered she was pregnant, Michael asked her to marry him. After she had tumbled from the tree, a bout of cold feet hit her, and she called off the engagement. My brother was going to propose to her again during their stay in New Orleans while they attended the wedding of their two best friends. If she agreed, they would be married there. I volunteered to help even though it was an outlandish idea.

He lowered his voice, "No, she remains clueless as ever. Thank you for getting the dress to the seamstress."

"You didn't see the gown, did you?"

He smiled, "No. I promised I wouldn't peek at it until next Sunday. You know I'm as good as my word."

"Yes, you are."

"How'd it go with the injured dog? Were you able to reach Kian?"

"Yes." I related the story to him. "I'm relieved to know the little dog would be okay."

"You did your good deed today. Kian will take great care of him."

"Who are you talking to?" It was Elizabeth's voice in the background, and then her face filled the screen. "Hi, Christina! It will be good to have you here tomorrow. Marcus is going nuts with the wedding plans, and Nancy is going crazy with his mother, Simone. If this continues, one of them might not make it to the church. The drama is real." She giggled.

Marcus, my brother's best friend, was marrying Elizabeth's friend and agent, Nancy the following Friday. I marveled at what a small world it was because if Elizabeth had not met Michael, then Marcus would have never met Nancy. If Marcus hadn't met her, it was possible he would have continued to pursue me. Thankfully, he was head over heels in love. Even though Marcus and I had a brief, albeit fun affair, I too was invited to the wedding. The outrageous thing? I was going.

After we had finished our call, I had one more to make. I pressed JuJu's name on my phone, and my personal assistant answered immediately. Her face appeared on the screen while she stuffed a slice of pizza into her mouth.

"Hey boss lady!" she exclaimed between chews. "I didn't expect to hear from you until tomorrow. Shouldn't you be at the cute little bed and breakfast I booked for you in San Francisco? Check in time was four o'clock." She looked at her watch. "Which was four hours ago."

I scrubbed my face with my hand. "Yeah, I know. I was waylaid here in Mintock."

"Is it a problem with the house construction?"

I explained the story yet again.

Her soft brown eyes looked sad. "Is the doggy going to be okay?"

"Yes. The dog needs surgery, but the veterinarian assured me he's going to be good. Listen, it's too late for me to drive to the airport tonight, I need to get some sleep. Call the inn and let them know I won't be able to make it, so they don't wait for me. Then put me on the ten forty-five flight tomorrow morning out of San Francisco to New Orleans."

"But that won't get you into New Orleans until six forty-five," she countered.

"The party doesn't start until eight. I'll change on the plane. Could you text Michael and Marcus with the flight information, so they are aware?"

"Yes, ma'am." She took a large drink of beer from her mug.

"I'm sorry to bother you with all this on a Friday night."

"Com'on Christina, I know it's part of my job. I don't mind."

"Still, I do appreciate it." I hesitated, "And there's one more thing I'd like you to do."

JuJu grinned, "There always is."

"Get me the data on an organization called Harry's Hounds. They are a..."

"A rescue group," she interrupted. "They rescue dogs. I've heard of them, and I've seen them on Facebook."

"Hmmm... Facebook? Interesting, find out what you can."

"Will do. Anything else?" She took another bite of pizza.

"Nope. That will cover it. Thanks again JuJu and I'll see you later next week."

She smiled broad enough to make her dimples appear. "You know where to find me until then. Let me know if you need me to bring anything else with me."

"I will. See you soon," I said before we disconnected.

As I rose from the bed, I caught a glimpse of myself in the large oval mirror standing by the bedroom door. The night had taken its toll. I looked awful.

My gaze traveled downward to my rain soaked blouse, it was see-through as it clung to my skin. I was tall like my brother and had the same sky blue eyes, sandy blond hair, and deep-set dimples. There the comparison ended. Where my brother was lean and muscled, I was not. I was curvy with big boobs. As much as I tried to lose a few pounds, they always managed to creep back on. My thighs rubbed together. There, I said it. My. Thighs. Rubbed. Together. I would never be a size six, or even a size eight. I was perpetually stuck at a twelve.

At least my curves were firm, and they didn't jiggle. I could use a bit more exercise ... I blew out a big breath and shuddered. I needed to stop having thoughts like that.

CHAPTER 3

The big black limo whisked me away from the airport toward New Orleans. The ever efficient and friendly Russell, who was Simone and Marcus' chauffeur, found me at baggage claim and safely seated me inside the car before he collected my suitcases. Even now that I was here, I wasn't sure how I felt about attending Marcus and Nancy's wedding. Of course, I had to be here for Michael, but even before we discussed having his wedding here, I had already accepted Marcus' invitation.

Elizabeth had quelled most of my fears and told me that Nancy had approved the guest list, including the other ex-girlfriends. Not that I had any feelings for Marcus other than friendship, but it was still awkward. At least it was for me. I would never invite my ex to my wedding if I ever had another one. I broke out in a smile, and a small giggle escaped my lips. No, I was confident my ex-husband would never want to see me again.

Russell glanced in the rearview mirror at me. Neither of us had rolled up the privacy screen.

"Did you say something, Miss Christina?"

I smiled and shook my head. "No Russell. Just glad to be back in your beautiful city."

His face filled with a wide grin, "There are some big doings up at the house this week. Mr. Marcus has hired five other drivers, and Mr. Frederick is doing the schedule. It sure is crazy!"

I knew the unflappable Frederick, who was the majordomo of the house, had everything firmly under his control. Nothing ever escaped his notice. He and Marcus' mother Simone ran a tightly organized household.

"I have no doubt that it's all exciting," I said.

"After I drop you at the party, I'll bring your suitcases to the hotel. You've already been checked in, and I have your card key."

"Thank you, Russell. I'm always impressed with the hospitality here."

My phone rang, and as I reached into my pocket, the screen between us discreetly closed.

"Hello?" I answered.

"Hello, Christina." Kian's velvet smooth voice greeted me.

"Oh, hello." My heartbeat quickened, and I swallowed hard. Trying to sound casual, I managed to croak out, "Um, how is the little stray?"

He laughed a little, "Your little stray is doing excellent. He came through the surgery and is waking up now. We're putting a little cast on him. Do you have a favorite color?"

"I do love the color of sapphires." I wanted to bite my tongue after I said it. Why did I have to mention the color of Kian's eyes? Big black leather limo seat, swallow me now. "Um, you know, blue," I stuttered on. I felt like a stumbling teenager.

"Well now, I think I know that color." And, there was the beautiful Irish accent. "I do believe we have cast material in the color of sapphires. You also need to name your little guy too. We can't keep calling him Dog Doe you know. You give it some thought, and when I call to give you the update tomorrow, you can let me know then."

My only thought was, oh goodie! Kian will be calling tomorrow! After we had disconnected, I felt a giddy rush. My heart was still beating fast. What was this? Schoolgirl crush? I was old enough to be his ... his older sister. I had to stop reacting to him every time I saw or spoke to him. I cleared my throat and tugged at my tight little black cocktail dress, which had inched up over my thighs. It wouldn't be good to flash the party attendees as I exited the limo.

Russell pulled up in front of Delmonico's. Marcus had reserved the entire restaurant for his pre-wedding party. Since he was the city's District Attorney, there were notable New Orleans' famous in attendance, which brought the paparazzi who were thick as flies on sugar. The flashes ignited when Russell opened the door for me. Legs together, I attempted a graceful exit from the car, but my saviors were there. Both Michael and Marcus were suddenly standing in front of the open door and reached in to lift me up on my feet.

Hugging them both, I whispered between them, "Thank you, guys! It's a good thing you are here or my hoo-haw would be on the front page of the Sunday morning paper."

I heard them both chuckle as they ushered me into the restaurant which was already in full party mode. The music was pumping, and the traditional layout had been changed to accommodate the standing room only crowd in the front room.

Marcus slipped his arm around my shoulders. "Com'on, I'm excited to introduce you to Nancy. You will love her!"

For as long as I've known Marcus, he always exuded sexual prowess from every pore. He could easily capture any woman he happened to fancy. Tall and dark-haired, his dark eyes shouted, *Come on over here! You know you want to.* I knew too about the six-pack under his shirt, and the marvels his body could bring. With all of that, still, he was too controlling for my tastes. And, he was tied to the city since he was the DA. As much as I loved The Big Easy, I could only take the weather in small doses. Somehow, we never fit correctly, Marcus, the weather, and me.

He led me over to a petite dark-haired woman with bright eyes and an engaging smile. Even though surrounded by a crowd, when she saw us approach, she held out both arms to me. "You must be Christina! I would recognize those Michael dimples anywhere!"

I grinned while Nancy enveloped me in her arms and gave me a hug. In those few seconds, she managed to allay all my fears and removed any awkwardness I had felt. There was an acute awareness in her eyes. She knew the score, but I could tell in those seconds that it didn't bother her. She had captured the hunter. He was hers now. Totally.

After she let go of the embrace, Marcus slipped his arm around her and pulled her close. "This is *Ma Petite*." He beamed as he said Nancy's nickname.

Nancy and Marcus met the previous autumn when Michael had set up the meeting with his New Orleans's friends. Nancy was Elizabeth's literary agent, and they had been touring the country promoting Elizabeth's newest romance novel.

An arm draped over my shoulders from behind. I recognized the scent, Coco Chanel. My arm enfolded her waist.

"Elizabeth!" I looked down. She had a pair of strappy, low-heeled sandals on her feet. "Where is your boot?"

She giggled and looked sheepish, "I am not going to wear the boot here. I clomp in that thing. I'm clumsy already, and it will make me fall for sure. Besides my ankle is healing well and the doctor said if I was careful and wore flat shoes I'd be okay." Her emerald-colored eyes flashed their stubbornness.

I don't think Elizabeth ever realized what type of an impression she made. When I first met her last Thanksgiving, I knew Michael had found the one. Almost six feet tall, with wavy, burgundy colored hair that fell to her waist and a face that a goddess would weep for, she made a good match to my blond-haired, blue-eyed brother. They were striking together, and they made heads turn. She wore a tight little black cocktail dress with the sandals, and although she was only five months into her pregnancy, the tiny baby bump was evident, especially when she kept her hand on it stroking lightly. When Michael joined our tight little circle, his hand possessively replaced hers over the bump.

"How is the dog you rescued last night?" Michael asked.

"Kian called me on the ride in from the airport. The surgery went well," I replied.

Michael nodded, and I saw Elizabeth's eyebrow rise in amusement.

"Kian?" she said with a smirk. "So you're on a first-name basis with the hunky veterinarian?"

My face bloomed with color. "Well ..." I stammered, "he asked me to call him Kian."

"Funny," Elizabeth said, looking over at Michael for emphasis, "he is still Dr. McDermott to me."

He laughed and pulled her closer to kiss the top of her head. "And he should stay that way with you. There will be no drooling by you over the new pretty boy in town."

"A girl can dream." She sagged in a mock faint.

Marcus and another man joined our group. Michael nodded to the stranger and held out his hand. "Scott, I didn't think you'd be able to make it down for the wedding."

"You know I wouldn't have missed a good time like this," he said shaking his hand.

My brother turned to Elizabeth and me. "This is an old college friend of ours, Scott Binder. We attended Santa Cruz together and then he and Marcus were in the same class at law school. Scott, this is my fiancée, Elizabeth, and my sister, Christina."

Scott's grip was one of power. Saying it was firm was an understatement, and his sharp and calculating amber eyes caught mine as we shook hands. Over his white collared shirt, he wore a navy-blue sports coat that blended with his earth brown colored hair, cut in a manner, which invited you to run your fingers through it. Well assembled with his dark denim pants and the navy calfskin leather Berluti loafers, he managed to look dressed but casual at the same time. His name was familiar to me and not because he was my brother's friend. I searched my memory to find why I knew his name.

Marcus laid his arm over my shoulder and whispered in my ear, "Big time corporate attorney for Silicon Valley, he specifically asked to meet you."

Bingo! That's where I had heard his name before. Inwardly I sighed and tensed myself, so what else was new? Someone trying to get in on the game. My game.

Marcus squeezed my shoulder and pointed to the next room. "We have tables set-up in the room over there. *Chér*," he said looking at Elizabeth, "I'm sure you want to get off your feet. I'll send over a waiter for your drink orders. Tommy and Marie should arrive shortly too, and *Ma Petite* will be joining you in a while. I expect her to tire out. She's still not used to our humidity here," he drawled in his soft southern accent. He was always the most gallant of the three friends.

Elizabeth, with a grateful expression on her face, leaned on Michael and limped toward the room.

Left with Scott standing next to me, and deciding to give him a break, I said, "I hope you'll join us."

His face brightened as he held out his arm for me to take. "I'd love to. I wanted to meet you."

I slipped my hand around his elbow, and we walked companionably. "Oh?" I raised an eyebrow. "Why is that?"

His amused face was infectious, and I gave him a toothy smile back.

"I've been an admirer of yours for quite some time. I was with AppSoft when you were negotiating with them to sell your company Find-It! You were brilliant, and looking back, I know they did not expect you to outmaneuver them. It was a billion-dollar deal, and you became a wealthy and famous woman." His shrewd comment was on the money accurate.

"Before I gave up control of my company, which was the love of my life, I wanted to make sure they were going to treat it properly."

He pulled out a chair at the table for me. "I think it was more than that," he stated as he sat next to me. "You brought legitimacy to the world of on-line search engines. You showed the industry with the right product you could give users a great tool and sell a ton of advertising. Tell me, do you ever miss helming the ship?"

"I didn't exactly run away from it. While I no longer have a controlling interest in Find-It!, I am on the board of directors of AppSoft and have shares in both companies. It's always a good idea not to put all your eggs in one basket."

The waiter stopped by our table to take our drink order, and the conversation turned naturally to the wedding.

True to Marcus' word, Tommy, the third man who made up my brother's trio and his wife Marie joined us soon after we sat. Tommy headed up the University of New Orleans's doctorate marine biology program and was one of the country's foremost experts on alligators. Of the three guys, he was always the most relaxed and casual with his country-southern style. I had to think hard about a time when I didn't see him in jeans and a t-shirt with his shaggy chestnut hair always looking in need of a trim. Marie, on the other hand, was a statuesque beauty with burnished copper hair and a mass of freckles. When she gave out her substantial hugs, she managed to squish everyone into her ample cleavage.

Marie and I had been in close contact over the phone during the past several weeks while I helped Michael plan his surprise wedding. Even as we talked about Marcus' wedding, we had to be careful not to let on about the other wedding hoping to take place on the following Sunday. Michael likened Elizabeth to a frightened colt, and he was afraid if she had even one whiff of what we were planning before he was ready to reveal the idea, she would immediately leave New Orleans.

Throughout the evening, the boys kept me busy on the dance floor, especially Scott, who as it turned out was quite appealing. Coincidentally, he was staying at the Ritz Carlton too and gallantly offered to escort me back to the hotel. I did inwardly giggle at the invitation considering Russell was driving the limo. Somehow, New Orleans spread a gracious southern charm over men like the thick powdered sugar over a beignet.

Once inside the hotel lobby, Scott pointed to the Davenport Lounge. "Would you like to have a nightcap? I don't feel like ending the evening."

It would have been normal for me to decline, but I knew Jimmy, the trumpeter who played the lounge. He was a friend, and whenever I visited New Orleans, I would try to connect with him at least once. Since I was still on Pacific time and not tired, I nodded my head in agreement. Although it didn't surprise me the room was full, we found an empty couch near the back.

When the cocktail waitress approached us, Scott looked at me and asked, "May I?"

Intrigued, I nodded.

"We'll both have the Nolet's Reserve on the rocks." He smiled at my raised eyebrows.

"A man who knows gin." I laughed, "And, probably the most expensive gin in the world. How did you know the Ritz would have it?"

He gave me a conspiratorial wink, "I don't want to give all my secrets away."

I lifted my eyebrow again, "And, you knew I liked gin. Well done."

His smiled turned self-satisfied.

We sipped our gin and listened to the music. Sitting together on a couch designed for two made it close quarters, and it would not be exaggerating to say it was clearly an intimate setting. Eventually, Scott's arm slipped around my shoulders as he ordered another round for us.

When the musicians took a break, he turned his attentive gaze toward me. His eyes matched the golden colored gin we drank.

"I suppose your entire week is taken with both weddings?" he asked.

"Yes, I'm afraid it is. I hope you'll be able to stay for Michael's wedding. I'm sure he would love to have you there."

Scott smiled, "He has already extended an invitation to me, and I am delighted to be included. Perhaps it will give us more time to get to know each other."

I took a sip from my glass and teased back, "Perhaps."

"How is it that we never met? I spent a lot of time with the guys in college."

"I was Michael's bothersome younger sister. By the time I entered college, you and Marcus were already in law school. Then I buried myself in my studies."

"And, your work. Your brother always spoke so highly of his brilliant sister. You're four years younger than him?"

"If that's a sly way of figuring my age, I'll just tell you, I'm turning forty this year."

"And no children?"

I looked down at my drink to hide my expression and took another sip before I answered. "Nope. No kids."

He stared intently. There was silence between us, but before it became awkward, he spoke again. "You sound regretful."

I took a deep breath, "No regrets. It didn't happen for me. By the time I decided that it might be good to have children," I paused and cleared my throat, "I was thirty-nine."

"You know, it's not too late for you." He picked up one of my curls and twirled it around his finger.

I slipped my hair from his fingers and tucked the long blond strand behind my ear. "No, it's not. Are you volunteering?" I laughed heartily trying to break the subdued mood.

He smiled broadly and winked, "Would you like me to volunteer? We could start tonight." He raised his eyebrows in a suggestive manner.

I smirked at him, "Um no, Mr. Binder, as much as you are trying to get into my executive suite this evening, that's not going to happen."

He laughed at the double entendre and jokingly leered back at me. "Well, maybe not tonight. You can't blame a guy for trying."

I finished my glass and reached over to put it on the table. Scott took the tumbler from me, "Would you like another?"

"No, I better not. I have a lot of errands tomorrow and should call it an evening." I moved to stand.

He took my hand, "I'd like to see you again."

"Oh, I'm sure our paths will cross during the next several days."

"No," he said more adamantly, "You know what I mean."

I stood with my hand still in his. "I'm throwing a little party in my suite tomorrow night. Why don't you come? It will be an intimate group, the guys, and their women. I've also invited Jimmy," I pointed to the trumpeter on stage. "There is a billiards table in the suite and a beautiful terrace. It will be a chance to relax. About six o'clock?" I squeezed his hand. "Thank you for the fun evening."

He stood, "You know the performer on stage?"

"Yes, I do," I replied. "Jimmy is a friend of Tommy and Marcus."

"Thank you for the invitation. That would be great. May I escort you to your room?"

"No, that's not necessary."

21

"I insist."

I sighed inwardly as we started walking toward the elevator. I dug out the card key Russell had given to me since it was needed in the elevator to go to my floor.

Scott looked amazed when he realized where my suite was located. "You have the whole floor?"

"Yep." I answered and smiled, "It's a large airy space."

When the elevator doors opened onto a small hallway, only my door was straight ahead.

"Shall I come in and make sure everything is okay?"

I put my hand on his shoulder to stop him from exiting the elevator. "No. Definitely not necessary. I'm familiar with the suite, I've stayed here before."

He nodded and stepped back. "I'll see you tomorrow night."

I was surprised but happy that he gave up so quickly. I waved as the elevator doors closed to take him to his floor.

Sighing, I shook my head whispering. "Oh, brother."

The suite was impressive by any standard. A formal dining room, master bedroom with an ensuite bathroom, a huge living room complete with an antique billiards table, and the best part was a lovely terrace overlooking the river. It was at least three times the size of my first apartment.

Russell had been thorough. My luggage was in the bedroom. Rounding the corner into the dining room, I found a plate of freshly baked pecan sugar cookies on the table. I smiled widely. These were special because they came directly from Marcus' family kitchen.

A handwritten note next to the plate read ... *A sweet treat for the best sister in the world. Cook made them especially for you. Thank you for everything you do. Love you, Michael.*

I bit into a cookie. "Oh..." I exclaimed, "these are so amazing."

I retrieved my cell phone out of my purse. A simple *Call me* text from JuJu flashed on the screen. I checked the time, it was before eleven in San Francisco, and I hit the screen for the call.

"Hey, boss lady," JuJu's enthusiastic voice answered. "How's Nawlins?" She drew out the words.

"Humid," I answered simply.

She laughed, "Yeah, there's always a trade-off isn't there?"

"What do you have for me?"

"I did the search on Harry's Hounds and your doctor Kian."

I interrupted, "He's not my Kian."

Her smile turned into a devilish grin. "Whatever you say, but he is one fine piece of man."

"You saw a picture of him?"

"All over his Harry's Hounds page on Facebook. He is a big hero. He has over two hundred fifty thousand likes on his page."

"Wow! That is impressive."

"Harry's Hounds is a non-profit that rescues dogs and then re-homes them. They have a few corporate sponsors, but most of the donations come from individual contributors.

He works out of his home in Mintock, which he recently purchased, his first house by the way. He currently is a contracted employee at the hospital. But has agreed to buy the business when the owner is fully retired.

He received his bachelor's degree with a full scholarship from UCLA, and his veterinarian degree from UC Davis, which is considered the best veterinary school in the country. And his grades were excellent. He graduated at the top of his class.

The doctor is known for his pro-bono work too. He regularly volunteers at zoos and sanctuary shelters. I bet your brother loves that!"

He's not married and never has been. And he's young." JuJu raised her eyebrows at me.

"How young?" He couldn't be that young, he had gone to school after all.

She laughed, and the grin returned, "Very young."

"JuJu…" I warned...

Now she smirked, "He's twenty-nine," she paused, "but he'll be thirty…" she continued, "in six weeks."

I rolled my eyes. "You make it sound like I want to date him. I don't. I'm only interested in his non-profit organization." I tried to make it sound innocent.

"I want to date him!" JuJu exclaimed. "As I said before, he is one fine specimen."

"You're married!"

She sighed, "There is more than enough of me to go around."

"Anything else?"

"I've emailed the full report to you, including his financials. He is still paying student loans, but he's doing well enough. There is a clear delineation between his income and the non-profit."

"That's what I'm looking for," I laughed, "not how old he is. I want you to run another search for me."

"On who?"

"Scott Binder, he's a corporate attorney in Silicon Valley. I'm not sure where he lives, but he may be based in San Francisco."

"Got it. Anything else?"

"No. I don't need it until Monday, so have a good rest of your weekend."

"You know I never mind."

23

"I know JuJu, you are spectacular!"

After the call, I zipped into the all-marble bathroom for a quick shower and then slipped in between the cool sheets. Sleep came quickly, and I dreamt of rolling green Irish hills, being surrounded by puppies, and Kian.

CHAPTER 4

Even with the time difference, I was up with the sun and enjoyed breakfasting on the terrace. I valued the quiet because, in a couple of hours, it would be a day full of wedding planning.

Michael arrived shortly after breakfast to review the last-minute details with me.

"I hope she says yes." I looked across the dining room table at my brother who sipped at an iced tea.

"I have no doubt," Michael replied confidently. "I know she wants to marry me, and she said yes once before. Elizabeth always needs a little prodding to push her over the edge. Let me see what the flowers look like."

I pulled up the pictures on my iPad and slid it over to him. He skimmed his fingers smoothly over the glass, moving the pictures.

"I saw you leave last night with Scott," he commented casually.

I raised an eyebrow. "He's staying here at the hotel. I also invited him to come tonight."

Michael nodded his head and then looked from the iPad. "He's a fun guy, but I don't think he's for you."

My breath huffed out, "How so?"

"He's too much like your ex-husband, Tim."

"And how's that?" I pressed my lips together to quell my growing impatience.

"Com'on Christina, he's a corporate attorney. That's somewhat bland in my book."

"Well, maybe I like ordinary," I retorted.

"Do not give me that, you have never liked dull people. Frankly, I don't know how you ever ended up marrying Tim. He wasn't even a real nerd."

I laughed with him. "You've got me there."

"You know Scott will try to impress you."

"He already has."

His face lit up in surprise. "He has?"

I smirked, "He has already *tried.*"

He raised an eyebrow. "How?"

I laughed. "Expensive Gin."

He grinned. "Have to give him credit. He knows your booze of choice."

"Damn, Michael, you make me sound like a drunkard!" I wrinkled my forehead in a frown.

He quickly changed the subject. "Hey, are there any left-over cookies from last night?"

I rolled my eyes, a mannerism I picked up from Elizabeth and retrieved the cookies from the butler's kitchen.

Michael smiled broadly and reached for a cookie. "I knew you weren't going to eat all of these," he declared in between mouthfuls.

I took a big bite out of one too. "These are so delicious. I have organic milk in the refrigerator. Want some?"

He nodded vigorously.

My big brother and I spent the morning over milk and cookies planning the final details of his surprise wedding. We wanted to make it appear to Elizabeth as if we threw it together at the last minute. No one but me could assemble this extravaganza at the eleventh-hour, and this was one of my unique talents. Anything could be accomplished with enough money and helpers.

At noon, Michael bent over and kissed the top of my head as he headed for the door. "I'll see you tonight. What time?"

"Six is good."

"An early night?" he responded opening the door.

"I had to start a little sooner. Jimmy will be coming up before he goes on stage in the lounge."

"I like him; he's someone you should look at. The last time I was here during Mardi Gras, he was so booked up we barely had time to even say hello."

"Oh nonsense," I said and shoved him out the door. "I've got things to do, and you better get back to Elizabeth."

Back at the dining room table, my cell phone rang as I began to review what needed to be accomplished during the afternoon. It was a video call from the animal hospital, and when I slid my finger over the phone to accept the call, Kian's face filled the screen.

"Ah... good morning Miss Hoffman, hope I didn't catch you at a bad time?" His voice was as bright and sunny as his face was.

"Good afternoon, Dr. McDermott." I smiled. His charm was

infectious.

He looked briefly up at something which I assumed was a clock and I could almost hear his gears shift. "Ah yes, that would be afternoon New Orleans time. I wanted to give you an update on your boy. Have you thought of a name yet? He'll need a name you know. We can't go around calling him boy or dog."

I shook my head. Why did I need to name the dog? He wasn't mine anyway. "No, I haven't Dr. McDermott."

"Kian," he admonished me. "I don't stand on formalities."

"But you called me Miss..." I paused.

"That's because you're in New Orleans, aren't all women known as Miss?"

"Yes, but, Christina will do." Great, now he had me babbling.

His eyes were so beautiful. And, his voice. I could listen to the melody of his accent forever. Snap out of it! What was wrong with me?

"Your boy is recovering on schedule. Today he stood and took some tentative steps. We have his leg in a cast now. He's being a good boy and not chewing on anything ... yet. He's still exhausted. He took a bad beating. The worst injury was the leg, it might be a little early to tell, but it should heal satisfactorily. Dr. Ashton did an expert job with the surgery. You should meet her. I think you two would get along quite well."

There was a sound of a cage door opening in the background, then the camera panned around, and I saw the little dog on his side. His eyes opened, and his cute tail wagged. He looked so small lying there. A towel was placed underneath his body, so he didn't rest on the cold steel of the cage.

Kian's hand reached in as he passed the phone to someone else. He petted the dog around his head, and spoke in soothing even tones, "How are you doing buddy? I have your ma on the phone. She's concerned about you, but you let her know with that first-rate tail of yours that you're going to be up and running around soon. You're a tough little guy. A fighter. There's no give up in you, is there?" The doctor's hands moved down the small body, and I could tell he was doing a quick examination. "Yes. You'll be chasing after some fat cats in no time, and will soon be dashing after a few slow squirrels too."

Kian stepped back and closed the cage door. His face came back on the screen.

"Thank you, Doctor. Thank you for everything you've done. He looks so much better."

He smiled, his deep dimples growing wider. "It was you who saved him. You stopped and picked him up, instead of ignoring the trash on the pavement which would have been very easy to do."

"No," I shook my head, "I did what any person would have done.

"Ah, Christina, you'd be surprised how heartless and uncaring people can be. He's doing well, and we should be able to release him early next week. Is it okay if I contact you again tomorrow for another update?"

"Please. I'd appreciate the call."

"Excellent Miss Hoffman. I will see you again tomorrow."

I smiled. "I look forward to it."

After we had hung up, I sat at the table quietly. I did not need to be attached to a dog or a man. No. My life was too busy. No. That was not going to happen.

CHAPTER 5

Lunch with Marie was at their plantation house. Located down in the bayou, it had survived most of Hurricane Katrina's ravages. The house was built in a classic design with large white pillars. The surrounding garden was an explosion of spring color. In the back, a gated boat dock and fence discouraged the alligators from visiting the yard. Their part of the bayou had all the charming elements, including low hanging mossy green trees, chattering birds, burping frogs, and at night twinkling fireflies and chirping crickets. Of course, there were the ever-present alligators too. It was like stepping into a Disneyland ride, except this was the real thing.

Tommy's great-grandmother, who lived with them, joined us for lunch too. Great Me-Maw was the matriarch of the family and spoke mostly in Cajun French. She had a special love for Michael, who would spend hours speaking to her in her native tongue. In my years of knowing the family, I had picked up snippets of French, but I was nowhere near the fluency of my brother. The Cajun part of the wedding feast would be directed from their side of the family.

I wasn't sure of Great Me-Maw's age, but she was a woman who wore her wrinkles on her round face like a badge of honor. Her big brown eyes, the color of espresso coffee, were quick. No one would fool her or get away with anything without her noticing.

My parents with my grandmother Helen were due to arrive in New Orleans in a few days. They'd be staying out at the house and helping with the Greek and German cuisine. This conglomeration of nationalities was perfect for Michael and Elizabeth. They were sure to love this crazy mixture of food and music.

Marie had laid out the menu in front of us on the table. Her old-fashioned kitchen was large enough for a big round table to seat eight people. This was my favorite room because the windows offered a spectacular view of the bayou and garden. The first floor had suffered the most damage from flooding during the hurricane. Fortunately, in this part of the bayou, the waters receded quickly after the storm.

"We are planning all of Michael and Elizabeth's favorites," Marie said indicating the menu.

Great Me-Maw said something unintelligible in Cajun, which she followed up in English, "Vegetables." And made a sour face.

Marie laughed, "Now you know Great Me-Maw, Michael is a vegetarian. He doesn't eat any meat."

Great Me-maw puffed out a heavy sigh, "All dat vegetable ruins my good *étouffée*." Then she grinned, "But my boy will eat the fish for his Great Me-Maw."

I laughed, "For you, yes, he will. I see you also have the famous bread pudding on the list."

Marie's eyes twinkled. "Oh, did you hear that story?"

I smiled playfully. "About how Elizabeth almost prostituted herself for your bread pudding. Yep. That story just keeps getting better each time it's told."

"I'll make a version of the whiskey sauce without the alcohol, so she can have her fill."

"I wouldn't be surprised if she disappeared from the reception and we found her holed up in some corner of the house with the whole bowl of pudding," I chortled.

Marie laughed heartily, "Don't I know it."

Shortly before four o'clock, I arrived back at the hotel. I took advantage of the time to take a long soak in the Jacuzzi tub in the tiled bathroom. As I dried off, the doorbell rang.

"What the hell?" I slipped into a robe and scurried to the door. Peering through the peephole, I saw Scott standing there with flowers and a bottle of champagne. Opening the door, I said unkindly, "You're very early."

"Am I?" He tried to look at his watch but the items he carried hampered his arms. "Didn't you say five?"

"No that was six. No one is here yet, and as you can see, I'm not ready."

"I think you look fantastic. I love after bath mistiness."

He stepped toward me, and I sighed inwardly moving aside.

"Why don't you finish getting ready, and I'll put the champagne on ice. I'll just make myself at home, shall I?"

Raising an eyebrow, I remarked, "I guess so." As I walked off toward the bedroom, I turned, "Would you let the caterers in when they get here? And, how did you manage to get up the elevator? You need a card key or an escort."

He grinned, which I had to admit looked cute on him. "I told you I have my ways, and I don't share all my secrets. Besides, don't you like a little mystery?"

Closing the bedroom door, I said silently, "Not when it arrives an hour early."

There was a small lock on the knob, and I turned it quietly. I decided not to let Scott's early arrival deter me from getting ready for my party.

After make-up and hair, I slipped on my new Marc Jacobs' black cross strap dress. Looking in the long mirror, I pivoted around. The dress gave me a flattering and elegant silhouette. It was perfect, and because I worked with the designer, it came in my size. It's a miracle! I finished the dress off with a pair of black Louboutin J-String pumps. I admit I didn't want to walk far in these shoes, but they did give me killer legs.

Opening the door, I looked down the hallway toward the living room. Scott stood by the French doors leading to the terrace. As he twisted off the cork from the champagne, he saw me, and the bottle's cork came out with a big pop.

He smiled appreciatively his eyes roaming my body. "Your timing is impeccable Christina! Champagne?"

I nodded, and he began to pour. I took the glass he offered. "What should we toast to?"

His grin was devilish, "How about us?"

"Is there an us?" I raised my eyebrow.

"There could be."

We touched our glasses together.

"You look very sexy tonight." His voice took on a husky quality, and the accompanying admiring look made heat run through me.

I gave him a smile while sipping the champagne. "Thank you, and thank you for this," I said lifting my glass. "And for the beautiful flowers."

"The caterers were here and have set up in the kitchen. They said they'd be back in fifteen minutes," he said after he looked at his watch.

"Thank you again for your help." I walked out to the large patio and was pleased to see several small couches and club chairs scattered around a small portable fire pit. Set up in the corner by one of the French doors was a bar filled with liquor and glasses. And in the other corner, a large barbecue heated. "They do an excellent job here at the hotel."

"Have you stayed here many times before?"

"Yes. I love New Orleans, and this hotel pampers me. I like their security too."

"I'm surprised you don't stay at Marcus' house."

I sat on one of the small couches and crossed my legs, which made my dress slide alluringly up my thighs. "Oh no," I laughed, "his mother is too bossy for my tastes. That is all I'm going to say about that subject. Tell me more about you." I patted the place next to me. I felt friendly.

31

He sat next to me. "I'm afraid my life isn't as exciting as yours."

"Married?" I asked with my eyebrow raised.

"At one time. It was a fiasco, and let me leave it at that. I'd rather talk about you and me."

After taking my champagne glass and setting it gently on the table next to us, he turned toward me and lightly trailed a finger along the spaghetti strap, which tried admirably to hold up my dress. His movements made a shiver run down my spine in a tempting way.

"There you go again, alluding to us," I murmured breathing in the musky scent of his aftershave.

He tucked one finger under my chin, to lift my lips to his. "I think us would be fun."

The chime at the front door surprised both of us. I rose to answer the door. Scott did not look pleased. Did the bell save me?

CHAPTER 6

Michael was front and center carrying a box, which contained his cue stick when I opened the door. He looked down at my feet.

"Holy hell Christina, what do you have on your feet?"

I smirked, "Those would be my shoes."

"Take them off. You're going to break your neck. You don't need to be so tall." He moved past me when he saw Scott standing in the living room.

I called out to my brother, "When did Mom put you in charge of my foot apparel?"

"Ignore him, Christina." Elizabeth wrapped her arms around me for a hug. "He's been Mr. Cranky Pants all afternoon." She leaned back from the hug to look at me. "I love your dress! You are gorgeous! And, I wish I could wear those shoes."

Behind Elizabeth, the quartet of caterers tried to be extra polite, but I could tell they wanted in. After introducing themselves, two went to the patio, one man to the bar and the other to do the barbecue, while the women would do the setup in the kitchen and serve.

After speaking with the wait staff in the kitchen, I joined my three guests in the living room. Michael already had a cocktail and now was racking the balls on the billiards table. In a short time, the bell rang again, and Marie, Tommy, Marcus, and Nancy joined us. Jimmy arrived about five minutes later.

Jimmy hugged me tightly, and Scott's expression did not look pleased. Jealousy? Interesting thought, we only met the previous night, what reason did Scott have for possessiveness?

"How's ya doing girl?" Jimmy grinned at me with his boyish good looks. Sandy blond hair with strawberry red streaks ran through it and complimented his freckles. His hello hug ended with a quick pat on my bottom

"Jimmy you are so rude!" I took his hand and led him into the living room. He casually wrapped his arm around my shoulders. "Have you met Elizabeth yet? And this is Scott Binder, a college friend of the boys."

Scott had a peevish look on his face again when he shook hands with Jimmy.

"How long can you stay?" I asked as I slipped away from Jimmy's arm.

"My first set is at nine." He accepted a beer from the bartender.

I showed Jimmy the terrace, and we both inhaled the smoky scent of the barbecue filling the air.

"Sugar, you know how to put on a party." His Louisiana drawl was soft like Marcus, and he drew his words out slowly.

I grinned at the compliment, "You know it is just my way. I'm glad you could squeeze this in tonight."

"I wouldn't miss it."

The sound of the crack of billiard balls from the living room floated outside, and laughter followed.

I grabbed Jimmy's hand, "Com'on. If Michael is playing this is bound to be a hoot."

He chuckled behind me, "I still remember beating him the last time. He doesn't like losing."

"He has to be bad at something. All those years he beat all of us at Monopoly, it's payback time."

I enjoyed a cozy evening of loving family, delicious food, potent cocktails, and lively conversation. Oh, and challenging men! Jimmy and Scott did themselves proud by vying for my attention. Jimmy and I knew we'd always be just friends, no matter how often he liked to grab my butt. But Scott ... there was something different. I was sure Michael was wrong about him. He proved he could keep his wits when the heated discussions threatened to implode and he certainly challenged me.

At the end of the night, after everyone else had left, Scott and I enjoyed one last cocktail out on the terrace. It was evident to both of us what he had been angling towards all night, and I was certain he was going in for the kill. But, I would seriously disappoint him tonight. I was not in New Orleans to be a conquest or make one.

We sat together on the comfy love seat, sipping our brandies. My naked feet, absent of the discarded shoes, dangled over the edge of the armrest as my back leaned against his chest. His lips brushed the top of my shoulders with light kisses, and his free hand stroked my arm.

"We're finally alone," he murmured.

I sighed softly, the kisses, the brandy, the strength I felt leaning against him made me want him. However, I was determined not to give in. I did not have room in my life for a relationship. My miserable marriage had proven to me that I was not cut out for the mated life. I did fine on my own.

"I'm not sleeping with you tonight, or while we're in New Orleans."

He sighed too, "Christina, you have this hard shell, like an M&M candy, but inside, you're all squishy and soft. Try opening up a little and let the soft interior out."

"I like my M&M's with peanuts," I quipped.

There was a long pause from Scott as he twisted to look at me grinning widely. "Are you saying you're nuts inside?"

With that, both of us started laughing, and we had to put our brandies on the table. He turned to me still grinning and kissed me on my mouth. The kiss was not necessarily passionate, but it was sincere.

When he broke the kiss, he leaned back to look at me. "I don't want to rush. I think there is something between us, and I felt the spark. I won't push you, but I would like to see you when we get back home. Is this possible?"

"Scott," I started, "I'm not looking for a relationship right now..." The disappointment appeared on his face, and I decided that perhaps I should give him a chance. "Okay, let's see what happens once we get back home."

"Good," he said as he leaned down to kiss me again.

This time I felt the passion injected into the kiss.

CHAPTER 7

Putting a wedding together without the bride's knowledge was not as easy as it sounded. I lost count how many times I almost slipped up around Elizabeth, and she began to wonder what I was doing all day instead of enjoying the activities of the other bridal party members. Frankly, all the planning was starting to exhaust me. It was Michael's job to keep her away from the hotel, especially as all the family and friends began to arrive. He was not doing such a hot job either because Elizabeth kept suggesting they drop by the hotel. We had her convinced there would be a raucous bachelor party the night before Marcus' wedding after the rehearsal dinner, which did not set well with her. But, it gave her something to ponder and chew on, and it kept her out of my way.

Scott was always lurking about in the background. I discovered he had bribed the security guard to give him access to my floor. I let him know clearly if he repeated the action I wouldn't even consider seeing him again, and I would have the guard fired.

And then, there was the matter of the dog. Kian, in his charismatic way, contacted me each day and gave me an update on Dog Doe. With each call, he requested I name him. And, just as smoothly, each time I avoided it. Really. What was Kian thinking?

And, what was I thinking? Every time Kian called, I became tongue-tied on the phone. Definitely not me. Was it the blue eyes? The accent? Or, the way he cared and spoke about the rescued dog? I knew it was the latter when I ran the conversation through my mind.

The clinic had been busy when he called, but there he was, all smiles for me.

"Good day to you Christina. How are you and New Orleans getting along? Are you enjoying the delicious beignets?"

I smiled deeply when I heard his voice. "So you know about the famous donuts?"

"That I do. If I breathe deep enough, I can smell the chicory coffee too. There is nothing better."

"I'll bring some coffee and mix for you when I return. It's one of my favorite treats. I actually make the beignets at home."

"Now you tell me you're a chef too! I'll look forward to them! I have a special surprise for you." He handed the phone to his assistant and gave her instructions, "Turn the camera toward the cage. There you go. Can you see, Christina?"

"Yes?" I said with curious anticipation

Kian opened the cage door and gently pulled the dog out. "Watch this," he said as he lowered him down to a rubber mat on the floor.

Looping a towel with a handle at either end around the dog's torso, Kian supported him as he lifted him to his feet. The rescue took some tentative steps forward and then stood still, not wobbling a bit.

"Oh, my gosh Kian! I can't believe it!" I exclaimed. "How wonderful. Look at him, he's standing."

When the dog heard my voice, his tail wagged. Okay, I'll admit it. The wagging tugged at my heart.

"He's doing terrific." The pride in Kian's voice was unmistakable. "I told you he was a tough little guy." The dog barked in the background. He laughed, "And, he does enjoy putting his two cents in too."

Kian knelt in front of the dog and rubbed his face and sides. Stitches were visible in what was left of his earflap. The dog did look a little lopsided, but it only added to his quirky appearance.

"You and the people in your clinic make miracles happen. Thank you for saving his life."

"Carrie told me about the donation you made to our rescue organization. That was very kind of you to pay for the entire surgery, and I appreciate it."

I could feel my face coloring a bit, and I don't know why I was suddenly embarrassed. "It was nothing really."

Kian's face came back on screen, and those eyes pierced through me again, making me feel feverish.

"Don't say that Christina. It means a lot to us and to the animals that are saved by it." He smiled broadly and winked, "Now, to the record keeping. Have you come up with a name yet? I'm growing tired of calling him Dog. He needs a proper name, and you're the chosen name giver."

I laughed and sighed at the same time, "You're really going to nail me on this, aren't you?"

He grinned, "That I am."

"Okay," I acquiesced, "I have one. How about Koa? It means brave and fearless. I think this dog went through quite a lot to come out through to the other side."

Kian smiled, "And in Hawaii, the Koa tree is gigantic. Our little Koa here isn't large in size, but he does have a colossal spirit, so, yes, I think this is a very apt name for him. Finally, we have a name!"

Inwardly, I was somehow relieved he liked the name. I don't know why, but perhaps I was feeling the stress. Or was Kian's approval so important to me?

"Well little boy, or should I say Koa, how do you like your name?" He smiled as he scratched the dog's head.

Koa wagged his tail and leaned into Kian's hand. And my heart melted yet again.

CHAPTER 8

The week flew by with all the details finalized for Michael's marriage. Instead of a career in financial investing, I could have easily become a wedding planner. Of course, it was more fun when you spent your brother's money!

On Thursday, while everyone was involved with the afternoon rehearsal at the church where Marcus and Nancy would be married, Russell and I collected my parents and grandmother at the airport. We drove out to the bayou plantation house where Great Me-maw greeted us with open arms. Grandmother Helen and Tommy's great-grandmother instantly became close friends. My grandmother deftly maneuvered her way through the kitchen. It amazed me how she did not pose as a usurper to another woman's territory. World leaders could take lessons from her. Even the language barrier didn't hamper the two of them.

My mother, Candace, could have taken a page or two of notes from my grandmother's playbook. Almost her first words after greeting me at the airport were, "Have you met any nice men yet?"

I bristled at the usual interrogation, which over time was what our conversations had become. This time, however, I came prepared.

"As a matter of fact Mom, I have met someone. He is an old friend of the three boys. He went to school with them at Santa Cruz and then attended law school with Marcus," I said.

My mother's interest was immediately piqued. "Oh! Where does he live?"

While looking down to pick nonexistent fuzz off my sweater, I nonchalantly replied, "In the San Francisco area." I knew she expected me to continue with more details, but I just stretched out my legs in the comfortable back seat of the limo. Was I mean to tease her this way? Probably.

Dad looked up from his smartphone. "Did you run a background check on him?"

"Yes Dad, it came out clear. No felonies. No convictions. And he isn't known for conning rich women. He's a corporate attorney who works mainly for Silicon Valley."

He nodded and looked down at his phone again.

My grandmother leaned over and patted my knee. "It would be good for you to be dating," she paused to wrinkle her nose, "he so sounds boring. A lawyer? You need someone who will stimulate you."

Mom immediately responded, "No she doesn't Mother. She needs someone to settle down with so she can have some children. She's not getting any younger. In fact, it may be too late already!"

Dad brushed his hand over my mother's arm. "Now Candy. Don't say that."

My mother became indignant, "I don't know about you Steve, but I'd like to have some grandchildren."

He laughed, "Candy, you already have two beautiful granddaughters, and another grandchild on the way! Not to mention a great-grandchild on the way too." He looked at me, "Ignore your mother honey. You do your own thing."

And there you have it. Silence for the rest of the trip out to the bayou.

For as liberal as my parents could be, my mother was stuck on the whole grandchildren thing. She adored Michael's daughters, and believe me, she normally did not dote ... ever. It could have been our Greek family. I had many cousins, and there currently was a grandchild baby boom happening. As the oldest, Mom had always been competitive with her sisters, and both my brother and I had been a source of pride for her and the family. Now her sisters, without any hesitation, were whipping out the grandchildren photos. As a result, she had been harping on me for the past several years bringing it up every occasion we were together.

Don't get me wrong, I did have the motherly instinct crop up inside of me, particularly since I was roller-coasting quickly to forty. When I was younger, there wasn't the money or the time. Now, I had the means, but the wealth made it even more difficult. Having to run background checks on men who wanted to date me was absurd, yet it was an essential part of my life. So far, I had not been very successful in the romance sector of my life. Perhaps that was the tradeoff. I enjoyed being the aunt, which meant it allowed me to butt my nose into my brother's business, and that was a win-win as far as I was concerned. If only I could move Mom off my trail. Maybe her new grandchild and great-grandchild would keep her busy?

After dropping off the family at the house, Russell returned me to the hotel. Michael planned to pop the question to Elizabeth at the rehearsal dinner, and I was not going to miss the event.

The party was hopping by the time I arrived. It was a smaller group than at the first party, but Marcus still closed the restaurant. A cadre of waiters passed exotic appetizers and champagne while we danced to a hot Cajun beat. Scott found me, and although not the smoothest dancer on the floor, the music infected him too. I loved to dance, but I second-guessed the wisdom of wearing five-inch heels.

Shortly before we sat down for dinner, the music slowed which was our cue to clear the dance floor. The moment had arrived. Michael and Elizabeth danced together in the middle of the floor. The crowd was hushed as the music slowed and then played very softly in the background.

Michael went down on one knee and gazed up at Elizabeth who looked like a doe caught staring into headlights. I half-expected her to sprint away. It was almost impossible to keep my emotions tamped down. I could feel small drops leaking out the side of my eyes. He asked the question. She blushed and looked flustered. However, I could see it in her eyes when she accepted his proposal for a wedding in two days. She saw only my brother and her answer was only for him.

I was so happy for both. My brother had found the one woman he'd been searching for and that thrilled me. Their styles and personalities complimented and they made a good team. I sighed audibly. I did love a good romance.

Scott was instantly behind me and gave me a glass of champagne, which Marcus had asked to be served.

"Jealous?" he whispered in my ear.

"What?" I asked while turning to him.

"Are you jealous? They look delighted." He pointed to the newly engaged couple.

I wrinkled my brow and gave him a bemused stare. "No. That's an odd question."

"Why do you think so?" he challenged. "This is the ultimate in romance. I believe every woman would want a proposal like that."

I shrugged my shoulders. "I don't know. But, I do know they worked hard on their relationship together to get to this place. As for me, I am not envious. I'm thrilled my brother found his special someone."

Scott smirked. "He didn't have much of an option, did he? She is pregnant."

I wasn't sure if he was stupid or just trying to aggravate me. He was doing so well at the second option.

"Really Scott? For someone who wants to get on my good side, that type of comment is not going to get you there very fast." I drank the glass of champagne quickly and placed it on a passing waiter's tray. "Please excuse me. I have some things I need to do."

"I'll save you a seat at dinner," he called out after me.

"No, I don't think you need to do that."

It was cute when Elizabeth finally figured out everyone had been in on the plans for her wedding. We didn't tell her everything, and she had no idea that both families were coming to New Orleans in the morning.

Elizabeth warmed to all the plans, and then she finally realized she did not have a dress to wear. "I suppose I could run out and find something in a local store."

I wrapped my arms around her shoulders. "Now, my dear sister-in-law-to-be, do you think for one minute that I wouldn't have a dress for you? Remember the dress I had shown you before we left home? The one you fell in love with?"

She grinned. "Do you mean?"

I squeezed her. "Yes, it just so happens, the designer was persuaded to make one for you that would allow for your little pooch."

"How do you know it will fit? I mean, how could you tell how big I'd be?" Her eyes grew wide. "What if it doesn't fit me?"

"Don't worry. Remember the shift Madame Bernard had you try on when she was altering your maid of honor dress for Nancy's wedding?"

Elizabeth nodded and raised her eyebrows. "Do you mean?"

"Yes, that shift is part of your dress. Madame Bernard has altered it, so your dress will fit perfectly on Sunday," I said patting her back.

The smile on her face grew wide, and tears ran down her cheeks while she captured me in a big hug. "Christina, I'll never be able to thank you enough. You are the sister-in-law I always wished to have! Thank you!"

Michael chuckled as he sat back down next to us. "Mutual sister-in-law love? Great, I'll never be able to go up against you two."

I turned to him. "You never had a chance."

I didn't last too far into the evening. I felt exhausted and blamed it on the wedding planning. Scott managed to insinuate himself back into my good graces, and he was attentive bringing me drinks. Although I couldn't put a finger on it, there was some about him that rubbed me the wrong way.

CHAPTER 9

The next morning, my cell phone rang loudly and wanted to throw it against the wall. Whatever idiot was calling me at ... I looked at the time and couldn't believe it was nine. How had I managed to sleep so late, and why did I feel like such crap? I expected my head would burst open any moment.

I croaked an answer, "Hello?"

"Christina, I hope I didn't wake you."

The voice was unmistakable. It was my Irish friend.

"Hello, doctor, er, ah Kian," I said as I tried to clear my throat and not hack up a lung in the process. "No, I was up."

He didn't sound entirely convinced when he answered, "If you're sure. I only called to give you an update on Koa."

I sat up in bed. "Oh, okay." The headache made me dizzy and my vision blurry. I didn't remember overdoing the champagne.

"Would you like to turn on the video so you can see him?"

Immediately I tried to angle to see myself in the mirror located across the room. It was as I thought, and I didn't want anyone to see me in this condition. How late had we partied the night before? I'm not even sure how I got up to my room. I looked over at the other side of the bed. Why did it look as if someone had slept there? The bed linens and comforter were in disarray. I usually kept to one part of the bed.

"Um, sure," I answered. I was naked, so I wrapped the covers around myself and switched to the video feed.

Koa was front and center, and he was white. Where was the little gray dog I picked up from the highway?

"Doesn't he look grand? The techs cleaned him up a bit, and lo and behold, you have a white dog! All that gray was dirt. He is a terrier mix, and probably has a lot of West Highland terrier in him. What a good boy he is." Kian kneeled in front of him and stroked the top of his head. "Yes, you're a first-rate little rescue."

Koa liked the attention and rolled over on his back so his belly could get the same action. I laughed watching them play together.

Kian stood and looked into the phone. "He's ready to go home. Are you expecting to return on Monday?"

Without thinking, I said, "Yes, my flight to San Francisco is on Monday, but I'm attending a board meeting in the afternoon, then it's off to see friends."

"We're open on Tuesday. The sooner he gets into his home environment, the faster he will heal."

His words didn't sink in at first, and then the realization hit me. I shook my head vigorously, "No, you don't understand. I can't take him."

Kian's face was one of utter disappointment and rejection, but he didn't say a word.

I, on the other hand, started to blab away, "I really don't have the time to care for a dog. I travel a lot. I wouldn't know what to do. I've never cared for one all by myself."

"You care for Michael and Elizabeth's dogs when they are away, don't you? I'm sure they would return the favor." His expression had not changed, but his voice became resolute. "At least consider fostering him, until I can find a suitable adoption family."

"How long will that take?" I asked, thinking I could probably care for him for a couple of weeks at the most.

"Not too long. Koa's a young dog and especially handsome now that he's been cleaned up some. I'm sure a family would snap him up quickly. He's a little skittish, but that should clear if someone works with him to socialize with people."

"I guess I wouldn't mind fostering him ... for a short time," I added with emphasis.

He rewarded me with a bright smile. "There you are then, we're all set now.

Somehow, I backed myself into fostering a rescue. Here I was an excellent negotiator and Kian's skills far outstripped mine.

"We'll see you Tuesday. I'll look forward to it," he added looking like he had won a poker game, which I suppose he had.

I spotted them as soon as the call ended. Black socks, on the carpet by the bed! I didn't wear black socks. A visible light illuminated the space underneath the closed bathroom door. Crap! Had I brought someone back to the hotel last night?

I didn't remember. Damn it! Why didn't I remember? How much did I have to drink? Then it occurred to me, I mixed champagne and gin last night. A particularly deadly combination for me because it apparently blew my memory. My head felt foggy. I hated hangovers and rarely over imbibed for that reason.

The bathroom door opened slowly, and I stared into Scott's face. Damn it, damn it, damn it.

He grinned at me while wrapping the towel around his waist. "Good morning! I've taken the liberty of ordering coffee. It should be here soon."

He looked enticing in the towel. It was easy to see why he was so self-confident. A broad chest covered with a smattering of dark hair, tapering down to ... never mind where it was leading. There was a tension between us, and I could feel the electricity. We stared at each other as the seconds ticked by. Whoever spoke first lost.

Scott laughed and sat on the edge of the bed. "Don't worry Christina, we didn't have sex last night, although I would have liked to. You were somewhat unresponsive when we got to your room."

I frowned. "And, you decided to stay? Why?"

He grinned. "You invited me! You said if I wanted, I could bunk with you! Who am I to say no? It was such a tempting offer. Besides, I like your rooms better."

Being under the covers became too hot, so I pushed them off and bravely strode naked to the closet to retrieve my robe.

He whistled, "You do look lovely naked."

I gave him my best withering look. "I suppose you undressed me?"

"No, you did that all by yourself. I wasn't feeling any pain last night either and I doubt I would have been coordinated to do that undertaking."

"You did manage to maneuver yourself in my bed." I tied the sash to my robe.

"You invited me."

I glowered. "Whatever. I suggest that you find your clothes and get dressed. I have a wedding to attend and am late already." I opened the door to the bedroom and pointed out. "You can use the guest bathroom." A loud knock on the front door interrupted me. "Now what?"

It was room service with the coffee Scott had ordered. They also brought orange juice, bacon, smoked sausage, eggs, French toast, beignets, and fruit. By the time the waiter had the dining table set, Scott had traipsed out completely dressed.

I sat at the dining room table, poured myself a cup of coffee, and reached for a beignet.

He sat opposite to me. "Is that all you're going to eat? I wasn't sure what you'd like."

I smirked. "So you decided to order it all?"

He sat back and sipped at his coffee. "Yeah, pretty much."

Picking up a plate, I filled it with eggs, bacon, and fruit. He chose the eggs, French toast, and smoked sausage. "Thank you for ordering breakfast," I said. "It will save me time. I have to be over at Marcus' house for the final fitting of Elizabeth's wedding dress in an hour."

"And then there is the wedding."

"Yes, today is Nancy's day. There are still a few details which I have to see to for Michael's wedding, but those will be easy."

He sliced his sausage into bite-sized pieces. "I hope you're going to save a dance for me at the reception."

I smirked again. "Who knows?"

I supposed I should have thanked him for rescuing me the night before and making sure I reached my room safely, but there was something ... I don't know, I couldn't put my finger on it. Scott was charming and good looking. He did have a pleasant personality. What was it that I didn't like about him? Were my brother and grandmother correct? Did I need someone more exciting?

Fortunately, Scott left my room without too much prodding. I quickly dressed in a sleeveless fuchsia colored cocktail dress by Prada. It had a matching jacket I could wear inside the church and then remove for the reception. I decided against the killer shoes and chose a more practical pair, three-inch Prada patent leather heels.

Russell delivered to Marcus' house where the girls dressed for the wedding. Michael and the boys had stayed at the hotel after the rehearsal dinner. I was glad none of them knew Scott spent the night with me. I would have never heard the end of it.

Simone greeted me in the entry hall of the magnificent Garden District antebellum mansion. The house grounds held a tent for the evening's reception and inside the house was an explosion of color with flowers covering all available spaces.

"Christina!" Simone called to me as she exited the library off the entryway. She kissed both of my cheeks to greet me. Her slight French accent always made me smile. "You look lovely. Prada is always one of my favorites." How did she know? "Of course you are here to see Elizabeth. She is up in the blue room with Madame Bernard having her wedding dress fitted. It is very dramatic. The dress is perfect for her tall frame."

Marcus' mother was a New Orleans's society darling. Her family roots and wealth stretched back generations and included family in Montreal. Always perfectly coiffed in her favorite Chanel suits, nothing was ever out of place with Simone. She ruled her family with an iron hand. She hadn't been thrilled when I dated her son since she would have preferred a society woman for him so he could expand his influence in New Orleans. When she discovered how much money I had, her opinion of me changed. Unfortunately, she did not care for Nancy either, but they had apparently called a truce, and the wedding proceeded peacefully.

"Thank you, Miss Simone. It is wonderful to see you. I hope you will spare me a few minutes tonight so we can catch up," I said as I headed for the stairway.

She called out to me, "Of course, of course." She turned toward the dining room, "Frederick!"

The house's majordomo was there in an instant. I shook my head in amusement. Frederick was the eyes and ears of the house. As the butler, he directed all the servants. He knew about everything that occurred in his domain. Frederick and Simone were the perfect pair.

I heard several voices inside the room as I knocked on the blue room door.

"Can I see?" I requested after the invitation to enter was issued.

My breath left me when I saw Elizabeth standing there as the seamstress zipped up the back of the dress.

"Oh, you look stunning!" My eyes watered, I knew Michael would love her in the dress. It was perfect.

Elizabeth moved to hug me. "I can't thank you enough."

Covered entirely in white lace, the mermaid style dress was so tight it surprised me she could breathe. Even though she was five months along, her pregnancy was successfully hidden. I didn't know how the designer managed, but she worked her magic. Nothing would ever be too good for my brother.

CHAPTER 10

While we were at the wedding and reception, Elizabeth's relatives arrived from Southern California, and were shuttled over to the Ritz Carlton. The rest of the family and friends landed with my assistant JuJu. She would oversee the remaining events so I could enjoy the wedding. I finally felt satisfied I had pulled this all together in the short amount of time we had.

And then there was Scott. What was I going to do with him? He was certainly persistent. Being who I was, I decided to take the direct route.

The wedding reception was outstanding, and it would be counted among the Crescent City's most lavish affairs for the year. Simone had outdone herself. I had attended one of their Mardi Gras parties a few years back and had thought it was magnificent, but it could not hold a candle to the opulence of this event. The guests would speak of it for years to come.

Open tents with tables and chairs were placed around the outside of the house. The entire bottom floor was available to all the guests, and I lost count of the number of bars serving cocktails and champagne. Waiters, dressed in crisp black and white uniforms, carried tray after tray of delectable appetizers. Different music surrounded me as I walked through the grounds and the house. A big band orchestra in the ballroom, Cajun, Zydeco, and jazz bands were tucked into other areas. All the bands were strategically placed, so one type of music didn't overplay another. World-renowned Chef Beau LaFonte was responsible for dinner, which showcased his masterpieces. Simone spared no effort or expense for her son's wedding.

As the sun began to set, the trees and grounds were lit up with thousands of tiny sparkling white lights. Everything took on an appearance of a fairyland, and everyone was enchanted by the effect.

I found a small table near the ballroom and Scott joined me after a visit to the closest bar. When he sat, he scooted the chair next to mine, and we watched as guests walked around or spoke in small groups.

"It's nice to be able to take a moment to sit and relax," he commented after taking a drink from his cocktail.

"It is," I sighed. "We're in for a long night."

"I think you're right. Did your assistant get all the relatives settled into the hotel rooms?"

"Yes, there was a problem with Katy's flight, my niece who lives in New York. But, she's due to arrive later tonight. Russell will take one more trip out to the airport to collect her, and then everyone will finally be here."

"I can't believe you pulled it off."

"It hasn't happened yet. The bride is still a bit skittish. Michael is doing everything he can to keep her emotions from taking charge. Her hormones are in overdrive. Everything is making her cry."

"I'm sure it will be alright, and I'm looking forward to spending another wonderful evening with you."

I turned to look at him directly, it was now or never. "So Scott, let's have a chat about that."

It appeared my comment intrigued him. "Okay. Let's talk."

"What exactly is it that you want with me? I'm having a difficult time figuring you out. I know I haven't been the nicest person to you, but you still continue to pursue me."

He laughed heartily, which was the first time I've seen him do so. Before now, it was as if he kept everything in reserve afraid of taking a misstep.

"Is that what I'm doing, pursuing you?" He wore a wicked grin on his face.

"Yes, it is. Admit it. I want to know why?"

"I told you before, I find your personality challenging. I don't meet a person with your capabilities every day. Why do you think I'm interested in you?"

I frowned. "I'll give you one guess, and it starts with M."

"I hoped you would give me more credit than that. Yes, you are an incredibly wealthy woman, but I'm successful in my own right. I work for a large, lucrative corporate law firm, and made partner last year. I'm an excellent attorney, handsome, and many women consider me a good catch."

His voice sounded slightly insulted, and suddenly I felt sorry for my mistrust. Why couldn't I relax around him? Is this what my ex-husband made me, a distrusting bitch with commitment issues?

I took a drink of my cocktail and found it to be the Nolet's Reserve. I knew Simone would not have stocked it and concluded that Scott must have brought it with him.

"Thank you," I said indicating to the drink. "This is very sweet of you."

He grinned making his smile bright. "The bartender has it tucked behind the bar. It's only for you."

"You're gracious, and I'm afraid I haven't been. Perhaps we could start over?" I extended my hand to him. "Hi, I'm Christina, Michael's sister. It's a pleasure to meet you."

He caressed my hand between both of his. "No, the pleasure will be all mine."

I giggled, the alcohol having the desired effect on me. "Oh, I hope so."

Since my brother, Tommy and the girls were part of the wedding party we were not seated with them for dinner. Instead, we sat with part of Nancy's family, and I laughed thinking about what the conversation surrounding the seating chart was like. As one of Marcus' former girlfriends, I was known on his side of the family, and most likely, they would have considered it awkward for me to attend the wedding. But, not Marcus or Nancy, or even Simone for that matter. For all their showy excesses, if they decided it wasn't important, then it became insignificant.

Halfway through the evening, I received a text from JuJu indicating Katy had arrived at the hotel. I breathed a sigh of relief. Finally, my job for Michael's wedding was done. Everyone else could take over now, and I would be able to enjoy the festivities. I never wanted to do this again and warned Michael this would be the last long distance nuptials I would arrange. Ever. I was serious. This event kept me up at night because Michael was such a perfectionist, and having to do everything behind Elizabeth's back killed me. She had become a friend to me, and I felt guilty sneaking around her while the affair was planned.

After dinner, we met up with the rest of the gang and partied the night away. Since the police chief, the mayor, and other important city people attended the reception, we didn't have any trouble with the police driving by because of noise complaints, besides all the neighbors had been invited to the festivities. We even had our share of locals and tourists who stopped to look through the fence and partied right along with us.

I enjoyed Scott's company. He was attentive and appeared to be seriously interested in me. I had a great time until I received JuJu's text.

You know Scott is divorced, she texted.

I texted back, *Yes. He told me. You told me.*

With a six-year-old son?

I frowned when I read the text. Should it matter that Scott had a child? No. But, why hadn't he told me? Did he think it would make a difference?

CHAPTER 11

"It had better be a critical problem, my dear brother. You just woke me from a sweet dream," I said answering my cell the next morning.

His voice sounded panicked, "We're at Defcon five."

"Elizabeth is ready to bolt?" I headed toward the bathroom. Glancing at the clock to notice it was already eleven in the morning. How had I managed to sleep so late?

"She became all weepy this morning about her Dad not walking her down the aisle, so I had to call him at the hotel and let her know that her family is here."

"Oh, is that all?" I said. "We're having the pre-wedding party tonight, and she'll discover that everyone is here for the ceremony. Did knowing her father was here calm her down? Does she know about the party?"

He sighed, "She doesn't know about the party. She believes we're meeting him and her sister for dinner. I think she's okay now."

I turned on the water in the shower. "There you go. We've skirted around the crisis. Michael, everything will be okay. Just relax. JuJu has all the details, believe me, she has it well under control. Everything will go smoothly tonight and tomorrow."

"Thank you, Christina. I'll never be able to make this up to you. You've been amazing!"

"Never again Michael. You know I loved doing this for you, but I will never do it again. I don't think anyone will ever entice me to look at another wedding dress."

"I can't wait to see the dress. I've heard whispers about it."

"You will be blown away. Elizabeth radiates in it. Damn, I don't know how you managed to get so lucky."

"It's all due to you."

"Yes, it is," I laughed. "Now stop worrying and get off the phone. I'll see you later."

After we had ended the call, I pressed JuJu's name on the phone.

"Hey, boss lady, up already?" she answered.

"I don't know how I slept so late."

She laughed, "Well, you were up pretty late last night ... and sending me drunk texts."

"Oh, JuJu, did I really? I'm sorry. We were having so much fun and then I received your message about Scott. I'll have to admit it sent me reeling."

"Don't worry. I'm surprised it didn't come up on the first pass. And before you ask, I'm doing a more thorough search now."

I grimaced, "Is that legal? I don't want you to do anything against the law."

"It skirts around it. I'm having Jeff help me," she answered.

Jeff, her police detective husband, helped us out from time to time when I needed to dig a little deeper into a background.

"It's really not a big issue. I'm not concerned that Scott has a son. I am only wondering why he didn't tell me about him. It doesn't matter to me."

"Okay, whatever you call it," she answered, and the smirk in her voice came through loud and clear on the phone.

"I haven't slept with him."

"Really?" she chuckled.

"JuJu."

"Sorry. Remember, I know your reputation."

I sighed, "I am trying to get past that reputation."

"Hey, this is JuJu you're speaking with, no apologies are necessary. I know who you are, and you don't have to worry about me."

"I know that, and thank you. How are the preps for the party going?"

She began to tick off the list. "Oh, and you need to call your mother."

"Is there a problem?" I asked with apprehension.

"I don't think so. Your mom needs a job. Both Grandma Helen and Great Me-maw haven't given her anything to do. By the way, is that right? They call her Me-Maw?"

"Yes. It's a Cajun reference for grandmother. Now, what about my mother?"

"Well, the grandmothers have everything all handled on their side. Tommy and Marie's cousins are crawling out of the woodwork, and everyone wants to help with the wedding. It's amazing. I would never have expected to see so many volunteers. Apparently, they all know Elizabeth and love her and her books. And there's a story too, something about bread pudding," JuJu explained.

I gave a hearty chuckle, "It's the infamous bread pudding that Elizabeth scarfed down when she was here last year. She couldn't get enough of it." What was I going to do with my mother? She was used to being in charge, so I understood this was probably killing her. "I'll give Mom a call. Maybe I'll take her shopping. She likes antiques."

We talked a few more minutes, and JuJu assured me all the plans were under control. I called my mother, and we organized a late lunch and a shopping trip for the afternoon. Mom suggested we invite my aunts and cousins who were all staying at the hotel. After I arranged to collect her from Marie's house and a small bus for our trip, I finally took my shower.

Much to my surprise, the shopping trip was a total success. Everyone jumped on the bus, including our friends from Mintock, and Elizabeth's family. Part of the fun for me was the ability to spoil everyone on our trip. JuJu came through for me again by scouring the nearby drug stores to buy gift cards for our passengers.

We made it back in plenty of time for the pre-wedding party. Everyone Elizabeth loved was there to celebrate her marriage to Michael, even the newlyweds managed to attend. The courtyard area of the hotel was set up with fountains, lighting that resembled gas lamps, small wrought iron tables and chairs, plenty of trees, flora, and fauna, and a small jazz band with Jimmy entertaining us. The event was large but still managed to feel intimate. I knew this is how the wedding would feel too.

Elizabeth turned on the waterworks when we revealed the surprise that everyone was here to attend her wedding. Okay, all the women in the place started to cry, and I spotted more than a few men wiping their eyes dry.

Finally, I managed to get a cocktail and to find a couch in the corner of the room. Since my feet ached, I slipped off the five-inch heels and rested my feet on the seat of a chair I pulled over. Scott saw me and made a beeline in my direction.

"May I?" he asked.

"Of course."

He sat next to me and leaned over to touch my glass with his. "This party is fantastic."

"Thank you." I took another slow sip from my gin and tonic. "Enough money can do anything."

He leaned back and watched the crowd with me. "It sure can. It all comes down to a matter of economics. Either you have the money, or you don't, and if you don't, you only have to figure out where to get it."

"Yep."

"Michael owes you big time for this."

I wrinkled my brow, "How do you figure?"

"You've spent a lot of money putting his wedding on. Especially flying all the family and friends in. It adds up."

"Not that it's any of your business, but Michael paid for his wedding."

He blustered, "I'm sorry Christina. I didn't mean to step over the boundaries. It was only an observation."

I blew out a big breath, "Scott, you make the strangest comments."

"Where are you off to when all this is finished?"

"Home and back to normal life. I have a board meeting on Monday, and I need to check on my new house. The construction has almost entirely stopped with the rain we've been having. And I have to pick up my dog."

Scott jumped at the word, "Dog? I didn't think you had a dog."

"Well, I don't really. Koa's not my dog, I'm only fostering until the rescue group can find a permanent home for him."

"They are a lot of work. They usually end up making a big mess," he remarked.

"This is a little dog. I rescued him, so I feel responsible. Besides, I'll be sticking around for a while, because I need to push the builder along."

"Why did you choose Mintock? It is such a small town. I would have expected you to be in San Francisco."

"I like it because it is a small town. My brother lives there, and my family lives close by. I lived in Manhattan for several years, and I want to slow down a bit now."

He moved a little closer. "I hope you'll allow me to continue to get to know you."

"Sure." I smiled. "As long as you tell me why you didn't tell me about your son."

He looked surprised at first but covered it well. "I'm sure I told you about Matthew. But, maybe I didn't. I don't let everyone know about him because he's part of my private life."

I nodded. Good recovery. "So then, you would have ultimately mentioned him?"

He smiled evenly, "Of course. I think we're making headway to that eventuality."

Leaning over, his lips found mine, and that was it. His kiss enveloped me. It enticed me to react as his tongue nudged my lips apart to explore more fully. I felt … nothing. No hunger, no ardent desire to return his kiss. I'll admit, I had always been slow to heat, but between us, there was no connection. I tried. His hands roamed, while his mouth moved along my neck and lower. Was it me? Or, was it him? How could I think so clinically about what was happening and still felt nothing at all?

I was hopeless.

CHAPTER 12

"Well, there you are!"

I was so grateful when I heard Tommy's voice.

"Ahem!" He cleared his throat loudly. "Scott, you want to pull your tongue out of her mouth?"

Anger flashed in Scott's eyes. He was not pleased. However, I was relieved for the interruption.

"What do you want? We were spending a few well-deserved moments alone," he said irritably.

Tommy merely gave Scott his *don't fuck with me* look.

"We're doing a champagne toast for the bride and groom. Michael's sister should be there." He pointed to Scott, "You, I don't give a shit about."

Whoa! What brought on the animosity between these two old friends?

I reached for my shoes and slipped them on. "I need to be there."

Tommy pulled me up to my feet and wrapped his arm around my waist. "Com'on baby sister," he drawled in my ear.

I didn't turn around to look but knew Scott did not follow us. We joined the crowd surrounding Michael and Elizabeth and was handed a glass filled with champagne.

Marcus held his glass up toward the pair. "My turn," he smiled. "Michael, Tommy, and I have been like brothers for over twenty years, and I think other than his girls, this is the only thing he has done perfectly. Elizabeth, you are our breath of fresh air and the sunshine on a cloudy day. We don't know how he managed to capture you, but..." he pointed to Michael and continued, "you have our pledge, we will always protect her as our little sister. To the bride and groom!"

Everyone toasted, and Elizabeth slipped away from Michael and kissed both Marcus and Tommy.

She whispered to them, "Thank you for making me feel like a member of the family."

Michael lifted his glass, "I'd like to thank my sister." He wrapped his arm around my shoulders. "And, where is she?" He looked around and spotted JuJu in the middle of the crowd. "Com'on over here."

She grinned wildly and put her arm around Michael's waist.

He continued, "I couldn't ask for a more perfect wedding planning team. Thank you my dear sister, and thank you JuJu. This party is amazing."

JuJu giggled, "Wait until you see what's happening tomorrow."

Elizabeth had her *doe in the headlights* look. "What is going on tomorrow? Christina! You promised a small wedding."

Both Michael and I said simultaneously, "Shush JuJu!"

Marie put her arm around Elizabeth's shoulder. "Don't you worry *Chér*, you know all the people here. This is it. It won't be a big deal. I promise. A little food, some flowers, a few chairs ... did I tell you, Great Me-maw is making you some special bread pudding?"

"She is?" Elizabeth asked.

Great Me-maw spoke up from the crowd, "*Ca c'est bon!*"

Marie translated, "She said it's good!"

Elizabeth laughed, "That much I can understand."

Michael lifted his glass again, "Tomorrow is the big day. Thank you all for traveling here to join us. And thank you to our wonderful family and dear friends for making this a dream come true for me."

"Me too!" Elizabeth added.

What can I say? We all had lied to poor Elizabeth, but she took it all in stride and was a beautiful bride the next day. During the first part of the wedding, my time was so occupied, I didn't have the chance to see if Scott was there. He found me during the reception when the food and music were in full swing. I was no longer the go-to person for anything and could relax. Even though it was a Sunday, I had a feeling that it wouldn't end until the wee hours of the morning.

Scott slipped into the chair next to me. "There you are! I've been looking for you. Nice wedding, you did a good job."

"Thank you," I replied. "I'm glad to see it finished."

"Isn't this the type of day you would like to have?" He flagged down a waiter and accepted two glasses of champagne. He placed one in front of me and raised his, "To the best wedding planner!"

I smiled and took a sip of the champagne. No expense was spared here, as I remembered all the bottles Michael and I had tasted before he chose the champagne.

"I've done the marriage routine before," I replied. "It wasn't very successful the first time. I don't want to repeat my mistake."

He raised his eyebrows, "Isn't every woman looking for their Prince Charming?"

I laughed ruefully, "He doesn't exist."

"Elizabeth seems to have found her's," he countered.

"My brother is one of the rare ones. He will make her an excellent husband. They both need each other."

"Is that what it comes down to?"

Taking a long sip of the champagne, I peered over the glass, "This conversation is too depressing. Let's dance!"

Scott took my hand and led me to the dance floor where he pulled me close. The song was a slow one, and I enjoyed the feeling of his arms.

He whispered into my ear, "Will you let me take you to dinner next week?"

"You know I live in Mintock now?"

"I guess if I want to see you, I have to come to you."

"That's the deal."

Tommy came up behind Scott and tapped him on the shoulder, "Give her up."

I winked playfully at Scott, "You can have me again later."

He did so reluctantly. Tommy whisked me away.

"Baby sister, you need to stay away from that bad boy."

I raised my eyebrow. "You really don't like him."

"He's an ass. You know he and Margaret had an affair."

"What? When? Does Michael know?" Margaret was my brother's ex-wife and was known fondly in our circle as the *bitch from hell*.

"No, or at least I don't think so. It wouldn't matter now, but Margaret saw Scot on the side when Michael was engaged to her. I found out years later after they were divorced. I ran into one of her sorority sisters, and she told me the dirty details. I figured so much time had passed by, that it wasn't necessary to dig up old shit."

I wrinkled my nose, "The last thing I want is Margaret's sloppy seconds. Does Marcus know? I'm surprised he would invite him to the wedding, especially how he felt about Michael's ex."

"No. Just you and me ... well, ... and Marie. We didn't want to upset the applecart by telling everyone this week. But, it looked like the two of you were getting kind of serious." He laughed and made kissing noises.

"Okay, enough of that." I slapped him playfully on the shoulder. I sighed, "Well, another one bites the dust."

"You weren't really interested, were you? He's annoying. Always trying to one-up us." He grinned wildly and spun me around. "Like that is even possible!"

I giggled when he pulled me in again. "Never!"

CHAPTER 13

With the fairytale wedding finished, I flew back to San Francisco the next morning. All my relatives stayed in New Orleans for a few more days, which meant I could enjoy peace on the plane. Even JuJu took a few extra days of vacation in Houston with her family.

I arrived in time for the board meeting, which was surprisingly interesting. The company was a small technology rich company looking for another infusion of cash for additional research and development. The discussion was right up my alley and would make most people insane, but for me, I enjoyed the discussion of stock splits and equity dilution.

Afterward, I spent the rest of the day at my best friends' house. Robert and Gary lived in a sunny yellow three-story row house in the Castro District of San Francisco. While I parked in their driveway, the garage door opened. Robert stood by the door leading into the house looking like a model straight from GQ. Tall and thin, he kept his dark brown hair cropped close to his head. His aquiline features could make him look haughty, but he was completely the opposite. His smile gave him away in an instant.

"She's here Gary! Move it!" he called out through the doorway behind him while holding a wriggling tri-color King Charles cavalier spaniel. "Oh baby, come to Papa!" Robert grinned, set down his beloved Buffy, and spread his arms wide.

"Bobby!" I cried out while hugging him.

Buffy immediately ran to me and yapped around my feet. I picked her up and let her give me kisses. Gary joined us, and we had a mutual three-person and a dog hug.

"Oh girl, look at those shoes!" Gary exclaimed in his deep Tennessee accent as he pointed to my feet. "Those are the new Jimmy Choo shoes, aren't they? I am dying here!" He fanned himself with his hands.

I stuck my foot out and modeled the black lace-up peep toe bootie. "Don't you love them?"

"Can you say jealous? They make your feet look tiny! Come on in. We just finished setting up in the back garden. Bobby is going to barbecue for us," Gary said as he wrapped his arm around my waist and led me through the kitchen.

With my shoes on, Gary was shorter than I was. He had tied his long blond wavy hair back and let it lay down his muscular back. The men were opposite in the looks department, Robert long and lean, and his husband with his muscle builder body.

Robert and I met in high school in the days before he came out of the closet. We had never dated, but he did take me to my high school prom. We met Gary while in college, and I felt the two men were destined for each other.

Robert tied an apron around his waist and shooed us out of the kitchen. "Everything is already outside. Let me do the finishing touches on the salad, and I'll be right out."

I followed Gary to the back of the richly decorated house into the garden, which was in a burst of color. Flowers of all different varieties bloomed around us. I sat in one of the heavily padded rattan verandah chairs, as Buffy jumped up and made herself at home in my lap. Gary, a landscape architect, was proud of his garden. The yard, which included a small greenhouse at the back of the lot, was a place where he could dabble in his love of horticulture.

He handed me a cocktail in a large hurricane glass. "I'm trying a new recipe. Let me know what you think."

I took a sip, it was icy cold and fruity flavored, and as soon as I swallowed, I coughed and sputtered. "What do you have in this? It's good, but it has a punch at the end."

He looked gleeful. "Do you really like it? Bobby thought it was a bit strong at first too, but keep at it," he laughed, "the burning will go away."

I shook my head giggling, "You guys are just trying to get me drunk!"

Robert came out with a platter of steaks. "You know it. You are a lot of fun when you're drunk. And then we'll take pictures and get rich when we sell them to the tabloids."

"What makes you think the tabloids want pictures of me? I'm not that famous."

"Oh, but you are." Robert picked up a magazine from the table next to him and handed it to me.

It was a Northern Californian magazine with a headline blazed across it, "*Being Rich in the Dot Com World.*" There was even a picture of me, which was not at all flattering. I grimaced and opened the magazine to the page.

"I remember this. The writer called me about six months ago wanting a few quotes for the article. At the time, it sounded harmless enough."

"And as your attorney, I've asked you to run requests like these through the public relations people," Robert said.

I quickly read through the article and frowned. "It makes me sound like a controlling bitch and a little crazy. The author probably spoke with Tim too. This sounds just like him."

Gary patted me on the top of my head. "The fact that you created a new way of searching the internet makes you a legendary crazy bitch, and that's why we love you, sweetheart."

I lay the magazine aside. "Am I really that bad?"

Both men grinned at me raising their eyebrows.

"Okay, okay," I acquiesced, "I'm bad!" Laughing, I pointed to the steaks, "Damn it, Bobby, get those steaks going."

Robert turned and opened the barbecue. "How were the hunky's weddings?"

I chuckled at the nickname given to my brother and Marcus. Their paths had crossed over the years. Robert was Michael's attorney too, and his firm had handled his divorce. The boys always commented about the drool-worthiness of Michael and his friends.

"Perfect and perfect. Two different styles for two different couples. I'm exhausted from the ordeal, though. It was a lot of work, but I'm glad I was able to give Michael and Elizabeth a great wedding."

Gary sat next to me on a matching chair and put his feet up on the ottoman to relax. "How are the mommies-to-be? I bet Elizabeth looked amazing in her dress. And Michael's daughter, has she calmed down about her pregnancy yet?"

"She was a beautiful bride. She felt the baby move during the ceremony. It was cool for us all to share in it. And yes, Tammy is looking happy. She's transferring to Stanford in the fall so she can be close to her boyfriend, Jason. She'll be taking her undergraduate classes there after her pregnancy."

Robert raised his eyebrows. "How much did that cost you?"

"Stop being a cynic. Who cares? I called in a few favors, and they'll be naming the building after me," I smirked.

They laughed as Robert put the steaks on the barbecue.

Gary turned to me and was solemn, "Have you given it any more thought?"

"What?" I looked puzzled, and then it hit me. He was talking about *The Baby*. I had been around two pregnant women and felt the clock ticking away. I seriously thought about motherhood. "Oh. That. You know I love you guys, and you would be the best fathers in the world, but even with all the baby stuff floating around me, I don't think I'm ready yet."

Gary nodded, "We understand. But the offer is there." He chuckled and shook his glass, "Baby in a cup. All we need is a turkey baster!"

I took another sip of my cocktail and coughed. "I think I'm getting used to this."

"See I told you." Gary grinned. "A few more sips and you'll be downing them like a drunken sailor."

"That's all I need. I can't since I'm driving back to Mintock tonight."

"Why? We have your room all made up for you," Gary whined.

I sighed, "Because I agreed to foster a dog and have to pick him up tomorrow."

Robert turned his attention to me with surprise … no, shock on his face. "You foster a dog? What happened? Did someone start the apocalypse and not tell me?"

"Com'on, I'm not that bad."

He pointed the tongs he held at me, "You have a hard time keeping houseplants alive. I can't even fathom what you'd do to a dog."

"That is true, I don't have the green thumb like Gary, but I've cared for dogs before. Besides, it won't be for very long," I argued.

We enjoyed the meal and the evening. Gary managed to ply me with enough of his new cocktail so I couldn't drive home. I ended up staying the night, and after they had fed me breakfast, I was on the road again.

On the way to Mintock, I questioned my sanity in agreeing to foster Koa. But, when I walked into the animal hospital, and he limped out to me, there was something in his face and eyes. I melted on the spot.

CHAPTER 14

Koa's tail wagged, then he looked at me. The cast on his front leg was dark blue, and I almost blushed remembering the conversation with Kian. It surprised me to see how small Koa was. On the night I brought him in, I didn't think much about his size. He truly was white too. It appeared the techs had gone to a great effort to clean him up.

I kneeled on the floor and put my hands out for him to sniff. He moved closer to me, and his tail wagged again.

"Hey boy, are you ready to spend some time with me?" I said softly.

I petted him under the chin and moved my hands around him. When I did, he became a wriggling ball of fur. Dancing in a circle, as much as the cast would allow, he lifted himself onto his back legs and leaned his body against me. He looked at me with soft brown eyes.

I melted some more.

Kian's voice behind us came crashing over me like a wave, "Koa is excited to see you."

I met his smile with my own. "He's in much better shape than when I brought him in. He looks great!" I picked up Koa. My heart beat a little faster, and it wasn't the exertion from standing.

"He's a trouper. Aren't you my little friend?" Kian said.

I watched those fascinating hands stroke Koa's head. He wriggled in my arms wanting to get down to the floor. Kian pulled two bottles of pills out of his coat pocket and handed them to me.

"Give these to him twice a day. They are antibiotics. These others you can give him if he needs them for pain. Keep him quiet if possible. No long moonlit walks yet, and bring him back to see us in ten days. We'll remove the cast and do some more x-rays to ensure everything is stable."

I nodded and dropped the bottles into my purse. "Thank you, Dr. Mc ... ahh ... Kian. Thank you for saving him. I'll take good care of him until you can find a family who will take him."

A shadow passed over his face, but it was brief, and then he leaned toward me as if to guard our conversation against the others in the waiting room.

"Have dinner with me Friday night," he whispered.

I blinked at him. Did I hear him correctly? Did he ask me out on a date? I must have looked confused because he repeated his invitation.

He touched my elbow as if to bring me back to reality, "Will you have dinner with me Friday night?"

"Um," I began, "ah, okay." A million thoughts bombarded my brain, and chief among them was Carrie's comment, *"He's not interested in older women."* He had to see I was older than he was.

Kian's smile brightened on his face, and he stepped back, "Good. I'll call you then?"

"Okay," I repeated.

"Let me help you out with Koa." He bent over and easily picked him up.

"Okay." Not one who was usually caught by a loss of words, I certainly had none at my immediate disposal.

He tucked Koa away in the crate I had purchased at the local pet store. Kian chuckled when he saw the two dog beds, leashes, collars, food, treats, and assorted toys in a box on the back seat.

"You're not going to be spoiled Koa. It will be bare bones for you, my friend," he said turning toward me. "I'll look forward to seeing you on Friday night."

"Thank you again." I felt awkward standing there, so I stuck my hand out. I wanted to conclude our conversation and get to the safety of the front seat of my car before I drowned in the deep blue pools of his eyes.

Fortunately, he didn't leave my hand dangling in the air. His hand enveloped mine. It was warm and soft. Yes, take me right now.

"I did the easy part, Christina, you did the hardest. You rescued him. It would have been very easy for you to ignore the little gray bundle, but you didn't. Now not only will his body heal but maybe his heart will heal too."

His words put a lump in my throat. Why did I get the feeling he was talking about something else besides Koa? I didn't know what to say. He squeezed my hand, and when he let go, my hand felt suddenly cold.

After I had pulled out into the traffic, I punched in JuJu's telephone number. It took three rings, but she answered.

"Hey, boss. Did you pick up Koa?"

"He's in the car, and we're headed to the cabin. Thanks for all the recommendations about what to get at the pet store for him."

She laughed, "No problem. Did you buy out the store?"

"Pretty much. The clerk also had lots of recommendations too."

"I bet she saw you coming."

"Probably. But, I like supporting the local stores," I said as I turned onto the main highway, which would lead me to the south side of Lake

Mintock. "By the way, did you have a chance to transfer the donation to Harry's Hounds we discussed last week?"

"Yes and no," she said. "The wire transfer has left our bank, but the organization won't be notified about it until tomorrow morning. I made sure their bank wouldn't charge them a fee for the transfer first before I flipped the switch on the fifty grand. Why is there a problem?"

"No," I answered. "Just curious. Thanks for taking care of it for me."

"You're welcome. Can I get back to my Tex-Mex? We're about ready to go into the restaurant!"

I laughed, "Yes, of course. Sorry for interrupting you. Have fun!"

So, the donation was not the reason for the dinner invitation from Kian. Part of me was happy for the discovery and yet I was still perplexed. It was also not the cause of the unusual words he left me with at the end of our conversation. This gave me plenty to chew on. What would be his reaction to the donation? When I gave instructions to JuJu, I hadn't even considered what he would think. All that had mattered to me was Harry's Hounds was a well-run organization that used its contributions wisely.

I turned off at the utility road that ran alongside the highway. This lane led to a group of houses along the lakeshore. First on the right, Debi and Don's house. They were good friends of Michael and Elizabeth. Don's father, Frank, was the Chief of Police in Mintock and his mother Annie, a high-ranking tribal elder for the area's Pomo Native American tribe. Then there was Lewis, the local Fire Department Captain, and his wife Angel. My new house was next, on the largest lot in the Cove. I drove by slowly surprised how far the contractors had come in only a few days. It appeared as I looked through the windows the flooring was installed on the bottom floor. The garage was completed, and the door was hung. I planned to walk to the house later to check out the progress that had been made.

Michael's house was next and then Elizabeth's cabin. I stopped at the back door of the cottage and lifted Koa out of the crate. He wriggled to be set loose, but I held him firmly to bring him inside. Once down on the floor, he quickly explored every possible inch. It was surprising how fast he could move with the cast. Then he circled back around to me.

"Does it meet with your approval?" I smiled with my hands on my hips.

He barked and set off to investigate the area again. I unloaded his food, toys, and beds. Elizabeth had made it into a homey little place. With only the two small bedrooms and bathrooms, the main room was a combination of kitchen, dining, and living room. She had spent some money upgrading it, with the addition of central air conditioning and modernizing the bathrooms and kitchen. The cabin still had a rustic appeal with pine walls and hardwood floors.

The view of the lake out the front windows and from the porch was spectacular. The home faced north, so it had a commanding view of the sunrise and sunset. I fell in love with this side of the lake the first time I visited Michael's house. It was quiet and well preserved with only the handful of houses along the road. The next cove over, while you could see more of the lake, had heavier traffic and far more homes which stretched up into the hills. What I looked for was solitude, and this area delivered. After the constant noise and crowds of New York, and even the substantial traffic in San Francisco, I relished this little slice of paradise.

It was different from Hawaii too, wealthy people surrounded me there, but the residents in this cove were regular people. Well, besides Elizabeth who was a bestselling romance author, and Michael, a world-famous wildlife photographer, and conservationist. My brother already considered me the resident babysitter, and frankly, I was overjoyed to oblige. I had cared for both of his daughters while they were young. Perhaps by being close to the new baby, it would stave off the maternal rumblings I felt.

When I finally sat on the couch, Koa came over, parked himself by my feet, and looked up at me.

"You want up?"

I leaned over and placed him next to me. Immediately the paw without the cast pressed on my leg, and as he dragged it across, he looked at me hopefully.

"Oh, okay. Com'on over."

I pulled him up into my lap, and he curled up into a little round ball. His eyes closed when I began to pet his soft little head, and he promptly fell asleep.

My heart melted again.

Then it began. The soft little snores emanating from him were becoming louder. I turned on the television and chuckled when I had to turn up the volume to drown out his snores.

After an hour of television, I was bored. I managed to slip Koa into his bed next to the couch. He stirred a bit and then fell blissfully back to sleep, snoring away. Grabbing my keys, I walked over to the construction site.

It was after five, and all the workers had already packed up and left for the day. It looked like perhaps there was still a worker hanging around because I spied a new Jaguar F Type convertible parked on the side of the house. I used my key to open the locked double front door.

I called out, "Hello? Is anyone here?"

Everything was eerily silent for a few seconds, and then I heard footsteps coming from the interior of the house.

When the man came into view, I dropped my keys and silently mouthed, "What the hell?"

CHAPTER 15

"What are you doing in my house?" My voice held the shock I felt.

"Ahh..." Scott began. With the intense stare I leveled at him, he shifted from one foot to the other. "I was in the area and remembered you mentioning building your house in Mintock, so I thought I'd stop by and take a look."

"By breaking and entering? How did you get in?" My anger rose quickly, and it took everything I had in me to remain calm.

He grinned and sauntered toward me. "It wasn't so much breaking as it was entering. Your patio at the back of the house is missing one of the large sliding windows."

I frowned. "A missing window does not give you permission to enter a house, as an attorney, I would think you'd know that."

His expression was sheepish. "I'm sorry. Most of the construction guys were still here when I arrived, and they didn't question me. When they left, I started to wander around. It's a fantastic house, a very creative use of space. It's all the talk in town about the big house going up using all this computer technology." He tried to placate me.

"I didn't realize you were so familiar with Mintock," I said. "It isn't as well-known as some of the bigger tourist areas around here."

The tension drained from me. Scott seemed to relax as if he were taking cues from my body language.

"A good friend of mine lives in Mintock. He's the mayor," he answered proudly. "We get together on Tuesday nights, for some..." he paused, "gaming."

I smirked. "Oh, the boy's poker night?"

"Yeah, you can call it that. I wasn't exaggerating," he said changing the subject, "the house looks great!"

I nodded, finally looking around at my surroundings. "Yeah, it's been a lot more work than I imagined. I've never built a house from the ground up before. I'm thankful Elizabeth's cabin was available to me."

"Will you give me a tour?"

I raised my eyebrow while I thought about his request. It sounded harmless, so I agreed. "Let me see if there is enough light." I pointed at a small monitor built in a wall panel close to the door. I spoke with the clear voice. "Spiti, corner lighting all rooms at seventy-five percent."

The panel beeped softly and repeated, "Corner lighting all rooms at seventy-five percent."

The illumination, built into the edges of the ceiling began to brighten slowly.

Scott wore a surprised expression, which made me happy. "I suppose all the rooms are lit now?"

"Yep," I said proudly.

"And Spiti is the name of the house?"

"It means house in Greek."

"Do you have those panels in all the rooms?"

"They handle more than the lights too. I can also use an application on my cell phone to do the same thing, even when I'm not at home. Let me show you the house. Careful, it looks like some of the floors are still not finished. This entry area leads to most of the rooms on the bottom floor; the kitchen, laundry facilities, the garage on the right, and on the left, is the entertainment room. If we go straight, that will take us directly into the living room. I don't think they've started on the kitchen yet. Let's try the entertainment room."

"Lead the way," he answered.

Scott followed closely behind me. He whistled when we entered. I agreed with his appraisal, the dramatic marble hearth was magnificent. The color was a rich rainforest brown with red veins running through it, and all on a dark gray background. Once the room was filled with the billiards table, dark chocolate leather couches and chairs, and floor to ceiling bookshelves, it would be the perfect area to entertain.

Looking up he paused and then turned to me with astonishment in his voice. "Is the roof retractable?"

"Yes, the outside glass walls fold away too. I don't want to try to open everything until my builder gives me the approval." I pointed to the monitor by the door we just entered. "The little panel opens everything. It's cool to watch, and surprisingly not noisy at all. The windows pull back to this corner behind the outside wall. A movie screen drops from the remaining ceiling in front of the bookshelves."

"This is unbelievable. When you told me it was technology rich, I didn't imagine this." He touched the cold marble of the hearth.

"The living room is through this door."

We went into the next room. What we could see of the gleaming dark hardwood floor was impressive. Most of the floors were covered with rubber matting because they were still working on the glass wall, which looked over the lake.

"I'm assuming this is also retractable." he said pointing to the wall.

"It looks like they are having trouble with it too." There was a small portion on the side that appeared to be askew, which is how Scott made his way into the house. I frowned, "The contractor should not have left that area unsecured. The last thing I need are vandals breaking in and destroying the interior."

Scott wandered over to the huge hearth against the back wall. The fireplace was made from luxurious dark brown marble, which matched the hardwood floors flawlessly. It was carved almost to look like wood.

"This is a magnificent piece," he said.

I grinned with pleasure. "I rescued it from a demolished house located in Canada. It's been in storage for several years. This room was actually designed around the hearth."

He ran his hands over it appreciating the fine detail of the carving. "I'm impressed, you know your design and architecture."

"I have a few friends who helped me with the design."

He leaned up against the fireplace and gave me a long look. "So, why don't we have dinner tonight? I believe I asked you out while we were still in New Orleans."

His words shocked me back into reality. I had been so focused on showing off my new home I forgot who he was. I had already decided not to see him any longer, especially with the news Tommy had shared with me. I shuddered inwardly; sleeping with my ex-sister-in-law showed me just how little taste he had.

"So, you slept with Margaret while she was engaged to Michael." I posed it as a statement and not a question.

"Ahh, I see Tommy spoke with you."

"Yes, he did. He was a little worried we were getting too close."

He scowled. "Tommy never could keep his mouth shut. Is that the reason you backed away from me in New Orleans?"

I looked at him with disbelief. "Aside from the fact that you're not trustworthy... you're a shitty kind of friend. What did Michael do to you to deserve that treatment?"

Scott spread his hands wide. "An opportunity arose, and I took it. Come on, it was over twenty years ago, you're not going to rake me over the coals, are you? Besides, I didn't think Michael would actually marry her."

My brother is a man of his word," I replied coldly.

There was a pause between us, which was as wide as the Grand Canyon even though we were not more than ten feet apart.

He broke the silence first. "I guess you and me don't have a chance?"

"I don't think there ever was you and me. You knew my brother, I wanted to be friendly."

He blew out a long breath, "What they say about you is true."

"And what is that?" Here it comes... I steeled myself.

"You're a tough nut to crack. You don't like letting people in. Some even call you a cold-hearted bitch."

My face remained stoic because I was practiced, it wasn't the first time I had heard that description. Like all the other times, the words pierced my heart, and I could feel the blood gush from the wound.

I nodded slowly. "You're right. I do have that reputation because I don't let anyone ride roughshod over me. I wasn't born yesterday. I stand by my principles."

His voice softened, "That can be isolating."

"I don't want a friend who doesn't stand by theirs, so if you call that lonely, then I welcome it. In my world, though, I don't have room for people who think only of themselves."

"Is that what you think of me?"

"So far your actions haven't proven otherwise to me. I love my family, anything that hurts them wounds me."

He shook off my response. "Your brother was not damaged by my sleeping with Margaret. They hadn't married yet anyway. No one was the wiser."

"Don't you think you compromised her into thinking she could get away with it?"

"Hey, don't blame me for her behavior. She came to me, and what is a guy supposed to do?" He again spread his hands out.

I rolled my eyes. "Look, I'm not going to argue with you about this. I don't care what you think about me. We are not a couple. I would appreciate if you didn't drop by again. And I certainly wouldn't expect you to be in my house again."

He looked disbelievingly at me. It told me he had not been asked to leave very many places. There was a menacing appearance about him. It felt borderline threatening.

Scott glared, and the hostility in his voice was evident, "You're not worth it. Dumpy and chunky were never my preference."

With those final words, he slipped out of the open window and was gone. I stood there not quite believing the encounter.

"Weirdo," I said aloud to the room.

Thankfully, I would never have to cross paths with him again.

CHAPTER 16

Sometime in the middle of the night, a thunderstorm complete with lightning flashes hit. The noise and light woke Koa, and he began to howl and shake, which woke me. He was already on the bed and insisted on sleeping next to me when we retired for the evening, so I wrapped him in my arms and held him until his shaking subsided.

I discovered right away that he loved to be petted and his affection knew no bounds. I lay in bed stroking his soft little head and whispered that everything would be alright. He whimpered a bit and moved closer if that was even possible. He had my number.

Finally, around five in the morning, the rain stopped. I decided to start my day because I wouldn't be able to go back to sleep. I jumped in the shower and made coffee. Afterward, sitting in my robe at the desk by the window, I watched the sun come up first over the hills, and then over the lake. Everything outside looked freshly washed and the sun hitting the water made a sort of steam rise above it. It promised to be a hot and humid day.

Suddenly, the sky clouded up again and turned a dark, ugly gray. Before I knew it, large drops were falling from the sky in rapid succession. A drenching rain, it was as if someone poured water from a pitcher.

A knock on the door yanked me out of my thoughts, I glanced at the clock, and wondered who was here so early? Koa woke up startled, barked, and hobbled to the back door. I wrapped my robe tighter around me and tugged it together around my throat.

I peered through the kitchen window and saw Kian standing on the back porch, soaked to the skin. He wore a gray sweatshirt with the hood pulled over his head. Koa snuffled at the door with his tail wagging furiously.

When I opened the door, he pushed the hood back off his head. There was already a puddle gathering under his feet, and I noticed a motorcycle behind him.

"I'm sorry for coming so early, but I saw your light on and took a chance you'd be up," he muttered softly while Koa was attempting to dance around him.

"Kian, you're soaked. Come on in, and let me get some towels so you can dry off."

"No, I can't. I don't want to mess up your floors. The rain caught me by surprise this morning. I thought it was behind us."

"Com'on," I drew him inside, releasing the death grip I had around the lapels of my robe. "I can't let you stand out there. Here stand on the throw rug. I can put it in the dryer later."

He grudgingly came in, and when he stood on the rug, he bent down to acknowledge Koa. "Hey little man, I see you've got it pretty good now. All cozy and warm for you."

I pulled several towels out of the linen closet in the utility room and handed them to him. Koa trotted away, no doubt to find a toy he could present to our guest.

Kian wiped his face and patted his head dry. "Thank you, Christina. I didn't mean to intrude on your morning. I don't want a puddle to form under me either."

I looked down and expected to find a wet patch under me instead. This man was hot while he was dripping wet. His clothes clung to him leaving no doubt about the physique underneath. I was likely to come down with a case of the vapors very soon.

He was silent. I glanced down and noticed why. When I reached for the towels in the closet, my robe had opened, and he had an extended view of my cleavage. I tried very casually to close my robe, but I saw the smile creep onto his face. How did I get myself into these situations?

"Um, would you like some coffee?" I asked hoping that I wasn't blushing.

He did have the good grace to look me in the face. "No. I don't want to trouble you this morning. I only came by to thank you."

Koa came back into the little utility room at that moment with a chew toy. He planted himself next to Kian's feet and proceeded to chomp on it as it squeaked unmercifully.

"No thanks are necessary. Koa and I are getting along just fine. He's quite a bit of company for me. I don't mind keeping him until you find a family for him."

"No, that's not what I meant. Although, yes, I thank you for taking care of him." He bent down with a bit of exasperation and took the toy from Koa. "There will be no more of that noise my good fellow." Koa sat up and barked at him. "No. You may not have this infernal thing back until I've left." Kian looked back at me. "I wanted to thank you for the generous donation. My accountant called me this morning to tell me what had landed in the fund. I can't believe you did that. You don't know what this means to us. We'll be able to finish the kennels now, which means we'll be able to rescue more dogs." His voice was full of emotion, "It's a magnificent thing that you've done. I wanted to thank you in person."

His gratitude made me feel warm all over.

"The Foundation did a thorough check of your organization, it's well run. You do a lot with little money. They noticed too, that while you do get corporate sponsorship, you get the bulk from individual contributors. That's important to us. The community and surrounding areas have applauded your efforts. Someone will be in contact with you to see how we can help in other ways too."

His face broke out into a big smile, "Then I was truly blessed the day you contacted the hospital about our little Koa."

I returned his beaming smile. "And we were fortunate that you dropped everything to come to his rescue."

"So, I'll still see you Friday night then? I'll pick you up at seven. Wear something comfortable, like jeans, okay?"

Intrigued, I nodded. "Okay."

He handed the towel back to me. "I better stop dripping on your carpet. Thank you again, Christina."

He held my hand in his. That was enough for me. Oh, those long luscious fingers. As he opened the door to leave, he bent back over to Koa to return his toy and gave him an affectionate pat.

I watched him get on the motorcycle and tried not to drool. He saluted me as he headed out toward the highway.

What was I doing? Kian was ten years younger than I was. I was not going to become one of those women everyone snickered about, what were they called? Cougars. Yes. That ridiculous term. Besides, he was not interested in me. Carrie had let me know clearly that I would not be his preference.

I sighed. "Yes, it's all for the best. I don't have time for this." I watched Koa who happily destroyed the toy. "Would you like some breakfast?"

As if he understood me, he wagged his long tail.

CHAPTER 17

By Friday, our little cove began to look like normal with everyone returning from New Orleans. Tammy collected Michael and Elizabeth's dogs from the boarding kennels. She cared for them while they took a week to Hawaii for their honeymoon.

I struggled not to think about my date with Kian. I tried not to be nervous but failed miserably. Intrigued by his direction to dress casually, I felt like a teenager rummaging through my closet to find the perfect informal attire. I didn't do casual well. I did designer and sweatpants; the in-between was difficult for me. After years of wearing jeans because it was all I could afford, I felt like Scarlet O'Hara raising my fist to the sky swearing never to be poor again. I didn't want to see another bowl of ramen noodle soup or a nasty frozen bean burrito again.

I did find a pair of jeans that fit and looked decent on me. The fabric was worn in the knees, and I had forgotten how comfortable they could be. I topped the pants with a simple navy cotton blouse which I tucked in and added a belt.

After feeding Koa, I sat down to wait. Nervously. When my cell phone rang, I almost jumped out of my skin. Frank, the police chief was returning my call from earlier in the day. Michael had suggested I contact him to find out about the driver of the black truck.

"Hello, Christina. Sorry, it took me so long to get back to you. We were stuck at the airport waiting for our luggage that decided to take another flight home. It wouldn't have been a problem, but Annie purchased so much stuff in New Orleans, we had boxes to retrieve also."

"Oh, I'm so sorry to hear that. It's good that you got home all in one piece ... or is that pieces?"

He chuckled. "Too many pieces. Now, you had a question about a tricked out black truck with the license plate that says BIG ONE?"

"Yes. Have you seen it around?"

"I'll say I have. It belongs to our mayor. Why do you ask? Is there a problem? I know he drives it too fast sometimes, but a lot of us do up here on our mountain roads, we are not used to much traffic."

"I think I had an encounter with him up on top of the mountain about two weeks ago." I described the event with Koa and the subsequent episode at the veterinary clinic. "I don't know what's happening with the mayor and Dr. McDermott, but I saw a person driving the truck on top of the mountain throw Koa from the truck."

Frank was silent for several moments before he spoke. "Did you see who was driving the vehicle? Can you make a positive identification?"

"No, I can't. I didn't see the person driving. I don't even know if there was more than one person in the truck. I am confident about the license plate, however. Kian… I mean Dr. McDermott, told me there are problems with dogfight clubs in the area. If you could have seen Koa, he was barely alive when I found him."

"Christina, who have you spoken to about this incident?" his voice was foreboding.

"Michael and Elizabeth know, Dr. McDermott and his staff, my parents, my nieces, and my attorney." I racked my brain trying to remember if I told anyone else. "Why?"

"We do have problems with this in our town, and the people associated with these rings can be dangerous. I don't want you to discuss it with anyone else for the time being. I have to follow-up on this, but it needs to be done carefully."

"Is the mayor dangerous?" I asked.

"This is the first time I've heard the mayor might be involved. It is hard for me to believe he is. He is a respected man in our town, and he is a tribal elder. It is counter to everything the tribe believes to participate in something like this. If he is mixed up in it, I must investigate carefully. Mayor Busch is well regarded and powerful in this region."

"What can I do to help? I have resources available."

"Right now, I want you not to speak about this to anyone else," he instructed. "I don't know if he is involved. I'll make quiet inquiries."

"Okay," I replied. "Would you keep me updated?"

"Certainly."

I drew a heavy breath, I felt better after our conversation but hoped I had made the right decision in confiding in Frank. Michael trusted him implicitly.

Koa sat at my feet and thumped his tail against the carpet. Seeing his sweet face, I said, "We will find out who did this to you. I promise."

He barked a millisecond before the loud knock. We both made our way to the back door. The butterflies in my stomach made my palms sweaty, and I brushed them against my jeans.

Seeing Kian who stood in front of me caused me to gasp. Standing there was raw sexual energy dressed in black leather. Why was it so difficult to breathe? From his shit-kickers and leather pants to the black wife beater t-shirt and well-worn leather jacket, it was a sight you'd see on the cover of a romance novel. A naughty romance novel.

He lifted his head and turned on the killer smile. Coupled with his sapphire eyes, I was done. Completely done. Take a fork to me and lift me off the fire.

His eyes raked me from head to foot, and he grinned again. Apparently, my wardrobe choice met his expectations.

Koa was all over him, and I just stood there. Mouth gaping open.

"Hello Christina, I see you're ready. Do you have a jacket?" He pointed to the motorcycle parked behind him.

"Um..." I paused because my brain had apparently stopped working. I had to reboot. "Yes," I said slowly. "Let me get it." I tentatively pointed to the bedroom door. "I'll be right back."

I left him standing in the doorway, and closed the bedroom door. It was then I freaked out.

I mouthed silently, "Oh my gosh, oh my gosh, oh my gosh!" What was I going to do? I pulled out my leather bomber jacket from the closet. What the hell was I doing? The butterflies in my stomach multiplied and made me feel almost nauseous. Shit!!

I looked at my shoes, those heels wouldn't do on a motorcycle. I changed them for a pair of Gianvito Rossi heeled ankle booties.

Walking back out to Kian, he helped me into the jacket. "Nice," he said as his hands stroked down my shoulders to my elbows.

I tried to think of a suitable reply. My brain clearly was offline. No intelligent responses were coming anytime soon.

CHAPTER 18

Kian handed me a large helmet when we reached the motorcycle.

"This is for you. Have you ever ridden on the back of a bike before?" he asked.

I shook my head.

"I want you to wrap your arms around me, and hold on tight. Okay?"

I nodded my head. I would not have a problem with that, touching inappropriate areas on his body was entirely different.

"Move your body in the same direction I do, okay?"

I nodded again. "Will you go slowly?"

He winked at me. "Of course, I will. Be sure to hang on tight."

Kian helped me with the helmet and to climb on behind him. Seizing my thighs, he pulled me against him, cocooning him tightly. My arms encircled his waist, and I was careful not to let my hands dangle lower.

Suddenly, I heard his voice in my ears, "Christina, can you hear me okay?"

I whispered my reply, "Yes."

Apparently, there was a microphone built into the helmet.

Being so close to him, my entire body felt electric. The engine roared to life, and his voice was inside my helmet again.

"Ready?"

"Yes!" I said breathlessly. "Slow okay?"

I heard him chuckle and we were off! The wind rushed against me, and all I thought was *I'm going to die!* His body was firm under my hands, even through his jacket I could feel his muscles tightening and relaxing as we rounded the curve to put us on the highway. Didn't I ask him to take it slow? We were passing vehicles at speeds I would have never attempted in a car. The vibration from the engine moved through me, it was the most erotic experience I ever felt, too bad I was too scared to enjoy it.

"Kian, please slow down. This is too fast for me."

He immediately moved over to the right lane and slowed his speed.

"Sorry, I didn't mean to frighten you."

"Okay, this is better." I straightened a bit, but still held him firmly. "Where are we going?"

He laughed, "I wondered when you were going to ask. Ahh, Christina, you are too trusting. Hopping on the back of a motorcycle like this is second nature to you."

His voice was alluring and combined with the rumbling of the engine, I wouldn't have been surprised if I climaxed right there on the bike. All my blood was now centered around my core and the heat it generated made me want to rub myself against him. What was I thinking? What was I doing here with him? Was it the danger he exuded? Wow, his leather pants had fit him like a glove in all the right places. Kian's words interrupted the fantasy running through my mind of him and me naked.

"There's a nice little restaurant between here and Ashley. They have good bands on the weekend. You know, the kinds that are good to dance to."

"Oh, okay." I tried to picture in my mind a restaurant that would be off this road. I had nothing... then I remembered... Michael had told me about a place and warned me not to go there. Sure enough, Kian signaled to exit the highway, and he turned into a dirt parking lot. In front of us stood Ray's Saloon. He was taking me to a biker bar! What the hell?

Yes, there were a few cars parked, but mostly it was motorcycles. Big expensive looking bikes. Some patrons were standing outside, and they gave us the once over as we dismounted. Okay, it felt like their eyes were boring into my back. They made no pretense about staring either.

Kian took my hand, and we approached them. Imagine my surprise when one of them greeted us with a nod.

"Hey, doc. How are ya doing?" his gruff voice called out, and he took another long drag on a cigarette.

The man looked at me with interest. He was probably older than I was as evidenced by his graying temples. At least I wasn't the oldest person here. Thank goodness.

"Doing decent Jim. How's Cherise?" Kian asked.

"Good," he replied. "Her fleas are gone. That pill really helped."

"Glad to hear it. Make sure you give it to her once a month."

Kian held the door open for me and as we entered another man said in a low voice, "Better not let Shelby see her." The men snickered as the door closed behind us.

We waited a moment while our eyes adjusted to the darkness of the bar. Kian held my hand, and he pulled me with him. We found an empty table in the middle of the room and set our helmets on a chair.

"Wait here. I'll get some drinks. What would you like?" he asked while he helped me out of my jacket, and then threw them both on top of the helmets.

What I wanted was for him not to leave me alone. What I really wanted was for him to take me home. Now. He squeezed my hand. Could he read my face?

"I'll have a beer."

Smiling kindly he asked, "What kind? Dark, light? They specialize in a lot of the small breweries in the area."

"I like dark beers. You decide."

"Got it." He winked and set off toward the bar.

I looked around slowly. This day was certainly going into the diary. Patrons sat at the tables around me talking and laughing, and blues music was piped in from somewhere. The video monitors on the surrounding walls played sports channels. Thankfully, no one was paying any attention to me.

Kian returned quickly, and he set down a black looking beer in front of me. He pulled the chair next to me close and sat, so our knees met.

Touching his glass with mine, he grinned, "Cheers!"

"What is it?" I asked pointing at my beer.

His lips turned up into a smirk, "That my dear is beer. I believe you ordered it."

"Kian!" I admonished him.

Laughing, "Oh, you mean what type of beer? That's a Guinness. Same as I'm having."

I nodded and took a sip. It was good, smooth, and creamy. They served it at the right temperature too.

"Is the beer okay?" he asked.

"Yes, it's delicious. I'm curious, why did you ask me out?"

He raised an eyebrow. "That's an interesting question."

I held my breath waiting for the answer. Maybe I didn't want to know.

Leaning in close to me, his fingers grazed my cheek and then my chin softly. "I think you are beautiful Christina and I like your compassion. I want to get to know you."

My breath caught in my throat.

"Now you tell me why you said yes." He leaned back in his chair.

I shook my head.

"It's only fair. I answered you." His grin went all the way up to his eyes.

"Well, I..." I faltered and somehow was saved when a bottle red-haired waitress came up behind us and threw two menus on the table.

The waitress glared at Kian. "Who is she? Are you her escort?"

He responded quickly, "Shelby, there's no need to be rude."

"You didn't call me," she scowled.

She wore black short shorts and a small low cut t-shirt that barely contained her, let alone her enormous breasts. Tied around her waist was a black apron. She looked young. I guessed no more than twenty-two or three.

I wanted the floor to swallow me. Now. Anytime would be good.

"And I told you I wouldn't." Kian's accent became stronger. "Perhaps we should talk about this somewhere else."

"No, I'm on duty. I have to work. I want to know why you didn't call me?" she insisted, her voice getting loud enough to draw attention.

"Shelby, let's talk about this later. You know why I don't call you."

She sighed and retrieved her pad from the pocket of her apron. "Do you know what you want to eat?"

Kian scooped up the two menus and handed them to her.

"Yeah, the fish and chips." He looked at me briefly, and I nodded, thinking Yes! Anything, just make her go away. "I'd like vinegar instead of the tartar sauce, and ketchup for the fries. Have Sam make the fries well done," he said.

She bent over and leaned against Kian giving us both a view of her ample bosom. "I know how you like it."

When she was gone, I asked, "Is she going to spit into our food?"

He winked at me, "Probably. But don't worry about that, the food is good here, and she'll forget soon enough that she's angry at me."

"Do I want to know why you didn't call her? Did you two date?"

"No, we did not date. Every time I come here, she makes sure she leaves her telephone number where I can see it. Somehow she took my friendly personality as interest in her."

"So you're not interested in her?" I asked with raised eyebrows.

"No, I am not," Kian answered flatly. "She's not my type. I like tall women who wear little high-heeled boots on motorcycles. Now, let's get back to the question you have neglected to answer. Why did you say yes?"

My voice faltered, he was referring to my shoes. "I don't know why I said yes." I could not say it was because he was big, beautiful, sexy as hell, made me squirm, and had luscious lips.

Grinning, he moved his head closer to me and put his arm around my chair back. "Are you sure you don't know? Was it my sapphire eyes?" He blinked several times.

"You are a big tease." I laughed tentatively. My face flushed. Was it suddenly getting warm in here?

It was him. Kian radiated heat. And he released it all in my direction. His hand came up to my face, and he stroked my reddened cheek with his thumb while his fingers curled under my chin. His face, no his eyes, mesmerized me. They were dark, languid pools where a woman could lose herself. My lips parted slowly. Was it because it was becoming difficult to breathe or due to his fingers gently tilting my chin down? I didn't know. His face drew closer, and everything moved in slow motion.

His lips touched mine so softly that I almost questioned whether they truly did. His arm came around me and then his mouth pulled me in. Teasing my lips with his tongue, my mouth parted further. I wanted this kiss. Badly. Kian took all thought away from me. This was raw. It was sexual. It could become an addiction. He delved inside with not a moment of tentativeness, and he claimed me. When his teeth pulled at my bottom lip, and he gently bit the corners of my mouth, I was lost for good. No one had ever kissed me like this. No one.

This kiss ended, and he pulled back only a few inches. Our eyes opened, and I could see the moment affected him as much as it did me.

Both of us breathing heavily, I asked softly, "Why?"

He replied huskily, "Because you needed to be kissed and I needed to do it."

I wanted to touch my lips as I could still feel the burning trace on them. Who was this man?

CHAPTER 19

What had I just done? Almost having sex with someone in the middle of a bar, with crowds of people around? Had I lost my mind?

I snuck a quick look around. No one gave us a second glance. The pool players continued with their games, couples were dancing to the music, and people stood at the bar ordered drinks. We weren't on their radar.

My attention went back to Kian who looked at me as if he was studying a puzzle.

"Tell me about the wedding," he said after taking a drink from his beer.

How he could switch back to a normal conversation was beyond me. My lips still tingled.

"Oh... it was wonderful."

Somehow, we began to find words. His laughter rang in my ears when I regaled him about the more entertaining events. Shelby delivered our food, and to my surprise, she acted normal and was pleasant. We ordered another two beers and dug in.

Our discussion eventually turned to Koa. I broached the subject, which I wondered about for the past two weeks.

"Do you know who abandoned Koa on the mountain road?"

Darkness passed over his face, and his voice lowered. "I have my suspicions."

"Is it the same man who came in and confronted you the night I brought Koa into the clinic? He drove the same truck I saw on the mountain road."

Kian's voice remained quiet, and he took my hand in his. "Like I said, I have my suspicions. Look, Christina, I don't want you talking about this to anyone. These rings have dangerous people associated with them. I don't want you to get involved."

"That's the same thing Frank said to me."

His face registered surprise, "Have you been talking to Frank about this? Who else knows?"

I gave him the same names I recited to our police chief earlier in the day. "I don't understand why you two are so secretive. We should expose them and be done with it."

"It's not that easy. The leaders are powerful men. They've made sure nothing leads directly to them. By you seeing Mayor Busch's truck up on Mt. Mintock, it's the closest we have come to linking him to this ring. You need to make sure no one knows you can identify the truck. It's not safe."

I frowned and sat back. "I'm not afraid of some small-town mayor. I have resources too you know."

He sighed, "Christina, this man is influential, and he has a lot of nasty people working for him. It's not difficult to arrange an accident. Please listen to us, and let it go."

Kian didn't know me. "I'm not going to let it go. But, for now, I will wait... but I want you to keep me informed." He raised an eyebrow as I spoke. "I saw what this man did to Koa. I will not stand for it."

His smiled warmed his eyes, and his voice softened, "I knew there was more than one reason why I liked you so much."

Our attention was diverted by a man who stood near us, we both turned to look at him. He was a medium built Hispanic man and looked like he worked as a ranch hand.

Kian stood, "I need to talk to him for a few minutes. Please stay here, I'll be right back."

I nodded, and Kian joined the man. They walked outside, and I watched the door close behind them. Turning back to my beer, I emptied it.

Shelby sat next to me, and she pointed to the empty glass, "Want another?"

I was too full to have another. "No thanks. I'm good."

She nodded. "So what are you to him?"

I didn't know how to answer her question. What was I to Kian? A first date? I, for one never had a first date kiss like the one we shared, and certainly not in the middle of a bar. Especially a biker bar.

"I ... well ..." I stammered, "um... it's our first date."

"Shit. What was it like to kiss him?" she asked wistfully. "It looked like quite a kiss."

I wished Kian would come back because I didn't want to have this conversation with her. My resting bitch face would not go over big with her. She was nice, but still, I didn't want to encourage her. How did I get myself into these situations?

"Um, it was a sweet kiss," I answered hoping this would be enough and she would leave me alone. I would not tell her his kiss blew my socks off. So much so, I wanted to be naked with him that very minute.

"I've been trying to get him to call me for four months. Now you come in here, he kisses you like that, and you tell me it's your first date. Shit. I don't stand a chance with him." She frowned. "You're older than he is too. I guess he's looking for a mother."

Admonishing myself not to make a comment to her statement, I sat there silently.

Shelby stood, "Yeah, I guess that's it for me. He's into the old chicks. You sure you don't want anything else to drink?"

I shook my head, "I'm good."

She walked away from the table. I breathed a sigh of relief. I was a cougar. Damn. I didn't want to be a cougar. In fact, I didn't want to be here any longer. The band was warming up, and their music sounded loud and cranky. And, by the way, where was he? I hated having to wait.

Frankly, I felt crabby. I don't know what I expected from this date, but if someone had told me, I wouldn't have believed it. Kian entered, and in an instant, all thoughts of leaving were replaced with a silent *wow!* Dressed as he was, he looked every inch a bad boy. Secretly I'd always been attracted to someone like him, but have never been brave enough actually to hook up with a dangerous looking man. Inwardly I giggled; Frank should have told me to keep away from Kian!

His stride was long, and his face was angry. I wondered what they talked about outside and whether he would share it with me. Reaching me quickly, he took me by surprise when he cupped my face in his hands and leaned over. His mouth met mine, and I was lost again. This kiss was not as long as our first, but it was nonetheless thrilling. The warmth of his lips and his tongue teasing mine sent a blast of heat and desire through me.

Pulling me to my feet, he wrapped his arm around my waist and whispered in my ear, "let's dance."

He didn't give me the opportunity to answer, and I found myself suddenly on the dance floor pressed up against him. The music was no longer loud, but soft and filled with blues. That surprised me, this placed should be filled with loud music.

I pulled back a bit and looked at him. He had lost the anger, and now his face looked suddenly melancholy and sad.

"What's wrong?" I whispered.

"Nothing."

"It doesn't look like nothing. You were happy, and now you're not. Is it me?"

He smiled that brilliant smile, but it didn't reach his eyes. "I said it was nothing."

I tucked my hand into his and pulled him back to the table.

Kian protested on the way, "I thought you wanted to dance?"

I pointed to his chair. "No. You wanted to dance. I want to know what's wrong."

I waved at Shelby and put two fingers in the air, and she nodded back to me.

"I don't want another beer. I have to drive." He was acting like a petulant child.

"If you don't want it, I'll drink it," I said firmly. "Now tell me what's wrong. You came back in here looking like you were going to kill someone. You gave me a wow kiss and then suddenly you looked like your heart was breaking. Please tell me what's going on. First, did you bring me here because you had this meeting set up?"

He grinned at me, and little bits of me melted. How did he do that?

"A wow kiss?" he said with a smirk.

I tried to look droll, "You heard me."

He blew out a breath, "Yes, I brought you here because I had the meeting. I also brought you for protection."

I laughed, I didn't know if I should be insulted. "Protection?"

"No, that's not quite the right word. More like a cover. I didn't want to appear suspicious, and having you along made it look like I was on a date."

Now I was sure I was being insulted. Was I an easy date? Someone desperate enough he knew would accept his invitation.

"I see." My voice was frosty. "Perhaps we should forget that beer and go home. In fact, I think I'll call a cab and not bother you any further." I moved to rise.

He caught my hand, "Please don't leave." His eyes were earnest. "I'm sorry."

"Well?" I said containing my anger.

"I asked you out because I wanted to get to know you better. It's not about the money you donated either."

I pressed my lips again. He had to say it, and of course, it was what I was thinking. "Go on."

"You're not going to leave, are you?"

"I'll reserve the choice."

"Fair enough," he replied.

Shelby sat our beers in front of us. She didn't make a comment before leaving, perhaps because I still had my hand on the outside of my purse.

I took a big drink from the beer.

Kian leaned back. He chewed on his bottom lip. Now that was sexy. I wanted to chew on his bottom lip too. What was I thinking? I needed to be serious. I knit my brows together. At least my face could be stern even if my mind wasn't. How did he make me lose my anger?

"I asked you out because I wanted to spend time with you and felt you wanted the same thing. Jose called me yesterday and said he wanted to talk to me. He has a small ranch with sheep and horses, right outside of Ashley. I've treated some of his livestock when his regular vet has been out of town..." he paused, and I nodded for him to continue. "One of the times I was out at his ranch, I asked him about dog fighting in the area. He said he keeps out of the mess, but he has overheard a few temporary ranch hands working at his place talking about the ring in the area. I asked if he could get more information. I warned him to be careful about obtaining it because I didn't want him to be involved."

"And he contacted you because he had information?" I asked leaning closer to him.

Kian took a drink. "Yes. He said that some of the guys who are involved in the ring come to this bar on a regular basis. I already knew that which is why I'm here."

"Oh, it's not for the fish and chips? Or Shelby?" I grinned.

He smiled, and this time it reached his eyes. "Now come on, you said you liked the fish and chips, although they are not as good as me mums." He slipped into a stronger Irish brogue.

I nodded.

His voice lowered again, "He told me tonight about a possible location where the fights are held. This is the closest we have gotten. They have different places, and it's hard to pinpoint. I'll call Frank with the information tomorrow."

His gaze diverted over to the corner where a group was playing pool. I leaned against my arm to look nonchalantly in that direction.

Turning back to face him, I whispered, "Are those some of the guys?"

Kian nodded.

"Christina," he said, "I don't want you to get involved in this. Promise me?"

I studied him.

"I'm serious." He took my hand in his. "I don't want you to get hurt. This is not something you want to fool with."

"I'm not stupid Kian. I don't want you to be hurt either. Where are the mayor's dogs?" I referred to the conflict he had with the mayor the night I was at the clinic with Koa.

"I have kennels at my house where I house all the rescue dogs I have yet to foster."

"Are they safe there?"

"Yes. They should be. I have them behind a locked gate in my yard. The gate and the doors are all alarmed. I have security cameras too."

I rolled my eyes. "Alarms can be cut, and locks can be broken."

"I know that, but his dogs won't be with me for long. I'm sending them to a group who do a unique retraining program for fight dogs. They have a good record on saving these types."

"Hey, doc." We stopped speaking as one of the pool players approached us.

If there was a definition of mean, this man embodied it. Long greasy brown hair pulled back in a ponytail showed his hard-lined face. His jeans and t-shirt appeared like they needed a good wash and the dirt under his fingernails completed the look.

"I think you owe me a game from the last bet you won off me," he challenged.

"That I do," Kian responded his accent thicker. He rose, and when I stood next to him, he wrapped his arm around my neck. "Come on baby. Let me show this guy why he shouldn't gamble with an Irishman. Usual stakes?"

As we followed him over to the pool table, Kian whispered in my ear, "Do not say or do anything. Okay?"

I nodded slightly looking at the men standing around. I wasn't planning to say a word. I hopped up on a barstool sitting off by itself and hoped that no one would notice me.

Thankfully, no one engaged me in the conversation during the game. None of the men had women with them although they were all very friendly with the other waitress, who kept bringing them beers. From my vantage point, I could see Kian was skilled at the game and thought it was interesting how much thicker his brogue stayed. When he bent over the table not only was I able to marvel at his hot ass, but a tattoo became visible, which appeared to cover most of his back.

As Kian continued to win, the man he played against became more agitated toward him. The others in the group were ribbing him at losing, and challenging Kian to beat him. At this point, while I wondered if we would make it out alive, the man had a spate of good luck and began winning.

I breathed a sigh of relief when Kian put a one-hundred-dollar bill into the man's hand and walked over to join me.

The man called out to him, "How about another one?"

Kian smiled, "No, too rich for my blood. I know when I'm beaten. Thanks for the game." He wrapped his arm around my waist and led me back to the table.

"You lost," I whispered.

He grinned, "On purpose. I know when to diffuse a situation. But, while we were playing, I did learn some valuable information. It seems there is going to be a big fight coming soon. Now I need to find out where and when it's going to happen."

CHAPTER 20

To say this was one of the weirdest dates I had ever been on wouldn't be a stretch. After the game, we danced a bit more and then headed for the cabin. When we arrived, Kian walked me to the front door. The ride home had been just as thrilling, although he did take it slower.

He leaned over and gave me a soft kiss on the lips. It wasn't anywhere near the kisses he had given me at the bar, but it was great nonetheless.

"Would you like to come in for some coffee, or tea, or whatever?" I asked, thinking I would prefer the whatever.

He smiled and murmured, "Oh, I better not. It would lead quickly to other things that perhaps we're not ready for."

I tried to cover the disappointment in my voice, "I guess it would. I had fun tonight. Thank you." It had been a unique experience.

"Did you now? Then perhaps we should do it again."

"I'd like that. Please keep me up to date on the happenings ... you know ... with the dogs."

"That I will do."

Kian cupped my face in his hands. And whoosh! It happened again! His lips took mine, and this time there was hunger behind them. When our tongues met in a frenzy, and my teeth captured his lower lip, his arms pulled me closer to him while his hands cupped my bottom. Desire, no lust, shot through me like lightning and there was no mistaking his appetite for me.

He broke away from the kiss. "Ahh, Christina, you're going to kill me." His breathing matched mine, both of us taking gulps of air.

"Are you sure you don't want to come in?"

Koa barked from the other side of the door, and Kian chuckled, "That's quite the watch dog you have there. May I call you in a couple of days?"

"Coward," I breathed hard.

He flashed me his brilliant grin, "Exactly. Now go inside, and I'll be on my way."

Koa was there with his wagging tail when I opened the door.

Kian petted him. "Take good care of my girl." He gave me a wistful look, "I'll call you."

We watched him leave.

After I had snuggled next to Koa in bed, I looked at my phone surprised to see three messages from JuJu. One calendar reminder about a meeting I had with the contractors in the morning, the second a text containing more information about Scott, as if I could give a damn about him. The third one made me laugh.

The text read, *Howd it go? Did u get a goodnight kiss?* Then a fourth message popped up. *Good grief! I hope ur not doing the big nasty tonight! Msg me back so I know ur ok*

I laughed aloud. I could always count on her to be the comic relief. I quickly typed back. *No big nasty tonight. In bed w/ Koa. Goodnight kiss achieved and a few more! Talk tomorrow.*

I received a smiley icon back. Then a devil one.

I placed the phone on the nightstand and closed my eyes. A ping sound announced another text.

"Really JuJu, you should be asleep!"

The text was from Kian. There was a graphic of big red lips making kissing motions. It simply said, *Thank you.*

I smiled broadly. An additional message arrived from him, which made me shake my head in disbelief.

And you can straddle my engine and be my back warmer anytime you want.

Giggling, I texted back. *Silly! I had fun too, thank you.*

I put my phone back and snuggled back down again. Kian. He made me feel young. Yikes! Ten years younger than me ... what was I thinking?

I stroked Koa's head, and he moved closer to me laying his head on my outstretched arm. What was I doing?

CHAPTER 21

The next morning, I felt better after chewing the contractor a new one. I didn't think I would have any additional visits from Scott, but anyone could have broken in with the compromised security of the window. After I spoke with JuJu and learned the new information she had about Scott, I felt vindicated in my earlier thoughts about him. Apparently, he was in severe arrearage with his child support payments. I knew he was slime.

When I left, I peered over at Don and Debi's house. Don's mother Annie was getting into her truck, she spied me and waved at me to wait. Her truck made its way down the utility road, and she stopped in front of me. Hopping out of the truck, I wondered how she managed to reach the gas pedal. She was a tiny but spry woman, and I always felt huge next to her. Dressed in her usual jeans and chambray shirt, she wore her black hair in a long braid down her back. Her warm face was beautifully unlined, and only her eyes showed the understanding wisdom that came with age. Her affectionate and sincere hugs always left me breathless, which was true today.

"I'm so glad I caught you. I was just coming down to invite you to dinner tonight. The whole family will be home, and I thought it would be a wonderful time to hear about the honeymoon and everyone's adventures," she said after she released me from a second hug.

"That sounds fun. Can I bring something?"

She patted my hand. "No. Just yourself. Our cute veterinarian Kian will be there too. I heard you two had a date last night."

How did she know? I reminded myself this was a small town where everyone knew everyone else's business. We had been outed.

"Um... yes we did."

"Good." She patted my hand again. "I think you two will make a good couple." She must have seen the surprise on my face because she continued. "Yes. I know what people will think, but you both like to rescue things."

"I" ... I stuttered ... "we ... are not a couple. There is nothing between us. I mean, we're friends. Just friends. We had dinner, that's all."

Annie smiled in the all-knowing way she had. "Yes, of course, my dear. I know, friends, which is what I meant to say." She climbed into the truck. "See you about five tonight?"

While I walked back to the cabin, a big SUV came down the road behind me. When it honked, I immediately grinned. Michael and Elizabeth were home! They parked behind their house.

"Hey, Christina! What great timing!" Michael called to me stretching his arms out.

I gave him a welcome home hug. "Need some help carrying things inside?"

Elizabeth slid out of the seat on the passenger side. "Hi! Do you have time?"

"Of course," I said giving her an equally big hug. "Did you buy out Hawaii?"

"Oh you know, gifts for everyone. And I found perfect stuff for the baby's room." She patted her tummy, which looked rounder since I had last seen her.

Michael looped his arm around her shoulders, "Babe, I want you to go inside and sit. Let us carry everything in."

She rolled her eyes. "I am perfectly fine to bring stuff into the house."

He pulled her toward the steps. "In. Don't give me any guff. Your ankle is swollen."

"That's because I've been on a plane for five hours!" she argued.

I began to pull suitcases from the back-cargo area.

Michael called to me when he came out of the house and back down the stairs. "I've got those Christina. They are heavy. Grab the bags in the back seat, they are a little lighter."

I didn't roll my eyes, but I did make a face. "I have them!" Wow! They were heavy. "What do you two have packed in these suitcases? They weigh a ton!"

He rushed to the back of the car. "I told you so! When will you listen to your big brother."

I grinned, "You're so bossy!"

He laughed, "Yeah, it runs in the family."

We managed to get everything into the house and piled it up in the dining room. I loved Michael's house. He had renovated the old house last year shortly before moving in. Whereas I tore down the building on my property, his exterior hadn't been in such bad shape. He created a great room, which combined the living room and dining room. The expanded deck outside led down to the beach, and his enlarged bedroom included a small office and bathroom. Upstairs he had two bedrooms for the girls. With the baby coming, they would revamp his office into a small bedroom.

When he did his renovation, I warned him he didn't have enough bedrooms. Never in a million years did I imagine a year later he would be married with a baby coming. It's strange how things happened.

Elizabeth called from the kitchen, "Do you want some tea? I'm making some."

We both responded with a "Yes!"

My phone rang, and I checked who it was. I walked into the living room when I saw Kian's name on the screen.

"Hi," I said.

"Hey Christina, I hope it's not too soon to call. I mean a guy is supposed to wait at least a week, isn't he?"

I giggled. Where did that come from? "No, of course not. It is good to hear from you." I was conscious of the quiet in the dining room.

"I had a great time last night."

"So did I. Thank you again."

"It's I who should be thanking you. I had the sexiest woman in the place with me."

"Oh stop it." Inwardly, his words thrilled me.

"May I pick you up for Annie's dinner tonight?" he asked.

"Don't you live on the other side of the lake; the same side they are on?"

"Yes, I do."

"Wouldn't it make more sense for me to pick you up?"

"Would you like to pick me up?" he teased.

"It does make more sense."

"We certainly don't want to get in the way of your common sense, would we?"

"Then I'll pick you up at four forty-five, okay?"

He laughed, "I'll be ready then."

"See you later."

"I look forward to it."

Michael walked up behind me, "Are you giving Elizabeth and I a ride too?"

"No."

He laughed.

Elizabeth came out from the kitchen. "What did I miss? What's so funny?"

"Apparently, Christina is picking up Kian for our dinner at Annie's tonight." He smirked.

Her mouth made a big O, then she giggled too. "That's exciting. How did this come about?"

I pressed my lips together...hard. I didn't roll my eyes, but I wanted to. "It's nothing. Kian and I had dinner last night."

Elizabeth raised her eyebrow, "A date?"

"Yes, and he took me to Ray's Saloon!"

Immediately the ire in Michael's eyes flashed, "Where did he take you?"

"You heard me," I said with the same smirk he wore moments before. "And, I rode on the back of his motorcycle."

"I can't believe this Christina. Are you crazy? I'm going to have a talk with our good doctor." He pointed to me, "You shouldn't be anywhere near Ray's Saloon. All types of nefarious people visit there."

Elizabeth clapped, "Oh it sounds like fun! I used to love when Don took me out on his motorcycle. When I spent summers up here with my aunt, we'd be on the bike the entire time."

I ignored Michael and his over protectiveness. "Can I help bring the tea in?"

She nodded, and we carried the mugs to the living room. Both of us curled up by the bay windows on the big chocolate brown couch.

"I want to hear all about your date with our veterinarian. I'm sure you had an enjoyable evening. He certainly is cute. He's got a great butt, doesn't he?" she whispered to me conspiratorially as she tucked her long legs under her.

Michael carried the bags into their bedroom.

I leaned toward her, "You should have seen him yesterday!" I described his leather pants.

"Oh!" Elizabeth fanned herself.

"He has a tattoo on his back too! I couldn't see what it was, but it looks big."

She almost draped herself over the couch and grinned, "Oh mercy! Tell me about Ray's Saloon. Was it exciting?"

I leaned back and took a sip of the hot tea. "Oh, it was not any big deal. Just a bunch of bikers. Most of them were harmless. The waitress is madly in love with Kian."

"Oh?"

"No. I don't think he's interested in her."

Elizabeth peered at me over her mug. "And the age thing?"

"Yeah. That is the thousand-pound elephant in the corner, isn't it?" I answered.

"Has he brought it up?"

"Not really. But it's not important, we are only friends. He's grateful because I've fostered Koa. By the way, where are the dogs?"

Michael walked back into the living room and sat in one of the chairs opposite the couch. He had changed into sweatpants, a t-shirt, and running shoes. "Tammy has them at the groomers today. She said they smelled bad when she picked them up from the boarding place. Why is Kian grateful?"

I pressed my lips together. My brother and his good hearing. I stayed silent.

He stood, "Why is he grateful?"

"I also contributed to his dog rescue foundation," I answered.

"Oh. That was sweet of you." He kissed the top of Elizabeth's head. "Babe, I'm going to run off a few miles."

"Okay, have fun," she said.

As he exited, he turned, "How much was the contribution?"

"None of your business," I answered pertly.

Michael leaned his arm against the doorjamb. "How much?"

"Fifty K."

"Wow." He nodded. "Good. The money will be used wisely and well. See you later." And with that, he closed the door.

Both Elizabeth and I raised our eyebrows simultaneously.

"Well," she said, "I didn't expect that."

"Actually neither did I. It does make sense, though. You know Michael contributes to many animal conservations funds."

"Yes, we've discussed it. Do you think Kian asked you out because of the donation?"

I shook my head, "He asked me out before he knew about the donation. I believe he wanted to thank me for taking Koa."

"Is Koa yours? Permanently?"

"No. Just until he can find a home for him. You know I shouldn't have a dog. I travel too much and have way too many responsibilities."

"When do I get to meet him?"

"Koa? I'll bring him to dinner tonight. I don't want to leave him all alone in the house for the second night in a row."

"That's a good idea. Annie and Frank certainly won't mind. They may even know someone who might want him," she suggested.

"I don't want to let him go until his leg has had a chance to heal. I think that would be too disruptive for him. He still appears to be a little shy and uncertain."

Elizabeth nodded her head, "You're probably right. It would be too disruptive. It would be better to let him recover with you."

"Well, you know, Koa does trust me," I replied quickly. "He's getting used to me."

"No, I think you're absolutely correct. He will heal faster with someone he knows and trusts."

"Exactly."

Later, I stood staring into my closet. I didn't feel like wearing jeans, even though it was that was the type of evening it would be. Jeans never looked good on me. They made my butt look big. I found a pair of black slacks. Black was an excellent choice. It was a slimming color. Normally, I wouldn't be concerned about my weight, but I didn't want to be the dowdy looking one in the group, especially since Kian would be there.

I swung the closet door firmly shut after I pulled out a pink pullover. I was ridiculous again. This wasn't me. I didn't care what people thought about me. I dressed for myself. Why was I reacting this way?

CHAPTER 22

I fed Koa a light dinner because he would undoubtedly charm nibbles out of everyone at Annie and Frank's house. He was good about getting into his crate in the back of the SUV. I had loaded a case of red Trousseau wine next to the crate and before I left, added a box of Chardonnay both from local vineyards.

After plugging Kian's address into the GPS, we were off. I drove through the town and noticed that the shops were already closing. This was a very family oriented quirky little town, with a large population of the local Native American tribe living here. Most of the businesses closed early on Saturday and remained closed on Sunday. During the summer when the tourists tripled the population, hours were different, but during the offseason, it was a sleepy village. And, that's how I liked it.

Once past Mintock, the car began to climb the mountain road. The map instructed me to turn off on a dirt road, which raised my eyebrows. It wasn't unusual to see homes in the isolated parts of the unincorporated area around Mintock. I drove slowly past a couple of homes. The lane was full of potholes and was probably a nightmare to drive when it rained. Kian's house was located at the end of the road. Literally.

The home had seen better days. It was an old ranch-style building with a covered carport. The paint was peeling from the wooden paneled front, and the landscaping was overgrown and mostly weeds. The house looked sad and saggy. Koa started barking in the back. When I opened the car door, I could hear it too. The thunderous sound of barking dogs.

Kian opened the front door when I stepped up on the porch. I could see six large dogs behind him all barking and tails wagging furiously.

His face was bright and welcoming. Oh, and the stubble on his face… it was obvious he hadn't shaved today. I didn't mind it at all. He was sexy personified standing at the door with jeans riding low on his hips and an old t-shirt advertising the Dublin football club, the Shamrock Rovers.

"So you found me!" he said as he stepped out on the porch.

"It wasn't easy," I replied. "That's some driveway you have there."

"Yeah, my neighbors hit me up for a contribution for paving the road when I first moved here, but when we discovered what it would cost, everyone lost their taste for the project."

"I see."

He slid his arm around me easily and bent to kiss me. "You look lovely. I'm afraid I'm underdressed."

"It's probably just the opposite. I never wear the right things to these types of events."

He raised his eyebrows, "Is it an occasion now?"

"You know what I mean."

He chuckled, "That I do. Come on in, let me introduce you to my boys."

He pulled me inside into the small living room. I was pleasantly surprised. The interior was utilitarian and plain, but clean and tidy with hardwood floors. The large dogs were sitting and staying in their position by the door. It was evident it was a strain for them to keep still, but they did. I counted two large black labs, three huge pit bulls, and a golden retriever.

"Okay boys, be nice now," he calmly told them.

When Kian released them, they all approached me with their tails wagging. They sniffed my hands, my pants, shoes, and of course, other more personal places and then sat down in front of me. I greeted each one separately with a scratch under their chins as he called out their names. Charger, Butch, Bert, Guinness, Carne, and the last one, the golden retriever, was Harry.

"Is Harry, the Harry Hounds?" I asked.

He grinned, "That he is. Harry has been with me the longest. I rescued him while I was still in vet school."

"Are they all rescues waiting for homes?"

"Well now, they are all rescues, but they have found their forever home with me. They are all special needs dogs. All of them are older too. Butch is blind and uses Charger to guide him around. They are brothers. Their previous owner died, and we couldn't split them up knowing how much Charger means to Butch." He pointed to Carne, "He doesn't have a tongue. Some crazy bastard cut it out. Dogs use their tongues to eat and drink. So, he must be specially hand-fed. He's a great boy."

"Oh my gosh!" I exclaimed and kneeled in front of Carne. We were eye to eye. I rubbed the side of his face. He leaned into my hand and grunted. "Oh, you like your ears rubbed? I know a few cocker spaniels who like this too!"

Kian stroked the top of the brindle colored pit bull's head. "Bert and Guinness were dog fighters. They had to go through special training to rid them of the aggressive tendencies, it was hard work, and I couldn't bear to part with them."

"They are beautiful Kian," I said as I tried to pet all of them equally.

"They're my family."

"Bert and Guinness aren't the mayor's dogs, are they?"

Kian offered his hand to pull me to my feet. When I rose to stand next to him, he held onto my hand. It was a sweet and comforting gesture.

He shook his head. "Those two are in the dog run in the back of the house. I keep them separated from the other dogs. They are too aggressive right now. I'll be sending them to a special camp. The people who run the site work with the dogs and decide if they can be placed in homes. Come on, I'll show you the rest." He tugged on my hand and lead me toward the kitchen.

"Oh," I said, "I didn't realize they might not be placed."

He looked grim, "Sometimes it's too late, or the dog cannot be changed. Then it just wouldn't be safe for us to home them. It's sad, but for safety reasons we sometimes have to make those difficult decisions."

"That must be hard."

"It is, but it's the only thing we can do."

Two teenage girls giggled in the kitchen. They were both pretty, and when they saw Kian, they both blushed.

Both girls greeted him at once, "Hey Doctor K."

He smiled, "All done with the food?"

They both pointed to the bowls of food placed on a cart by the back door.

Kian turned to me, "Would you like to join us for a bit of dinner?"

"I'd be delighted!" I answered enthusiastically.

"Betsy and Sue are two Harry's Hounds volunteers," he introduced us. "And this is Christina, our newest volunteer. She is taking care of Koa for us."

I immediately recognized Betsy, a cute and petite brunette, being Don and Debi's daughter.

She spoke up, "I know Christina. She's building her house close to where I live. Is she your new girlfriend?"

Kian flashed a smile and winked, "Yes, she is. Although I'm not sure if I'm her boyfriend yet."

"Come on, enough of that kind of talk." I pushed him ahead of me toward the door.

He chuckled and opened the door while he pulled the cart behind him. Everyone, including the dogs, trooped outside. We were met by two teenage boys. They appeared to be close in age to Betsy and Sue. It also was very evident that although the girls thought Kian was dreamy, they were far more interested in these young men.

Both boys worked hosing off the large patio. The concrete was separated with chain link fencing which led out to a large green lawn. These were the dog runs, and they curved around to a large building attached to the house. When the young men saw us coming outside, they turned off the water and rolled up the hoses.

Kian called out to them, "It's food time. We're ready to go. Meet my friend Christina. This is Luke," he said referring to the freckled teenager with strawberry blond hair. "And that's Jesus," he pointed to the dark-haired youth.

They both greeted me with a wave. Kian grabbed a stethoscope from the cart and handed another one to Luke.

Kian held out his hand to the dogs. "Stay," he commanded.

All the dogs stopped and did not follow us into the building. The interior was like a clinic. The floor was made of a flexible rubber material, which was all one piece. One area had counters and cabinets, in the middle was an examination table, and on the opposite side, sat a row of built-in kennels the length of the wall. Each kennel was outfitted with a small doorway, which led to the dog runs on the outside.

We were greeted with barking when we entered. Most of the dogs gathered near the front of the cages. I hung back as the team worked. They were a well-oiled machine. Each of them had a job to do. Each dog was brought out and checked by Kian. He allowed the team to take turns medicating the dogs, examining and feeding them. The dogs appeared to be used to the routine too.

While I watched, Kian explained each case to me. These were the rescues that needed medical help before they could be released into foster care or up for adoption.

"And thanks to you Christina, we'll be able to add more kennels so we can accept more dogs that need medical help first." He smiled as he lifted the last dog, a young yellow lab onto the examination table. Kian buried his face into her neck as she nuzzled him. "Hey girl," he said gently to her. "How are you doing little momma?" Kian pressed her sides softly, "Puppies," he said by way of explanation. She has another week to go. She was abandoned on a road embankment. We'll hold onto her until she's done with the puppies, then we'll find homes for everyone."

Seeing him work with the dogs and the kids tugged at my emotional heartstrings. He was kind and informative with the teens, even when they made mistakes, he didn't lose his cool. After he had finished, he gave instructions to the teenagers and then lead me outside.

"They'll take care of everything else and spend time with each of the dogs while they wait for Leonard to arrive. He's is my roommate, and he keeps an eye on things when I'm not here. Are you ready?" He noticed the hatchback open at the rear of the car. "Did you bring Koa?"

I nodded. Koa cried when he heard our voices. Kian opened the crate door and petted him.

"Hey boy, living the good life here I see. Yeah, you'll get attention tonight from all the pretty women." He looked at me. "Good idea to bring him along, it will help with his socialization."

"I thought so too."

When we were settled inside the SUV, he tapped the GPS on the dashboard, "Do you know how to get there?"

"I think so. I've been to their house before. Ready?"

I followed the bumpy dirt lane back to the main highway.

"You're very polite," he commented.

"I am?"

He laughed, "Yeah, not a single word about my gravel road."

I smirked, "Good thing you're not reading my mind."

He leaned over, and the stubble on his face brushed against my cheek. "Tell me what you really think."

The silly grin on his face made me laugh. His eyes, though ... I would kill for those eyes.

"You really don't want to know. I'm thinking how the hell do you drive this road when it rains?"

He chuckled, "If it rains then I stay home and have a nice fire in the fireplace. Then, I make hot chocolate, you know the kind with the little marshmallows."

I grinned, "And some whipped cream?" I asked.

"Oh yeah, lots of whipped cream! Tell me, do you ever spray it straight into your mouth from the can?"

"Um... yes... I have."

"Will you tell me about it?"

I laughed and pressed my lips together, "I don't think there is much to tell. It's just point, squirt and..." I paused, teasing him, "then swallow."

He paused first and then laughed. I was pleased to have caught him off guard.

"And you always swallow?"

"Always," I answered.

"I think we'll get along great."

When we hit the main road, he indicated to turn to the right.

I pointed to the GPS, "It says to make a left."

"Sweetlin', that way will take you through town again. You don't need to do that. The GPS doesn't always know the best way. Make a right turn, I promise the way is shorter." He had the Irish lilt in his voice now. It appeared he used it specifically when he wanted to get his own way.

So I made the right turn. He was correct, the trip was shorter. I turned the GPS off because it kept bleating at me that I was going the wrong way. Sometimes computers don't know everything.

We teased each other the rest of the way there. The sexual innuendo was high as was the erotic tension between us. It was remarkably laid back with Kian though. He made it easy. There were no veiled threats of superiority or one-upmanship.

When we entered Annie and Frank's long driveway, I couldn't help but point out that it was paved.

He chuckled, "Just goes to prove they have money to burn! And think of all the hot chocolate time they're missing!"

Kian lifted Koa out of his crate and carried him into the house as Frank greeted us at the front door. Frank handed me a beer that had been freshly opened.

"Is this the famous Koa?" Frank asked as he gave Kian a dark beer. He bent down to scratch Koa's ear. In response, Koa's tail was wagging furiously. "You didn't bring Betsy with you?"

"No, she is still working with the rescues. She said to let you know she'll be here in time for dinner." Kian answered.

Annie came into the living room from the kitchen. She wiped her hands on her apron and then hugged both of us. Her arm linked with mine. "I'm so glad you brought Koa. Mandy will enjoy the company. She has been quite miserable since we had to put Susi-Q to sleep."

"Oh, I'm so sorry! I didn't know you just lost a dog," I said.

"It was her time, but she was still much loved. We did everything we could, but we needed to let her go. She waits for us at the Rainbow Bridge, and until then, she chases all the slow squirrels!" She waved her hand for Kian. "Com'on. Everyone is outside by the fire. I think we will be sitting inside tonight because it's going to be too cold to be out there after the sun sets."

Kian caught up to us, and he slipped his arm around her shoulders. He leaned over and kissed her cheek. "It's always good to see you, Annie. You're going to let me know when you're ready to raise another pup. I have a pregnant girl at home. Probably be at least six puppies."

Annie nodded her head. "I don't know if I have enough energy for a puppy. But, we'll talk about you bringing over an older dog. One who will sit on my lap at the end of the day."

He smiled, "I think I might have a couple who might just do the trick for you."

She threw her head back with laughter, "Now it's a couple?" She led us outside. "We may have to think about that. We certainly have room and enough love to go around."

We greeted everyone outside, Don, Debi, and Michael, Elizabeth, and Tammy. We traded hugs and kisses. Don brought us chairs, and we drew close to the big bonfire.

Their house was on the reservation land, which butted up against Mt.

Mintock. It was a rambling, two-story ranch style home with a beautiful view of the lake. About 200 feet away, a large barn contained their horses.

Tammy spent a lot of her time here exercising them. She had plans to go to veterinary school after she graduated from college. Her pregnancy put a hold on some of that, but she made it clear, she was in it for the long term. She needed to be, her fiancé was going to medical school.

Tammy pulled up her chair next to mine and draped herself over me. I hugged her.

"Whatcha thinkin' kiddo? How do you feel?" I asked.

"I'm ravenous all the time… well… when I'm not throwing up my guts."

I brushed her bangs from her face. "That bad?"

She laid her head on my shoulder. "No, it's not that horrible. I'm driving back down to Stanford tomorrow. The little house you got for us is great. I'm having so much fun decorating it. Going to school there will be awesome too. You and Dad have been so fantastic to help Jason and I out."

"Still going ahead with the wedding?"

She nodded, "We decided we'll just do something small and then after the baby comes, Elizabeth said she'd help me with something bigger."

"She did?" I asked. That surprised me. Elizabeth wasn't known for her organizational skills. I didn't think planning a wedding would be her forte'.

Tammy giggled softly, "Of course, we both know that it would be a disaster. She's trying to be helpful and be like a mom." She nuzzled closer to me and whispered, "But, when we start planning it, can you be there in the background to guide stuff along?"

I smiled and patted her back. "Of course I will."

Tammy sat up abruptly. "But don't let her know okay? I don't want to hurt her feelings."

I regarded her seriously, "Absolutely not. My lips are sealed."

She laid her head back on my shoulder, "Good. Thank you. It's going to be great because once I'm married to Jason, our families will all be connected."

"You're looking forward to having Debi and Don as your in-laws?"

"Oh yes! They're fantastic. She has been helping me decorate the baby's room. So, you came with Dr. Kian tonight? I think he is really cute."

"Yes, I picked him up from his house."

"Are you two dating?"

"We're becoming friends. You know I'm fostering Koa."

"Oh, I know. I think that is awesome. Poor little guy. Who would do something like that to a dog?"

"A very crazy person apparently."

"So, is Kian like young enough to be your son?"

My beer almost came sputtering out of my mouth.

"No!"

She laughed, "Gotcha!" She stood. "I need more water. Want anything?"

"No thanks."

I looked over at Frank and Kian engaged in what looked like an animated conversation. I knew exactly what they were talking about and I was not going to be left out of the discussion. I walked over to stand next to them. They both stopped speaking at once and stared at me.

"What's so exciting? Is it our favorite current subject? The mayor and his abusive ways?" I interjected. "What I'd like to know is what is going to be done about it? Are we going to turn a blind eye?"

Kian pressed his lips together, "I was asking Frank the same thing."

"What you two fail to realize is that Mayor Busch is a very powerful man, not only in the town but also in the county. He's wealthy, and we don't know who he has in his pocket," Frank expressed.

"I'm rich too. I'm sure this goes wider than the county too," I said.

"If we can prove the gambling, we can get the Feds involved in the case. I'm afraid the charge of animal abuse can only go as far as the county sheriff," Frank said.

"They are bound to slip up somehow. Their operation is getting large," Kian said.

Annie came up behind us and stood next to Frank. We were all silent again.

"I know what you're talking about. Frank told me about the problem, and since Mayor Busch is a Pomo elder, he thought that perhaps I could get the council involved. He is right, Busch has friends in some high places, and he has a ruthless streak. He is not an honorable man. All elders must take an oath to be a reflection of the tribe and to live outstanding lives. Given enough evidence, I can bring it to the council, and he will be removed from the tribe," Annie said.

"What it sounds like, is we need witnesses to come forward," I concluded.

Frank nodded, "We do need witnesses. But most of the likely ones are people on his payroll."

"Then perhaps we need to bribe them to bring evidence," I said.

Frank chuffed, "That would be a bullet in their head."

The shock was evident on my face. "Really?"

"Christina, these are criminals who are dangerous," Frank said.

"Damn it, what kind of mayor does this town have?"

"A very sick one I'm afraid," Annie added, "but, I'm working on that."

"How?" I asked.

Kian grinned, "She's thinking of running for mayor. There's an election scheduled this summer."

I beamed, "Wow! Annie, you'd be perfect … everyone loves you!"

"I'm not sure yet, but I'm doing an investigation," she said. "Come, let's join the others, and let this conversation lay for a while. Kian, tell me how is my granddaughter doing? She is thrilled to be one of your volunteers."

"Betsy is an accomplished volunteer and has her priorities in the right place. She cares for the dogs deeply but is also interested in the medical side too," Kian said.

I giggled, "And it doesn't hurt that you have two handsome hunks working with you too."

He grinned, "That too, is something to be considered. I wasn't just born yesterday, and I know how to motivate others."

No, I thought, he wasn't born yesterday, just the week before. I sighed inwardly about our age difference. What was I doing?

Kian took my hand and held me back. His eyes trailed over my face, "Are you okay?"

"Why do you ask?" I wondered what showed on my face.

"You looked unhappy for a moment."

I shook my head, "No, I'm fine."

He slipped his arm around my waist, I noticed how it was feeling very familiar there, and I liked it. A lot.

"Okay, let's see what they have to munch on. I'm hungry, and I'm sure dinner won't be for a while." He looked around and found the snacks on a table set up on the patio.

Michael called out to me, "Christina, didn't you bring wine?"

My hand flew to my mouth, "Oh! I forgot all about it."

"Give me your keys, I'll get it," Kian offered.

"The doors are unlocked, it's in the back. There are two cases. I'll go with you."

"I've got it."

"I insist."

He chuckled and opened the door for me to step into the house. "Of course you do."

We walked out together, and he sped up a bit and opened the hatch before I had a chance. His actions made me smile. I tried to reach in, and he blocked my way. It surprised me at first, but then I discovered his motives.

Kian wrapped his arms around me and pulled me against him. It was great to feel his hard body pressing mine.

"I've been waiting to do this," he whispered as he lowered his head and his lips tasted mine.

It was one of those kisses. Long and deep. I loved his kisses, they made me feel hidden, almost like I was tucked away somewhere.

"So good," he whispered, and his tongue teased mine with short strokes. Even though I tried not to, I let out a soft groan.

My hands splayed over his back. His hard muscles bunched and moved under my fingers. His hands were likewise occupied except lower. Much lower. He pressed his fingers under my butt to pull me closer, and when he did, I could feel his firm arousal pressed against me.

"Oh shit!" My brother's voice rang out clearly. "Do you two need to get a room? Kian, get your hands off my sister's ass. Christina pull your sweater down!"

I popped my head up above Kian's shoulder, "What? What are you doing out here? Can't we have any privacy?" Being caught by my big brother. Why did I feel like a teenager again?

Kian appeared reluctant to move away from me, but he finally took a step back.

"What? In Annie and Frank's front yard? I wouldn't call that private!" Michael said tersely.

"Why are you out here?" I answered back.

"They sent me to find out why the wine was taking so long," he said as he brushed me aside to pick up one of the cases.

Kian winked at me and grabbed the other box. He mouthed the word "later" behind Michael's back. I smiled, and my stomach tightened.

Michael quickly outed us when we went back inside. "I found them out there making out like a couple of teens."

"We were not!" I protested.

Kian was keeping himself out of the fray by taking the case of wine he carried to the kitchen. When he joined me again, he put his arm around my shoulders

"Let's go get some snacks," he said.

I piled two plates with chips, dips, vegetables, cheese, crackers, and other munchies, while Kian went for a refill on our beers. We met by the bonfire. Annie had been correct, with the sun setting it was chilly, but the fire kept us warm for the time being.

Kian's eyes were big when he saw the two plates piled with the goodies, "Ah, a woman after my own heart."

He set both beers on the small table next to us and scooped up dip with a chip. Koa seated himself between our feet and looked at us expectantly. Kian slipped him a baby carrot, and Koa happily settled down to chew on it.

"Carrots?" I asked.

"Yeah, a few vegetables are good for him."

"Hmmm... I'm learning new stuff."

He bumped my shoulder with his. "Stick with me kid, I'll teach you a lot of things."

I laughed, "I'm beginning to see that. So," I hesitated, "the kiss by the car?"

"I like kissing you. You have wonderful lips, and I get the feeling you like kissing me."

"I do. A lot."

He lifted the bottle of beer to his lips and took a long drink. "Everyone seems to think we are dating."

"Yes, they do."

"What do you think about that?" he said leaning over from his chair to gaze at me.

What did I think about that? How do I answer? What did he expect? He was definitely expecting an answer because he hadn't moved. The reflection of the fire danced in his eyes. His smile quirked to the side bringing out the dimple in his cheek.

"No games," he whispered while he ran his finger along my lips. My lips parted slightly, and I was tempted to touch his finger with my tongue. "Be honest."

You mean to be vulnerable. I can't be vulnerable. I could be truthful.

"I like that they think we're dating," I answered quietly.

A wide grin filled his face. "So do I. I like it a lot," he said using my earlier words. "In fact, if it's okay with you, we could prove them right and say we're dating." Cupping my face between his hands, he touched his lips to mine. "What do you think?"

I took a deep breath hoping it wasn't too audible, "Yes. I like that a lot."

He gave me another soft kiss, which was interrupted by Michael, clearing his throat. We both looked up and saw him behind us. He held his beer and loomed.

"Michael!" Elizabeth's voice rang out. She shuffled up to us, I could see she was wearing her boot.

"Ankle hurt?" I asked.

"Yeah. The flight home today made me feel all bloated, fat, and ugly. Get me a chair honey," she said.

"Coming right up!" He dragged two chairs over to us, and they sat."

Elizabeth spied my plate of goodies. "May I? I haven't had anything to eat since we left the house."

I quickly handed her the plate, which she accepted with a grateful smile.

"We stopped to see the eagles before we arrived here. Michael wanted to see if the eaglets were still in the nest," she added.

"Were they? Did you see them?" I asked.

She frowned and wrinkled her nose, "No. I didn't. He," she said pointing to her husband, "wouldn't let me. I had to stay in the car and wait, but then he showed me the pictures when he came back to the car."

"I didn't want you to slip. Everything is wet from the last rain, besides your ankle was causing you pain already," Michael defended while he bent to kiss her. "The eaglets are not in the nest, but they are close by, I saw them flying over the lake and through the trees."

I cleared my throat.

Michael grinned at me, "This is what you get when you are married."

"Do you have the pictures with you? I'd like to see them," Kian said.

Michael whipped out his cell phone from the holder he wore on his belt.

"Wow," Kian whistled, "you took these with your phone? They are excellent."

Michael beamed, "Thanks."

I leaned over Kian's shoulder. "Nice, but then I wouldn't expect anything less from you."

We were slowly joined by the others while the sun set over the horizon. When it became too cold for us to stay outside, the men extinguished the bonfire, and we went into the house. Inside the large den, we ate lasagna, salad, and a delicious peach crumble Annie had made from her own canned peaches. Then we played charades and sang karaoke.

These people were becoming family. Making the decision to come to Mintock was the right one. The town began to feel like home to me. Over the last ten years, I had moved so much trying to find the right place. Here it was, right next door to my brother and his new wife. A year ago if anyone had suggested it, I would have never believed them.

Kian… what about him? Was I actually dating someone ten years my junior? He didn't act immature. Instead, he had a youthful vitality, which drew me in like a moth to a flame. I had to be so careful because many men saw me simply as a cash cow. In the past, I put up guards and wouldn't let anyone in beyond those barriers. What was Kian looking for? Had I vetted him enough? He certainly believed in what he was doing with his rescue organization. Seeing him today interacting with the dogs and teenagers showed me his character. He wasn't putting on an act for my benefit. I decided when I saw the small clinic and kennels set up in his home, that no matter what happened between us, good or bad, I would continue to assist him in his efforts.

Frank, being the lawman he was, cut off the alcohol right after dinner. Surprisingly enough, no one objected. Annie did point out the extra bedrooms in case anyone wanted to stay. Everyone was content though to drink soft drinks and play games. Their family was like my own - loving and kind. Mine though was much more boisterous and outgoing. We would not have cut off the drinking, though, and many times I remembered waking up in my grandmother's living room after having spent the night on the floor tucked into a sleeping bag with my cousins surrounding me. My parents and relatives would nurse hangovers in the kitchen by drinking thick black coffee, which had literally been boiled on the stove.

While we were in the middle of charades, a cell phone rang. Don, whose turn it was, looked at Kian, "Don't answer it!" It was the men against the women.

Kian looked at the screen, "Sorry, this one I have to take." He stepped away from his group and answered, "What do you have Leo?" He paused, "Damn. How bad? How many? ... No, take him to the clinic, I'll meet you there."

CHAPTER 23

Every eye was on him when Kian turned to face us. A hush had fallen over the room.

"I'm sorry, I have to go. That was Leonard. Some idiot shot a dog in front of my house and left him there. The dog is still alive," Kian said, already walking toward the front door.

I rushed to him and dug for my keys in my purse. "Let's go."

Kian looked at the guys. "Leonard is taking him to the clinic, there's nobody at the house…"

He didn't need to finish the request, all three, Michael, Frank, and Don were up.

"We'll go. Annie, could you take the girls home?" Michael requested as fished his keys from his pocket.

"Of course," she responded. "Please keep us informed. We'll stay here for a bit. Christina, Don can take Kian to the hospital."

I shook my head, "I'll take him. I know the way."

Frank came out of the back room wearing his holster and carrying a shotgun. He had his cell phone and was speaking to dispatch. "Have Deputy Grant meet me at Doc McDermott's house." He called to Kian, "Give me your house keys. We'll check everything out."

Kian threw him his keys. "Someone will need to stay to look after the dogs."

"Don't worry, we have it covered," Don said as he kissed Debi. "I'll meet you at home."

Elizabeth called to me as we were leaving the house, "We'll look after Koa!"

Shit! How could I have forgotten Koa? I gave her a grateful smile. "Thank you."

We didn't waste any time reaching the car. I hit the accelerator, and the tires spun as we drove down the road toward the main highway.

I felt so sorry for not remembering Koa. I was a terrible mother.

"Do you think it was the mayor and his gang?" I finally asked.

"It has to be. Leo said he saw a pick-up truck tearing away from the house."

"Oh! I wonder if it was the mayor's truck?"

"I can't imagine he'd be that stupid. Frank will check everything out."

Kian had a white-knuckle grip on his knees. I placed my hand on top of his. His grasp relaxed, and he looked at me.

"Sorry," he said. "This is the worst time for me. Not being able to do anything."

"I understand." I squeezed his hand, and he lifted mine to his lips and kissed it.

"Thank you for coming with me."

"Of course. I can't believe I overlooked Koa," I said.

He smiled, "Not to worry. I forgot him too. The women have it covered."

The roads were clear, and every light was green as we passed through town. Silently, I said a small prayer as we pulled into the clinic's parking lot.

"Pull around the back," Kian instructed. "Leonard will have the rear door unlocked."

I parked the car, and before I had it shut off, he had hopped out.

"Are you coming in?" he asked.

I wouldn't miss this. I nodded and followed him inside.

He flipped the lock on the back door after he had pulled it closed behind us. His whole demeanor changed. He put on his white coat, which hung on a hook by the back door, and pushed through the double doors. Leonard, the technician I had met previously, hovered over a table. A medium-sized, brown, scraggly looking dog lay on the stainless-steel table panting heavily. There was blood on the table and caked on both the dog and Leonard.

"How is he doing?" Kian's voice commanded.

Kian pointed to a swivel stool, which was out of the way. Right away I knew he wanted me to sit there. I did. No additional prompts were necessary.

"I gave him a sedative for the pain. It looks like the bullet didn't pass through him. See there's an entry here." Leonard pointed to the dog's thigh.

Kian cursed and picked up his stethoscope and used it on the dog's chest. He pressed his hands over the dog's body while softly speaking, "There's a good boy. What a good dog you are."

The dog yelped and lifted his head. Leonard was there quickly to hold him down. Kian spoke in soft, soothing tones. "Sorry about that my friend. We're going to fix you up."

Kian pulled the stethoscope from his ears. "Let's prep him. We need to get in there now. The bullet is still in there, and it feels like his femur is shattered."

"Shit," Leonard muttered softly.

"Shit is right."

"Do you want me to call anyone in?"

Kian sighed and looked up at the clock located over the double swinging doors. "No. I think we can do this together. Let's get him under anesthesia and then you can tube him. I'll get the surgery room ready. I'm going to need you to glove up too."

Leonard nodded as Kian readied a syringe. "Pictures?"

"Yes, we'll need a few." Kian turned to me. "This is going to take all night, or at least several hours. Will you call the guys and let them know?"

"Yes," I said. "Can I help in any other way? I'll be glad to stay."

"Really?"

"Yes. Can you use me?" I asked already pulling my cell phone out.

"Yes. Absolutely. Would you go to the break room and make some coffee? It's down the hall on the left."

"Cream and sugar?"

"Just a bit of cream," he answered.

"Leonard," I asked, "coffee?"

"Coke with lots of ice. It's in the refrigerator."

"I'll find it."

I found their break room. It reminded me of Kian's house, tidy and functional. Everything had a place. They even had a one-cup coffee maker.

I spoke to Michael and let him know what was happening at the clinic. He told me both Frank and the deputy were looking for any clues the shooter may have left behind. My brother assured me at least two of them would stay at the house until either Leonard or Kian arrived back home.

By the time I carried the drinks to the main room, the dog had been placed on a surgical table in an adjacent room. Inside, music played, and I smiled when I recognized The Airborne Toxic Event. Kian had good taste in music.

Both men scrubbed their hands at a large sink outside the surgical room. Kian lifted his foot from a pedal and the water shut off.

"Thanks, Christina, please put them on the small table next to the laptop," Kian said.

He motioned to two packages sitting on another table. They had been opened, and surgical gowns were sitting on both.

"Grab it by the strings and hold it open for me," he asked. When I did, he slid his arms through the sleeves and turned. "Please tie the strings in the back. And then help Leonard."

There was a small laptop on the table where I placed the drinks.

"I'd like you to take notes for us. I'll dictate what I need you to write."

"Okay." I pulled a small swivel chair over to the table with the laptop.

They settled themselves around the small operating table. The bright lights were focused on the dog who was breathing peacefully. The tube coming out of his mouth was hooked up to a ventilation system, which hissed softly.

Kian looked at another clock mounted to the wall. "Okay Christina, mark down that we're beginning at one sixteen a.m."

I clicked away on the laptop and then looked up just in time to see Kian pass a scalpel along the smoothly shaved thigh of the dog. The blood pooled up, and he dabbed at it with a surgical sponge. The cut became longer and longer. I swallowed deeply, not realizing until that moment that he planned to take off the leg.

As he progressed, Leonard was right there being an extra hand when needed. After the initial cuts, I was surprised how little blood there actually was. Kian would dictate observations to me and procedures he used. Then there was the nauseating smell of the flesh being cauterized. I knew he had to do that to staunch the bleeding, but I wasn't sure I could take it.

At one point, I must have looked pale because Kian called out to me, "Are you okay? There's club soda in the break room."

My face reddened a bit. "No, I'm okay."

Huh. If he could do this, then so could I.

At four a.m., the men looked wiped out. I wasn't feeling any better. It appeared they were almost done. I peered at the disposed leg lying on a nearby table. It now merely looked like a piece of meat, raw and red. The dog still breathed peacefully through the tube. As he closed the massive wound, Kian began to sing along with the music. He was listening to Young the Giant now, and his movements went in time with the beat.

Leonard rose and stripped off his gloves. He took a long drink of his coke, which must have been terribly watered down. He stretched and started to clean the area.

Kian stood too and stretched his arms out. "Okay, Christina. Mark the time as four thirty-nine a.m. We're done. Leave everything Leonard, the crew will clean up when they get here. That's only a half hour away. You go home."

"What about you?" he asked as Kian removed his own gloves.

"I'll finish up the notes and wait for the crew. Go home. Relieve the guys that are at the house, and get some rest." Kian smiled and patted the man on the back. "Good job tonight."

After Kian had cleaned the dog, he carried him to a cage located inside the large room and laid him gently inside. Then he looked at me, "Well now, you must be as exhausted as I am!"

"I am tired." I felt the fatigue rush through me suddenly as if the adrenaline was keeping me awake and now that the crises had passed, I had nothing left to go on.

He looked over my shoulder at the laptop screen, "Good notes. Ever thought about becoming a vet tech?"

I laughed, "I don't think taking dictation qualifies me for that."

His hands rubbed my back.

"Thank you for your help tonight. It was much appreciated. By you volunteering, I didn't have to call someone in and away from their weekend." He bent and kissed my cheek. His now day old beard brushed against my cheek, and for some reason, it felt right. It made me feel alive.

"Is the dog going to make it?"

"He should. He's a young dog. He didn't have any other injuries, and that's in his favor. We'll check to see if he is microchipped and the shelters to see if anyone has inquired about him. If not, we'll add him to the list and find him a forever home too."

"I'm so glad." I looked around, "Do you have to clean this yourself?"

"No," he said, "I don't. I have a crew who comes in on the weekends to check on the dogs. They'll clean up." He glanced at the clock. "Would you mind if I crashed at your place? I hate to make one of them take me home, and I don't want you driving the road this late."

"You mean this early?"

As I spoke the words, we heard the back door open. Voices followed the footsteps down the hallway.

A rush of surprised expressions joined us in the large room. After Kian had explained what happened to his technicians, both went to check on their newest patient. He left instructions and told them he'd be back in a few hours.

He took my elbow and led me to the back door. "Don't worry, I just need sleep. No funny business."

I laughed, "Of course, you can crash with me."

He crossed his heart, and his voice took on more of his Irish lilt, "I promise. You can trust me."

He did have an evil glint in his eyes, though.

CHAPTER 24

When we arrived at the cabin, I showed Kian around. We stopped in Elizabeth's fantasy bedroom complete with the enormous sled bed and more pillows than one person could ever want.

He chuckled, "Elizabeth really is a princess."

I grinned back, "Yes she is."

"Michael did find the perfect person for himself, didn't he?"

"I think so. She gives him the opportunity to be the hero. None of the other women in his life let him."

"Is this where you sleep?"

"No. I sleep in the guest room. You can sleep in here. Elizabeth doesn't mind."

He took my hand, "Then I'll sleep with you in the guest room. Is that okay?"

I eyed him.

"No sex. Not tonight. You are the most ravishing creature on this earth, but I'm exhausted. I need to sleep, but I need to hold someone too. I know it sounds strange. Is it okay?"

It did not sound weird to me. I understood the rawness of the evening. The shock of what happened. From a fantastic night to a night filled with horror and blood.

I nodded, "Do you want to take a shower?"

"Do I need to?" He sounded so earnest.

"No, you don't. Neither of us does. We need sleep." We needed to heal.

I led him to my room. He grinned when he saw the plainness of it. I pulled back the covers and fluffed up the pillows. He had his shoes and socks off by the time I turned around.

"No need to be shy around me." He took his t-shirt off and reached for his belt buckle.

I turned my back to him, I couldn't watch him undress. I simply couldn't. This was too surreal for me. I pulled my sweater over my head and heard him unzip his pants. They flew into the chair next to me and then the bed rustled. I slipped out of my jeans and flipped off the overhead light. Thankfully we were in the dark. We wouldn't be for long because dawn was on its way.

He patted the space next to him. I slipped into the bed. This was too odd. How could he make me do these things?

"I'm so tired," he whispered. He pulled me against him, and we spooned together.

Even though I was just as tired, I laid there for a while. It felt great to have his arms holding me close. It had been a long time since I had that. His breathing became even, and it lulled me finally to sleep.

I was woken abruptly by shouts. Kian was having a nightmare.

Curled into a tight ball, he yelled, "No! No! Don'a 'urt de puppies. No!" His voice was almost childlike, and his accent had a thick Irish brogue. His body jerked violently.

I switched the small lamp on and shook him. "Kian, you're dreaming. Kian, wake up!"

His beautiful eyes opened, and he had tears in them. Surprise covered his face, and he looked around at his surroundings as if he couldn't remember where he was. When he realized, he took a deep breath and scrubbed at his face with his hands.

"I'm sorry." He sat up, and the beautiful tattoo on his back was visible.

A Celtic cross with roses entwined through it. It covered most of his back, and the intricacies amazed me. He pushed back the covers and then I saw the horrible scarring he had on his side and lower back. The scars were old and white, but it was evident they had been deep. I reached out to touch them, and he caught my hand, brought it to his lips, and kissed it.

"What? How?" I sat up next to him.

"The scars? They happened a very long time ago. I forget I have them. I usually warn women ahead of time. Sorry."

I pressed my lips together. Great. I didn't want to know that he warned all the women. I didn't want to know how many he had.

He flopped back on the bed and moved his arm over his head.

"That was a bad nightmare you had. You were all curled up."

"Yeah. It's a reoccurring dream. I have it when I'm exhausted or feeling exposed. I'm sorry I woke you."

Did he feel vulnerable?

"Do you want to tell me about the dream?"

He blew out a big breath, "It's an old story."

Lying next to him, I put my head on his shoulder. "I have time."

"Well ... I was seven years old, and my family lived in Ireland, in a small town not far from Dublin. My mother was a microbiologist, and my father, a teacher. We lived on a family estate that was owned by my da's family.

His older brother, my uncle bred horses and dogs. We didn't know he was running a dog fighting ring."

My eyes grew wide, "The problem has been around that long? And in Ireland too?"

"Yes, in Ireland too, dog fighting has gone on for centuries, he said grimly. "One of his bitches had just given birth to a bunch of puppies. I was so enamored with them. The first thing I did when I'd come home from school, was to run to the barn and visit the new puppies. One afternoon, as I was going out to the barn, I overheard my uncle speaking with one of his workers. He was in a rage because one of his dogs had just lost a fight. He called the dog all sorts of foul names and said that it wouldn't be allowed to breed. He wanted to get rid of the worthless issuance he had in the barn."

"Oh no, Kian. He wasn't going to ... the new puppies?"

He sighed heavily, "I don't know how I knew. But, I ran so fast ... I passed him outside of the barn doors and ran to the puppies. He was so furious, he planned to stomp them to death. I threw myself on them. I curled up in a ball to protect them. My uncle warned me to get out of the way, but I wouldn't budge. I just kept screaming."

I placed my hand on his chest and could feel his heart racing. "You don't have to tell me."

"No. I need to. I haven't talked about it in so long. I've tried to bury it. My uncle yelled if I didn't get off them, he would do to me what he planned to do to them. I didn't budge. I didn't think he'd do it. He was my uncle, after all, my father's brother. The first kick from his boot hit my side. The explosion of pain was something I'd never imagined to feel, but I knew I had to protect those puppies. The kicks kept coming. He finally picked me up by the shirt and threw me to the side."

"Tell me he didn't." I trembled at the thought.

"No, he didn't. My father heard my screams, and he came running into the barn. He hit his brother with a shovel. Knocked him out cold."

"What happened?"

"The puppies survived. My uncle served one year in prison. Ma insisted that we move and that's how we ended up in Los Angeles. We had some family living there. They wanted to get me far away from the situation."

"He only served a single year? He could have killed you."

"But he didn't. The local judges were in his pocket. He had to serve some time, but most of the time he was under house arrest at the estate. Both of my parents were furious. My uncle told my da that I deserved the beating for being in the way. The puppies were his, and he could do as he liked with them."

"Is this what lead you to become a veterinarian?"

He chuckled, "Oh, I think it chose me." He turned on his side to face me. Trailing a finger down my cheek to my chin, he then ran it over my lips. "I'm sorry I woke you."

"I'm sorry you had the nightmare, but what happened to you is even worse and to have to relive it through your dreams is awful."

"I'm used to it. I've even seen therapists about it. They blab at me about needing to let go and forgive."

"What? How could you forgive what your uncle did to you? An innocent boy?"

"No, my sweetlin', forgive myself. I blamed myself for what happened."

"How could you? You saved the puppies."

"In the mind of a seven-year-old, I found fault with myself. Don't worry about me. The experience has made me the man I am today. Had it not happened, I probably wouldn't be here."

Not here. That was a terrible thought. True, I guess, all the events, which happen to us, bring us to where we are now.

He brought me out of my thoughts by giving me a soft kiss. "Can we sleep another couple of hours?"

I looked at the clock, it was only seven thirty. "Take the time you need."

"Stay with me," he said.

His eyes showed hurt, I knew he was putting on a brave front. He had the same haunted look when he saw the injured dog. Although last night he had his professional mask on, I knew he was afraid that he may have caused the injury to the dog by keeping the mayor's dogs. It was evident the shooting was retribution of some kind.

"Yes," I answered softly. What was happening here? Kian was in my bed. I was fostering a dog? My life didn't have room for this. Everything was too out of control for me.

His arm wrapped around me, and as he rolled onto his back, he positioned me with my head on his chest. It was an intimate action, our bodies pressed together. His chest, hard with muscles, would be one any woman would dream to have to pillow her head. Smooth skin, with a smooth chest.

I woke and heard the shower running in the guest bathroom. The spot next to me was empty. Koa was curled up on the foot of the bed. How did he get there?

The bathroom door opened, and Kian came walking into the bedroom with a towel casually wrapped around his waist. He didn't have problems with nudity.

"Ahh, you're up. I've made coffee. May I bring you some?" he said as he picked up his jeans and t-shirt.

"No, I'll get up." I pointed to Koa, "How?"

He grinned, "Elizabeth and Michael brought him by about thirty minutes ago. Your brother was very surprised to see me answer the door."

"Yeah, I bet he was."

"Your sister-in-law looked like a cat with a canary. Don't be surprised if it's all over town later today."

"I guess we'll be doing the drive of shame through Mintock as I take you home."

"No need. Frank is coming by to pick me up. He wants to talk to me about yesterday's assault. I also want to stop at the clinic and have a check in on our patient."

Great. Yeah, I wanted Frank to know that Kian slept here last night. Now Annie will know too. Wait, she's going to know anyway, Michael will tell her.

I pushed off the covers. I had felt strange sleeping in my bra and panties last night and questioned why I didn't put on a nightgown instead. I wasn't thinking straight. Now I had to face Kian in my underwear.

I stood, and he looked at me with a big grin on his face.

"Christina, you are quite sexy in your underwear." He took the few steps toward me.

I wanted to cover myself with my hands. I didn't though. I was glad at least I wore a matching set and didn't have on my granny panties.

He placed his hands on my hips and pulled me close. He kissed my shoulder leading to a trail up my throat and ended at my lips. His kiss was divine. Soft, warm, and inviting. I wrapped my arms around his shoulders and stepped in close, so our bodies touched.

"I do want to ravish you, Miss Hoffman. Will you give me that opportunity?" he whispered as he continued kissing me. His fingers moved around to my backside, and he filled each hand with a butt cheek. He squeezed and massaged me while our tongues tangoed.

Slipping his hands under my panties, his strokes became more intimate. The caresses sent heat through my blood to my core. I dropped one arm around his waist and pulled at the towel. Kian obliged me by moving his hips, so the towel fell at his feet. When we came back together, I was greeted with the feeling of his hot swollen flesh pressing against my belly. His cock was hard and ready, just the way I liked it.

He pulled at my leg to wrap it around his hip, and when he did, his erection pressed down between my legs. Now the only thing between me and this ultimate pleasure were my damned panties. They needed to come off. Now.

All the while his tongue was stroking mine making me feel ready to orgasm on the spot. His fingers unsnapped my bra, and when he pressed me back on the bed to a sitting position, my breasts were exposed. I looked at him. His blue eyes were on fire with appreciation. My gaze traveled down his incredible body, and I rested on his magnificent straining erection.

117

"Ahh sweetlin', you are mine now," he said possessively as he knelt in front of me.

Cue the knock on the door. Both of our heads whipped to the side where the back door was located.

"Fuck!" he grimaced.

"Frank?" I barely whispered out. Perhaps if we were quiet, he would go away?

Kian rested his hands on my parted thighs. "He's here to pick me up."

I sighed, knowing this scene was over.

"I'm sorry baby. I completely forgot. Seeing you in your panties, well, you are sweet hotness."

I smiled and ran my fingers through his tousled wet hair.

He lowered his head between my legs, pushing them apart further and kissed the material covering my begging core. Then he moved my panties to the side while his tongue nudged inside, licking my swollen clit.

My hands fisted in his hair as I twisted and moaned into the pillow.

"I had to have a taste of your honey, and you taste just as I thought you would. I will be back for more, is that okay?"

"Oh, yes, please," I gasped.

He kissed me. "Later. I'll call you."

"Fuck," I echoed as I felt him stand. I laid there on the bed not moving while he dressed.

He closed the bedroom door when he left, and I could hear him speaking with Frank a few seconds later.

Frank's truck drove away a few minutes later. I looked over at Koa. He laid there at the end of the bed and wagged his tail.

"What?" I asked the dog.

CHAPTER 25

What was I getting myself into? I hoped my drive to San Francisco would help clear my mind so I could figure out what was happening to me. Kian was cute and sexy… but smart, intelligent, and sexy was even better in my book. Ten years younger than me. What was I thinking?

The more I thought about his age and the fact he was a friend of my brother, it depressed me. Everything led back to the money. Why else would a man who looked like that be interested in me? Maybe he wanted to score for his organization. At least it would go to a good cause.

When I arrived in the city, I dropped Koa off at Robert and Gary's house. I didn't want to appear too eccentric by bringing him into my meeting and having one of the secretary's care for him. Koa would have to eventually acclimate himself around their dog, Buffy. The drive did help sort my thoughts, and I decided to stop second guessing Kian's motivations.

The meeting was boring. Financial sales types were trying to convince me to invest in their company. I looked forward to my house being completed, and then I could drag business associates out to my neck of the woods. I didn't mind the drive to San Francisco especially if I could couple it with a visit with my best friends, but it was a drain on my energy.

When we were finished, I told them to send all the information to JuJu. She would not thank me, but I rarely gave out my personal number to business acquaintances. I arrived back at Robert's house and noticed Gary's car parked next to his in the garage. That made me smile, two of my favorite guys for lunch!

Delicious aromatic smells greeted me when the garage door opened. Gary hugged me by way of a greeting.

"What is that smell? It makes my mouth water," I asked him.

"Roasted chicken, I put it on the rotisserie. New potatoes, carrots, and salad," he replied as he held the door open for me.

"A real Sunday dinner? Wow! I'm starving too. They didn't even offer me any snacks at the meeting, can you believe it? I drive all the way out here on a Sunday, and not even a miserable store bought cookie!"

Gary covered his mouth in mock surprise, "The devil you say! Well, it would serve them right if you didn't invest in them. Cheapskates! By the way, we're keeping Koa. He has fallen madly in love with Buffy. They would make delightful puppies."

"He's fixed," I replied.

Robert greeted me in the kitchen by saying, "Who would cut off the precious boy's nuts?"

"It appears Dr. Kian did it. Part of his philosophy to cut down on the number of homeless pets," I said.

Robert picked up Koa who was wagging his tail around me trying to greet me. "My little man, they have taken your family jewels away. Can you believe it? There will be no whoring for you!" Koa licked his face, and he laughed, "I agree, I like boys better too!" Robert set him back on the floor, and when he straightened, he had a serious expression.

I had seen that face before, and it wasn't good news. "What?"

"Go on, tell her," Gary said.

"Let's sit down." Robert motioned to the kitchen nook chair.

We both sat, and Gary brought us glasses of chilled white wine. Robert reached for a large white envelope and pulled out a stack of eight by ten photos.

My eyes widened. It was easy to see that I was the object of the pictures and where the pictures had been taken. It was the hotel in New Orleans. I picked up one of the pictures. I was in bed with enough of my body showing. I began a slow burn, "That son of a bitch!"

"So you know about these pictures?" Robert started. "There are all sorts of different positions."

I frowned, "No I do not. They are not very flattering, are they? They make me look like a drug user and a prostitute."

"Who?" he asked.

"That asshole, Scott Binder. I woke up the morning after the party, and he was in my bathroom. I certainly do not remember inviting him to my room the night before."

"He probably drugged your drinks," Gary said as he joined us. "You're not that heavy of a sleeper. For him to have put you in some of those positions, you would have to been completely out of it. Do you know who the other man and woman are?"

I examined more of the pictures and shook my head. "No, they don't look familiar at all. It doesn't matter because it's my face that's visible." I snapped my fingers and laid my palms up out flat. "Let's have it. What does he want?"

He handed me a typed letter written on white copy paper. I read it and threw it down. There were no names on it. It was very clear what he was after. Money.

"Ha! He thinks my reputation is worth five million dollars."

"If he releases the photos to the tabloids, your membership on all the charitable boards certainly will be jeopardy. You know that crowd shies away from any scandal," Gary said.

I shook my head, "Son of a bitch. How was this letter delivered? It's Sunday, there's no mail delivery."

Robert put the pictures back inside the envelope. "A courier dropped it off shortly after you left."

I jumped on this, "A messenger? We can trace that."

"Already done. No one is answering the phone at the service. It seems they are closed on Sundays," he said as he closed the envelope. "We'll see if we can lift some fingerprints from the letter and photos tomorrow. I would recommend not involving the police right now."

"Why the hell not? I know who did this," I shouted angrily. "I do not give in to intimidation."

Robert rubbed my back. "I know you don't. The pictures are bad, and you don't want them to be spread all over the internet, which will happen if you let the police in on it. They would be leaked all over. Let me see what I can do with my connections. I would rather protect you from the fallout."

"Damn. I know who did this. I pissed Scott off last week too when he visited me at my new house."

Robert looked perplexed, "He visited you at your new house?"

I nodded, "I think he actually thought he had a chance with me. The creep. He called me fat to top it off!"

Gary was indignant, "He called you what? The bastard! If you are fat, then what does that make me? You are not fat! Not even close!"

I leaned over and kissed him on the cheek, "Thank you, my friend."

"We have to stick together girl," he responded.

I pointed to the envelope, "I think he's also involved in the dog fighting ring that's plaguing the area."

Robert tapped his chin, "Hmmm… I wonder if we can use that? Let me think on it. He gave us a week to assemble the funds. We're supposed to call him on this cell phone number when we have the money. And yes, I've already checked the cell phone number, it's one of the disposable kind."

I jotted Frank's name and phone down.

"He is the chief of police in Mintock and is heading up the investigation into the dog fight ring. I want him to know about the photos," I said.

Robert took my hand in his, "Are you sure Chrissy? These pictures are raw."

I patted and squeezed his hand, "Yes Bobby, I'm sure. Frank knows me now. He knows I don't do that sort of stuff." My skin prickled as I said it.

He nodded, "Okay. Let's have some lunch. I'm hungry."

We had a filling and healing meal, and it was just what I needed. Before I left, I took pictures of the photos with my cell phone. If they were released, I wanted my family to see them first. The boys also promised to visit Mintock and see the progress on the house over the following weekend.

Back in the car, I bristled every time I thought of the pictures. I would have to call JuJu in the morning since she'd be back from her vacation. I knew what she'd say to me. She would advocate the quick death of Mr. Binder. A quick, very painful death.

My thoughts led to Kian. Was I stupid? What could he possibly want with me? He was young and good looking ... strike that ... he's totally hot. I liked him. I felt like I could relax around him, be me, and not have to put up the mask I wore in public. Just me, a geeky girl who loved computers, technology, and figuring out if an idea would work or not. I laughed to myself, a nerd girl who also loved wearing designer clothes and stiletto heels.

And mister dreamy eyes? With his hot body, quick wit, sexy Irish brogue, a bit of a bad boy plus being a doctor, and yeah, Superman too, by saving dogs. How did our divergent paths cross?

Just as I passed Ashley and started up the mountain road, my cell phone rang. Kian's name popped up on the dashboard of the SUV.

"Hi," I answered, and a thrill ran through my body, especially as I remembered the morning's event.

"Hi, back at you. How are you doing? Are you almost home? How was the meeting?"

The barrage of questions almost made me feel dizzy. "I'm fine, and yes, I've just hit the mountain road. The meeting was boring because the people who were presenting were annoying."

"Do you want to come over to my house? I can pick up a pizza, and we can watch a movie or something."

I smiled to myself, I liked the or something activity. "I have Koa with me."

"That will be okay. He knows my dogs, I introduced them before I gave him to you."

"You did?"

"Yeah, I wasn't sure if you were going to take Koa, so I thought I might have to take him."

"You didn't think I would take him?" The thought hurt me a little.

"No Christina, it's not like that. I thought that perhaps you'd end up being too busy, or perhaps that maybe something would come up and you'd not be able to care for him. I don't know, I always have a contingency plan in the background."

"Well…" I said.

"Come on Christina, please give me a break. Don't be so hard on me. It wasn't an easy day. I received plenty of ribbing from Frank in the truck on the way to the clinic."

"Oh, okay. If you're tired, perhaps we should postpone to another night?" I teased.

"Damn it! I'm picking up the pizza. If you make it to the house before I do, Leonard should still be there. He's going to stay with his girlfriend tonight."

"Oh? So we'll have the house to ourselves?"

"Yes, if you don't include the pack of dogs, then we'll be completely alone."

"If you put it that way, I'd be delighted to come to your house for dinner."

After we had disconnected, I smiled a wicked grin, three nights in a row. I completely forgot all my arguments about Kian.

Leonard was feeding the dogs when I arrived. He added Koa to the pack and fed him too. Koa was a little shy with the other dogs at first, but after eating, he laid down with the rest of them to snooze off his dinner.

I appreciated Leonard staying with me until Kian arrived, after what had happened the night before, I didn't feel 100% safe in his house. We watched the Golden State Warriors basketball team fight it out with the Los Angeles Lakers. I had no idea about the nuances of the game, and bless him for trying so valiantly to explain it to me.

As soon as Kian arrived with two hot pizzas, Leonard left with one of the pies, bidding us both a good night.

I joined him in the kitchen, and after he had set the pizza on the table, he pulled me into his arms.

"Come here, woman. I've waited for this all day you little minx, teasing me like you do."

His breath was hot on my neck as he nibbled his way up to my chin. His lips claimed mine, and his tongue found its way into my mouth, after stroking my lips to coax them open. At the same time, his hands were busy as ever under my thin sweater. The clasp on my bra gave way, and his hands were under the material quickly caressing my breasts. His thumbs brushed against my already hardened nipples, and a gasp escaped my throat as electricity pulsed through my body and came to a stop at my core.

He had a wicked grin on his face as he pulled away from me. Before I knew it, the sweater was off over my head and on his kitchen chair. My bra too found a home next to it.

His lips. Oh, his lips, they worshiped my breasts. Teeth grazed against my tender nipples making them ache for his touch. My fingers combed through his hair as he continued to suck one and then the other. I felt his hands under my butt as he lifted me onto the table. When he did, I grabbed for his t-shirt, and he helped me pull it over his head.

"Just a minute," he said as he turned with the pizza box in his hands. It went into the oven.

I giggled ... my practical thinking doctor. Then he turned back to me and rubbed his hands together. His hair was so tousled. He looked like a mad scientist.

"Now my sweetlin', I will have you, and I will have you thoroughly."

"Here in the kitchen?" I asked. I've never had sex in a kitchen.

He pulled me to my feet. "This way." He grabbed my sweater and bra. We kissed all the way to his room.

The bed was large and straightforward. A couple of pillows and a comforter covered it. Several large windows faced the backyard.

"Sit," he commanded

I did as he requested.

"Let's get you naked," his voice was deep. I could see the anticipation on his face and his body. His erection strained against the material of his jeans. I remembered why I liked younger men so much.

"I want you naked too," I purred.

"Oh, that's easy," he said as he undid the button and zipper of his jeans. His shoes were off, and the jeans followed.

He stood there in black briefs, which were gone in a flash too. Stepping toward me, I felt myself becoming liquid. I melted. This man was not shy in the least. He enjoyed me looking at him. I surprised myself because I actually looked, unlike this morning when I hadn't had a chance before we were interrupted. My previous question had been answered, he certainly manscaped.

"Now you," Kian murmured.

He knelt in front of me and reached for my waistband. My hands flew to the button to help him. He batted my fingers away. He slowly unzipped the zipper. I aided him by lifting my hips so he could slide my slacks down. He lifted each leg up, and after he had removed my shoe he kissed my insole, then he slid the pants off. Again, I was glad I didn't wear the granny panties. I needed to get rid of them.

Pushing me gently back, he hooked his fingers under the thin material of the underwear and slowly brought them down. As he did, he kissed my exposed flesh. The stubble on his cheek brushing against my skin made me ache for his touch. The removal of the rest of my clothing was agonizingly deliberate. When that scrap of material finally was gone, I almost sighed in relief.

His hands parted my thighs unhurriedly. Everything was going in slow motion.

"I want to savor you," he whispered.

I felt his breath on my flesh, the trail of his tongue along my inner thigh, and his fingers lightly teased me. He led a path around my center.

"Mine," he said.

"Yes," I whispered. "Yours. Oh, Kian I want you." I lifted my head, and our eyes met. There was an incredible connection between us.

His head dipped again toward me, and I felt his tongue tracing the same circle his fingers had only done moments before. He was killing me ever so sweetly.

The feeling of his tongue dipping in and brushing against my clitoris made me cry out, "Oh yes!"

"So very wet. I think you do want me." The more aroused he was, the thicker his accent became. "Tell me what you like."

"Oh, I like everything you are doing," I panted, my fingers brushing through his hair trying to bring him closer.

Teasing me with his tongue, he licked my nub until I felt I couldn't take any more of the pleasure he offered. Spreading my outer lips wider so he could fully access me, his fingers gently probed me deeply. I could feel my body being taken to the top of the peak, my hips moving against him as I fisted his hair. I was so close. So close.

"Tell me what you like," he whispered again and then focused entirely on my clit with his mouth.

"Oh Kian, I'm coming!" While he sucked me deeply, my body hit the crest of the wave, and I felt myself shatter into crush after crush of orgasms.

I laid there trembling and panting as the aftermath of the explosion in my body continued. He moved slowly up my body and pulled me to him. Holding me, he kissed my face, my eyes, my nose, my mouth, my chin, and my neck.

I moved to stroke him, and he stilled my hand.

"Shh… We have all night for that. Nothing is going to happen to it. First, you … breathe deeply."

He kissed me again. His hands caressed me as his fabulous kisses rained down. I felt so soothed by him. So relaxed. I hadn't realized how tense I had become.

I returned his kisses ardently. My hands slid along his side and to his back. His firm flesh pressed against my stomach. This part of his body craved my attention. Slipping my leg in between his, I gently lifted his knee with my leg, parting his legs so I could reach between them.

My fingers brushed his balls, and he uttered a curse, "Damn woman, you have tricky hands."

I smiled and pushed him on his back. His cock was so thick and hard, it lay on his stomach. I firmly ran my finger from the crown all the way to the base, and his erection responded by jumping against my hand. I found a bead of his clear liquid at the tip, and I dipped my head down. My tongue peeked out as I lapped up the precious drop.

Kian groaned loudly, "Ahh, sweetlin'. What you do to me. Ye are gonna kill me for sure."

I giggled, "You are quite randy. I will need to teach you a lesson here." I wrapped my hand around his tool and licked around the crown. His taste was thrilling. Earthy and clean, my tongue and lips wrapped around him as they slid down his swollen shaft. The weight and feel of him aroused me and made my slick, wet flesh ache for him. I had a driving need to have him deep inside of me. He studied me as I licked around his crown again.

His hands stilled my movements. "I need to be deep inside of you," he echoed my thoughts.

I grinned and took as much of him as I could into my mouth and sucked him hard as I slowly drew him out. His entire body shuttered in response.

"That's it! I'm fucking you until you can't take it anymore!"

I giggled, "Promise?"

"You will beg me to stop," he challenged.

In one fluid movement, I was on my back under him. He had my legs up around his waist, and I was spread wide as I possibly could be. My core was on fire! I wondered if I was drenching the sheets because I had never felt more alive, sexier, and more aroused than right at that moment.

The head of his shaft was at my entrance, and my body was so greedy for his, but he had other ideas. He pressed the top into me ever so slightly, just barely inside. My hips snapped up to try to take more of him.

"Oh!" I panted, "More. More."

He pressed again further, and this time when he withdrew, he moaned into my shoulder.

Kian's eyes were pools of liquid again, and as he withdrew, I could tell it was the most difficult thing he had ever done. My hips snapped again and this time I couldn't still them while I undulated under him.

"Tell me what you want," he growled into my ear. "Do you want my cock?"

"Yes. I need you. I want it all."

Those words did the trick. He was inside of me with one swift motion. Buried up to the hilt and I tightened my legs around him because I never wanted him to withdraw. The feeling of being filled with him was incomprehensible.

The moment he started moving inside of me, his massive throbbing flesh touched every part of me. The pleasure was overwhelming just as he warned.

"My woman. So wet, so hot," he whispered in my ear and then took my lips.

That was all it took. The orgasm took me by surprise. My body arched against him, at once trying to get closer and trying to writhe against the exquisite torment. With every deep thrust of his body into mine, I came over and over.

I felt his body tighten against mine and knew he was close to his own release. I reached down around his ass and stroked his balls.

He groaned in delight, "Now you've gone and done it!"

His hips snapped, and he buried himself so deeply I could feel him against me, which triggered another orgasm in me. My body milked his release as his body shuttered again and again.

Collapsing on me, we became an entangled heap.

CHAPTER 26

Being there in Kian's arms was sheer bliss. My head on his shoulder and palm on his chest, we laid on top of the sheets. Both of us tried to cool down, as the perspiration dried on our skin. It was quiet in the house, and the dogs had surrounded the bed on the floor. I was glad none of them had tried to jump on the bed during our intimacy.

He stroked my back slowly. "Are you hungry? We have the pizza in the oven."

I smiled, "No. I'm okay." I lied. I was starved, but I didn't want to move. I didn't want to let go of Kian. His body felt too right next to mine. I was too exhausted.

The grandfather clock in his living room began to chime, and I counted eight. How had it become so late? Just the thought made my mutinous stomach growl.

He laughed, "Not hungry? Well, after that workout, I am! You stay in bed, I'll get the pizza, and we can eat it here."

Kian moved to get up, and I protested, "No, you don't have to. I can go with you in the kitchen."

"No. Stay here. I will bring it to you. Do you want some wine, soda, or water?"

"Water would be nice. I'm thirsty after all that activity," I grinned.

"I'll be right back. Do not get dressed. If you get cold, pull up the comforter," he said walking away.

I called out, "Why don't you want me to get dressed?"

He winked at me, "Because, I don't want to have to undress you again. You don't think we are finished, do you? We're not. I told you, you are going to beg me to stop!"

I giggled, and after he had left the room, I clapped, "Oh goodie!"

While he was gone, from the middle of his bed, I looked around his bedroom. Like the rest of the house, it was utilitarian. A few framed Irish landscape scenes were on the walls. There was an adjoining bathroom at the end of the room near the windows. Instead of curtains on the windows, he had shades, and they were all pulled halfway down. Everything was neat, tidy and in its place. He didn't have the typical bachelor's pad with clothes piled everywhere and dirty dishes stacked on every open surface. I assumed it was the medical training in him.

The thought of him and me together again so soon was intoxicating. I stretched languorously on the bed. The way he looked at me made me feel desired above all. He was unabashed in his praise as if he sincerely meant the compliments. I wouldn't let them go to my head because certainly, they were not true, I knew they were just the heat of the moment. Every man says things he doesn't mean when he is having sex. Even so, it was charming to hear.

He returned quickly with pizza piled onto paper plates and napkins, then he retrieved ice-cold bottles of water. Climbing back on the bed, he took a slice of pizza and leaned against the headboard. I joined him with my own piece.

The pizza was surprisingly good even though it had sat in the oven for over an hour.

"This is good," I said munching away, "did you get it at Vincenzo's?

He nodded and swallowed. "Yeah. They make the best thin crust pizza. I'm glad it's on my side of town. They know me, all I do is to call, and they hear my voice. They say, 'twenty minutes.'"

I couldn't believe I was sitting in bed, eating pizza, naked, with a man. If anyone had ever told me that was in my future, I would have called them a liar. I looked down at my stomach. It was not flat. Pizza should not have crossed my lips. My hips were too wide. My thighs? Still touching when I walked. I frowned and then looked up.

Kian was watching me. He laid his half-eaten slice on the plate and took a drink of water. He scooted down so he could put his head in my lap if he wanted to. He didn't. Instead, he laid a soft kiss on my stomach and then my thighs. Positioning his arms on either side of my legs, he placed another kiss very close to my mound.

"I love your curves. I think it's wonderful that you can eat pizza with me in bed. Most women would never dream of doing that because they are too worried about what they look like to a man. I love that you have a quiet confidence in yourself. Your body is beautiful to me. When I hug you, I don't feel all bones, there is something for me to hold onto. I want you naked. Your body arouses me, even when you have clothes on. The way you move is so incredibly sexy. When I see those high-heeled shoes, I want to fuck you while you're wearing them. You make me hard every time I see you. In fact, …" he paused to roll over, and when he did, his cock sprang to life, standing straight out from his body.

"Oh," I whispered.

He laughed heartily and finished the slice of pizza. Then he slapped his hands together and rose to his knees.

"Now, where was I?" he said lustily. "Oh yes. I was about to have some desert!" He gripped my thighs and pulled me down until I laid flat.

"Aren't you going to turn off the lights?"

"No...," he said drawing out the word. "I like to look at my desert! Mmmm... sweet honey. I am going drive you out of your mind!"

I blushed. I never blushed except around him!

"Isn't it my turn, you know, to do you?" I met his eyes.

He grinned, "Don't worry," he handled his cock, "this is not going anywhere."

"Promise?" I giggled.

He flashed me a grin and dove in between my legs. I was ready for him, and he didn't make me feel self-conscious at all. Somehow, this whole thing began to feel completely natural.

"Mmmm... mine, mine, mine," he murmured as he took complete possession.

I giggled again, "Kian, you sound like a romance novel."

He quirked a smile, "I'll have you quiet woman! Stop interrupting me." His Irish was coming out again.

I shook my head, closed my eyes and let the sensations pull me under.

If I thought our first round was fantastic, well then, the second installment, which went on until the early morning hours, ruined me. His lovemaking was intense and so pleasurable that indeed I told him several times during the evening I couldn't take any more. In between, we ate cold pizza, opened an excellent bottle of Bordeaux, talked, explored each other's bodies until all knowledge was memorized.

He allowed me to examine his scars closely and showed me the ones that hurt when the weather was bad. I lay on his back and traced the lines of his tattoo. I could see more, what was hidden in the leaves that intertwined their way around the cross. I found roses, a face of a dog, an apple, and a dove. Kian told me there were ten symbols hidden among the leaves representing hope, life, honor, faith, unity, balance, transition, temperance, ascension, and navigation. I asked if he would explain them to me one day.

Very early in the morning, he finally wrapped his arms around me, and both of us looked for sleep. I felt his body relax against me and knew he found it first. I marveled at his gentle touch, his giving nature, and the sense of wonder he had for my body. Never had I ever experienced anyone like him. His deep feelings for the things he cared about were more than evident in how he acted. I began to believe he cared about me too. What were my feelings for him? I didn't have long to ponder the question because sleep quickly claimed me too.

CHAPTER 27

Kian was up when I woke. His side of the bed was empty, and it was barely dawn. He was visible from the windows throwing balls while the dogs chased after them in the backyard. As each one came back with a ball, he petted the dog and then threw the ball out again.

Koa was with me on the bed sleeping. That made me smile because the only way for him to get on the bed was if Kian placed him there. It was too early to get up, and I wanted to sleep more. But I felt a little awkward. What if he wanted me to leave? Should I get up now? What did he expect from me?

The chasing games ended outside, and I heard Kian open the door to the kennels and the mini-clinic. It would make sense that he would feed and care for the dogs in there also, after all, it was Monday, and he'd be going to work in a couple of hours. I blew out a breath, his day started early. I didn't know where he took all his energy from and then I remembered, yes, he was ten years younger than me.

I decided to get out of bed, and dressed in yesterday's clothes. Ugh. I hated doing that. I used to carry a change of clothes in my car for the times I had an unexpected sleep over. The task was finding my underwear. I looked under the bed. Nope. In the adjoining bathroom. Nope. Had we left them in the kitchen? No, I remembered still having them on when we moved to the bedroom. Where had he tossed them? Nothing under the pillows, or mixed in with the sheets? This was ridiculous. I found my bra, which I needed more than the panties. Damn. I gave up and put on my slacks. When I found my shoes, there were my briefs, crammed into the toe. How they ended up there, I would never figure it out. I stuffed them into my pants pocket.

Once in the living room, I quickly hid my panties in my purse. Moving on into the kitchen, I noticed Kian left a full pot of coffee, and a clean mug sitting next to it. I checked in the refrigerator, and it rewarded me with real half-and-half. There was nothing else in there. I take that back, there were bottles of Guinness, and a bunch of old take-out boxes, no real food, though. Nothing else, except packets of soy sauce, ketchup, and jam. Typical bachelor.

The contents of his cupboards brought back my student and starving days of my business. The shelves revealed boxes of cereal, most of them open and practically empty, a box of processed cheese, quick cook rice, macaroni & cheese, and a couple of jars of salsa. So much for trying to fix breakfast. He was obviously a meal on the run type of guy.

He came into the kitchen wiping his hands on a towel. When he saw me, his face spread wide with a grin. He wrapped his arms around me and gave me a kiss, which took my breath away.

"Good morning sweetlin'. You didn't need to get up so early. I hope I didn't wake you with my playing with the boys. I like to give them a little exercise in the morning because otherwise, they are couch potatoes all day long."

"No, it's okay. Did you see your patients in the kennels?"

"That I did. Many of them need medications two to three times a day. I like to keep an eye on them. I opened their doggy doors so they can go outside too." He grabbed a mug out of the cupboard and poured himself a cup of coffee.

"Are they here all by themselves during the day?"

He reached inside the refrigerator and snagged the cream. "No. I have local junior college students who volunteer for school credit, and they come in and help the organization. In turn, I give them instruction on veterinary technician techniques and their teachers test them with the material on their exams."

"That's impressive," I remarked. "It's a win-win for both of you."

"It is," he nodded and took a sip of his coffee. "Harry's Hounds couldn't possibly afford to pay salaries to them, so the volunteers are incredibly important. The high school students I had here the other day are on a similar program. It works for all of us.

I'm sorry I don't have anything in the house for breakfast. Normally I would have picked up some donuts or milk for the cereal."

My eyebrows quirked, "Oh, you mean when your other girlfriends stay over?"

He looked candidly at me. "Stop it, woman." He pulled me against him. "Have I dated before you? Yes, I have, as I am sure you have too. Don't look for ghosts where there are none." He gave me another breathtaking kiss.

I gazed into his eyes while he still held me and looked for deceit. But, I couldn't be sure. I was never skilled at discerning matters of the heart from people. I have always been a bit of a sap and believed what people told me. This always led me to trouble.

He released me. "I'm going to take a shower," he said, "I need to be at the hospital by eight."

I nodded, "I have to go too. I have a few things that require my attention." I hadn't told Kian about the photos the son-of-a-bitch Scott sent to me. I wanted to speak to Frank about them. Perhaps there was a connection to the dogfight club? I was convinced Scott was involved in it in some way. No one could be a buddy of the mayor and not be involved. "Will you let me know how the dog that was shot is doing?"

His smile brightened, "Yes, I will. He looked good yesterday when I left him he was already up on his three legs and walking around."

"Wow! That is fast!"

"Dogs do very well on three legs. Soon he won't miss it at all."

"Will he have a long rehabilitation?" I asked.

"No. I've already contacted one of my foster people, and they are getting their home ready for him. He'll stay with them for a time. They can care for him while he heals, and we'll begin the search for a forever home for him."

"You do work quickly."

He nodded and finished his coffee, "I have to. There are so many dogs out there needing rescue. The more I can move out to foster places, the more I can bring in. It's difficult for me to turn the hard cases away."

"Like the ones you have in your kennels?"

"Yeah. I'm adding a few more kennels, but there is only me giving medical treatment and only so many hours in the day."

I agreed and wrapped my arms around his waist. Putting my head on his shoulder, I said, "You're an awesome guy, you have so much love for neglected ones."

Did I include myself in that corner, one of the neglected ones?

He returned my hug and whispered, "Someone has to do it."

Kian packed Koa and me into the car. He kissed me goodbye and said, "I'll call you later?"

"I'd like that," I said and then waved goodbye.

I turned the Cadillac around and gave him one last glance in the rear-view mirror. He stood there in his jeans and sweatshirt and waved at me until I reached the dirt road. When I reached the main highway, I gunned the engine and headed toward Mintock, stopping at the town's only Starbucks. I used the drive-through to get coffee and a scone. Michael would have had a heart attack if he knew.

I reexamined the photographs that were copied to my phone. It made me sick seeing them, and my heart sank. I hadn't thoroughly looked at them yesterday. They were so crudely done. It was still too early to call Frank, but I knew my brother would be up.

When he answered his cell phone, I said, "Hey, do you have some time?"

Michael heard the tone of my voice, "Sure. What's wrong?"

"I have to show you. Can I come over?"

"Yeah. Don't knock on the door, Elizabeth is still asleep."

I left Koa at the cabin and headed over. Michael was making coffee when I walked into the kitchen.

"Want coffee?" he asked.

"Yeah." Okay, it would be my third cup this morning, and I was already wired enough. But, I couldn't turn it down.

I sat at the small table in the cozy kitchen he had designed. Filled with all the latest appliances, it showed my brother loved to cook, and he was comfortable working in the room. I waited while he hunted in the refrigerator. He found a large container of plain Greek yogurt, along with honey, raisins, dates, and nuts from the cupboard. He put everything on the table and pulled out a couple of bowls and spoons. I spooned the yogurt into the bowls and squirted honey into each, then sprinkled the nuts and fruit on top. Michael plugged in a small cooker and filled it with milk and oatmeal. He set it to start cooking.

He sliced up a baguette of bread and went back to the refrigerator for the brie cheese. By the time he finished, the coffee was ready, and he poured us both a cup. He put the creamer in front of me and then sat holding his own mug.

"So, what's up?" he asked. His face reflected my serious tone.

Pouring cream into my coffee and then scooping up a bit of yogurt on my spoon, I pressed my lips together. I called up the pictures on my phone.

"Please forget I'm your sister when you look at these," I said handing him the phone.

I watched him as he flipped through the pictures. His face showed no reaction. He didn't look at all of them. He placed the phone face down and brought his attention back to me.

"These were taken in New Orleans," he said it as a statement and not a question. "I recognize your room. Do you know the couple in the pictures?"

I shook my head. As strong as I was, tears started a path down my cheeks.

"Oh, baby sister," he said soothingly and put his arm around my shoulders.

The fountain started then. I sobbed. The tears wouldn't be held back. I couldn't stop them. My big brother held me while I cried, not saying a word, only stroking and patting my back. He was such a good guy. Where would I be if I didn't have him in my life?

Michael pressed a napkin into my hand when my tears started to ebb. I wiped at them and blew my nose.

Finally, he said, "You were obviously drugged. It shows clearly in the pictures you were out of it. How did this couple get so close to you? You spent most of your time with us, and when you weren't with us …" he paused, "fuck." And he said simply, "Scott."

"It had to be him," I said blowing my nose again. "The pictures were sent directly to Bobby."

"How much?" Michael asked.

"Five million."

He blew out a breath, "He has a large set of *cajones*."

"I'd like to cut them off," I retorted.

I took another drink of coffee and picked up a piece of bread, slathering it with brie. Never let it be said that the Greek's don't bury their sorrow in food.

"I assume Robert is working on this?"

"Yes. I want Frank to know about the pictures too," I said.

"What pictures?" Elizabeth padded into the kitchen. She kissed Michael on the top of the head and gave me a squeeze.

He rose and checked the oatmeal. "Oatmeal is done."

Elizabeth smiled, "Okay. Let me have a bowl for the yogurt too, please."

He outfitted her with a bowl, plate, spoons and a knife. He also spooned up a big bowl of oatmeal for her.

He looked at me, "Do you want some?"

I shook my head, "Blech."

"Michael makes it taste great. I love it!"

She made me laugh. "No thanks, I can do without a bowl of paste this morning, as delicious as it may be."

"Suit yourself." After covering her oatmeal with the nuts and fruit, she squeezed a big blob of honey into it and then stirred it around. Then looking up at us, "Now, what pictures?"

Michael glanced at me, and I nodded. He picked up my cell phone and handed it to her.

"Christina is being blackmailed, we think by Scott."

She looked at a couple of pictures and setting the phone face down as Michael had, she blushed. "Now I know why I didn't like him. There was something creepy about him. What are we going to do about this? These were not taken with your consent."

Elizabeth made me smile. Ready to pitch in help, I knew why my brother fell in love with her. She made no judgments about other people. I brought them both up-to-date.

"I think it's a good idea to let Frank know about this problem. If Scott is implicated in the dogfight club, this would be more ammunition for Frank," she said.

Michael agreed, "Definitely. Although, you probably won't need to show him the pictures. I think a description will do."

I frowned, "I know. I feel so violated. It's like I was raped."

He leaned his head against mine. "You were raped if the pictures are any indication. Oh, sweetheart, I'm so sorry."

I felt the tears coming on again. I didn't want to cry. I don't know why I felt so much emotion now. I didn't feel it yesterday. I should have. It wasn't until I showed my brother that I felt the full impact. I felt dirty.

"Does Kian know?" Michael inquired.

"No. I didn't tell him. How could I? I don't want him to think badly of me."

"Why would he think badly of you?" he demanded. "You didn't do anything wrong. So are you dating him?"

"I guess so," I chickened out with the response.

"You know you're ten years older?"

His expression of disbelief was all I needed.

"Yes. Of course, what's the big deal? He knows, and it doesn't seem to bother him."

"He's only a few years older than Katy," my brother continued to argue.

Elizabeth put her hand on his forearm. She shook her head, "Honey, I think they are old enough to make their own decision without your assistance."

Michael looked at his wife and harrumphed.

I laughed, "You sound like Dad. I didn't think I'd ever say it, but you are becoming him."

He smiled and tried to hide it, "No I'm not."

Giggling, I said, "Yes. Yes, you are. You even make the same noises Dad does."

I was glad I had confided in them. It was the right thing to do. I knew I would have to tell my parents eventually if it progressed in that direction. My parents were strong, but this, I was certain, would devastate them.

After breakfast, I went back to the cabin and showered. I wanted to scrub the memory of the pictures out of my head and knew I wouldn't be able to.

Kian called me during his lunch break. I could hear him eating in the background. I hoped he was eating something healthy, but doubted he was. It was sweet of him to call me and let me know he was thinking of me.

"I'm okay," I giggled. "I need to get some sleep tonight. I'm exhausted."

He laughed heartily and then lowered his voice, "I told you I'd tire you out. Though, I'm a bit tired myself too. We haven't got much sleep in the past two nights."

"And whose fault is that?" I murmured over the phone.

His voice became a whisper, "There you go again making me hard. If I didn't have appointments right after lunch, I'd drive over and ravish you some more."

"Oh, you're such a tease!" I giggled again.

I marveled at this man. He made me laugh. He forced me to open up. Kian was so uncluttered, it was refreshing. There were no games with him. If he wanted me, he came out and said it. I didn't have to read his thoughts or pick up subtle hints. I never met anyone quite like him, and I wasn't sure how to react.

Frank called me during the afternoon. He had already spoken with both Michael and Robert and suggested that both he and Annie stop by the cabin after dinner. I appreciated that he did not insist I go down to the police station.

Annie pulled up in her pickup truck a few hours later with Frank right behind her in the squad car. When I let them into the house, she gave me a warm hug. I had made tea, and a small coffee cake and they made themselves comfortable at the dining room table while I put servings on plates. After I had poured the tea for us, I pulled out my cell phone.

Frank said, "I've seen the pictures hon. Robert sent scanned copies over to me this afternoon."

I nodded and set the phone down.

"I haven't seen them. Is it okay if I look?" Annie said.

I handed her the phone. She only looked at the top one and then placed the phone face down on the table.

I began to tremble. My voice shook, "Um... I don't know what to do. I can pay him the ransom without a problem. That's not the issue. Those pictures will make their way to the internet sooner or later." So far, I was holding it together, but I was near the breaking point. "My parents will be appalled, and my grandmother…" I trailed off.

Annie slipped her arm around my shoulder. "How can they be my dear? You did not participate in the pictures, and that is certainly evident. You are a strong woman." She squeezed me. "And you will need to use all the strength you have to get through this, but mark my words, you will get through this."

"Robert told me that this Scott Binder person visited you here in Mintock last week," Frank interjected using his professional voice.

I know why he brought Annie along. Frank did not strike me as an emotional hugger type. This subject matter was delicate.

"Yes. I caught Scott walking around the interior of my new house. One of the windows was not closed properly, and the builder left it unsecured. He helped himself and walked in. It surprised the heck out of me. I had just arrived and noticed a car sitting at the side of the house. I figured it belonged to one of the contractors," I said.

"Did he mention anything about the pictures to you at the time?"

"No. We had a bit of a fling in New Orleans, I mean nothing happened between us. I didn't sleep with him. I inferred that I wasn't interested in pursuing anything with him. When I found him in the house last week, he tried again, and I rebuffed him again. While we spoke, he is the one who told me he was friends with the mayor and that he comes up to Mintock frequently for what I thought was poker night. Now, I'm sure he's involved in the dog fight club. He has to be."

Frank pursed his lips together and sighed heavily, "I think you're probably right. He must know also that you know who is blackmailing you. You are not without your resources either. You are a wealthy woman."

"This is why he is blackmailing me. He knows I have the money. I thought it was a little strange that Michael had said he hadn't heard from Scott in years and only invited him to the wedding to be friendly because he was attending Marcus' wedding. Even Marcus said he hadn't heard from him in quite some time until he showed up down in New Orleans a couple of months ago."

"It sounds like he was testing the waters when he came for his visit last week." He took a drink from his mug. "I do have some good news for you now."

"You do?" The surprise was evident on my face.

"Since you are being blackmailed, we have invited the FBI into our little drama. Five million in blackmail gets onto the Feds radar quickly. They are assigning two agents to us, and they'll be here tomorrow. So, I don't want you to do anything unwise like contact Scott, okay? We're going to hand this over to them. Our small little town doesn't have the resources they have, and we're welcoming the takeover."

"What about the dog fight club investigation? Will they also start investigating that too? It's so obviously linked together."

"The agent in charge assured me they would look at that too, especially with the note we found at Kian's house," he replied.

"Note? What note?" Again, he surprised me.

"Didn't Kian tell you?" Annie asked.

I frowned, "No he did not."

Frank scratched his upper lip as if searching for the words. "We found a note near the front door when we did our investigation that night. It basically said if Kian didn't get his nose out of things that this type of shooting would become a regular occurrence."

"Oh," I murmured, "poor Kian. I can imagine why he didn't want to tell me."

Annie squeezed my hand. "I know this is all very hard for you."

"What about the other veterinarian who retired? The one Kian replaced. Was he in on all of this?"

She sighed, "He is an old gentleman. I don't think in the past few years he noticed much of anything. He treated the dogs as they came in and didn't ask many questions."

"How does a man like this Busch even become mayor?" I said with a disgusted tone. "Is it because he has friends in high places and is on the tribal council?"

"Regretfully," she sighed again, "he does come from old money. His father was part of our governing body, which is how, when his dad retired, he was voted into the council seat, much as I was. My dad was an Elder also, and he never had much time for the senior Mr. Busch. He said he didn't trust him. I never had confidence in the junior one either. I always felt he was just past the shady area. He runs a large interstate trucking company, which was suspected of having ties to organized crime. No one was ever able to prove anything, but a large number of rumors floated around. He was furious when the Board of Elders voted down the casino plan. We were approached by a major casino to build a satellite casino here."

I raised my eyebrows. "Really? That could have been very lucrative for not only the tribe but the town as well."

"We felt it didn't fit in with our culture. Most of our tribal members do well. They own businesses here in town, and they contribute to our economy. We did not need it. We've seen other tribes tear each other apart because of what the money from a casino does. Mayor Busch was very much for the casino, and like I said, he was not happy with the vote," she explained.

"The agents will want to speak with you when they arrive. I'll call you so we can arrange a time," Frank said.

I looked at my hands, not replying.

Annie reached out to me again. "I know this is going to be difficult for you. But, you are a resilient woman. You have it in you to get through this."

"I thought I had protected myself enough to insulate against attacks like this. I was stupid. Too trusting. I won't make that mistake again."

"It's hard when the person who strikes you is someone your family knows. Normally we do not have defenses against those situations. Your friends will help you through this too," she said.

"Thank you, both for your kindness. Your acceptance of me into your community has meant a lot to me. I feel I have another family here."

"Of course, my dear," Annie said, "I hope you don't mind another mother, I tend to be one to everyone."

I grinned, "I welcome an additional mom, especially if it is you."

She beamed at my declaration and gave me a long hug.

After they had left, while I cleaned up the table, I thought about having to speak with the federal agents. I wanted Robert with me when I did. I called him, and he agreed to come out for the appointment. I didn't relish the thought of speaking with complete strangers about the photos. And Kian. What about him? I couldn't show him the pictures. What would he think? No, I concluded, it was best if I kept this to myself.

I needed to think about protecting my family. The photos would destroy them. I couldn't do that to them.

CHAPTER 28

After my visit with Frank and Annie, I felt miserable. Tired from a couple of nights of no sleep, I turned in early. Somehow, Koa had picked up on my mood, and after I had settled into my pillows, he crawled up from his normal position at the foot of the bed to lie close to me. As I petted him, he licked my hand. When he was thoroughly finished, he settled back into me and let out a big sigh.

"I know it, boy," I whispered. "My heart is so heavy tonight." A small tear leaked out from the corner of my eye, but I blinked hard trying to hold them back. I wasn't going to give into tears. That would not solve anything. I had to pull up my big girl panties and attend to this crisis just as I did with everything else. I had to make a plan.

As much as I didn't want to involve the FBI, I knew it was the smart thing to do. Scott needed to be locked up. If he thought he would get the better of me, he had another thing coming. My resolve began to harden; this was the person in me I recognized the most. Nothing would beat me down. I would win out. The nerve of that son-of-a-bitch. Who the hell did he think he was? Blackmail me? Over my dead body. It was with these thoughts that sleep came.

I don't know how long I slept, but Koa's slow menacing growl woke me. He was standing on the bed, ear perked straight up, tail at attention. His body was rigid. At first, still half asleep, I thought he was growling at me. Instead, he looked at the window.

I didn't hear anything outside, but he was alerting me to a problem. I crept out of bed and peeked between the opening in the curtains. A black truck was parked next to my SUV, and two men dressed all in black were prowling around quietly. I didn't recognize them or the truck.

Shit! I shifted silently to the other side of the bed, and Koa followed me. Picking up the receiver from the old-fashioned landline, I pressed the buttons for nine one one.

The operator came on the phone quickly asking me to state the nature of the emergency.

"Two men are prowling outside my house, and I can't identify them. Please send someone immediately," I whispered.

The operator confirmed the address and told me the police would be there shortly and to stay on the phone with her.

I wanted to call Michael. I picked up my cell phone.

"Christina?" he answered sleepily.

"There are two men prowling around the cabin," I whispered into the phone.

"Stay in the house!" he instructed. His voice told me he was instantly wide-awake.

"I have the police on the other line."

"Good. Are you in your bedroom?"

"Yes," I hissed.

"Why didn't the flood lights come on?"

I could hear Michael's movements in the background.

"I don't know, but everything is black outside."

I heard a noise from the lake side of the house, and Koa went ballistic. His barking was fierce. I lifted him off the bed, and he shot to the door in the living room.

"Turn the lights on!" Michael shouted.

I reached for the light switch in the bedroom and flipped it up. The lights were out!

"Shit!" I said, "No lights." I looked at the bedside clock, and it was dark. "No electricity."

There was another noise at the back door, and Koa came flying. He barked and growled ferociously against the door. I looked out the window, but at this angle, I couldn't see anything.

I saw Michael's house lights through the window, and his huge flood lights lit the entire area. It was then I could see the two men at the rear of the house. They had caps pulled low over their heads, and I still couldn't see their faces.

My brother's back door opened, and their dogs rushed out. When the men saw them, they ran for their truck and jumped in. The dogs followed the pickup almost all the way down the entire utility road, barking and making a ruckus.

When Michael reached my door, I finally unlocked it and let him in. He was carrying his gun and a flashlight. A police cruiser pulled up shortly after with its lights on.

We greeted the officers on my porch and spoke briefly to them. Michael suggested that we go over to his house since the cabin had lost electricity.

I picked up Koa and held him in my arms. He was still shaking and alert.

I buried my face in his fur and murmured to him, "My good little boy. You saved your mommy, didn't you?"

My brother said with a smile, "He's a barker, isn't he?"

I raised my head. "Yes, he is, and I'm thankful he was there. I would have never heard them had it not been for Koa."

As we walked over, all the homes had their lights on, and Don and Lewis were walking toward Michael's house. Elizabeth was up and had already put water in a kettle on the stove. She was talking to Debi on her cell phone assuring her everyone was okay.

We sat at the large dining room table, and Elizabeth came in with an afghan blanket, which she placed over my shoulders. I had held Koa in my arms, and when she suggested that I could put him on the floor, I shook my head almost violently.

"No. He stays with me," I said.

She wisely backed away and went back to the kitchen to make tea.

The officers asked their questions. No, I couldn't see their faces. And no, I didn't catch their license plate number. Were they serious? It was dark until Michael's lights came on. I couldn't see anything. They went back over to the cabin with Michael and the neighbors to investigate the area. With it being as dark as it was I doubted they would be able to see anything at all.

Elizabeth padded in with two large mugs of steaming tea.

I took the one she offered to me. "Great Me-maw's tea?" I asked.

"Yep. The very same. It will fix what ails you." She stared at me with her kind eyes. "It's been a busy couple of days for you, hasn't it?"

"I hate when everything happens at once. I dislike a chaotic life. You know me, I want everything to line up correctly. When everything is in disarray, it makes me nervous."

"You haven't had much sleep either," she commented as she probably noticed the dark circles under my eyes. "Katy's room is all made up. You have to sleep here tonight, or what's left of it."

I opened my mouth to protest, and she held her hand up to stop me.

"You and I both know Michael will not let you sleep at the cabin tonight even if they are able to get the lights on. That is definitely not on the agenda."

I frowned, "You're probably right."

Elizabeth chuckled, "Oh girl, you know I'm right. I wouldn't let you either. Any idea what those men were after?"

I shook my head, "I have no idea."

I squeezed the bridge of my nose with my thumb and forefinger. A headache that had been brewing when I went to bed, now started to throb. I could only guess the excess adrenaline in my system let it escape out.

She noticed my movements and guessed. "Do you need some aspirin?"

"Yes, please."

Elizabeth returned with a bottle of aspirin and a cup of water and set them down in front of me. Koa had fallen asleep in my arms, so I pulled out the chair next to me and laid him on it. After downing the aspirin, I put my head on my arms on the table. I hoped my headache would go away quickly.

A light shone through the window, and Elizabeth sat up tall from her seat to look outside.

"Oh! It looks like your lights are back on. Those men didn't cut the line; they must have just flipped the main breaker. That's good," she said.

I replied with my head still on my folded arms, "Good. Then I can go home and go back to bed."

I heard Michael's voice as he walked into the room.

"There is no way you are going to sleep there tonight. Go ahead and use Katy's room."

Elizabeth piped in, "I already told her the same thing!"

He nodded and pulled out a chair. "Good. I think both of you should go back to bed after you've finished your tea. The police will take your statement tomorrow. They don't need to do it tonight."

It looked like I was now giving a statement to the FBI and the police. How did my life get so complicated suddenly?

Michael continued, "There is not much to see over at the cabin. Looks like the men cut out the screens in Elizabeth's old bedroom and they were going to try to get in that way. There was one window slightly ajar."

"I would have never left a window open!" I said.

She said, "Don't worry about that! There's a window that never closed completely. Even though it looked locked, you could easily push it open."

My brother looked shocked, "Now you tell me this?"

She rolled her eyes, "No one can see the window is unlocked. Stop worrying."

He frowned, "We're going to have that fixed the first thing tomorrow, and I'm installing an alarm system. Also, I'm putting a big lock on the breaker box too."

I stared at him, "Don't you think that's a bit overkill?"

"I do not!" he adamantly replied. "Now you both should go back to bed."

"You've gotten bossy in your old age," I gave him my best glare.

Secretly, I was glad that my brother was being cautious. This episode scared me. I didn't know what these men were after or whether it was a simple break-in. Was this connected to Scott and Mayor Busch somehow? I had no idea what they would want.

Bed sounded good. While we were sitting at the table, my headache ebbed. Both the aspirin and tea were helping. Michael went back to the cabin to join the others and do their men standing around thing.

I carried Koa upstairs, and he curled up falling back asleep. My brave little dog probably saved me from certain horror tonight. I'll never forget how he stood so courageous at the unseen forces trying to break their way in. Switching out the light, I snuggled down into the covers. Now, I was utterly exhausted. I promised no matter what happened, I would sleep late.

If promises were wishes, I told myself when Koa woke me. He was crying softly at the door to be let out. I didn't even want to know how he managed to get off the bed. Kian wouldn't be happy with me if he knew I let Koa jump down off the bed, particularly since he had warned me against it. The little dog didn't look any worse for wear sitting by the door, he wagged his tail when I made my way out of the bed.

I picked him up and padded down the stairs quietly. It was just after dawn, and I didn't want to wake up the entire family. I wondered what time Michael and Elizabeth managed to get back to sleep. I carried Koa out through the kitchen and was surprised to see Michael sitting at the table with a cup of coffee.

"Hey," I said, "what are you doing up?"

"Up? I haven't been back to bed. The police just left. What are you doing up?"

I pointed to Koa. "Bathroom break. I forgot to take him before we went back to bed. Why so late? I would have expected a fairly quick investigation."

"Frank called the guys and told them to be very thorough. He is getting the Feds involved in this too as soon as they arrive."

"Wow, really?"

"He doesn't want to be embarrassed by a sloppy investigation."

I nodded, "Makes sense."

He drank the rest of his coffee and rose from the table. He kissed me on my cheek.

"I'm going to join my wife and try to get a little sleep. Thankfully, we don't have anything scheduled today, and we can sleep late. I've been worried about Elizabeth. She starts to do too much and gets fatigued. It's not good for her."

I agreed, "I'll be going back to sleep as soon as I take care of my little hero here."

Michael chuckled, "It's a good thing you have him."

"You said that right!"

I carried Koa outside and let him sniff the grass a bit and then we both went back upstairs. I lay in bed for a few minutes before trying to sleep and reviewed the day that was ahead of me.

I'd have to talk to Robert and bring him up-to-date, and then I needed to speak with JuJu. And then there was Kian, ever in the back of my mind.

What would he think about this mess?

CHAPTER 29

I woke to the ringing of my cell phone. It was Frank, the Feds wanted to do the interview during the afternoon. Robert was already on board, and we would all meet at the cabin.

Even though it was light outside, the thought of going to the cabin gave me the creeps. An alarm system in the house would make me feel safer I had to admit, but as my brain began to process everything that had happened, it was still disconcerting.

It was quiet as I crept through the house. I wondered if Michael and Elizabeth were still asleep. Once outside, I saw my brother's jeep parked in front of the cabin. The back door was open, and he had some workmen working around the house. Elizabeth came out of the cabin and waved at me.

How had he managed to have work done to the cabin so quickly? I had to admire him, he was better at it than me.

"Did you talk to Frank?" he asked.

I nodded, "Yes. We're all set."

"You may want to use our house for the interviews. I want to make sure everything is completed here."

"I thought the same thing. Thanks," I said going into the cabin.

Elizabeth greeted me with coffee. "Good morning. You look better. I'm glad you slept in, you needed it."

"What I really need right now is a shower."

"Go right ahead. I'll feed Koa if that's okay."

After showering and with fresh clothes on, I took my briefcase and let everyone know that I'd be at the house. I needed to finish up paperwork and make phone calls.

Michael called to me to say that Vincenzo's would be delivering sandwiches and drinks. If they stopped at the house, I was to direct them to the cabin.

I tried calling Kian first but was told by Carrie that he was in surgery. She was pleasant to me on the phone. I guessed word had gotten out that the doctor and I were a thing. She said she would have him call and then she asked about Koa. I let her know he was a big hero in my book.

Robert was on his way to Mintock when I reached him. He let me know he'd be there within the hour. This was after we had a long conversation about the previous night and I reassured him I was perfectly okay.

Lastly, I called JuJu. She looked well rested on the screen. She did not say the same thing about me. I brought her up-to-date on the happenings of the past few days. Her first questions were about Koa and the dog that was shot. I assured her that all animals were okay and in good shape. She breathed a sigh of relief. Then her real questions started. Before I had a chance to tell her otherwise, she said she was packing her bags to come to stay with me for a few days.

"Absolutely not JuJu," I said adamantly.

"You need someone to stay with you!" she protested, waving her arms around her head.

"No. Thank you, sweetheart, but there are enough people here who are already in line to help. Honestly, I need you to stay home and assist me in other ways."

Finally, she acquiesced.

"What I need you to do however is check on what the travel restrictions are for traveling with a pet companion."

Her face showed puzzlement, "Where are you going?"

Pressing my lips together in hesitation, "I'm not sure yet."

"Traveling with Koa?"

"Maybe."

Sighing, she turned toward her computer and starting typing. How is it this woman could read me so well?

"Definitely not Hawaii," she said.

"No, it needs to be somewhere out of the way. A small population area."

"If you stay within the continental United States, you know there are no restrictions. You can board a plane with a dog. It would be more undercover if you fly private." She stopped and took her time to look at me. "Christina this isn't like you. You're not a runner."

Chewing on my lip, I acknowledged, "I know. It's more than me JuJu. It's my family. If the pictures hit the internet, the press will be crawling out of the woodwork. I could take it, but my family…I don't want to put them through it."

"Whether you disappear or not, your family will still be in the center of the circle."

"People will get bored with the story if they can't reach me. It will be bad for them for a couple of weeks, and the story will die. I'll send my parents and grandmother somewhere. I'll put them on a yacht in the middle of the ocean. Away from everything. But if I stay around, the story will take on a life of its own. I can't do that to them." I sighed heavily thinking about the maelstrom that was on its way.

"Are you thinking Canada? Or maybe Mexico?"

"Maybe. It needs to be somewhere out of the way. Somewhere I wouldn't be recognized."

"That's a tall order. If it hits the news, your face will be everywhere. You will be recognized. But let me put my thinking cap on."

"Thank you," I said.

I was so grateful to have her working with me, she always had my back.

After talking with JuJu, I could cross off several items on my to-do list. Even though I faced a crisis, the financial empire I ran still had to be attended.

Robert arrived just as the catering truck came. I snagged a couple of sandwiches for us and sent the truck down the road to the cabin. My friend had a box full of documents, which he carried into the house and set on the dining room table.

He took a long look at me, "You need to get some sleep."

I grimaced, knowing I looked awful and having your best buddy confirm it was never good.

"Well, thanks, Bobbie."

He put his arm around my shoulders and brought me in for a squeeze, "Com'on, if I can't be honest with you, who can?"

Hugging him back, I said, "I know. It's getting to me because everyone is telling me how bad I look."

"You don't look horrible; you only look tired." Robert took off his jacket and rolled up his sleeves. Lifting the lid from the box, he set it aside. "I have a bunch of foundation documents you need to sign. There are also some board requests to review."

I sat at the table and dug a pen out of my briefcase. Taking the first document, the pages that needed my signature or attention were marked with little color tabs.

"This is the donation of the laptop computers for the elementary school outside of Saint Louis, which was destroyed by the tornado."

I nodded and signed on the tabbed pages. "Have they received them yet?"

He grinned, "Have they ever!" Digging around in the box, he pulled out an enlarged photograph, depicting a group of students posing in front of a large cement block sign reading Matterson Elementary. Behind it, where a building should have been standing only rubble remained. They held a big banner in front of them that read, *Thank you, Miss Hoffman, for caring!*

My smile was as wide as Robert's. This is what it was all about. Since the foundation was in my name, we could send out the donations quickly and worry about the paperwork later. My parents, who assisted me with the running of the organization, made it easier for me. We didn't have tons of bureaucracy. It was simple. With only a few people needed to run it, we could make decisions fast. Everyone employed felt comfortable enough to approach me about any concern.

Next, he handed me the documentation for the Harry's Hounds donation.

He chuckled, "And how goes it with your veterinarian?"

I gave him a coy look, "It is just fine Mr. Noseypants."

He laughed loudly now, "I think he's the reason you're not getting enough sleep!"

"Think what you like." I tried to put my professional face on, but it wouldn't stay. I laughed with my best friend, "Oh, he is such a fricken hottie!"

"I'm glad you finally got some. What a dry spell you've gone through!"

"I know! Right?"

"Now he's not the reason you're donating to Harry's Hounds, is he?"

"Robert! No. Don't even suggest that!"

"You know I had to mention it, especially with what happened to you in New York."

"I understand. New York was different, that guy was scamming me. Kian isn't like that. I've seen his organization in action. The separate clinic he has set up at his home is full of rescue dogs being treating and waiting for homes. The money is being used wisely, and the organization is making a positive impact. He is grateful for the money for Harry's Hounds, moreover, though, I believe what is going on between the two of us is different. I know our relationship muddies the water, but we are both aware of the situation."

We continued to review paperwork together until Frank, and the two FBI agents arrived. Koa barked when they entered, but not even close to the barking he had done the previous night.

The agents, Sue Martin and John Goings, were what I would have imagined typical agents to be. Both wore black suits with white shirts. Agent Martin wore a comfortable pair of black pumps, which made her taller than Agent Goings. They carried weapons, and I could see the bulges from their holsters under their jackets. Needless to say, they were both imposing, but they each had friendly, if not businesslike, faces. These were people I could relate to easily.

I was relieved to have both Frank and Robert there with me. I didn't want my emotions to take over. Then Michael arrived. His presence made me feel weepy. Even though he had already seen the photos and I knew he was there to help, I didn't want to discuss those pictures with my big brother in the room.

Reaching deep down inside of me, I pulled up enough courage to make it through the interview. The agents were especially interested in the near break-in the previous evening. We all communicated everything, which had happened up to this point. They saw the same patterns we did and came to the same conclusion that the events were interrelated.

We began to talk about the dog fighting ring and found they had not been informed about the shooting in front of Kian's house. The agents had a meeting scheduled with him on the following day and added the topic to their list.

I mused to Michael afterward that the meeting was like nothing I had ever seen on television. Instead, it was just like a business meeting, one I had attended thousands of time.

He agreed, "They were very professional, weren't they? No emotion on their faces when you described Koa's injuries."

"Yeah, I would have at least expected a few sniffles from them!" I quipped.

After the agents left in their nondescript American made car, that, at least, was like the movies, we joined Robert and Frank outside.

"I'm off," Robert said, "I'm driving back to the city. Hopefully, I won't run into much traffic."

I hugged him, "No, you shouldn't, you're going against traffic now. Thank you for coming and call me tomorrow."

Elizabeth walked up from the cabin with the dogs. She wrapped her arms around Michael's waist and put her head on his shoulder.

"I'm all done in the cabin."

"Need a before dinner nap?" he asked as he put his arm around her shoulders and drew her close.

"Yep," she responded.

"Okay. I'll be in to join you in a few minutes."

"I'll see you guys later," she said and went into the house.

Michael handed me a key. "This is the key to the breaker box. The alarm is installed and is live with the alarm company. There is a panic button on the wall in the bedroom by the light switch. And," he indicated, with his cell phone, "download this app onto your phone. It also has a panic button."

I looked at his phone, "Great. I like that. This will make me feel safer. Thank you, big brother!" I hugged him.

He knew me too well. He was aware that I would sleep in the cabin tonight.

"The security lights will go on at dusk and stay on all night. Sorry." He apologized. "We'll have to get some blackout curtains for the bedrooms. Our security lights will be on too. I don't want to take any chances."

"I know," I replied. "I do have the world's best watch dog, though."
He grinned, "Yes you do."

CHAPTER 30

While we said goodbye to Frank, Kian pulled up on his motorcycle. Koa's tail wagged madly before he even hopped off the bike and removed his helmet. He looked sexy, there in his jeans and his well-fitting Alice Cooper's, "Welcome to my Nightmare" t-shirt. The muscles in his arms bulged out of it in a most delightful way.

Immediately he had me wrapped in his arms and gave me a long hard kiss.

When he broke the kiss, his eyes, those deep pools of azure, bore into mine, "Why didn't you call me last night? Why did I have to hear about what happened from someone else?"

I looked around, both Michael and Frank had excused themselves. Cowards.

"I …" faltering, I didn't know what to say. "I didn't want to wake you. You haven't gotten any sleep either the past few nights. I couldn't rob you of the few you get."

"That's bollocks, Christina! Don't lock me out, not when I've let you into my life."

I put my palms on either side of his face and again was lost in those eyes. "I'm sorry Kian. Truly."

He pulled me in closer and whispered, "*Thabharfainn fuil mo chroi duit.*" Then his lips met mine again, and his kiss tore me apart.

I felt like I had shattered into little pieces all over the ground. I leaned against him, and the tears began to fall. How could he do that to me? How could he dig so deeply inside of me and find the most vulnerable place where I hid all my secrets?

How we ended up inside the cabin, I didn't know. There we were, sitting on the couch with his arms around me, and me crying soul wrenching sobs. How had he broken through? I thought the wall I erected was tall and thick enough.

He whispered, "*A grá,*" which I knew meant my love in Gaelic. "Are you going to tell me?" he asked, in a thickly accented voice.

While he held me, I told him everything. I showed the pictures to him. His reaction to the photos surprised me completely.

The fury showed on his face immediately. "I'm going to kill the son of a bitch who did this to you!"

Shock flooded through me. "Kian. Please don't overreact. I know it looks bad."

"I'm sorry, but I can't help it, knowing your body the way I do. This asshole violated you. You should be worshiped not abused!"

"Thank you for feeling this way, but please Kian, don't do anything. Okay? I don't want to worry about you."

He looked defiant, "Okay, I'm sorry. I won't go looking for this asshole, but I do promise if he ever crosses my path, I will make damn sure he never thinks about touching you again."

I smiled and kissed him lightly.

"You and Koa are my heroes!"

Kian brought me in for a deeper kiss. "I am an unworthy hero."

I looked puzzled. "Why do you say that?"

"Look at you. I feel so inadequate! You have more money than God. You're brilliant when it comes to financial investing. And yeah, you created world-changing software. I feel undeserving of being in the same room as you. I can't ever imagine why you'd be interested in me. I'm a small-town veterinarian, who is poorer than a church mouse."

I laughed and crawled into his lap straddling his thighs. Leaning forward for a kiss, he rested his hands on my hips.

"Look at you. You have more compassion in your little finger than most people have in their entire body. You are not a poor church mouse," I whispered into his mouth, "you don't look anything like a mouse." I squirmed against his growing erection, which was very evident as it poked between my legs. "And you definitely don't feel small!" I giggled. "In fact, I like your size a lot."

"You do?" he murmured thickly, as his grasp on my hips pulled me down so I could grind against him, which was obviously not enough for him.

He lifted my butt slightly with one hand while the other hand unbuttoned and pulled his zipper down. I was disappointed that he wore underwear but knew that would be remedied soon. Liquid heat circulated through my blood stream and sent everything to my core. Looking straight into his eyes while his hands roamed my backside squeezing and caressing me, it was evident the heat was rising in him also.

After he had pulled off his t-shirt, I ran my hands along the hard curves of his chest. I nipped at his lips with my teeth and then caught his lower lip pulling it out. His groan spurred me into action. There were no thoughts now, only deeds.

Kian's hands moved up to the edge of my t-shirt, and he tugged it off over my head. The chilly cabin air caught my skin but didn't make me shiver. His next move forced me to tremble. Without removing my bra, his lips captured my nipple through the thin transparent material. My nipples were already erect, but this made me arch to press myself to him.

My hips slowly circled against him as he sucked each nipple in turn. I took fistfuls of his hair while moaning softly. He pushed my bra up to uncover my breasts, my nipples glistened a dusky rose with the wetness from his mouth. His teeth scraped against one and then the other as I cried out in pleasure.

"Oh, Kian. Yes… oh please."

My breasts ached for his touch. His teeth closed around one, and the slight pain was exquisite. The carnality of the gesture made the intense heat pooling between my legs almost unbearable. My entire body burned with the anticipation of what was to come.

I couldn't wait any longer. Sliding quickly to the floor from the couch, I nestled myself between his legs and drew down his jeans. I could see the evidence of his stiff straining arousal through his briefs. He lifted his hips and was out of his pants and briefs in a flash. It was only then I noticed he had already taken off his shoes. Such a smart man.

His heavy breathing indicated I was on the right track. I wrapped my fingers around the thick base of his erection and the weight of him in my hand was glorious. I could feel his throbbing pulse, and when I gently squeezed him, his low guttural groan told me how much he liked what I did.

It was hard to believe his massive shaft fit so well into me. The memory made me squirm, adding more licks of heat to my core. I slowly ran my tongue along the full length of him. It was his turn to fist massive amounts of my hair as he tried to bring me closer.

"Oh, baby. Right there," Kian rasped out as my mouth reached the top of his cock.

I licked over and under the head. There wasn't any way I could fit his whole engorged flesh into my mouth, he was too big and long, but he seemed to be pleased with the area that I slowly drew in.

"Oh fuck, yes. Suck me." He let out the words between his clenched teeth.

I couldn't take any more. My own body was ready to explode with desire. I needed to feel him deep inside of me. I gazed at him, and he seemed able to read my mind. At this point, I would have done anything he wanted to give him the pleasure he deserved.

"Up," he said as his hands helped me to stand.

He unbuttoned my jeans and then slid them down my legs. I assisted by pushing down my panties along with my pants. He picked up the bikinis as

I stepped out of them and held them to his nose taking a deep breath.

"I love that they are wet, and they smell of your arousal," his voice growled.

I clasped his hands when I straddled his erection between my legs.

"They aren't the only thing that is wet." I kneeled above him and took his hand between my legs. "This is what you do to me," I said as I ran his fingers through my wetness.

His fingers circled my swollen clit. I shut my eyes tightly as he rubbed my super-sensitive nub. Then two fingers entered me, and I threw my head back. How could his fingers feel so good? His mouth clamped on my nipple, and as he sucked the stiff peak, his fingers swirled in my slick, wet heat.

Our breaths caught in our throats as he slowly lowered me and replaced his fingers with his hard shaft. We both shuddered when I sheathed him completely inside of me. The intense pleasure of our movements together made me close my eyes again.

"Open your eyes, look at me," he commanded through short gasps. "I want to see you."

I did as he asked and was swallowed inside of his sapphire pools. The thrusts of his hips were answered with the perfect arching of my body to meet each possessive plunge. Our rhythm was seamless. We were no longer two separate people, but now conjoined, and moving as one in a continuous fluid motion.

Our lips joined in an all-consuming kiss that reached inside us and stroked at our souls. Hard breathing was followed by ragged gasps as our bodies climbed together searching for the perfect release. The building pleasure was sheer torment, but we couldn't get enough of each other.

I could feel it coming, the powerful conclusion. It was within my grasp. "Oh baby, I'm almost there."

"Come for me woman. I need you to come," his voice growled.

I moaned as his body answered my declaration. I didn't know where my body ended and his began. The hot exploding waves were all around me as I shuddered and spasmed in his arms. My eruption led to his, as his body jerked with mine he released fiercely into me. Our cries of pleasure combined as we tried to breathe in gulps of air.

I stilled against him still sheathing him inside of me. Our bodies slick with the perspiration of satiated lovemaking, he leaned his head against mine and whispered again, "*Thabharfainn fuil mo chroí duit.*"

When I could speak again, I asked, "What does that mean? Is it Gaelic?"

He took a deep breath and spoke into my hair, "Yes, loosely translated it means blood of my heart."

I moved slowly off him, but he kept me on his lap with his arms around me.

"It means you are the blood that makes my heart beat." He smiled and kissed me, "They are words you would say to your lover."

I grinned broadly, "Is that what I am to you?"

He didn't hesitate, and he didn't try a coy answer, "Yes, you are."

Koa came to the front of the couch and barked.

I glanced at the clock in the kitchen. "He wants to be fed."

Kian looked down at his feet, "You can wait a bit my little pup. Your mother and I aren't finished yet."

"We're not?"

"No, we're not," he grinned when he looked at my questioning and eager eyes. "I want to sit here with you on my lap and have the pleasure of holding you in my arms while I remember the best orgasm I've ever had. Damn it, woman, you blew the top of my head off."

"I did?" I sounded pleased. "I don't think I've ever done that before. I like that."

"After I've held you and we've talked a bit, we'll order some pizza, feed Koa, drink some wine, and shower. Then I'm going to take you to bed where I can worship your incredible body and mind."

I lay my head on his shoulder, "I like your plan very much. Will that adoration include your wicked tongue?"

He ran his tongue over my lips, and when I opened my mouth, he plunged in to meet mine. "You can count on it, and my tongue will be very busy."

Just the discussion of his plans had me squirming in his lap, and it made him chuckle. "Do you need a little precursor to the action?" he suggested.

I couldn't believe that I wanted him again. So soon. My core sent signals to my brain that it thought this was an excellent idea indeed. I could feel the tightness between my legs as the notion formed.

I didn't say a word, but he caught the look in my eyes. Kian was the type of man who would think about sex even after having a massive orgasm. I was one lucky woman.

He bent his head forward and captured a nipple that had already begun to tighten with anticipation. A moan low in my throat filled the air.

"Oh yes," he whispered, "I think you'd like some more."

I felt like a starving woman and was lost in the only man who could feed me. Gently pushing me back on the couch cushions, he lifted one of my legs and placed it on the top of the back of the sofa. I was open to him.

Trailing his fingers down from my breasts, over my stomach and down to the junction of my thighs, he made me squirm for the anticipation of his touch.

"I love your curves. Please never hide them from me." His voice was husky, and it made me happy that he was as affected by this as I was.

"I won't," I promised.

"This ..." he said as he passed his hand over my rounded belly and my thighs that still brushed together when I walked, "this makes you a woman. A soft, warm woman. A place where a man can rest his head when the day has made him weary."

His fingers delicately touched the outside of my mound. I yearned for that touch. It was soft and feathery and made my body respond with a pool of moisture. "If you had curls here, would they be naturally blond?" He referred to my Brazilian bodyscaping. "You know I don't mind a few curls here if you'd like."

I made a mental note, cut back on the Brazilian.

"But I do like the very smooth surface you have here." He bent over, and his tongue made a trail from the top of my mound to the end.

I gasped, feeling the rasp of his tongue, so close to my clit. It was swollen again with need, and it wanted Kian's attention now. My fingers brushed through his hair and rested on his shoulders. I wanted to urge him forward, but he was having none of it. He was taking his time. He could be such a tease. I looked up and noticed his hand brushed along his cock. He was beginning to harden. How could that happen so soon? When I saw it, I wanted to wrap my lips around him.

Immediately my attention was back to me when I felt his velvet tongue touch my clit. Oh, yes! He circled it and teased it making the excitement pulse through me. His tongue traveled down to my opening and slipped inside. He then lapped up my wetness, and I heard his familiar groan vibrating inside of me. He replaced his tongue with one of his beautiful long fingers. He had the hands of a surgeon, and his fingers were an expert at the ministrations. The pad of his finger rubbed against my G-spot. He actually knew where it was and could find it. He made subtle, slow circular motions inside my silky softness. I could feel the waves of a crest approaching, and my hips responded to his strokes by moving along with them.

"Oh baby," I cried softly, "that's so good. Oh, yes, ..." I trailed off because he trailed off. He removed his finger, and it left me panting feeling somewhat lost.

"Too soon," he murmured. "I want your pleasure to last."

No. I cried inside, not too soon. Now. Please now. Kian's tongue jolted me back to reality. His head moved up my body, and I could feel as he did the pressure of his swollen shaft pressed against me. His erection was thick and hard. And as his mouth clamped down on my nipple, I wrapped my hand around his arousal. I felt the shock register in his muscles of his back as I stroked him.

"Woman, do you feel what you do to me. No other woman could have coaxed this out of me except you."

While he sucked on my nipples and squeezed my breasts gently between his hands, I stroked the firm hard head of his shaft. His hips were moving him between my fingers. And he tore himself away from my breasts to still my hand.

"I want you to come again," I whispered. "I want to feel your explosion."

He removed my hand, and he growled, "You will feel it, but first I will drink from you. I will make your body cry out to have me deeply buried inside of you."

His head was once again at the apex of my core, and this time his attention was on my nub. His tongue played and pleasured it, and each time as the climax would come so close, he'd change his position or rhythm. It was maddening.

When I thought I could go no further, I rose up against his mouth, and the wave hit me over and over as my orgasm crashed into me. My entire body pulsed as I writhed against his burning caresses and took agonized gasps of air.

He moved quickly and plunged himself deeply inside of me. He was fast and hard as my body fought for more oxygen. The orgasm that had just subsided came again, and with each urgent thrust of his hard cock, my body responded with clenching spasms. It wasn't long before his groans became a deep primal growl and as he stiffened, he rode the wild ecstasy in unabashed abandon.

Finally, his collapse on me, proving his absolute satisfaction, made me feel complete. So virile, and so much a man, he made me feel like a woman who was strong and feminine.

And his words affirmed it, as he rolled off me, "You are my woman, make no mistake about that." His brogue was thick, but the words he spoke sounded thrilling.

His arms wrapped around me to pull me close. Koa barked again, and we both laughed.

"Once I get my sea legs back, I'll feed Koa," he said.

"And I'll throw something together for dinner. We don't have to eat pizza. I have enough food in the refrigerator."

"Would you do that for me?" he asked.

"Of course."

He bent his head to kiss me softly, "*A grá.*"

CHAPTER 31

After we took a quick shower and dressed, we tackled dinner. Kian graciously only put his jeans on and skipped his t-shirt so that I could feast my eyes on his chest. A personal request of mine.

While I cooked the pasta, and found shrimp for scampi in the freezer, he prepared Koa's dinner. Kian shook his head when he noticed that not only did Koa get his regular kibble, but I also sprinkled a bit of cooked chicken over his food. I protested that my sister-in-law taught me that trick.

"If I do the chicken, then he isn't so finicky about eating his kibble," I explained.

Kian wrapped his arms around me from behind and nuzzled my ear. "I bet he isn't finicky. You're spoiling him." He kissed my neck and released me.

"I'm not spoiling him." I turned up the flames under the pan for the scampi. "You said he was probably a stray for a while. He deserves a little extra TLC."

He chuckled, "He has your number."

"It doesn't matter what you think."

"Oh?" He paused at the sink. One eyebrow was quirked up.

"Yes. I've decided that you don't need to find another home for Koa. He's perfect where he is now. No one can care for him like I do. He belongs here with me," I declared firmly.

Kian's smile was broad and warm. "I'm happy to hear that. I think you'll make Koa an excellent mom." His voice was thick with emotion as his arms wrapped around me.

I loved feeling the broad expanse of his back and was even becoming used to the scars on his sides. His head bent to kiss me, and tears brimmed in his eyes. It was all for the love of a dog.

Koa's bark made us both look down at him.

"You better feed him," I said. "I don't think he is going to tolerate much more of a delay."

He set the dog dish on the floor, and Koa dispatched the food in the bowl quickly. He then stood patiently by the doggy door waiting for Kian to open the latch.

I pulled lettuce and tomatoes from the refrigerator.

"Salad?" Kian asked. "Shall I?"

"Yes, please. You can dress it with the olive oil, and there should be some balsamic vinegar in the cupboard." I pointed behind me.

He opened the cabinet and reached up to pluck the vinegar from the shelf. "Got it!" he said as he set about making the salad.

Watching him made my heart beat a little faster than normal. "Do you want garlic bread too?"

"Do we have garlic bread?" He turned to me flipping a piece of tomato into his mouth.

"I have some French bread in the freezer, and there's butter in the refrigerator. All we need is a little garlic powder." I opened the cupboard and surveyed the spices. "There we go," I said as I spotted the targeted seasoning.

"Wow! We're having a feast! How do you do it?"

"It's always easy when you have the ingredients in the kitchen. I don't cook often, but when I do, I like to have everything handy."

We prepared dinner together, and I enjoyed his companionship in the kitchen. He didn't feel the need to augment the conversation by turning on the television. He watched over my shoulder while I made the scampi and marveled at my skill, which I found adorable.

While we ate, and drank a delicious early Chardonnay, we talked about our family histories. Before now, we hadn't had the time.

"Okay, let me get this straight," he said as he took a sip of wine, "you got the idea for "Find-It!" in college? Where did it come from?'

"I was a computer major and attended a lecture about the future of the internet. I began to correlate a way to open the platform. The idea was quite radical. Those were lean days," I explained.

"Were you already married when you designed it?"

I shook my head as I wrapped pasta around my fork. "No, and thankfully I wasn't, that's what actually saved my company. Tim and I were dating at the time. He was attending engineering school and working at a company selling copy machines. I worked as a waitress, went to school, and wrote the software during every free moment I had. I wasn't a very good waitress either," I laughed. "So usually I didn't make much in tips. My parents slipped money to me here and there, but they didn't have much extra cash either.

Tim, also known as *the asshole*, and I were married for about six months, and my new search engine attracted a lot of attention including big media attention. I was approached by AppSoft, and they offered me one hundred thousand dollars for it."

He grinned again as he finished off the shrimp. "I know this part. You didn't take it, did you?"

"I did not. Tim was furious with me. He was ready to cash out. He thought I had gone as far as I could with it. A hundred K was a lot of money. It would have paid off our student loans and set us up in a small house. But, I knew that I could go further, and I refused to sell out for such a paltry sum."

"So what happened with Tim?" he inquired.

"I borrowed money from my family and bought him out. It cost me fifty thousand dollars in divorce court, but the company was mine, free and clear. I worked another two years improving the engine and then I hit a breakthrough. AppSoft came back to me, and this time the offer was different. Far different. I had literally changed the internet." I saw him quirk his lips. "And, yes, I'm not humble about it either."

He laughed and his lips pressed against the back of my hand. "And my dear woman, you would not be you if you were humble about it."

"Pretty much the way it happened. But, let me tell you, my parents, grandmother, and brother saved me. Had it not been for them, I wouldn't have been able to stave off Tim."

"You mean the asshole?"

I giggled. "Yes, the asshole."

"I for one, am glad you got rid of the asshole."

"You are?"

"Yes," he said, leaning over to kiss me. "Otherwise, I wouldn't be doing this..." he kissed me longer the second time.

I sighed and leaned on my arms to gaze into his eyes. "And I really like when you do that."

He leaned in for a third kiss. "So do I."

After dinner, I dished up a couple of scoops of ice cream for dessert, and we sat on the couch.

"I suppose you know everything about me," he said after he set his bowl on the side table and lay down with his head in my lap.

"I don't know if I know everything. I do know your parents own an Irish pub in Los Angeles and it is quite successful. That's as deep as I went. My foundation investigated your organization financially, and your schooling, but we don't generally hit the families unless there is an unsavory trail."

"I understand why you have to do it, but it does leave a man feeling a little violated."

"Surely, this isn't the first time someone has looked into your background. You've had other corporate sponsors. They would have all done a search on you since you're the principle."

"I know, and yes we do have corporate sponsors. Although none have been as generous as you."

"We need to talk about that later. You have a huge following on Facebook. You should be able to tap into that to increase your sponsorship."

He groaned, "Let's not talk about that now. That stuff drives me crazy. It takes away from the core task we have at hand."

I smiled and ran my fingers through his thick silky hair. "Then tell me about your family. Why did they choose Los Angeles, and why a pub? Your mom had been a biochemist and your dad a teacher."

"Ma did work as a biochemist when we arrived here. It was difficult for Da to get a job as a teacher. He took a job as a bartender at a small restaurant in Santa Monica. My sister, who is ten years older than me ... hey... she's your age!"

I thumped him on the stomach. "Continue the story and knock off the age references."

He chuckled, "You know I was just trying to tease you. You're going to need thicker skin. Wait until you meet Seamus, my oldest brother. He's the world's biggest tease. Anyway, my sister was graduating from high school, and she had already been accepted to the Riverdance Dance Company. She was going to go back to Ireland."

"Oh my gosh!" I declared. "Is she a part of Riverdance?"

"No, she isn't. Her real love is ballet. She's petite, like my Ma. Her dance teacher recognized her talent, and when she was in Ireland, she studied ballet for years. She is retiring from the San Francisco Ballet Company."

"Your sister is a ballerina?"

He smiled with pride, "Not only a ballerina but a prima ballerina. She has starred in each ballet company she has danced with."

"And she dances with the San Francisco Company? That's impressive. They are an international company. I love ballet." I smiled. "I've probably seen her on stage."

"She did Bolero in the autumn last year. It was impressive." He grinned with a smirk in the corners of his sexy mouth, "Especially for someone her age."

I raised my eyebrows at him, "Be careful, youngster. Or you'll be sleeping by yourself!"

He raised himself up and pulled my face toward him. "Would you do that to me?" Nibbling on my mouth, he then placed a loving kiss. "I love teasing you. You make it easy. But, let me make this perfectly clear to you, the years between us are trifling. You have a youthful way about you, probably because you're a nerd."

I laughed and quickly kissed him back. "So now nerds are young? I didn't think they had an age."

"They don't. They are just nerds. Always buried in their phones or their computers."

"You have a point there. I do usually have my nose buried in technology. But you, my dear," I ran my fingers over his soft full lips, "are a bad boy, in the worst way. You and your leather pants, and your motorcycle and tattoos."

"Oh," he leaned in again, "I think you like bad boys a lot, don't you?" He laid his head back in my lap.

"Yes," I whispered. "I like you a lot."

He gave me a satisfying grin. "Now my middle brother, Sean, he's a nerd too."

"He is? Is he a computer genius?"

"No, he's an engineer. He lives near the beach, but what good does it do him? He doesn't date, too shy. Ma tries to fix him up with women from the parish, but he's not interested."

"Is he gay?"

"It wouldn't matter to me if he was, but we all think he's a guy who likes to be left alone."

"Your oldest brother, what does he do?"

"Seamus? He's a priest."

"You have a priest in the family?"

"Yes, we do. My parents are especially proud of that. He's my Ma's pride and joy."

"Does he live here in the United States?"

"No, he's back in Ireland. He's the priest of our parish back there."

"Is he a lot older than your sister?"

"Only by two years," Kian replied. "He was in seminary school when we immigrated to the States."

"Do you ever get to see him?"

"He's made it here a few times, once when Siobhan was married, and then again when her daughter and son were baptized. We all try to visit home when we can."

"You're an uncle too?" I asked.

"Yes, I am. And a proud one at that. Now that my sister is retiring from the stage, I hope to see them more often."

"Your sister is married?"

"No. Her husband walked out on her when the kids were small. It was tough on her when she had to travel. When they were little, she took them with her and hired a nanny. As the children grew, they stopped going with her, and she left them with the caregiver. It tore her up too, but she had little choice. She didn't get much support from her ex-husband. The bastard. He took off with the first nanny. Decided he didn't want the responsibility of children."

I frowned, "Some men just can't step up. It's easier for them to run away, and then the woman has to shoulder everything."

"My sister did it gladly. She loves her children madly. I think she could have been even more famous, but she turned down jobs to be with the kids. She stuck with American companies instead of joining companies like the Bolshoi."

We were quiet for a moment, and Kian looked over at the clock. "I guess I should be going."

"You're not going to stay?" My disappointment was evident in my voice.

"You'll have me do the walk of shame into the clinic tomorrow morning wearing the same t-shirt?"

I laughed. "You'll put on your lab coat, and no one will notice. Besides, no one will remember that you wore that t-shirt today."

"What? You think they won't remember Alice Cooper? Have you any idea how many people I had to tell who Alice Cooper was today? They will definitely remember."

"Oh, I'm sure I have a t-shirt in the closet that you won't drown in … too much."

"Hello, Kitty? I can just imagine something with pink and lace."

"Well, if you don't want to stay."

He caught the look in my eyes and immediately sat up. Swinging around to face me, he took my face in his hands. His thumbs brushed against my cheeks.

"Sweetlin', I do want to stay. Shall I stay?"

I nodded my head. Sometimes his age did creep into our relationship. He was so ready to please me, to make me happy. Men my age wouldn't bother. Or at least the ones I knew and dated, didn't.

"Good," he said, "then I'm staying." His kisses started on my forehead, then he moved slowly down, pressing his lips against my eyelids, my cheeks, nose, and finally my lips. I would never get enough of his kisses. They were never only our lips meeting; they were so much more. Lips touching, tongues exploring, inhaling each other's every breath. His kisses reached down to my toes and back up again.

After we had cleaned away the dishes, we went to bed. The light outside the window was a little distracting, but it did allow me to gaze and get lost in the sweetness of his face. Yes, his face had angular features with a strong square jaw and high sharp cheekbones. He had the kind of masculine handsome that would make a woman pause and take a deep breath, but there was also such incredible sweetness there too. The kindness in his eyes, they could cradle you, and you'd be lost forever in the deep blue pools of warmth.

His hands, the tools he used not only to repair broken bones and heal hurts, were the hands that would hold puppies close and comfort them. His hands eased the pain of all creatures. Including mine. My pain had begun to bubble to the surface.

The years of betrayal. All those men who only wanted me for the money. My heart was frozen over. But as we made love, I could feel my heart begin to thaw.

We moved together bit by bit, gently discovering more about each other as we had done a couple of nights ago. As much as I enjoyed our usual frenzied pace, this was my favorite. It was not so much about racing to the end, but instead, it was the building and stoking of a fire that would not go out even after we crested together.

Later, we wrapped around each other and slept until dawn peeked through the curtains.

CHAPTER 32

The next morning, I blissfully found Kian still wrapped around me. I expected him to be up, showered, coffee made and ready to start his day. He stretched out lazily and pulled me along with him.

"Good morning handsome," I purred into his ear. I rubbed my cheek against his stubble enjoying the feel of the prickle, which touched my skin. I nipped his earlobe with my teeth, and he groaned, stretching again. His body had his early morning happiness on. I liked that and ran my hand down his chest under the covers … well yes … to his triumphant manhood. Would I ever tire of his readiness?

"Come now woman, you can't possibly want me again?"

Teasing him, I moved my hand away. "If you don't want me then…" I trailed off.

"Now don't go and do that," he said putting my hand back. "You keep that right there and continue doing what you like."

I giggled and rolled up to straddle him. Leaning down, I grazed his nipples with my teeth that elicited a deep growl from him.

"What I like is…" I inched my way down, leaving a trail of kisses along the middle of his chest, "driving you slowly out of your mind."

Which I proceeded to do. Very happily, I might add.

When we finally started our day, we left separately and met at the small diner across the street from the hospital. We weren't fooling anyone. Talk spread quickly in a small town like Mintock. In the course of a few days, everyone knew we were together, … as a couple. When I walked into the restaurant, the hostess pointed to the back where Kian had already been seated. I nodded and made my way to the rear.

Several people greeted me as I walked back. Both Michael and Elizabeth were popular residents of the town, so it made sense that I would get lumped in with their family. Building a house and hiring local labor didn't hurt either. I slid into the booth next to Kian.

"Did you order coffee?" I asked as I picked up the menu and perused the breakfast selections.

He didn't need to answer because the waitress arrived at the table with two mugs and poured coffee into both. After she had taken our orders, we settled down with our coffees.

"It's surprising how busy this place is on a weekday morning," I commented looking around. Every spot was taken.

"If you get here before seven it's not bad, but a minute after, and forget it, you're in line. We order lunch for the clinic on most days, they run it over to us. It's very convenient."

"I know the food is excellent."

I was hungry. We had already worked up an appetite this morning. I loved this! After spending an incredible night and morning having the best sex of my life, and then being here with him in kind of a homey couple's type booth, I was reveling. But then every bubble must burst at some time, and my pin walked through the door at that moment.

Mayor Busch, with what could only be described as an entourage, walked into the diner. What were the chances?

Every table was full, and I couldn't imagine where the hostess would seat the party, but then I underestimated the man's power. They brought out a new table for them from the back and moved other tables with customers sitting at them. Apparently, Mayor Busch gave no consideration to the inconvenience of those surrounding him.

I said a silent prayer that he wouldn't see us. Why did that never work? Kian caught my hand and squeezed it when it was evident that the mayor had seen us and was on his way back to our table.

I doubted that either of them would make a scene since the restaurant was packed with people, but when I flashed a look at Kian, his face changed my mind. His eyes were filled with venom as he looked at the man who approached us.

This was the first time I got a good look at Mayor Busch. Yes, this fellow appeared as if he was used to eating out. He carried all of his weight around his mid-section. Dark hair and a more olive complexion than Annie's, there was nothing at all attractive about him. His large bulbous nose and cheeks were reddened which reminded me of late stage alcohol abuse. His comb-over only compounded his failed attempt at admitting he was losing his hair.

Kian didn't change his posture and barely gave him a glance as the mayor leaned against our table. The only thing that gave him away was the flexing of the muscles in his biceps each time he squeezed my hand.

"Dr. McDermott," Mayor Busch began, "I would have expected you to be already at your hospital instead of having a leisurely breakfast with your friend." He sneered at the word friend. This was not a nice man.

"I'm sure you don't have the time in your day to concern yourself about my schedule." Kian pronounced each word in his familiar Irish accent.

The mayor leaned in over the table, and I quickly moved my coffee cup out of the way because the bottom of his tie was aimed straight for it. "I thought I made it clear to you that I want my dogs back."

Kian straightened upright in the booth and with a lowered voice that was close to a growl, said, "And I thought I made it clear to you I'm not returning the dogs you have abused."

The mayor stared at him for a moment. This was a man who was used to getting his own way and rarely heard the word no.

"Did you enjoy the present I left for you at your front door?" he mocked. "You know I will continue to leave you presents like that."

Where was a cop when you needed one? The mayor had just admitted to us he was responsible for the dog shooting.

Kian didn't say a word. I was so proud of him. This was not the place for a confrontation. We needed to get evidence against this asshole. Hard proof that would lock him up for a very long time.

Mayor Busch flicked a glance at me, "Miss Hoffman, you are so much more attractive in person than your pictures portray."

The intentions of his words were clear to both Kian and me. It was my turn to squeeze Kian's hand because he looked like he was going to blow a gasket.

I would not let this odious man have the last word.

It was probably stupid of me, but I leveled my eyes at him and with a loud, clear voice said, "Mayor Busch, have you met our two FBI agents who arrived into town yesterday? They're here to investigate some suspicious activity having to do with a possible dog fighting ring here in the area. Can you imagine anything so heinous as to pit dogs together to fight to the death? I actually found a poor dog that had been almost torn to pieces by another dog, up on the mountain road a couple of weeks ago." I pulled my hand out from underneath the table and patted Kian on the shoulder. "Dr. McDermott saved the poor baby for me. In fact, that was me who was sitting in the lobby on the rainy night you rushed in. I recognized your truck. That's your truck isn't it, the one with the clever license plate? I would have said hello to you at the time, but it appeared you were quite upset about something. It is interesting to meet you finally. I've heard so much about you from a mutual acquaintance of ours. I believe Scott Binder is a very close friend of yours? Well, I'm sure the agents will stop by your office to meet you. They probably have a few questions for you."

First, the surprise registered in eyes, then the alarm, and finally the rage.

I put my resting bitch face on, the one that I negotiated with. I was famous for it. Men hated and feared it. The waitress came up behind him carrying our breakfasts.

I brightened up. "Oh, look our meals are here. I'm sure it would be interesting to keep chatting with you, but I don't want our food to get cold. Please excuse us. Have a nice day." I gave him a dismissive wave.

Internally I laughed. Michael loved and hated that wave. He loved it when I did it to someone else and hated it when I did it to him.

I looked over at Kian as the waitress put our food in front of us. "Mmmm… this looks good! How does yours look?"

The mayor still stood at the table, as if he couldn't believe he was just sent away by a weak woman who he had obviously seen very nasty pictures of, and I looked back at him with a glare, which clearly said, *why are you still here?*

One of the mayor's underlings came up behind him and tugged on his arm. He looked confused at first, then regained his composure and stalked off not saying a word.

Kian bit into a piece of bacon. "Woman, now you have gone and done it. You've let the cat out of the proverbial bag. I don't think it was a secret that the agents are here in town, but now, everyone definitely knows."

"Good!" I said. "He needs to know people are on to him, and that we've put him and that slime Scott together. I wanted to slap that self-satisfied smirk right off his face, if only in punishment for what he did to Koa and the newest dog. Stupid jerk! By the way, have you named the latest dog yet?"

"I just hope it doesn't drive him underground. If he knows he's being investigated, nothing prevents him from closing shop here in this area and moving it somewhere else. And no, I haven't named the new dog yet, do you want to give it a try?"

"I don't think the mayor will move anywhere else. His power base is here in this town. He doesn't have people in his pocket in some other place. That would take effort on his part, and he probably doesn't have the ambition or the drive to start over." I chewed on a small piece of sausage slowly. "Yes, I believe I'll give it a whirl."

"Give what a try?" he asked.

"Naming Dog Doe. I'll come up with a name. Can I let you know this afternoon?"

He laughed and put his arm around me holding me close.

"I love being around you because•you are an amazing woman," he whispered

His smile made my heart leap and do little lively jigs.

"Thank you for not attacking the mayor."

He laughed and continued to eat his breakfast. "He's an asshole. I don't care what he thinks he's going to do to me. I'm glad I didn't have to pull you off him. You're scrappy in an elegant sort of a way when you're angry."

"Is that a compliment?"

He touched his orange juice glass with mine. "Only in the highest sense my sweetlin'. I believe it is why we get along well because we don't take bullshit from anyone."

I picked up my glass and toasted him back. "That's right. We don't."

We finished our breakfast in peace and lingered awhile over our coffee. The restaurant's clientele had thinned out, and soon no one was waiting for a table. We left together, and I was relieved to notice when we left Mayor Busch was no longer there. As brave and confrontational as I was, I didn't feel like taking him on a second time in one day.

CHAPTER 33

"The dog's name should be Conlan. It means hero or wise one," I said to Kian on my cell phone while I stood in my new kitchen.

"I already know exactly what it means," he chuckled. "I do speak the language. So, you think he is a hero?"

"Absolutely," I jumped up and sat on the counter, "he is a casualty of war, and he should be honored as one."

"Your wish is my command." He winked at me. I could even see the sparkle in his eyes through the screen. Then he lowered his voice, and I saw him walking down the hallway to his office, where he closed his door. "I'm not going to be able to see you tonight."

"Oh?" The disappointment was evident in my voice. "Did something happen?"

He drew a hand through his hair and sighed deeply, "Yeah, I have another rescue coming in. She was abandoned out on the old highway and tied to a signpost. Thankfully, a trucker saw her and stopped. She has a bad case of mange, and there might be some other health problems too."

"Oh." It was all I could think to say. The rescue business opened my eyes to an entirely different world. Who abandons their dog on a deserted highway and ties them to a post? "Do you know how long she was out there?"

"I'm not sure yet. She allowed the man to pick her up. We'll see."

"Do you need any help?" Suddenly I was not so enchanted with my kitchen. It didn't matter.

"No sweetlin', I have this. It's what I do. I'll get her checked out and treated. We'll clean her up. If she has mange, then most likely she isn't pretty to look at. When I'm done with her, she will be."

"Okay. I'll miss you."

"Not as much as I will miss you. Take advantage of the night off and get some rest. Something tells me you'll need it." His chuckles were music to my ears.

"Don't forget his new name is Conlan!" I reminded Kian.

"Right, I got it. I'll change the name on his chart."

After we had disconnected the call, I placed the phone on the counter next to me and sat there with empty hands.

I'll miss you.

How did that happen? Where did it come from? How had he gotten past my barriers? I thought they were high enough. I was used to saying no, as much as my brother thought I didn't.

Damn. My feelings for Kian weren't going to make this any easier. If the pictures were leaked to the internet, I would have to disappear. I wouldn't have a choice. I couldn't do that to my family. Oh! I couldn't think of that now. I hoped that the FBI would figure something out before Friday.

I turned my attention to the new appliances in the kitchen, running my hands over them and loving their newness. I probably wouldn't have time to enjoy them, not if I had to leave. Damn!

I was enjoying Kian too. Not only was he the sexiest man alive, but he was also brilliant and could carry on a conversation. He was fun, and I even delighted in his teasing. I liked to be around my bad boy. Wait! When did he become *my* bad boy?

Opening the pantry door, I took a step back, I didn't realize how big it was. This was not a closet; it was a room! I didn't remember it being so big on the blueprints. Not all the shelving had been installed yet, but the wine refrigerator was already in. Putting wine on my mental shopping list, I'd have to christen it when I had the chance.

I slipped out of the house trying to keep out of the contractor's way. The house would be completed in a few of weeks. It was moving fast now. My entire life seemed to be speeding up. I went back to the cabin to see if I could try to slow it down a bit.

After I had made myself comfortable, I poured a glass of wine and didn't even wonder if one p.m. was too early for alcohol. I watched TV so infrequently. I didn't know what would be broadcasted during this time of the day. I pulled Koa into my lap, and we sat peacefully. He slept, and I channel surfed. I found an old sitcom and started watching. A special news bulletin alerted about a wildfire on the mountain highway outside of Mintock.

It was very early in the year for us to have wildfires, but it had been a dry winter, and we were in the fifth year of a severe drought. A careless cigarette thrown out of a car window was all it would take. I remembered Annie and Frank lived close to that side of the mountain and hoped their house was okay. There weren't many homes in the area. It was mainly reservation land and was sparsely populated with ranches filled with horses and cattle.

The aerial coverage showed only a couple of structures were involved now, but they expected the typical spring winds to kick up making the fire worse.

I pressed Annie's number on my cell phone. She didn't answer, and the call went to voicemail. I left a quick message of concern and asked her to call me when she had a chance.

As soon as I disconnected the call, my phone rang. It was my mother.

"Hey mom, how are you doing?"

"Are you okay? Dad and I are watching the fire coverage on the news," her voice came clearly over the phone. Mom was never one to mince words or begin with niceties if there was a crisis brewing.

"Yeah, we're okay. The fire is on the other side of the lake, off the mountain highway."

"Oh thank goodness. I was so worried. All you need is your new house to go up in smoke."

"I have a sophisticated sprinkler system running through the entire place, including sprinklers on the roof."

"I thought you had mentioned something like that to me. I'm so glad you think ahead. Honestly, I don't know what your brother was thinking, buying a wooden house in a high-risk fire area."

"Oh, you know Mom, Michael likes his rustic style, it goes with his rugged persona."

"Oh yes, the nonsense of him being a rugged outdoorsman. I should tell everyone when he was a little boy he was scared of spiders."

"He's changed quite a bit since he was seven."

"He still won't step on a spider."

"No, that's because he's a vegetarian and believes in the sanctity of life."

"Ach! Don't you believe it, he's still afraid of spiders!"

How did I manage once again to go down a rabbit hole with my mother?

"Well, we're all safe here Mom."

"Good. Let me know if you need any help with the new house. You know I am an excellent decorator."

I rolled my eyes, "Of course I will Mom. Everything is almost done, though." I wasn't going to tell her about the near break-in or the pictures. Not yet. It was too soon.

"Okay, keep your eyes out for any embers blowing over your way. You know that can happen."

I rolled my eyes again, "I sure will. I love you guys. Talk to you soon, okay?"

"Oh, now I remember the other thing I wanted to talk to you about. Michael said you had something to tell me. What is it?"

He did, did he? I rolled my eyes for the third time and now planned on the slow and cruel torture I would put him through.

"No," I answered. "I can't imagine what he could be talking about?"

"Hmmm… he said it was very important. Now, what was it?" I could picture her tapping her front teeth with the eraser at the top of her number two pencil. She had done that forever. I knew she was trying to picture it in her mind.

"No. Not a thing."

"Yes! Now I remember," she said suddenly. "You have a new boyfriend!" She announced it triumphantly.

I was going to kill Michael. It would be a painful and very slow death indeed. And I would make him watch. I tried not to sigh heavily.

"He's not really a boyfriend. We've been on a couple of dates," I said, not adding that we've also had wild, crazy, and amazing sex. No. That was not a mom discussion point.

"Oh, darling. I'm so happy. How did you meet him? Does he live in the city?"

"Um, no, he doesn't live in San Francisco. He lives here in town. He's the veterinarian here."

"But…" my mother paused, "I thought the veterinarian is in his twenties. Are you referring to the new one?"

How did she know so much about Mintock's veterinarian? My mother got around a lot more than I thought.

"Yes, I am. Dr. McDermott is almost thirty years old."

"Oh dear, isn't he a little young for you? I mean you're nearly ten years older than him. Doesn't that make you a cougar?"

Yes. My mother got around way too much.

"I am a bit older than he is, yes, but we've only just started showing interest in each other."

"I hope he's not showing interest in you just for your money. Have you had him checked out? You don't need another dating disaster like the one you had in New York."

I cleared my throat, "Yes Mom. I've vetted him and did a background check, but you know it's difficult to determine if someone is after me for my money. You know the man in New York was pulling a major scam with me. Everyone was fooled. The background check hadn't shown what scum he was."

The donation I had made to Kian's organization was another discussion point removed from Mom's conversation table. She would not understand. I hated that she brought up New York. I had learned my lesson with that guy. It would have been an expensive lesson too because we had almost married, but fortunately, I had overheard a telephone conversation he was having with his real girlfriend. Chalk up another humiliation for me.

"Exactly why you need to be super vigilant. I just find it curious someone so young would be interested in someone your age."

Oh, Mother, just slide the knife into my heart.

"I don't want to see you hurt again, Christina. I worry about you," she said

"I know. Thank you. Listen, I need to go. I'll talk to you soon."

"Okay sweetheart. Keep in touch with news about the fire, alright?"

"Will do. Bye, Mom. Hug Dad for me," I said and quickly pressed the disconnect key.

I was so done. I hit my head on the back of the couch. And, my brother was going to die. He was fortunate however because speaking with my mother was especially draining today so I would wait for another day to kill him.

I was also disappointed about not seeing Kian. I would admit this to no one else, but I missed him. I enjoyed being around him. He didn't take the world so seriously. Well… he did ... I guess it was himself he didn't take seriously.

Koa looked at me when he heard my loud sigh. I wasn't one for afternoon naps, but I was tired. Laying down now was not an option, I knew I had too much to do, but none of it held much appeal for me. I wished I wasn't being held in limbo.

Kian's appointment with the FBI was at four, and he probably gave them an earful about my artful conversation with the town's mayor this morning. I hope it wouldn't get me into trouble. Especially since I tipped our hand. But had I really? Mayor Busch surely had his ears to the ground to run his operation. How had he kept himself so clean? I didn't doubt that the mayor had people to do his dirty work. I also didn't know why he would want to break into the cabin, but I was certain he was behind it. Not many people knew I was staying in Elizabeth's cabin. The assumption was that I stayed with them at their house. So why try breaking into the cabin? It must have been to get to me. That thought made me shudder.

CHAPTER 34

Kian called me early the next morning to report on the newest rescue.

"She is absolutely adorable. The sweetest little girl I've ever met. She has a bad skin condition acerbated by the sarcoptic mange, but it will clear up, and her hair will grow back. Wait until you meet her. You will fall in love."

"I think I have only room for one in my life at a time."

"All I am saying is to wait. She will be living over at the clinic for now because we must isolate her since it's transferable to the other animals. But, once we get rid of it, she'll be able to be around the dogs, and we'll need to keep an eye out for any reoccurrence. She is a honey of a dog. She eats up the affection and personal contact."

"Are you going to get mange?" I laughed. "I don't want you giving it to Koa." Or me, I thought.

"No. She'll be okay with the initial treatment and then some subsequent shampoos. The big thing is to clear up her skin. She looks like she was probably a family pet and her condition got too much for them to handle. She's well fed, about 18 months old. There's evidence too that she had puppies. Recently, and if that's the case, there's a good chance the puppies will have mange too. We'll have to keep an eye out for them."

I looked at his face. He was so enthusiastic in his description of the newest rescue.

He continued, "So, I'm thinking how about you pick me up after the clinic closes tonight, you can meet our new pup and then we can go to dinner, and then..." His voice trailed off, and his look was intense.

"And?" I asked staring hard into the phone.

"I thought we could go back to my place," he said finally.

"Oh? Is there a hockey game on?"

He smiled wickedly, "No, but I thought perhaps we could play some tonsil hockey."

My evil boy.

I packed a small bag and loaded Koa into the car. Kian and I decided we would call ahead to the restaurant and do take out. This was okay with me because then I could slide into my jeans and wear a sweater instead of getting dressed up. This was a first for me. Usually, I would have dressed to the nines for any date with a man. Kian was different, though. He made me feel relaxed, and I didn't have to impress him. He liked me just the way I was.

I arrived at the clinic a little after six and went in through the front doors with Koa. I was surprised the doors weren't already locked, but Carrie told me they were waiting for me to arrive.

She and I weren't best friends, but our relationship had changed … dramatically. She was friendly with me and now always gave me a bright smile when I saw her.

"They're waiting for you in the main room," she said as I walked in.

I nodded, "Thanks."

I walked around her and passed through the double swinging doors. Kian leaned against a counter with one leg crossed over the other. Leonard sat in a swivel chair and had a portable table with a laptop on it in front of him. They were alone in the big room speaking quietly.

"There she is!" Kian's smile was big and his dimples deep. It was a look that always made my heart skip a beat.

"Hey! Sorry, I'm late. The traffic light was out, and you know the rush hour traffic."

Both men chuckled, and Leonard said, "Yes, that and a duck crossing can screw up any commute. Hey, Koa! He's looking good!"

Koa's ever wagging tail moved back and forth at a frenzied pace. He crouched down in the play position as much as his cast would allow and made his wanna play bark.

Leonard picked him up and ran a friendly hand over his body. "Are you ready for your x-ray? I'll have him right back." They both disappeared into another room.

Kian wrapped his arms around me and gave me a soft kiss. "Damn, I missed you."

I grinned after the kiss, "That's what I like to hear." My hands moved down to his butt, and I squeezed him through his lab coat.

"Careful woman, I'll take you right here!"

I batted my lashes at him, "Promise?"

He laughed and patted my bottom, "You are so going to get it tonight."

I kissed him, "I better! Are you going to show me your new rescue, or are you going to stand here all night copping a free feel?"

He squeezed me one more time, and I'll admit that it was exciting to stand there out in the open having a make out session. Breaking apart from me, he reached for a box holding latex gloves. "Yes. Let me introduce you." He handed me a pair of gloves. "Put these on."

I almost made a face, but I squelched it quickly. I didn't want Kian to think I was a coward, and I wasn't, but if it was bad enough to wear gloves, then how contagious was she?

He led me into a room, which had several kennels. Even though the lights were low, I could see her clearly lying on a small mat. She looked up as we approached. I had to squelch my shock at seeing her condition. Most of her fur was gone, and her skin looked red and raw with open sores. What little coat she had left was in tufts here and there. Kian switched on a light over her kennel. It was not bright but gave us enough illumination to see. Her eyes were alert. She slowly rose and stood by the door, her naked tail moving back and forth.

My hand went to my mouth, "Oh, poor baby."

He opened the door slowly. "Hey, there little girl. How are you doing? Feeling better? I bet you are."

I knelt in front of her and reached out. "Is she in pain?"

"No," he answered softly. "We've given her something to make her more comfortable so she can sleep a little easier. The mat she's lying on is soft and warming. It is made of a special material we use for burn victims. It's perfect for her too. We're treating her with antibiotics so that the lesions will heal." He sat on the floor and spoke in soothing tones to her.

My eyes started to leak, and soon I was having difficulties trying to hold back the tears.

"How could anyone let this happen?" I asked him. "Why?"

"If I only knew the answer. Don't cry. She's getting the help she needs. Soon she'll be with a loving family in her forever home. There are so many out there who need to be saved. It's hard for me when I think of all of them. But, I can only rescue the ones I know about. I can only bring in the dogs that I have room for here in the hospital or up at the house."

I petted her where her sores didn't seem to be too plentiful. She lay on her mat and closed her eyes obviously enjoying the attention and the touch. "Will she be okay?" I asked as Kian handed me a tissue from his coat pocket.

"She should be. I know she looks bad, but I think she'll respond well to treatment. She's not afraid of us, so I don't believe she was abused. Her previous owners probably didn't know how to get help for her or couldn't afford it. This type of problem just gets worse and worse without treatment. We have her all vaccinated, and she'll rest comfortably in here. In a few days, she'll be able to graduate from isolation, and we'll put her with the remainder of the population."

He helped me to my feet and closed the kennel door softly. As we left the room, he shut off the extra light over her. She slept peacefully.

We stood together outside of the room stripping off our gloves. He took mine from me and tossed them in the trash. I had not recovered from the meeting.

Kian wrapped his arm around my shoulder. "Are you going to be okay?"

"I think so. It's a little jarring to see. When you read about something like this or see pictures, it's not quite the same thing as viewing it live and in person."

He sighed deeply, "It's why I bring high school students in here to volunteer. They will be the dog owners of the future. Sometimes you can't adequately describe some of the horrors you see. But, this is my mission in life. I will make their lives better, even if I have to do it one dog at a time."

I held him close. "You are an amazing man, Kian. You have such love and strength. You fight for the underdog. It makes me proud to know you," I whispered, "and I'm so inadequate."

"My *a mhuirnin*, my darling love" he whispered softly in my ear. "You could never be inadequate in my book. In my book, you are an angel. It is you who have come in and saved us."

Cupping my face in his hands, he gave me gentle kisses. They were not meant to light passion, instead to heal.

A clearing throat interrupted us, and we both saw Leonard standing in the doorway. "Excuse me Kian, I have Koa's x-rays ready if you'd like to see them."

"I'll be right there." He turned back to me. "Don't be sad for our new girl. She's one of the ones being saved. I promise."

We walked together arm-in-arm to Kian's office. He flipped on his computer monitor and studied the x-rays on the screen.

"Koa is looking good," he remarked. "Everything is healing as it should. We'll take this cast off, remove his stitches and recast the leg with a softer one now."

They worked on him for forty-five minutes then we were ready to go. We stopped at the restaurant, and Kian ran in while I waited in the car. Everything was ready, and we arrived at his house fifteen minutes later.

You could smell the thick smoke in the air from the wildfire from the day before.

"Do you know if they've been able to put out the fire completely?" I asked him as he carried our dinner into the house.

"I think they have it contained. It was a miracle there was only one structure destroyed. They said the fire moved fast."

Kian's dogs were excited to see us, and I was happy to see Koa was accepted quite naturally with them. We popped the dinner into the oven to keep it warm and went out into the backyard to care for the dogs in the kennels. I even helped.

The two pit bulls, which had belonged to Mayor Busch, were due to be picked up in the morning by the group that would try retraining them.

Kian had already prepared me for the fact that sometimes they were not successful. There was a dark side to animal rescuing because sometimes a dog didn't make it. I didn't want to hear it. It was too hard.

After feeding all of them, I spent some one-on-one time with the pregnant lab. We sat together, me stroking her soft fur as I spoke gently. She laid her head in my lap and closed her eyes. My back leaned against the wall. It wasn't the most comfortable of positions, but I wouldn't move for anything to disturb her. Her eyes would flutter open every now and then, and she would huff out a sigh of approval at my petting technique.

"Hey, you!" Kian called to me. "Do you want some dinner?"

"Yes," I said. I was hungry, but I didn't want to leave this golden girl.

He bent down and stroked her fur too. "Come, let her get some sleep, she was outside with the kids most of the day. Let's have some dinner." He pulled me up to my feet and closed the cage door.

The table was already set, and a bottle of wine opened.

"When did you do this?" I asked.

He chuckled, "While you had your love fest with our girl out there." He pointed to the clock, and I couldn't believe it was already eight o'clock.

"How did it get to be so late?"

"Time has a way of slipping away when you're lost in the dogs."

"I guess it does."

We sat together, ate and drank wine. We were subdued and didn't speak much. The dinner was good, but I wasn't hungry, and the lack of sleep had caught up to me. We put the dishes in the dishwasher and straighten the kitchen.

I walked into the living room so we could watch television and he caught my hand to pull me toward him. I went willingly.

He wrapped his arms around my waist. "I have a new plan," he whispered, "let's take a bath and turn in early tonight. I think both of us are tired."

"That sounds good," I answered.

Following him into his bathroom, he grabbed a few towels from his linen closet on the way. The freestanding claw-footed bathtub looked like it would fit two people and I was ready to give it a try. He put the stopper into the drain and turned on the faucet. As the tub began to fill, he opened a bottle and poured in some of the contents. The room filled with a fragrant scent of lavender, it smelled like him. He always had a slight scent of the flower about him.

I breathed in deeply, "Oh, that's lovely!"

"My aunt in Ireland makes it and sends it to me. She grows lavender on her farm."

"Is this your mother's sister? The one you told me about, Aunt Maeve?"

"Yes, she's the one. She has a cottage industry making soap, bath products, and raising champion Irish Wolfhound dogs. Her dogs are much sought after as hunting dogs."

I inhaled again. "She certainly has captured the lavender, it's not too sweet. It can be used by both women and men."

"Now come here," he said pulling me closely. "Let's get you out of your clothes so we can enjoy this bath properly. My muscles ache."

I grinned slyly, "Is this what the doctor is ordering?"

He pulled my sweater over my head. "This is what the doctor is demanding."

My bra was gone in a blink, and my nipples became pointed peaks as the surrounding cold air hit them. I shivered a bit.

"Let's get you into the water, it will warm you up," he insisted

Shoes, socks, jeans, and panties went quickly. Kian held my hand as I stepped into the tub. The water swirled around my leg. It was hot. I crouched into the tub, and as the water touched my skin, I exhaled sharply.

"Woo…" I hissed, and the water covered me up to my waist in the deep tub.

I watched Kian undress. With the bright light of the bathroom, the scars on his sides were clearly visible. They were white with age, but no matter what, they looked like they had been painful. The cross on his back was beautiful. I marveled at his body. His broad chest and shoulders, the abs, which looked as if they had been carved by an artist, leading to a narrow waist and hips. Muscular thighs, and yes, in the middle of his body a surging rampant cock. Standing at attention. How did he do that so quickly?

He switched off the big overhead lamp, the bathroom was suddenly in darkness. Then he turned on a small night light at the door that bathed us in a soft glow. He climbed in behind me and slid down into the tub. The water level went up suddenly and covered my shoulders. I looked around the edges, but we were not yet close to sloshing water over the rim of the tub.

He turned the faucets off with his feet.

"Let me wash your back," he whispered.

He applied the lavender bath wash to a cloth and slowly rubbed it on my back. It felt heavenly. He sluiced water down my back to rinse the soap away. His fingers then kneaded my shoulders.

"You are so tense," he murmured.

"Your hands are helping." My body relaxed as he continued to massage my back.

I twisted and picked up the washcloth from the water. I ran it along his shoulders and down his chest to his belly under the water. He leaned back against the tub and closed his eyes. My hands kneaded his thighs.

He moaned, "That feels so good. You have good hands. All the aches are going away."

Kian pulled me back against him. Picking up the washcloth again, he ran it gently down the front of my body. His hands cupped my breasts and thrummed my nipples with his thumbs. The heavenly scent of lavender surrounded us. We didn't have bubbles in the water, so nothing was hidden from our sight.

I could see his hands kneading my breasts. His touch and the vision made everything below my belly tighten with delicious anticipation. I would have him inside me tonight, perhaps more than once. I didn't have to worry about that conclusion. All I had to do was to concentrate on the feeling he was eliciting in me, and how amazing his body felt in my hands.

While he caressed my breasts, my hands again stroked his thighs. I could feel his muscles move under my hands. He, in turn, ran his hands between my legs. Fluttering his fingers over me made my body tighten more, and my breath quickened when his fingers brushed against my clit.

"Kian." I moaned as his finger zeroed in on my nub, making it sensitive to his expert touch.

"You like that?" he asked quietly. When I nodded, his fingers slipped inside of me. At this angle, he was in the perfect position to hit my G-spot. He stroked me while his thumb continued to brush against my clit.

I groaned, "I'm so close baby. Don't stop."

I felt his cock rub against my back as I rocked against his fingers.

"I'm not going to stop. I want you to come hard for me."

The orgasm hit me by surprise, one second it wasn't there and the next I was riding the crest while my hips bucked against his hands. My core tightened around his fingers in small eruptions, the spasms running from my toes to my head and back again. And his fingers continued to pleasure me until he knew I was utterly spent.

His arms raised and tightened around me.

I purred his name, "Oh Kian. You do that so well."

He lifted my chin, and his mouth found mine. Our tongues met and brought pleasure and exploration.

"I want you in my bed now," his voice rasped. He stood gracefully and wrapped a towel around me. His hands gently dried me with the towel, making my skin feel electric.

"Go get into bed before you get cold," he instructed. I did as he said and heard the plug being pulled from the drain. The gurgling sound from the tub draining its water made me smile. He was so practical.

Pulling the sheet and comforter away, I tossed the towel on the nearby chair and slid into his bed. The sheets were cold, and my body was already cooling down. I still felt the incredible calmness that an orgasm always brought to me. Kian stood by the bed in a flash. His towel landed in a heap on top of mine.

"Scoot over," he said as he bent. I complied, and he slipped smoothly in next to me.

Strong, warm arms enveloped me. I had decided it was okay to feel vulnerable with Kian. My heart was opening to him. I hoped I wasn't romanticizing it, but I felt he was releasing to me too.

He faced me in bed and lifted one on my legs to wrap around his hip. In this position, our parts were pressed together. He still had his erection, and he pressed it down, so it lay firmly in between my legs. He moved his hips back and forth, and his cock rubbed against me. I reached down and positioned him so it would rub against my still swollen and sensitive clit.

I hissed air between my teeth and pressed against him. "That feels good baby. You're making me wet again."

Smiling he murmured into my mouth, "That's the way I always want you. Wet and wanting me."

His erection became slippery between my legs enabling him to push further against me.

Suddenly, he lay there panting. "Don't move he whispered, or this is all ending right now."

I didn't twitch a muscle. I too had been close. And my body ached to continue to move my hips against him. I didn't though.

He kissed me and slowly disengaged himself from me. I laid there panting, needing his touch more than ever. Positioning himself on his elbow, he stripped the covers off us. This was a good idea because I had grown increasingly warmer. He trailed a finger down between my breasts. They ached for his touch, and I whimpered as his fingers came close to a nipple. It stood straight out from my body, and even in low light, I could see that it was swollen.

His head lowered, and I whimpered again in anticipation. Holding my nipple between his thumb and forefinger, he lifted slightly and slowly began licking and sucking my nipple with his tongue. My whimpers turned into moans. His teeth nipped at me, and he bit just hard enough to meet that delicious junction of pleasure and pain. He knew how to drive me out of my mind. He played with both breasts as his hips slowly rocked against me. His straining hard-on pushed against me, and he moved slowly toward my center. When he was close enough, I spread myself wide for him.

By this time, he was over me and in between my legs. Leaning on his elbows, he looked into my eyes. "Do you want my cock?" He nipped at my mouth with his lips. Grabbing my lower lip between his teeth and pulling gently.

"Yes. I want it hard. I want you now," I whispered.

Kian lifted one of my legs over onto his shoulder. "I want to go deep baby. I need you so badly. All I want to do is to slam inside and take you."

I reached in between us and cupped his sack. I squeezed him gently, and it was his turn to gasp.

"Fuck me hard," I commanded.

That was all it took. I came almost immediately with his first few thrusts. It made me breathless. He slowed as I rode the orgasm, but then he began again in earnest. I couldn't find a breath. They all eluded me. The pleasure of his lovemaking was so incredibly intense it robbed me of all my senses. The only world that existed for me now was our two bodies meeting and combining. Every movement was a sheer pleasure for our gratification.

I could tell he was so close to his release, but he was fighting it. He did not want to give in. Suddenly his body stilled, and he let a low guttural groan. He whispered, "*A stór mo chroí*, my heart," as his final release came. Finding my mouth, his kiss was deep a full of satisfaction.

Our bodies were slick with perspiration, and when he rolled over, he moved the covers over us. "Baby, I am spent. You have utterly pulled everything out of me."

I rolled over and put my head on his shoulder. "You have satiated me." I kissed his neck. "Thank you." I murmured into his ear.

"No, thank you, my love. You give yourself so freely to me. You are so beautiful. I feel the need to worship your body."

I loved his words. A lot. Even though I knew they were only after-glow pillow talk, they still meant so much to me.

We cuddled closer, and sleep took us both.

CHAPTER 35

The barking dogs woke us both. Kian scrubbed his face with his hands. The dogs were running from the living room into the bedroom, back and forth. They were excited and bothered about something.

"Maybe it's a prowler. Koa behaved like that the other night," I said sleepily glancing at the clock, which read three. I was doomed, a night full of rest was not going to be mine -- ever.

Butch came up on Kian's side of the bed and laid his massive paws on his arms. When he didn't get the reaction he expected, he tugged on the comforter with his teeth.

"Okay, okay," Kian grumbled reluctantly. Grabbing his jeans from the bathroom, he slid into them and padded out to the living room. All I heard was "Oh fuck! The back yard is on fire! Christina, quickly! Get dressed!"

I never leaped out of bed faster. I was in the bathroom throwing on my jeans and sweater and never mind the underwear. Shoes? Where were my shoes? I turned the light on and found them behind the door. After sliding my feet into them, I ran out to the living room.

Kian was already in the back yard with the garden hose, but the flames were moving too quickly. The fire had already jumped the nearby fence and was quickly eating up the dry grass at the back of his property.

"Call 911!" he shouted. "I need to get the dogs out of the clinic."

I ran back into the house and looked for my purse to find my phone. Damn it! Where did I leave it? Then I noticed a phone sitting on a side table in the living room. Thankfully, Kian had a landline. Quickly dialing, the operator answered.

"We have a fire in the back yard. We need fire engines immediately!" I tried to keep my voice calm as I listened to the operator. She wanted me to confirm the address. How the hell did I know what street he lived on? I saw my purse lying on the couch and dived for it. My phone list was in my favorites file. Confirming the address, the operator indicated the fire trucks had been dispatched.

Running back outside, I almost cried out, the flames were right at the edge of the dog runs. Kian was nowhere in my range of sight, and I guessed he was inside the clinic.

I ran to the door and called to him. "The fire department is on their way. The fire is already past your property line. What can I do?"

"I'm back here. I need to move these dogs quickly. Put my dogs into the back of my pickup truck. Tell them to stay. They'll stay there. I don't want them to get hurt as I try to move these dogs."

"Okay." I turned and called to the dogs.

They were running around making a huge racket. Thankfully, the dogs listened to me when I called them. I scooped up Koa and led the rest of the dogs out the front door."

Lifting down the back tailgate of Kian's truck wasn't easy, but when I finally could wrench it away, I again called to the dogs. They complied quickly, and I closed the tailgate locking it in place again.

"Stay. Sit," I said as Kian had instructed. And what do you know, they all sat down to wait.

I put Koa into his dog carrier in the back of my SUV and turned back to the front door. Kian came out toward me carrying the pregnant lab.

"She's gone into labor. I need you to stay with her and help her. Let me lay her on the back of your SUV," he called to me as he crossed the threshold of his front door.

He held the pregnant dog in his arms and waited for me to lift Koa's kennel out of the back. I laid a blanket down, and he set her down gently. I was going to say something light about not knowing anything about birthing puppies. But this was not the time or the place. The worry on his face was evident.

He grabbed my upper arms and stared directly at me. "Promise to stay here. I need you to stay and help her." He turned toward the house again.

"Please be careful Kian. Please be…" I don't think he heard me. He was running back inside.

The smoke was getting thick. Where were the fire trucks? I saw a truck pull out of his neighbor's driveway and head toward me. The truck came to a jarring stop next to Kian's truck.

A man, about Kian's age, jumped out of the truck. "I'm here to help!"

"He's in the back trying to get the dogs out. Please help him!"

The other neighboring house was also backing out their truck. The cavalry was coming!

My charge started whimpering and wagging her tail. She wanted to get out. I immediately blocked her with my body. "No baby. You need to stay here, honey. Come lay down." I stroked her body and urged her to lie down again. I didn't know what I was doing!

The new truck pulled up. An older man and woman jumped out, just as the first younger man carried out one of the dogs. He put him in the back seat of his vehicle.

"Ed," he said to the older man, "can you take Kian's pickup to the main highway? He wants his dogs out of here. I think we can put the rest into my truck and Christina's SUV."

"How bad is it Bob?" Ed asked.

"Bad," Bob said.

Ed nodded. "Alice can take his truck. Let's use mine for anything else."

Kian staggered out, with a large dog. Bob ran up to him. "We need to move faster. The clinic is…" He started a coughing fit. I noticed his clothes were singed.

"Com'on guys. Kian, where are the keys?" Ed asked.

Kian fished in his pocket and threw his keys at Ed who in turn tossed them to Alice.

The two men went into the house. Kian moved to follow, and he called out to me. "When the puppies come, rub them briskly in a towel to make sure they are breathing and then lay them next to her. She'll know what to do."

"Okay. Hurry, and be …" Again, he didn't hear me.

I saw the flashing lights of two fire engines coming up the road. Finally, I thought. Behind them, another truck was close. As the vehicle drew closer, I recognized it. Annie and Frank were inside.

I called to them, "The fire is in the back. They are trying to save the dogs in the clinic."

The firemen nodded. Some of them ran into the house, the others unfurled a long fire hose. I realized at that moment, the second fire engine was a water truck.

Frank followed the men into the house and Annie joined me at the back of the SUV. She looked over my shoulder just as a puppy was making its appearance.

"Oh, Annie! Do you have any towels?" I cried.

"I do!" She ran over to her truck and pulled out two bath-sized towels. She handed them to me. "They are clean too!"

I lifted the newly born puppy and held it in inside the towel. I rubbed briskly as Kian had told me to, and I could see the small newborn opening its mouth to breath. I laid it next to its momma, and sure enough, she took over and began to clean the puppy.

"Oh, my gosh!" Tears ran down my face. I turned to Annie, "How did you guys know about the fire?"

Annie gently put her arm around my waist, "Frank listens to the police scanner. He heard the call come in."

We both turned when we heard the large crack. The roof of the house was on fire. One of the firemen approached us. "Ladies, you're going to have to move your vehicle. It's about to turn into an inferno here, and it's not safe."

I stuttered, "I can't... Puppies," I said as a way of explanation.

Annie patted me on the back. "You climb into the back seat and keep your eyes on the mommy, I'll move you down to the highway. I called Michael. He's on his way too."

Everything went dark. The fire had claimed the electrical power pole and the outside flood lights all shut-off. I heard more thunderous cracks and cries of men.

"Oh, Annie! Someone is hurt!" I moved to run to the house.

She pulled and held onto my sweater. "You're not going anywhere!" she commanded. "Get into the back seat now! We need to get to the main road. We are in the way!" Shoving me into the back seat none too gently, she closed the door on my ass.

She sat down in the front seat and yelled, "Keys?"

I dug in my jeans pocket and pulled them out. Handing them to her, I asked, "Are you afraid?"

"Damn straight I am. But if we stay here we risk hurting the effort more than helping."

Lights from the fire truck came on, and they bathed the front of the house as we pulled away. At the last glimpse, I could see a man being dragged out of the house by two firemen. He held a dog in his arms.

Two paramedic trucks passed us as we moved slowly down the utility road. I leaned over the back seat as number two, three, and four were delivered in rapid succession. Annie pulled us over on the main highway behind Kian's truck.

Alice and Annie knew each other, and as we stood there to wait, I kept a firm eye on the new momma as delivered number five and six.

Michael pulled up shortly after we arrived. He was driving Elizabeth's new Land Rover, and I was surprised she was not with him.

"She's at home. This is too dangerous," he indicated.

I agreed. When the dogs in the back of Kian's truck saw Michael, they became restless. He jumped up into the truck and calmed them.

"Do you know what's taking so long?" he asked.

"The house lost power shortly before we left," I said. From our vantage point, we could see the fire glowing, and the lights from the fire truck illuminated the area.

Another two fire trucks arrived.

"They are trying to contain it here. Since there are two homes so near, they are working very hard, so it doesn't spread," Annie said mostly to Alice who looked upset.

"We're fortunate, there is no wind up here tonight. Usually, the wind blows right off the mountain in this area," Michael observed.

I didn't feel like chitchat. We comforted the dogs as much as possible.

Finally, the pickup trucks and an ambulance came down the utility road. All of us strained to see who was inside the trucks and if anyone was in the ambulance.

I cried out when I saw Kian sitting inside the ambulance. An oxygen mask was around his face, and his shirt was off. The ambulance stopped on the highway, and I ran around to the back door flinging it open.

"Kian!"

"He lifted the mask and coughed, "I'm alright!"

"No, you're not! You have oxygen and... and..." I paused because that's when I noticed a burn mark on the back of his shoulder. "Oh, Kian, you've been injured!"

"I'm okay. It hurts like shit. But, I'm okay," he answered.

"I'm coming with you!" I jumped into the back.

"Miss, you can't just ride along." The paramedic tried to tell me.

"Watch me. Close the door and tell the driver to go," I insisted.

Annie popped her head in, "We'll take the dogs to the clinic. Michael will take Koa."

Kian lifted the mask off his face again, "Leonard is going to meet you there. I've called him. He's close by at Lori's house. Ask him to have a look at each of the dogs. Some of them may need oxygen too. How is our new momma?" he started coughing again, and I helped him put the mask back on.

Annie held up seven fingers, "I think she's done now. We'll take care of all of them." She smiled at him and then lifted her eyes to me. "Take good care of him, Christina. We need him."

The paramedic shook his head but knew he was outnumbered.

The trip to the hospital took no time at all. Kian had not taken the time to grab his wallet, but everyone knew the town veterinarian, so his treatment wasn't halted as the staff completed the endless paperwork. I had stuffed my wallet into my jeans pocket with my phone when I ran out of the house with Koa. I offered to guarantee any treatment he needed, but the admittance nurse just smiled at me and let me know they had it handled.

They didn't allow me to follow the gurney down the hall insisting that I stay in the waiting room. Have I ever mentioned that I am not patient? I called Michael, and he confirmed all the dogs were okay. I breathed a sigh of relief. I needed to get word to Kian somehow.

Approaching the nurse on duty, I asked if she could get a message to him. She came back with even better news. He'd been asking for me and was getting quite riled up when they wouldn't let me back to see him.

My spirits were raised when I heard the comment. I followed the nurse back to the room and found him lying on his stomach on an examination table.

"Miss Hoffman?" The doctor looked up at me. "Our patient insisted on your presence. I hope you're not squeamish. You can take a chair over there in the corner."

Kian's first words for me, "Have you heard from anyone at the hospital?"

"Yes," I answered. "All the dogs are safe. I spoke with Michael. He said Leonard checked all of them thoroughly. Some of them were scared, but they all were doing okay."

It was his turn to breathe a sigh of relief. "Good." He yelled out in pain, "Hey doc! Do you need to be so rough? Shit, this hurts like a mother fucker!"

The doctor who was treating him said, "Be glad it hurts so bad that means it's more superficial than deep. You have a second-degree burn on your shoulder, and it's going to hurt for a while, but it should heal without any problem. I'm more worried about the smoke inhalation you suffered from. You spent too much time breathing the smoke."

Both the doctor and nurse worked efficiently. After treating his shoulder, they applied a dressing over the injury.

"I want you to go for breathing treatments for the next several days as a precaution. You'll need to go to your regular physician tomorrow or urgent care, don't wait for Monday. This type of injury can get infected easily. You need to take it easy for a few days too." The doctor held his hand up to stop him from protesting. "Don't start with me."

Kian nodded begrudgingly. The doctor helped him sit up.

"The nurse will get your paperwork signed off, and then you can go." Both the nurse and doctor left the room.

I pulled my phone out of my pocket and pressed Michael's name. "Hey, Kian's ready to be discharged. We don't have a car."

Michael chuckled on the other end, "Annie dropped your SUV off at the hospital. She gave the ER attendant the keys. I'm just getting home now. How is he?"

"Second-degree burn on his shoulder and perhaps some smoke damage in his lungs," I said.

"No fucking smoke damage in my lungs," he said while he coughed.

I gave him a disapproving look as I pressed my lips together, and continued my conversation with Michael. "As I said, the doctor said there might be some lung damage, and he is to have some breathing treatments."

My brother chuckled, "Oh, my little sister, you have your hands full, don't you? I'll talk to you in the morning."

Looking up at the clock on the wall, which read seven a.m., it was already morning.

The nurse entered the room with a wheelchair and paperwork for Kian to sign. After all the paperwork had been finished, I retrieved the Cadillac. The nurse and I helped Kian into the front seat and all the while, he hissed air through his front teeth. This was with the pain shot the doctor had given him. This wasn't going to be pretty.

When I situated myself behind the steering wheel again, he turned to me slowly.

"I guess we should go back to my place. I need to get cleaned up and get to work," he said.

I gave him a slow stare. "Seriously Kian? What house were you planning on going back to? You can go see it later, to see what's left of it. For now, we'll go back to the cabin and get you cleaned up. I need to put some underwear on."

He laughed and laughed, "Oh sweetlin', do not make me laugh, it hurts too much. Is this the longest you've ever been dressed without underwear on?"

"It's not funny. My girl parts are rubbing against my rough jeans."

He continued to chuckle, "Don't tell me that. I am in no position to help you!"

"Kian," I said trying to use a disapproving tone, but I couldn't convince myself either, and laughed along with him. "Oh it's not funny, it's actually tragic."

He leaned over to me, and I could see the laughter tears in his eyes. "No, it's not a disaster. All that burned are things. The dogs are okay, you and I are fine, that's all that matters."

I kissed him, "You're right, that's what counts."

CHAPTER 36

Kian protested when I put him into Elizabeth's room in the cabin. First, though, I drew him a bath and bathed him everywhere except around the dressing. He smelled of smoke. His clothes were ruined. I would have to run to the local store later to find some substitutes.

I was tired and sore, but not nearly as worn-out as he was. The pain medication started to take effect, and I had him in bed before he knew what was happening. Elizabeth's bed was bigger and better suited for Kian. I propped pillows around him to pad his shoulder. He could barely keep his eyes open. I thought he fell asleep once and moved off the bed to creep away, but he grabbed my arm to pull me down again.

"Don't leave. Come lay with me for a while. I know you're tired too," he murmured sleepily.

I was beyond exhausted at this point, and there was too much to do today. It was Friday. I needed to contact the FBI agents to talk to them about the transfer of the blackmail money. I didn't know what they intended to do, but I planned to pay the money. Those pictures could not be released on the internet.

I tried not to sigh too loudly and sat again on the bed. Stretching out along his length, he spooned against me, draping his injured arm over me. I closed my eyes and drifted off to sleep.

An hour later, I woke to his soft snores. I moved quietly and tried not to jostle him, replacing my body with a big pillow. He wrapped himself around the pillow and continued to sleep.

Jumping into the shower, I washed every inch of my body twice. My hair was smoke filled and smelled just as bad as Kian's.

After dressing in a pair of dress pants and a blouse, I searched for my phone. There were two messages from Robert. I listened to his voicemails, and apparently, the FBI had been trying to reach me. I wondered why they didn't just call me. Then I checked the phone, there were six missed calls from them last night. Oh, I guess the Feds didn't do voice mails.

There was also a text message from JuJu, and it contained only one word. *Juneau*. Okay, and now I was supposed to become a mind reader.

I called Robert. He answered immediately.

"Where have you been?" demanded Robert. His face fell when I described the night's events.

"Are you okay? Is everyone okay? The dogs? Kian?" he asked.

"Everyone, Kian, dogs, and me, we are all okay. Kian suffered a burn on his shoulder when part of the roof collapsed in the clinic, but they could reach all the dogs. The poor dogs were terrified of the fire, and the only exit had partially caved in from the heat."

"Oh, girl! What you get yourself tangled up into."

"Robert, who knows right now. You know that we've had wildfires up here. We had one just the day before, and it destroyed a big barn. Frank and the Feds will investigate it. Speaking of them, have you heard from the FBI agents? They called me, but didn't leave any messages."

"I did," he said. "They are balking at paying the ransom."

"What the hell Robert? I want it paid. I do not want those pictures released."

He let out a long breath. I could always tell when he didn't want to reveal something. "They feel if you give into his demands, he is just going to release the pictures anyway and you'll be five million dollars poorer and still have to face the fallout."

I gave a sigh of exasperation, "It's easy for them to say that. Their reputation and integrity are not on the line. It's all me. I will be the laughing stock of Silicon Valley, not to mention the toll it will take on my parents and grandmother. I will not allow that, ever. If we can stop it, then I say let's try!"

"Christina, think about this clearly. The pictures plainly show you are not participating. Everyone who has seen them indicates that you undoubtedly appear to be drugged."

"The pictures are crude and pornographic! I could give a fuck what people think about me in the pictures, but I will not drag my family into this. I can go away until everything dies down. The embarrassment caused to them would be immeasurable." The harshness in my voice was distinct. "Damn it, Robert, you know how this will affect them. We need to do everything we can to stop it."

"And that's what the FBI is trying to do. They don't want the pictures released either."

"It certainly doesn't look that way to me. Sure, if the images are released, they say oh well, and go on to their next case!"

Robert became quiet, and this usually meant he was tired of arguing with me. "Look, Christina, both agents feel they are close to tracking this all back to Binder. He thinks he's smart, but even the clever ones always leave a trail. They are close. Please consider listening to their advice."

I pursed my lips together, "I want to meet with them today."

"I can arrange that," Robert said. "Let me give them a call now, and I'll get back to you, okay?"

"Alright."

I went into the kitchen to make coffee, which I should have done an hour ago. Now I needed it. After the first sip of coffee, I felt the first hunger pains. I missed having Koa too.

My phone rang again. "What?" I answered the phone harshly.

I smiled when I heard Kian's voice. He used the landline in Elizabeth's cabin. "Hey, good morning woman. Can you make me some coffee? I have a terrible pain medication hangover."

I went into the bedroom with a mug of coffee.

"How are you feeling? Any pain?" I asked, setting the cup down on the nightstand.

"I feel awful. I hurt, and my head is fuzzy. I need to get up and get to work." He moved to sit up and then slipped down against the pillows again.

"I think you should stay in bed for a while. I'll make you some breakfast, and that should settle your stomach. I can give you something to make your headache go away. Would you like that?"

He nodded yes. I laughed to myself. My big hero. I retrieved the ibuprofen and a cup of water.

"Do you want these or one of the pain pills the doctor sent home with you?" I waved the pill bottle at him.

"No," he said firmly, "I definitely do not want those pain pills, damn, they knocked me out. The other should be okay."

"I know the pain pills are strong. I had a hard time getting you out of the bathtub."

He sat up slowly and took the ibuprofen. "Did you? I don't remember that. All I remember is you bathing me. Thank you, by the way, in case I didn't thank you earlier. I appreciate you coming to the hospital with me. I remember you telling me the dogs are okay. Do I recall that correctly?"

I sat next to him. "Yes, Michael called to let us know they were all okay. Leonard is taking care of them. By the way, why wasn't Leonard there at the house last night?"

Kian rubbed his hand over his day-old beard. "Leonard stays most nights at his girlfriend's house. He just keeps his stuff at my place." His hands rubbed his face again, "Damn, I wonder if there was anything left of the house. When I left in the ambulance, my whole house was ablaze."

My arm went around his waist. I didn't want to touch his shoulder. "I'm so sorry Kian that you lost your house."

"It was just a house sweetlin'. That's all. I'm thankful you're okay, and all the dogs. I would have never forgiven myself if something happened to you," he murmured against my hair.

"I feel the same way. When I saw the firemen carry you out, I was sick with worry."

"Were you?" He gazed at me, and I was lost once again in those blue pools.

"Yes."

We sat there for a few minutes in the quiet. No dog. No other people. Just us. He brushed the hair away from my face and cupped my cheek with his palm.

"*A grá*," he said so softly and kissed me.

I knew the translation of those words. I didn't have to ask. I also didn't know what to think. We couldn't do this. Not if I had to leave. Oh, I hoped I didn't have to go. I so wanted to use those words with Kian. Did it mean I was in love with him? Where did it come from? How?

CHAPTER 37

Fortunately, Kian had extra clothing at the hospital. One of the technicians drove them over in Kian's truck with Koa. I was happy to be reunited with my dog. Kian was glad to be finally dressed again. He insisted on visiting his doctor by himself, and he had to go to the clinic to check on all the dogs. I made plans to stop at the market and stock up the refrigerator. Kian was now homeless and I told him sleeping at the animal hospital was not an option.

I verified with Elizabeth, and she was more than happy to lend him the use of the cabin. The clinic was now gone so the dogs he had been treating would stay at the hospital in town. His other dogs would be brought back to the cabin in the evening. Kian and I would be living together, at least in the interim.

I also made plans to have a meeting with the FBI agents at police headquarters. Robert had spoken with them, and he was driving up to be here for the afternoon. It would be a busy day.

Finally, Kian agreed to allow JuJu to buy some clothes for him. She could have all the shopping done in the afternoon and courier it to us.

Figuring that we would have a busy house, I arranged with Vincenzo's to cater in dinner. I knew Michael and Elizabeth would come by, and figured others would stop by too.

Robert was waiting for me at the police station when I arrived. He had a grim look on his face. I knew him too well, hi look spelled bad news.

"What is it?" I asked as he took my elbow and lead me into the lobby.

"It's not good."

I rolled my eyes. Great. Just great.

We were ushered into a private conference room where we were joined by the agents and Frank.

Agent Martin began, "We are also investigating the two wildfires."

"Really?" The concern in my voice and face was evident.

"We think the fire, the dog fighting ring, your blackmail, and break-in are all connected," Frank said.

"How?" I looked at Robert, and he nodded his head. "And shouldn't Kian be here? It was his house that was destroyed."

Agent Martin cleared her throat, "This is true. We spoke to him earlier in the day. He let us know that he still has Mayor Busch's dogs."

"He hadn't told you that? I thought he did," my voice was incredulous. Kian and I would have a serious talk when I saw him next.

"No," she shook her head, "he didn't, until now. We think everything is related because the wildfire which began the day before yesterday, burned down Mayor Busch's home and barn."

The statement surprised me, "Both the house and barn? They didn't mention it in the news!"

"Right. We suppressed the news," Agent Goings commented. "We had a chance to search the rubble of the barn, and there is evidence that this was most likely the site of the ring. A few telltale signs were left behind in their haste. We have not been able to contact Mayor Busch or Mr. Binder. They both seem to have disappeared."

Agent Martin continued, "We are pursuing some leads. Mayor Busch also owns property in Southern California near the Mexican border."

"The interesting thing is that Kian had cameras installed in the front of his house and driveway a few weeks ago when the trouble with Mayor Busch began," Frank said. "The cameras were motion-activated. We think we may have caught some visual clues from last night. Our lab is examining the images to see if we can clearly see the vehicle or license plate. We think it may be Mayor Busch's truck."

I had no idea Kian was so technically savvy.

"Were the cameras working the night the dog was shot?" I asked.

All three nodded their heads. "Yes. And we're examining that video feed too," Frank remarked. "Those videos are proving key in our investigation."

"Wouldn't it be stupid of the Mayor to use his own truck?" I asked. "He drives a very recognizable pickup."

Frank grinned, "Arrogance always gets them in the end. They always figure they will never be caught."

Robert spoke up at this point, "The problem is Christina, no one is answering the phone number we were given to pay the blackmail payment."

"What?" I had almost forgotten about the ransom. "What do you mean? How inept are these fools? No one is answering the phone? So where does that leave me?"

Robert frowned. "I'm afraid, we don't know where to pay. Remember we weren't given the instructions in the note. We only had instructions to call the number today."

"Oh great!" I rose and paced around the long table. "This is just great. By calling in the FBI, we effectively scared them off! Wonderful."

Robert reached out for my hand to still me. "We still may hear from them. This doesn't mean we will stop trying to contact them. The agents agree with us. If we can get more information from them on where to send the money, they said they might be able to narrow down their whereabouts."

I sat back down again. "Okay, let's be realistic about this. If Mayor Busch owns property near the border, it will be very easy for them to slip across to Mexico, and believe me, the internet works just fine in Mexico too!" I scrubbed my face with my hands.

The reality of me leaving was coming closer and closer. I didn't want to leave. Shit.

Agent Martin stretched her hand toward me. "Please Christina, don't think all is lost. We still have options and avenues to pursue. This is not over by any means. We have an excellent forensics team, and they are going over every inch of the barn. We have also searched Binder's home. It appears he has hasn't been there in days. We may have found some evidence that he shot the pictures of you. We don't think this is the first time he has done this because the couple with you in the photos are in some of the other images we found. Apparently, he is an experienced blackmailer."

"We also spoke with his co-workers at his firm," Agent Goings remarked. "He had bragged to a few of them that you were dating him."

I lifted my eyebrows, "He was living in quite the fantasy world then."

Robert laughed, "Yes, he was. As if you'd ever be really interested in him."

"You're right there. Son of a bitch!" I cursed.

The agents had given me a lot to think about during the drive back to the cabin after I completed my shopping. I did have fun at the supermarket picking up man stuff, like razors, shaving cream, and a toothbrush. I felt so bad for Kian. He had driven to his property and told me everything was gone. But only he would think of his neighbors. Their homes had been saved.

Staring at him through the phone I said softly when he showed me the devastation, "Everything can be rebuilt."

The grim look on his face, however, told me he had his doubts.

"Come on home Kian. We'll have a nice meal and talk about our day," I said slowly.

"I'm not very hungry," he said. I could see the tears forming in his eyes.

"Then come home for me. Would you do it for me?"

He let out a sigh, and there was a long pause. "All my dreams went up in smoke. Damn, my dogs could have been hurt or worst yet, killed. If I get my hands on the person who did this, I will snuff their life out." He said it with such vehemence, I felt he meant the words. "Not everything can be rebuilt, Christina. We had love and hope here. Now it's gone. All gone. It took so much work to put it all together. So much sweat, and it's all gone now." His face showed the terrible shadows of exhaustion and hopelessness.

"Please, Kian. Get into your truck and be with me. I need you here tonight. Do you understand?"

"Yes. I'll be there."

I blew out a big sigh of relief. This was not going to be easy. Of course, he would rebuild with my help. Wasn't that what having money was for to be able to rebuild something that was taken away? I said a quick prayer to be granted both strength and patience.

He looked tired when he arrived at the cabin and didn't look happy when he saw the gang. He pulled me into the bedroom so we could speak alone.

"I wasn't expecting everyone to be here," he said as he sat on the bed and pulled his t-shirt over his head. The doctor had re-dressed his bandage today. He grabbed a new t-shirt from the pile at the end of the bed and put it on.

"I'm sorry Kian. They are all worried about us. They are here to lend their support." I tilted his chin up so our eyes could meet, "You know, like family?"

"I'm drained."

"Come on out and have a bite to eat. I had some Italian catered tonight so we wouldn't have to fuss with the cooking or cleaning. Paper plates, plastic cups, everything is disposable. Easy button pressed. After you eat, excuse yourself and go to bed. They will understand. I'm sure they won't stay late because this isn't a party."

He brought my hand to his lips and kissed my palm, "You always make so much sense and always sound so reasonable. Thank you for being here for me."

Wrapping his arms around my hips, he pulled me close as he lifted my sweater and planted a kiss on my stomach. My belly fluttered with the tender kisses. He rested his forehead against me, and I bent to kiss the top of his head.

"Everything will be okay Kian," I whispered softly into his hair.

He answered dully, "Okay. Let's eat."

During dinner, Kian got a second wind. He started speaking with everyone about rebuilding his house. He was the most concerned with his Harry's Hounds organization. We all knew he ran it on a shoestring, but not once did he broach the subject of money with me. He did still have the fifty grand from the foundation, and it would help to rebuild. He was so used to doing without and doing with no one's help.

After dinner, everyone went out to the front porch to enjoy the dessert and drink the last glass of wine. Elizabeth stayed with me in the kitchen to clean up the remaining food.

I patted her middle as she leaned with her back against the sink. "I can't believe how pregnant you are! You went from nothing to major!"

She laughed and rubbed her belly, "I know. Nothing fits me anymore. Bras, panties, pants, even my sweaters are tight. I swear this baby is going to be huge."

"It makes sense, both you and Michael are tall. You can't go against the genes."

"Michael is such a mother hen." She smiled but looked wistful, "I love that in him too. Your big brother is the happiest when he is caring for someone. He is always spoiling me with some kind of surprise."

"Caring for someone he loves," I said. "He doesn't do it for everyone. Sure, he is a great guy and does for others, but the smothering thing, that comes from genuine love."

Her laughter had such a twinkling quality to it. It always reminded me of what a fairy might sound like, pure and clean.

"And you seem to have captured someone's heart," she broached lightly.

"I don't know about winning a heart," I countered.

"Oh yes," Elizabeth nodded. "You should see it from the outside, the way he looks at you when you are around him. His expression lights up. Our dear doctor could be quite broody when he wanted. But, when you are around him, he's different. The way he looks at you, well, it's hot."

I waved her off, "Oh, that's only the sexual side of things. Look at him, he's twenty-nine years old, and he is an Adonis."

Elizabeth giggled, "Don't forget that sexy accent too."

I smirked, "Most of that accent is when he wants to play someone or when he wants to be cute. He can alternate between the two accents very easily."

"Does he speak Gaelic? I always thought that was so romantic."

"Yes, he does. Sometimes he talks in his sleep. When he does, it's usually a mixture of Gaelic and English."

"Well, you're practically living with him now, aren't you?"

"I guess so. But, it looks like he is anxious to rebuild his place such as it was."

"A real bachelor pad?"

"Not quite that bad. He is very tidy. His place was very sparse, though. There was a small television across from the couch in the living room. The barest of essentials in the kitchen. Truthfully, I don't think he lost much in the fire. The biggest loss for him was the attached clinic. Now that was where everything was. It was almost like a duplicated veterinary hospital. It was impressive. He even had a special floor installed. I wonder if he had it insured? I bet he didn't. His regular house insurance wouldn't cover something like that either. The additional insurance rider would have been expensive."

Elizabeth buffed her nails on her shirt. "Then it's good he has a really rich girlfriend."

"That's the thing. I'm not sure if he would accept help from me. He had mentioned something to me very briefly today when I tried to broach the subject that he didn't want our relationship muddied. That makes no sense at all!"

"He appears to be a proud man. Nevertheless, he is at the very least smitten with you. I would even propose the 'L' word."

"That's nonsense, Elizabeth. We just met. We've only started dating. There is so much for us to discover about each other."

She raised her eyebrows, "Whatever you say. Remember, I write romance novels. I can recognize the difference between infatuation, lust, and the real thing."

Annie came into the house from the front porch. "Are you two going to join us outside? There is a marvelous sunset happening."

Elizabeth called out to her, "We'll be right there Annie." She turned to me, "I've got to get off my feet. Are we finished here?"

I nodded.

She put her arm around my shoulder and squeezed me. "Give what I said some thought. Watch how he looks at you. Watch his eyes."

Yes, I rolled my eyes. Elizabeth's habit was now firmly mine.

Kian and me? No. This was purely an infatuation on his part. I knew his reputation in town. He had gone through some women since arriving in town. He had broken some hearts too. Gently from what I heard, but broken nonetheless. My heart was not on the auction block. I had to make sure the walls I was good at building stood firm.

Later in bed, after Kian fell asleep I laid there for the longest time thinking about what Elizabeth had said earlier in the evening. She was right, our relationship was moving fast. It reminded me of when I first met Tim. That relationship had gone quickly too, and look where it ended up. I thought Tim loved me too, but it turned out to be a lie. Sure, we were infatuated with each other when we were first together. Then, it changed and became all about the money. He had never understood what I was doing, or in the early days, what I was trying to do.

Every time I thought about it, it made me angry to mull it over. I always came to the same conclusion; the money was more important than I was. All my ex-husband wanted was the quick fix, the immediate gratification. I learned that money could fix just about anything if you threw enough at the problem. I sighed, I had to sleep. Thinking about these problems was not getting me any closer.

As I finally relaxed into Kian enough to bring sleep on, I felt his body shudder.

Oh, no, I thought as the nightmare began all over again.

"Puppies, no. Puppies. Dona' hurt them. I won't let you hurt them!" Kian's voice began softly and then it grew to a shout. His body jerked and shook.

I sat up immediately and shook him. "Kian, Kian! You're dreaming! Wake up, baby. Everything is okay!"

He opened his eyes. "Oh shit. I'm sorry. I'm sorry." He buried his face in the pillow.

I switched the bedside light on, and the bedroom was flooded with light.

"Are you okay?" I rubbed his back.

He turned over slowly. "Yes. I'm sorry. Damn, that dream was so real."

"Was it the same one? About your uncle and the puppies?"

"Kind of, it started out like they normally do, but then suddenly I was fighting with Busch. I mean fighting him like we were in a dog fight ring and we were going after each other. I was trying to keep him from getting at all these dogs that were behind me." He scrubbed at his face, "Shit. It was so real."

"Are you going to be okay? Do you want me to make some tea?"

He smiled and reached for me pulling me down to his chest. "Switch the light off baby. I'll be okay. It just took me by surprise, that's all."

I did as he asked and snuggled back against him.

"I need to stop taking those pain pills because they are giving me the strangest dreams," he chuckled, "I'm afraid I wouldn't be a good drug addict."

"I'm glad for that!" I said.

"I wanted to make love to you tonight. The spirit is willing, but the flesh is too weary. I never thought I'd ever say that."

I kissed his chest. "You go back to sleep. There will be plenty of time for that later."

CHAPTER 38

The FBI concluded their investigation of the fire and confirmed it was not a wildfire as we first supposed. It was definitely manmade as they found evidence of the use of an accelerant. The damage to Busch's house and barn were also arson. Besides, his disappearance made him look guiltier, and fingers pointed in his direction. If only we knew which direction that was. I was sure he and probably Scott, had already skipped across the border.

Kian had the nightmares nightly now. He hesitated to fall asleep because he knew what it would lead to. All the dreams were now a variation on the theme. Often they would include the mayor and the dogs Kian had rescued.

Speaking of the dogs, we had them all living with us in the small cabin. Fortunately, they were well behaved, but Koa wasn't a happy camper. It appeared he felt he needed to compete for my attention with the other dogs. We had also temporarily taken the lab who delivered the puppies the night of the fire. Kian had a foster who had volunteered to take her and the puppies, but she was on vacation when the fire happened, and we waited for her to return.

There were a lot of dogs. Too many. I went from not having any dogs around me, except when I visited Michael, to a house full of dogs. I was in overload. I had to keep a bright outlook though because a depression had come over Kian.

His homeowner insurance was not going to cover the loss of the home clinic, so he lost everything there. He had voiced many times how he was not going to be able to rebuild, and he was so discouraged because there were so many dogs to save. We had not discussed my helping him. I could tell he was not open to it. I couldn't figure out why either.

With the missing Mayor Busch and Scott, the FBI decided to pull back on their probe. We still had not been able to contact anyone with the phone number we were given. The Feds said they'd continue with the investigation on the back burner.

I received a surprise phone call from Kian on Thursday morning, an invitation to lunch.

When I pulled into the driveway of the clinic, he was at the back entrance in an embrace with a petite dark haired woman. The embrace, while not a passionate one, made it evident he was thrilled by the hug. He bent down and kissed her on the forehead. I caught his eyes and noticed he had been crying. He said something to the woman, and she turned to look at me.

She was beautiful. Her facial features were so strikingly delicate she reminded me of a fawn. Her long black hair was held back in a ponytail. Where her face was fragile, her hair was not. I felt sorry for the band that needed to contain her mane. Considerably shorter than Kian, she only went up to his mid-chest. Then she smiled. Even I, who had few jealous tendencies, felt immediately inadequate.

Kian wrapped his arm around this woman and led her over to me as I exited the SUV. I towered over her, feeling gangly and awkward.

He smiled broadly, "Siobhan, this is Christina, the woman I told you about. Christina, this is my sister," he said smiling, obviously delighted to have us meet.

Siobhan held out her hand, "It's good to finally meet you. Kian has gone on and on about you." She gave me another one of her sparkling smiles.

The name and the strong family resemblance finally made it all click. "You dance with the San Francisco Ballet Company. I have seen you many times. It's a pleasure to meet you."

"I'm now a former dancer with the Company. I'm retiring at the end of the month."

Her comment caught me by surprise, "Retiring?"

I couldn't remember how old Kian said she was, but surely, she was too young to retire. Her face was smooth and unlined, almost as if her face had captured her youth to keep it forever."

She gave out a bold laugh, "Yes, I'm retiring. I've been dancing for twenty-two years now. All the abuse I've been dishing out to my body has now caught up with me. Besides, it's time I step aside and allow the younger more agile dancers take my place."

Kian squeezed her around the waist. "They will never replace you! You are a prima ballerina."

"My little brother has blinders on too! So are you ever going to feed me? I'm starving!"

If I imagined that she would eat like a bird, I was wrong and found out when we continued our conversation at lunch. We ended up at the diner across the street, and soon Siobhan was regaling me with stories of Kian when he was young. I also discovered we were the same age. I didn't know if that made me feel better, but she certainly didn't mention that I was dating a much younger man.

"I drove up from San Francisco to see if I could help. I was so happy to hear that all the animals were okay. It is very kind of your sister-in-law to open her home up to Kian," she said.

"Michael and Elizabeth have been great. Wait until you meet them," he said munching on his burger. "In fact, the whole town has been so kind. You are going to love living here."

I almost dropped my fork onto my salad; I didn't, but I know Siobhan caught the surprise in my face.

"I know I will." She patted his hand.

"So you are moving here?" I tried to sound nonchalant.

She nodded and smiled. "A couple of months ago Kian offered to open his home to my children and me until we can get settled. I'm tired of living in metropolitan cities. He convinced me we needed a slower and quieter life. Now with the fire, I'll have to find an apartment in town. I thought of going back to Los Angeles to live with our parents, but that perhaps is a little too drastic. I've danced with many different companies, so it's been hard to put down roots in any one place. My son and daughter are in high school, and I'd like them to be able to attend the same school."

"You don't have much of an accent," I said.

Siobhan laughed with a wicked grin as she too munched on her burger. "I can do an Irish accent for you! But I only bring it out on special occasions," she winked. "I'm not like Kian, who used to use his to pick up women."

"He still does," I winked back at her.

"Now ladies!" he interrupted.

"Oh no, you don't. I'm wise to you my little brother. I will fully inform Christina of all your faults!"

"I can't win here. I should never have introduced you!"

"Well now, she and I will have to compare notes won't we?" Siobhan laughed.

The three of us had a delightful lunch, and at the end, I felt I had found a new friend in Kian's sister. She was going to melt right into our little family we had here.

Later that night, I asked Kian if he was looking forward to having his sister around.

"She's family Christina. Family are the only ones you can truly count on. They'll somehow come through for you no matter what happens."

I sighed contentedly and snuggled on his chest, "You're right. I owe a lot to my family too."

CHAPTER 39

My cell phone jarred me awake. I reached over for Kian and remembered he was going the hospital early. I looked at the screen, and only a number appeared. Strange. No one except my family and close friends had my number. It was a damned wrong number, but to be sure, I answered it anyway.

"Hello," I said in my most stern, don't be a telemarketer, voice.

"Christina Hoffman?" the voice asked tentatively.

"Yes?" I said it against my usual better judgment. "Who is calling?"

"This is Jeff Nevlen from the New York Times. Would you like to make a comment about the photographs of you which appeared this morning on the internet?"

"What?" I sat up in bed. "What did you say? What?"

"Are you saying you don't know about the nude pictures which were released?"

Oh, fuck. I disconnected the call. I quickly switched to the internet browser, and there was my name trending. When I pressed the link, I didn't want to look at the screen. When I opened my eyes, I knew I was done. Utterly finished.

I understood what I had to do. I slipped out of bed and called Robert from Elizabeth's landline in the living room. My phone was now worthless since the number had somehow become compromised.

Robert answered the phone with a muddled voice.

"It's Christina. The pictures were released," I said it quietly. There was no time for recriminations. I had to act quickly now. The clock on the kitchen wall read five. "I've just been woken by a reporter from the New York Times wanting my reaction."

"I'm sorry. How do you want me to handle it?"

"Send security over to my parents and my grandmother. I'm going to call them now, and I'll let you know what we're going to do. The rest of the relatives will have to deal with it on their own."

"Consider it done. Do you want to make a response to the press yet?"

"No. Let me get my family out of the way first, okay?"

Disconnecting the call, I took a deep breath and dialed my parent's number. My mother answered the phone. "Elizabeth? Is everything alright?"

"What?" I asked, then I remembered I was using Elizabeth's landline. "Mom, it's me. Please wake Daddy and have him pick up the extension."

Whether she could hear the tension in my voice or not, she listened to me. It took only a minute, and my Dad's gruff voice was on the phone, "Baby, are you okay?"

Hearing his voice made we want to curl up in a ball and cry, but this was not the time to lick wounds. This was a time to plan, and to execute.

"Mom, Dad, I have some difficult news." As I told them about the pictures, my voice came out in a rush. I looked up and saw Kian standing in the kitchen. He walked over and sat next to me on the couch. I couldn't look him in the eye. If I did, I knew I would lose it all.

"Christina, I'm sure the pictures aren't as bad as you make them out to be. Are you sure you're not overreacting?" Mom said in her practical, no-nonsense voice.

"No Mom. I'm not exaggerating. They are disgusting. I was drugged, and it's evident in the photos, but I'm afraid that's not what people will see. I've already been contacted by a reporter."

Kian began rubbing my back, and I almost told him to stop. I couldn't take the intimate contact. I felt dirty.

"What do you want us to do Christina?" Dad's calm voice interrupted my mother.

I sighed heavily, thankful he was always the reasonable one. "I need you to get Grandma before they get to her. I need you to explain to her what's happening. I will talk to her, but…" I paused trying to catch my breath.

"We can do that." Dad was with the program immediately.

"Robert is sending security to both of your houses. But I think you need to get to her first."

I heard rustling on the other end of the phone. My parents, I loved them. They trusted me enough and took my word that shit was hitting the fan. They understood. Many years ago, we had spoken that something like this could happen and I never believed that it would occur in this way.

I had a home in Hawaii, which was in a small private community fortified with a fence and security. They could have a little peace there and be tucked away from the press. The good news was that my Grandmother loved visiting there.

When I hung up the phone, I turned to Kian.

"Is it bad?" He whispered.

I nodded. The tears were burning my eyes, but I resolved to remain strong and not to cry. This was not going to break me.

He wrapped his arms around me, "We can weather this storm too."

I shook my head, "No. No, we can't Kian. You have no idea. It is going to get far worse than this. I will be the center of the storm. Reporters will descend on this town like a horde of locusts. Anyone who knows me will be at the mercy of the press and the weird onlookers."

I could see the realization hit his eyes, "Are you planning to leave?"

I nodded slowly.

"Why? I don't understand. Why do you have to leave? What does running away accomplish? They will just hunt you down."

"Exactly Kian. They will leave you alone. They will come after me if they can find me. They will leave you alone. I'm the news story. Then after a while, after I become yesterday's news, I'll be able to resurface again. Things won't ever be the same, though. My name will always be tainted with those damn pictures."

I broke away from his arms. I needed to think, and he was making it difficult.

"Christina, leaving is not an answer. We can weather this storm together." He reached out for me, but I stepped back.

"No, it's better this way. You can rebuild your life with your sister, and get your rescue organization back on track. My life and my problems muddy the water too much for you."

He scrubbed his face with his hands and leaning over, he rested his elbows on his knees. "How long?"

"I don't know," I said it quietly and with finality. "It will take time for things to die down. The PR firm I have will work on it."

"And your house? You're just going to leave after you've built your dream house?"

I knew he was grasping at any straw he could find.

"Michael will make sure it's finished. I know I cannot do this to Mintock. I don't want them to be referred to as the town where the rich internet woman lives who had the smutty photographs taken."

"You don't have to do this Christina. There must be another way. Please don't do this to us. We're just beginning here."

Those beautiful blue eyes were swimming with tears.

How could I do this? I had no other choice.

"I just can't stay Kian. Please understand. I need to keep my family safe, and to protect you." I stood up and went into my bedroom to pack.

"I don't need your protection Christina," he bit back.

"You think that now. Do you have any idea what the press is like? They will hound you here, at the hospital, anywhere you go. If I leave, they will spend their time looking for me. I'm the story." I picked up my phone and showed him the internet screen. "Look. Do you see the trending numbers? Do you think this is just going to stop? It's not."

"Where are you going?" his anger rose. He followed me into the bedroom as I pulled out my suitcase. "What the fuck are you doing? Are you leaving today? Have you been planning this all along?"

"I can't tell you where I'm going. The fewer who know, the easier it will be for me," I explained.

"You can't just leave and not tell me where you're going. Do not block me out like this. You're irrational. We can do this together." His face ... no, his eyes pleaded with me.

I felt the wall rebuilding around my heart. This time I would reinforce it with more steel. I wouldn't let anyone tear it down again. I couldn't. My face grew impassive, and I didn't reply.

Kian stared at me. For a moment, I thought he was reaching out to me, but he picked up his jacket. "Fuck this. Fine! Do what you want," he shouted as he turned on his heel and left.

I heard him open the back door, and his truck fired up. I watched from the bedroom window as my heart broke into little pieces.

The tears came then. Yes. They came hard.

By the time I finished packing, my phone had shown over fifty voice mails and texts. As I scrolled through them all, most of them were from numbers I didn't recognize. I had two from JuJu and one from Robert.

The first call was to JuJu. She picked up the phone immediately.

"Hey," she said in a sympathetic voice.

"Hey back at you. So, it's Juneau?" I finally figured out what she meant. She was suggesting I go to Alaska. It was a good idea. The only way into the city was to fly or take a boat. The location would make it more difficult for people to track me down, and it was still in the United States. I liked the city too.

"I have a private plane booked for you out of Sonoma County Airport. They will be ready for you whenever you want. Just give them a call when you leave the house. There's a private car service that will drop a car off for you when you arrive. I'll text the details to you. I found a lovely rental home on the outskirts of town. The landlady is going to leave the house keys under the backdoor mat. I'll email pictures of the place. You'll like it, it's very rustic."

I raised my eyebrows, "Just how rustic?"

"Very."

I pursed my lips, "So God help you JuJu, there better be indoor plumbing!"

"Don't worry Christina, would I do that to you?"

"Yes."

"I didn't. No, I think you'll like it. It's fully furnished, everything is included. The owner rents it out to business people who have to stay in Juneau for long-term visits. It has everything -- internet, electricity, and I think she said the toilet was inside. I'll double check with her."

"JuJu!"

She laughed. "No. I'm sorry. We need to be serious. This is bad. Wow, those are some crazy pictures of you."

"You didn't look at them, did you? Oh, damn, JuJu, I'm so embarrassed now."

"Don't worry."

My voice lowered, "JuJu, those pictures are going to live with me for the rest of my life. I need to figure something out. Damn, they will always be connected to me. I don't know what I'm going to do. My poor parents. My grandmother. I can't believe this."

"I understand Christina. This will give you some time to think. If you want to stay long term, you can change your name and buy a house. Juneau is a small community city, but people can blend in easily. You'll be okay. More importantly, your family will be safe."

The tears started to come again.

"I'm sorry for crying. I don't mean to," I cleared my throat and wiped the tears away. "Okay. So, I'm taking Koa with me. I hope the owner is good with dogs."

"I told her about Koa," she said. "She let me know not to let Koa out at night. The area is rural. There are bears and wolves, and I'm sure lions and tigers too!" Giggling, she blinked innocently at me.

I sighed. JuJu meant well, but I did not appreciate her sense of humor at that moment.

"Will you contact a local veterinarian. Kian is still treating Koa's broken leg. I want a doctor there to continue Koa's treatment."

"Got it. By the way, how is Kian taking your exit?" she asked.

"Not good. He doesn't understand. He thinks we can get through this together. He doesn't realize how this will impact him, his practice, and his rescue organization. Everything that has my name associated with it will be tainted. This way will be better for him. He can tell people we aren't dating, that he barely knows me. They will leave him alone, and he can continue with his life."

"I hope you're right Christina."

"Of course I am. I'll have Michael take me to the airport. I'll let him know to contact you if he needs any help with the contractors on the house. He can always call me, but give him a hand if he needs an onsite person."

"You know you can count on me."

"Thank you JuJu. I'll change the sim card on my phone on the way to the airport and change my number. I'll text the new number to you. Please give it out to only my close family. Don't give the information to my extended family. Most of them can be charmed by a good reporter to give up the number, which is what I think happened," I sighed heavily. "I'll be in touch with you. I'm sure I'll think of a million other things."

"I'm here when you need me. And Christina…" she paused, "I'm very sorry this happened to you."

"Thank you JuJu, me too."

I waited to call Michael because they had been sleeping late. Elizabeth suffered from insomnia during her pregnancy, and he stayed up with her. When I finally called, I could hear the dismay in his voice. Thankfully, my brother understood his crazy sister and knew why I was leaving.

I explained what was happening and that we needed to move quickly. He, like Kian, disagreed with me about my moving. He also thought we could weather the storm together, although he was happy I made arrangements for our parents and grandmother.

Last, I spoke with Robert again. He had already notified the FBI and Frank. They were working on tracing the original photos and the site that had put them up. Robert was sharp and an excellent attorney. He would maneuver through the internet and for the sites located in the United States, threaten to sue them if they didn't remove the pictures. I doubted that he'd be successful at stemming the tide, though. I made him aware of my complete travel plans.

Michael pulled my Cadillac into the cabin's garage. We'd take Elizabeth's Land Rover to the airport. I didn't want to be followed.

After we had left, he reached across for my hand and squeezed it. "Are you sure this is the right thing to do?"

"Yes. Michael, it is. You and Elizabeth should get away for a few days. At least until the reporters discover I'm no longer here."

"Don't worry about us. Frank is going to erect a barricade at the start of the utility road. I let him know you'd pay for private security to monitor the street."

"Yes, of course, I will."

"It's all private property, the road, the beach, anyone caught trespassing can be arrested."

"That's good. Okay. Good plan," I responded. "Hey, stop looking so glum. It's not like you're losing me. I'll be away for a while, that's all."

"When are you coming back then?"

I bit the inside of my cheek. I didn't know the answer to his question. How long would it take for me not to be front-page news? Damn it.

CHAPTER 40

I strapped myself into the airplane seat. Koa sat next to me. One convenient thing about flying private, the flight attendant didn't get all up into your business. There were rules, which had to be followed during take-off, and landing, but everything else was off the table.

Did I want a mimosa? Yes. I did.

I sipped at it slowly, enjoying the taste. It reminded me of New Orleans. Then there was a sour taste in my mouth. That son of a bitch ruined New Orleans for me. I'd never again be able to think with fond memories of the Big Easy. I'd have to rectify that one day. As soon as it was safe to escape the frozen Alaskan wasteland of glacier forests. What was JuJu thinking, sending me to Juneau?

I let the flight attendant know I wasn't hungry and lunch didn't have to be served right away. I would continue to suck down mimosas, though. Maybe I would get drunk then cause a scene at the airport. Yes, that would be just the thing.

I flipped the footrest up on the seat, laid back and cuddled with Koa. I missed Kian and wondered what he would be doing. He'd be at his clinic, fixing all those sweet animals. I wanted to call him and let him know I had made the correct decision.

My softie big brother had tears in his eyes at the airport. I'm glad he had Elizabeth now. He wouldn't miss me as much.

I finished off the second mimosa, and the flight attendant immediately offered me another one. Was she watching me? I felt hungry and asked her to prepare my lunch. I declined the offer of more alcohol and asked for coffee instead.

Koa's nose went up in the air when I was served a delicious piece of salmon with a creamy dill sauce. He managed to score a bite of fish from my plate. I didn't care what Kian said, Koa could have anything he wanted. He was my dog.

Smiling at that thought, I realized how much Koa meant to me. He was a good listener. He heard about all my problems and never once offered up a stupid opinion of disagreement. I wondered if I'd be able to find his brand of dog food in Juneau. I did bring some of the food with me, but anything could be flown into the city.

Desert was just as good too. A heated slice of apple pie with vanilla ice cream. JuJu must have told them about my favorites. The coffee afterward hit the spot, and for the first time in the day, I finally felt relaxed. I stretched out and snoozed for a while. I was so tired. The lack of sleep over the past several weeks finally caught up with me.

When we landed, a representative from the car service company met me on the tarmac with the keys to the car. It was a nice big Cadillac SUV, like the one I drove at home. This one was brand new, though. It smelled of luscious leather. The rep loaded the luggage and Koa's crate in the back and off we went.

I hoped the GPS would take me to the house. JuJu was right, it was on the outskirts of the city, almost where the road ended on the other side of Juneau. Bigger than I anticipated, it was situated right on the water. The view from the front of the home was breathtaking. The serene bay and the majestic mountains with snow on their peaks surrounded me. It was colder too than I thought it would be, but the sun was shining which I had been told was rare. The inside of the house, while being rustic with light pine walls and floors, was outfitted with a sleek modern kitchen. The interior had more of a Norwegian style to it. The furniture, simple and elegant did not detract from the rustic interior. The high vaulted ceilings in the main rooms gave a ski lodge feel to the place. A ranch, rambler style house, it was long because almost every room faced the spectacular view of the bay. I hadn't noticed any other homes nearby, so I guessed it was isolated here, which was exactly what I wanted. I built a fire in the fireplace in the main room off the kitchen and put away the groceries I purchased after leaving the airport. As the house warmed up, I opened a bottle of wine and sat with Koa enjoying the view.

I spoke with my parents and was glad to hear they and my grandmother were getting ready for their flight to Hawaii. JuJu had set them up at the Fairmont in San Francisco since they had reporters camped outside their house earlier in the day. Michael also called and indicated it was a zoo in Mintock. Frank had successfully closed the utility road, which led to all the homes, but it was still a hassle for the residents.

It was one of my cousins who had blabbed and gave the reporter my cell number. It was an innocent mistake.

Michael told me Kian had been furious when he discovered I had gone. "I guess he figured you would swing by the hospital before you headed out of town. I don't know Christina; I think you're making a mistake by not trusting him. I think the two of you could weather this together, but I don't want to get mixed up in your drama with him."

"There is no drama with Kian. It was a nice little fling, and we're done now. It's better for everyone."

"If you say so. I thought you two were good together. Anyone who would take your bullshit had to be a special guy," he said chuckling.

"Michael!" I yelled at him so loud Koa looked up from his nap. I patted him gently, "It's okay baby. Mommy is just dealing with her bothersome brother."

"Gee thanks, Christina. You treat the dog better than me."

"The dog treats me better."

"Don't get your panties in a twist. I'm just teasing you. So, have you heard from Robert or the FBI?"

"No. But they have my new number, I'm sure they'll be in touch as soon as they find anything."

We spoke a bit longer and agreed to connect the following day. After the call, I looked at my watch, I was still on west coast time. Juneau was one hour behind, but that didn't matter. Koa looked up from his nap when I mentioned dinner.

I didn't feel like cooking, but I couldn't very easily order a pizza or run into town for takeout. So, I studied the interior of the refrigerator until I decided upon a grilled cheese sandwich and because it was so cold, I decided to add a can of tomato soup to the menu.

I turned in early and dreamt what was becoming a very familiar dream. Green hills and being surrounded by a bunch of white furry puppies that were climbing all over me. In the dream, I looked up, and Kian was standing over me. He took my hand in his and kissed me on the lips. When I woke with a start, I could almost feel the touch of his mouth on mine. A wave of sadness came over me so suddenly. It washed over me, again and again, like the tide I had watched in the afternoon.

A full moon high in the sky lit the bay with its light. It was beautiful. I touched the window and almost jumped back. Even though the glass was double paned, the window was freezing cold. I wouldn't even dare to open the French door that led to the verandah. This weather was going to take some getting used to. But the tradeoff was the most magnificent view I'd ever seen.

The heater kicked on and off throughout the night, but Koa and I were snuggled together, and we made a toasty pair. We woke to a misty and foggy morning. It was cold, and I put a jacket on to take Koa outside. He made quick business of it and hustled back inside where it was warm.

I hadn't yet looked at the news on the internet or watched television. It was too soon. I was too raw with emotion every time I thought about it. And every time it crossed my mind, I wanted to put my hands around Scott's neck and squeeze the life out of him. This reaction surprised me. I was not a violent person, ever, but there was something about what he had done to me that I couldn't let go. He had violated me in the most disgusting of ways. A wave of nausea overtook me when the visions of those pictures flooded my mind.

And if I didn't think about it too hard, I wouldn't think of Kian either. Of course, Koa was a constant reminder of him. Kian's voice whispering in my ear, his hands moving around my skin, and his kisses, which were so tantalizing. I missed his, "Woman, where is my coffee?" command early in the morning, and when I would finally rouse, he'd bring coffee to me.

Michael told me Kian hadn't asked him for my new telephone number. He had only spoken about what a bother the press was being on the utility road. That hurt. So, I guessed the uproar affected him after all.

I spent days out on the verandah bundled up in my coat, some of them were sunny, but most of the time, the sky would drizzle with a light rain. Sometimes I'd see fishing boats from homes in the area out on the bay. They'd see me and wave but would go on their way. The eagles flying overhead were breathtaking, especially when they would swoop low to catch a fish and carry it off in their sharp talons. When the tide changed, it dramatically uncovered flora in magnificent tide pools ripe for exploration.

It was incredibly lonely too.

I hungered for the sound of other people, and I chatted with JuJu, Michael, and Robert on the phone. Unbelievably, the Wi-Fi signal was strong, and I had no trouble with my phone or computer. Still staying away from the news, I drove into town a couple of times and ate dinner by myself. It almost reminded me of the solitary days I spent when my business started. Fortunately, my financial situation was far better now, and I could afford to eat out. I even hit a few of the tourist spots, but still, I was afraid of being spotted by someone.

Two weeks after I arrived, Koa's appointment with the veterinarian popped up on my calendar. JuJu had found a small, single doctor practice on my side of town.

The clinic was modern and clean. The doctor was from the area. After he had gone to veterinary school in California, he came back up to Alaska to practice. Koa checked out fine. The doctor was very interested in the story of how he was rescued. He said they had the same problem with dog fighting in Juneau. We concluded the problem must be everywhere.

It was determined that Koa could go without a cast and he seemed to be happy to be without it.

"Do you mind if I email a copy of the X-rays to his previous vet? I always like to make sure records are complete. He received excellent care at the other facility. Everything has healed nicely, the doctor said after he brought Koa back to me.

Koa looked remarkable without his cast. He needed a bath and a clip too. The area, which had been covered by the cast, did not smell great. In fact, it reeked.

"Yes. That's not a problem. Go ahead and send the paperwork to Dr. McDermott, in Mintock. I'm sure he's interested in how Koa is doing. Can I schedule a grooming appointment? Do you know of a good groomer in the area?"

The veterinarian rubbed his bearded chin. "We have several in the area. Monica at the front desk can help you with the information. But let's wait a few days for the leg to settle down before you have him groomed. He might limp for a couple of days, but that's a leftover from having the cast on. It will go away. Oh, and keep the exercise to a minimum for about a week. Let his muscles firm up again."

"I will," I promised. I did not tell the doctor that Koa had already been running along the shoreline with the cast on and it was hard enough already to keep him out of the water.

We were both tuckered out after all our activity, and we turned in early to bed. Koa's noxious smell had dissipated somewhat as the evening grew, but it still was a barely tolerable stink, especially when he wanted to cuddle with me. What a mother will do for her child.

The same dream plagued me again on this night too. Instead of ending with a kiss, Kian kept trying to tell me something, but I could not understand what he was saying. It was beyond frustrating for me because in my heart it was something I wanted to know. The puppies were such a fun part of the dream, the little bundles of snow. And Kian's kiss. That was always the most exciting. I would wake up panting and missing his touch.

The dreams made me physically ache. It was bad enough that I thought about Kian all day long, but now he invaded my dreams becoming a regular fixture in them. I wondered if he still had his nightmares. He still hadn't addressed the main problem that caused the bad dream, which was his uncle.

My dream shook me so much, I made a pot of tea, then sat next to the fireplace watching the dawn approach the bay. I climbed back into bed at eight a.m. thoroughly exhausted, knowing I would probably sleep until noon.

How was I going to make it here? I was so lonely. I needed to be with people. I needed to be with Kian. Was this whole thing a mistake? No, I told myself. This was for my family and friends. I needed to go away to protect them.

CHAPTER 41

I awoke to Koa's barking. He stood on the bed ramrod straight, barking with his teeth bared.

Oh, what now? Then I heard the knocking on the door. Very insistent knocking. I put on my robe and glanced at the clock. I had slept in late, it was two in the afternoon. A thought crossed my mind, as I padded out of the bedroom following Koa to the door, I couldn't help but think it could be reporters at the door. How had they found me?

Koa was pawing at the door, and his tail wagged furiously. He bent down to sniff under the door and then dug at the door again, crying and barking.

"Okay boy, back up." I opened the door slightly expecting to see faces and cameras.

It was Kian. I closed the door to take the chain off.

He had found me! How? How had he found me? Which one of my relatives or friends gave me up?

He looked strange standing there in his jeans and leather jacket. The jacket did not offer much protection against the cold. His face looked earnest but determined.

"Open the door Christina and let me in." It was a command and not a request.

I re-opened the door and held it wide. Koa was jumping on him and crying. Kian picked him up in his arms and held him while Koa licked his face thoroughly.

"Okay boy, that's enough. Damn, I missed you, my little guy." He set him back down on the floor.

I stood there with my arms down by my side, not believing he was standing in my living room. I wanted to wrap my arms around him, but something held me back.

He stared at me, looking at me up and down. I must have looked a fright after being up all night and then sleeping in until the early afternoon.

"I missed you too woman." He said it very plainly and didn't move as if he was giving me time to adjust to this new reality.

Tears ran down his face. That's all it took for my waterworks to begin.

He wrapped his arms around me and whispered, "I can't live without you, Christina. I love you. I've been miserable every day you've been gone. Nothing else matters except you. You can go anywhere you want to get away, but I won't let you go alone. There is nothing more important to me. I haven't done anything except think about you every day and night."

My arms went around his shoulders, and I clung tightly to him. "Don't leave me Kian. I need you too much. All I've done here is think about us. I've missed you so much. Koa has missed you. I can't be without you either. I love you too."

"We can do anything together sweetlin'. I will stick with you no matter what happens. Don't leave my side and I'll slay any dragons you have."

"My dragons are mighty."

"There you go lass; my sword is mightier." His words were the music I needed.

His voice alone soothed my soul. It quieted the restlessness I had felt during the past two weeks. We had only known each other a short time, but when we were together, I had discovered a destiny meant for me. He made me complete as if my other half was finally found. Wrapped in his arms, I could think clearly again. I was so wrong to run away from him. Even though I could protect myself, he had my back. We looked out for each other, we were a team. Oh. We. Were. A. Team. Together.

His lips found mine. We kissed the ecstasy of reunion, they were moments of longing, of regret, and of true love. Overflowing with happiness was the only way I could describe my heart.

He kissed my tears away as I did his. Our mouths crushed, tongues teased and explored, teeth bit with an untamed sexuality neither of us had experienced before. He threw off his jacket, and I was out of my robe in an instant.

"Bedroom?" he rasped, as his lips never left my skin.

I pointed directly behind myself. To my amazement, he picked me up in his arms and threw me over his shoulder and carried me like a fireman.

"Put me down Kian," I commanded.

"I'm not listening. I am never letting go of you again!" His voice came with such force and challenge it surprised me into submission.

When he finally found the bedroom, he bent over, and I fell on the bed. I felt giddy. My body was surging with the desire that was pointed straight to my core. He didn't wait. Off came his sweater, and he knelt on the bed between my legs. As he pushed up my nightgown beyond my knees, he laid a trail of kisses. He alternated between soft bites on my flesh and kisses.

The surge of need I felt for him made my body ache. He kissed my knees, and I lifted my hips so he could remove my gown. He spread my legs wide and because I faced a window without curtains, the light came streaming through giving him a complete view of me. His fingers fluttered over me.

I moaned loudly, "Yes. Baby, please, now. I can't wait. I need you now."

Kian unbuttoned his jeans slowly and then pushed them down his hips. Oh, sweet man, he was naked under his pants. He was mine, and I would never let him go.

I reached for him, and he pushed my hand away. "No, not yet. I will take you, but you'll wait."

Oh, I liked this commanding Kian. A lot.

"First, I'll see just how ready you are," he said as he placed his hands on my thighs.

I'm ready! I'm ready! I wanted to scream it, but I didn't move and waited to see what he was planning. I had missed this!

He bent over, and his tongue licked my length. Then he made a curious rounding motion circling my sensitive nub. I was going to come very quickly if he kept up that movement. He sucked at it gently. That was it! I was out of my mind with longing.

"So sweet, so juicy," he murmured. "I could stay here forever, and give you orgasm after orgasm until you pass out. I could make you wait, but I love your sweet nectar too much to deny myself."

His tongue made more several circles around my clit. His motions had me moaning loudly. I was glad there were no neighbor's around because I had a feeling this was going to be a noisy and long afternoon. He moved over me, hovering just above so his cock brushed against me. He rubbed himself back and forth, and I thought my eyes would glaze over from the intense pleasure.

"Oh fuck, that feels so good." His voice growled against my throat.

I lifted my hips. "Do it. I can't wait. Don't make me." My voice was raspy and thick. "Please," I begged. When it came to Kian, I wasn't beyond pleading.

Suddenly he flipped me over on my stomach and pulled my lower half up against him. I felt the force of his erection pressing hotly against me. Then Kian's naked thighs rubbed against mine.

"Lean on your elbows," he commanded.

My butt was now up in the air, and I was dizzy with anticipation. On my knees, I widened my stance. Completely exposed to him, I couldn't help but undulate my hips. I wanted this so much.

One arm wrapped around my hips and I felt his fingers find my clit, and he let out a moan of approval. My clit was swollen and ready to burst. I was on the edge of an orgasm. It wouldn't take much. One more pass of those caressing fingers on me.

I felt the head of his cock pressing against my entrance. He was big. How would he… I didn't have time to finish the thought. He slid into me hard, sheathed up to his balls the with the first push. That was all it took. My body tightened in convulsions. The orgasm hit me hard. Like a cement wall. He took possession of me, and with every push, my body reacted by thrusting against him. I was screaming, moaning, and groaning, making noises that were even unrecognizable to me. The sensations kept coming over and over, my body reacted to his in the only way it knew.

The pleasure was immense, there was nothing else that mattered in this world except him.

"Oh woman, I'm coming baby, it's too soon," he moaned as his hands continued to caress me bringing me to another orgasm.

"Don't stop Kian!" It was my turn to command.

His body stilled and then jerked against me. He was buried so deeply inside of me. I was surprised how long his orgasm lasted, but at the end, we both collapsed on the bed. Both totally spent. Both totally satisfied.

After a few moments, he moved gently off of me.

"Let me get a cloth and clean you," he said in a whisper.

I grabbed his arm. "Don't you dare move out of this bed. We'll worry about that later. I want you right here." I was afraid this was a dream and if he left the room … I knew it was a silly notion, but I couldn't stand the thought of him being away from me.

He smiled, and when I turned over, he wrapped his arms around me, "My sweet *leannán*."

"What does that mean?" I murmured softly.

He tipped my chin up, "*Leannán*, means lover." His kiss was soft.

"I love when you cuddle me like this after we make love," I purred.

Kian whispered, "Then I will always do that, my *a grá*."

Then he smacked my bare bottom!

He sat up, "Do you have any food in this house? I'm starving!"

Laughing, I sat up too. "Of course. Pizza delivery is a little difficult."

"I would say so. Could you have found a place more on the outskirts of nowhere? I didn't think I'd ever find the house."

"Speaking of which, which one of my relatives am I going to have to kill? Who told you my address? Was it Michael? Did you worm it out of him?"

He grinned, "No. None of your people would help me. JuJu, Robert, and Michael were all tight-lipped. I think Elizabeth would have told me, but Michael knowing her hadn't given her the information. Frank is so by the book, he wouldn't give it up either, I almost got it out of Annie though, she felt sorry for me."

"Yes, you and those puppy dog eyes of yours."

"And, remember the Irish accent too, I work miracles with my voice!"

"So Siobhan told me! So how did you finally get it?"

Laughing, he winked at me, "Those lovely records and x-rays your new veterinarian sent me had your address written all over them. Since you were so considerate to agree to release them, the doctor included your personal information too!"

"I don't believe it! Foiled by my own courtesy!"

He pulled me up from the bed and led me to the kitchen. I bent for a robe, and he snatched it from my hands, throwing it back on the bed.

"Let's be naked for a while."

"I don't like to cook in the nude."

He pulled me into his arms and nuzzled my neck. "Let's live a little on the wild side, shall we? I like to smack your ass when I get the feeling."

I spanked his bottom. "What's good for you, I can do too!"

He growled in my ear, "Now that's just going to get me hard again."

"One can hope for big things," I smirked.

"Oh, I've got big things for you. Feed me first and let's see what happens. Have you ever made love on a kitchen table?" He took my hand, and we went to rummage for food.

At first, I felt odd walking around the kitchen naked, but Kian's eyes glowed when he looked at me. He made me feel beautiful even though my thighs still rubbed together. Later that evening after we had a second round of lovemaking, I watched Kian stand in front of the large window looking out over the bay. The moon shone enough light into the room, and I could see his outline clearly, including his glorious firm ass. I loved squeezing his butt.

He turned and gazed over at me, then climbed back into bed. He arms went around me, and I laid my head on his chest.

"It's so beautiful here, and so peaceful," he murmured while he stroked my back.

"Who is minding the shop while you're gone?"

"Leonard and Michael," Kian replied. "I'll have to make some long-term plans for the practice and the rescue organization. And get my dogs up here."

I sat up, "What do you mean?"

"Christina, I'd like to have my dogs with me wherever we end up."

"No, you can't stay here. You're needed in Mintock. The organization is your life."

He sat up and framed my face in his palms. "No. You are my life. I am not going to be without you. You are my woman. We will face this together."

I buried my face in his neck. "I can't do this to you. I cannot allow you to tear your life apart."

"*A grá*," he whispered as he held me in his arms, "my life is torn apart without you."

CHAPTER 42

The following day turned out to be bright and beautiful, and I delighted in sharing my Juneau with Kian. Neither of us spoke about the future or about my current problems. We both relaxed and spent the time just being together. For a late dinner, we found a restaurant off the tourist trail that served mainly to locals. We had a booth in the back, and the waiter left us alone to enjoy our food. The grilled salmon was the freshest I'd ever tasted, and we sat in our booth blissfully eating.

Being with him gave me time to think and formulate a plan in my head. He made me feel brave when he told me about the comments the residents of Mintock had made to him. Of course, everyone had been shocked by the pictures, but no one blamed me. And they told the reporters who had flooded the town that I was a victim of blackmail and had been drugged.

I raised my eyebrow. "And just how did they know that?"

Kian kissed me. "Some stories need to be told."

"You didn't?"

"Maybe."

"Kian!"

"Yes, woman?"

"What am I going to do with you?"

He kissed me again, this time tugging at my lower lip with his teeth. "You'll think of some way to punish your bad boy."

I grinned and reached under the table to the zipper on his slacks. My hand massaged his already swollen cock.

"Oh, I can think of plenty of punishment," I whispered.

His hand held mine. "Careful, once you let the tiger out of his cage, how are you going to get him back in?"

I laughed, "I want to touch you." I squeezed him again.

Kian's eyes closed momentarily, but then he opened them and said, "There will be time later for all the touching you want."

"Now," I insisted.

"What do you mean now?"

"I want to feel your hard flesh between my fingers."

"I'm not going to be able to talk you out of this, am I?"

I shook my head. I loved this feeling he gave me. The danger. The discovery. It made me feel free.

He pressed his lips together and slowly drew his zipper down. "Now do not pull me out, just slide your hand in. And when I say stop, you need to listen, okay?"

I nodded my head with a glint in my eye.

"A child in a candy store," he murmured.

He made a small gasp as I reached into the opening he created for me and grasped his erection. He adjusted his hips to give me easier access and moved the long tablecloth to cover us.

"Damn, baby that feels good," he breathed through his teeth.

His eyes hooded over while I stroked his cock, paying particular attention to rubbing my thumb over the crown.

"Stop Christina," he gasped out, grabbing my arm.

I leaned over, and bit his lip, whispering, "No. I want you to come in my hand."

His body twitched, and I could tell he was trying to keep himself still. What was happening under the tablecloth was another matter completely. His cock jerked in my hand spreading his release inside his pants and through my fingers. After, when I withdrew my hand slowly, he watched me.

With a satisfied glint in my eyes, I held up my hand to him to show him the silky white emission. Pressing my fingers against my lips, my tongue luxuriously licked at them.

"My dessert," I whispered triumphantly.

He pulled my hand to his lips and kissed my palm. Kian whispered, "You are a bad girl, my wonderful woman."

The waiter approached our table. He smiled, "Is everything to your liking?"

Kian grinned, "Everything was perfect. We'll take our dessert to go, and you can bring me the check."

My phone pinged with an incoming text from JuJu. *Sorry forgot to remind u. Tomorrow is Kian's bday. I know he's there w/ u.*

After we had arrived back at the house, we had our dessert and so much more until the wee hours of the morning. Before my head even dropped on Kian's chest from exhaustion, I had my plan formulated in my mind.

CHAPTER 43

I woke before Kian and snuck out of bed to the living room. I needed to move fast before he was up. I called the newspaper in Mintock. I had briefly met the owner's son before the entire mess started. He was an award-winning investigative journalist who wrote at one time for the Washington Post.

"Good morning, Christina Hoffman for David Walker."

The receptionist put me on hold, and I was immediately greeted by David. "Christina, is this really you? You know the world is looking for you?"

I laughed, "Yes, I imagine it is. Do you have a moment to talk?"

"For the biggest news story to hit the internet ever? Absolutely."

"I want to give you my story. I do not want my PR firm involved or my lawyer. Just you and me. Are you interested?"

"You're handing me this Christina? Of course, I'm interested."

We spent the next thirty minutes talking. It was mostly me, but he interjected a couple of questions.

"This is all connected to the dog fight ring? Mayor Busch was involved?" he asked.

"All connected. Will you run with this story David?"

"You know I'm taking this to Washington Post first? Mintock's paper will get it, but I want it in the Post."

"I don't want anything less than where you earned your Pulitzer," I joked.

Next, I called Elizabeth.

"Hey Christina, it's good to hear from you. Are you trying to reach Michael? He's out running all the dogs," she said.

"No, I wanted to talk to you. Would you be interested in selling your cabin to Harry's Hounds? I want to use it as the new headquarters for the organization."

"I won't want to sell it, but I'd be glad to donate it as a lease for zero dollars if the business would like to use it," she immediately replied.

I loved my sister-in-law. "Thank you, Elizabeth, I knew I could count on you."

"Does this mean you're coming home?"

"Yes," I answered.

"Good. We miss you."

My last call was to JuJu.

"Hey, boss."

"Hi, please book the private jet for me. Kian, Koa and I will leave tomorrow. Bring us into San Francisco, I want to meet with Robert on the way home. And have a limo pick us up."

"Consider it done. So you're coming home? It's good to have you back."

I smiled, it was good to be back. I disconnected the call and looked up. Kian was standing in the doorway. And he was naked. I loved when he was naked. He stood there looking sleep-tousled. Oh, I just plain loved him.

He crossed his arms over his chest and leaned against the doorjamb, giving me a cocky eye, "So woman, you've decided to go home? And you're interrupting my vacation by making me leave tomorrow, are you?" His accent became thicker.

I walked toward him and slipped out of my robe. When I reached him, I pushed him backward toward the bed, "We can leave anytime you want, but I thought you'd like to celebrate your birthday first, with me, alone, in this big bed."

He grinned when I pushed him back onto the bed. "Ahh, woman, I think you want me only for my body."

I straddled his hips, "Maybe I do," I teased.

He moved suddenly and before I knew it, I lay across his lap with my butt sticking in the air. "Well now, woman, you'll not be having me until I make your arse good and red for the public performance last night." He smacked my bottom firmly. It tickled but didn't hurt.

"Oh, no you're not. I'm supposed to punish you!" I screamed in a fit of giggles.

Kian rubbed circles on my ass with his palm, then, he spanked me again! His fingers slipped in between my legs.

"Miss Hoffman, I do believe you're enjoying your punishment too much."

I wriggled my butt in the air and felt his erection pushing into my breasts. "I'm very naughty, and I need to be spanked again!" I giggled.

He obliged me, and this time he pushed two fingers inside of me. "Oh sweetlin'," he lay back on the bed, "I think you need to ride this birthday boy's pony."

And I did.

Later in the afternoon, we snoozed in bed surrounded by the remnants of lunch because Kian loved to eat in bed.

I lay on his back and traced the outlines of his tattoo. "You were going to tell me what all the symbols mean that are on your cross."

"They are all about my past, present, and future. Touch a spot," he said.

I pressed the bird in the upper corner.

"That's the dove. It stands for hope. The rabbit next to it is for life. The hands clasped together mean honor. The entire cross is my faith, not only my Christianity, but my faith in man to do right."

"This is beautiful Kian. How about the double spiral?"

"That's my sign of unity. Even though we have polar opposite energies, they must work together. The much larger spiral around it means balance to me. The world has to balance on all the different powers."

"How about the sun and the moon?" I asked as I traced the delicate drawings.

"Those are the transitions between night and day, and to reflect the seasons. The apple is temperance. And the dog is ascension. We can only one day hope to reach their level."

I murmured, "You're right about that. And the three spirals?"

"The last one is navigation. My personal navigation through my life," he rolled over to look at me, "we'll talk about that one another time."

I smiled and nodded. "How about the roses, are they just decorative?"

"No." He smiled. "They represent the women who have been important to me."

"Oh," I cast my eyes down to look at my hands. Why did his tattoo have to represent other women?

He took my hands and kissed them, "*A grá*, they are for my mother, my grandmother, my sister, and my Aunt Maeve. Perhaps I need to add another rose soon."

"Oh," I whispered, and my heart sang.

He pulled me in close, "Now, let's take a nap. I need regain my energy so we can make love all night."

We celebrated our last night in Juneau doing just that.

CHAPTER 44

Who the hell was Scott to dictate my life to me? I was not going to give into him or anyone. I contacted my parents and let them know we were on our way home. The three of them were thoroughly enjoying their island getaway, and they wanted to stay in Hawaii longer. They were happy when I told them they could stay as long as they wanted.

Both Michael and Frank were surprised when I asked them to take down the road barriers. The press could deal with me directly, and if they bothered any of my family or neighbors, I would have them arrested for trespassing.

Robert had successfully worked with the FBI in getting many of the sites located in the United States to pull the photos down. My friends at Find-It! worked to have my name removed from search sites. They had brought the search engine farther than I would have believed and now they could suppress searches for the photos. Who knew that could be done?

David's article on me was a huge victory. I was surprised too when I found the press and the public to be on my side. The charitable boards that I was on did not ask me to step down either. They removed my name from their websites for a while, which was understandable, but after some time had gone by, my name went back up on their board of director's listings.

I was also in regular contact with the FBI. They had placed the case on the back burner suspecting that both the mayor and Scott had disappeared into Mexico.

On the flight down, I finally broached the rebuilding of the Harry's Hounds clinic with Kian. I told him about the massive cash infusion his organization was about to receive. At first, quite naturally, he balked, but then I reminded him gently, the more money the charity had, the more dogs he could rescue.

To use the additional land on the other side of Elizabeth's cabin, we had plans drawn up for a new clinic and state of the art kennels. We weren't just any organization now, we had the funds and the know-how.

My house neared completion, and I was more than ready to move in.

With all the dogs, it was cramped in the cabin. We added to the pack because we were overflowing with testosterone. The sweet dog that had puppies the night of the fire, we named Shauna. Her puppies had homes already lined up, but we decided to keep her. The adorable girl who had mange was taken by Annie and Frank and named her Hayu, which simply meant dog in the Pomo language.

Kian, of course, hesitated about moving into my new house. He said he could easily rebuild his home on the other side of the lake. I told him he could do that, but the dogs were now living with me. If he felt he could do without his dogs then so be it, but if we were going to do a house divorce, I was taking custody of them. He understood my reasoning, and I think loved me more for it.

He told me that I would have to figure out what to do with Siobhan. She was moving to Mintock soon, and he hated to have her in an apartment.

Siobhan met me for lunch at a little Spanish restaurant near Robert's home in San Francisco. She was curious why I would invite her out, but I wouldn't let on about the reason.

We chatted lightly until we ordered.

"So now, are you going to tell me why you invited me to lunch?" she asked after taking a drink of Sangria.

I like that about her. Direct and to the point. We were going to get along fine.

"Yes. My house is going to be finished this weekend. We're finally vacating that tiny cabin of Elizabeth's. And her place will become the new headquarters of Harry's Hounds."

"We?" She stared at me with raised eyebrows.

"Yes, we. Kian is moving in with me, and we're taking all the dogs."

She laughed, "Well, I'm glad for that. You are good for Kian. You keep him from becoming so morose. You know he has quite the dark side to him. I'm sure you've heard the story about his scarring."

"Yes, I have. He also keeps me grounded and real. When you have a lot of money, a person can become unrealistic in their expectations. I try to use my money for good, but many times I'm shielded from the dark part of the world." I explained.

"Fair enough. Now I'm guessing, we are here to discuss me. I don't have to move in with Kian. I like the little town he's now calling home, and I want to spend time with him. There's ten years' difference between us, and even though my family is close, we're at the opposite end of the spectrum. I couldn't spend a lot of time with him when he was growing up. I want to now."

I nodded, "I don't question your motives for wanting to stay with your brother, whatever reason you have is valid."

"I'm planning on opening a dance school in Mintock. There isn't one. It will give some purpose to my life in retirement even though I will continue to consult with the San Francisco Company. I'll be judging new talent they bring in and handling some of their choreography. I need to keep my toes in my one true love."

"Those are great plans. Kian still has his property. He wants to rebuild the house and have you move there. You could design it any way you'd like. While it's being built, you and your children can stay with us. There is more than enough room in the house. I think Kian would like it."

At first, she gave me a look of disbelief and then was suspicious. "Christina, I don't need charity."

"No. Siobhan, you mistake me. You said you didn't spend a lot of time together when he was growing up. Now is your chance. The new house can be used as an investment for Kian, so he doesn't feel like he's living off my money."

Her face still showed disbelief. "I don't understand why you're doing this?"

"Because I love him. He loves you. It's simple math, A plus B equals C."

She looked at me for a long moment. She reached across the table with her hand held out. "Okay, you've got a deal."

My face lit up with a smile, and I took her hand. We shook on it.

She looked as if she didn't quite believe what she had just done.

CHAPTER 45

The night we moved into the big house, we threw a small party. The usual gang was invited, plus my besties. At the last moment, Kian called to let me know he'd be late. He had another rescue dog come into the hospital, and he had to see to her comfort first. I was used to this by now, and I looked at the four-legged crew who surrounded me in the kitchen as they waited for dinner. Tammy, who was visiting for the weekend, helped me assemble all the dog dishes as our family and friends arrived at the house.

It wasn't going to be anything fancy tonight, just a potluck, where everyone brought dishes. According to Annie, it was a Pomo Tribe tradition. Michael, Frank, and Don built a big bonfire on the beach, and Elizabeth and Debi were responsible for the lighting of the torches. I couldn't wait for summer to hit.

Siobhan arrived with Robert and Gary from San Francisco. They had carpooled. I even invited someone new. David, the journalist who helped me with the article for the newspaper. His son, Luke worked for Harry's Hounds as a volunteer and was about to be made our first part-time employee.

We all were in the great room. It had been warm enough during the day, so the glass wall was opened. It made the room feel like we were outdoors.

"Okay everyone, this isn't the official toast yet," I said holding up my champagne glass next to the doorway leading to the kitchen. "We'll wait for Kian to get here and then Annie can give the house her blessing. But I'd like to thank every…"

Suddenly, every face turned from smiles to absolute horror. A set of arms grabbed me roughly from behind! My glass crashed to the floor. I heard a harsh voice in my ear, as he pulled me into his body.

"Everyone stays perfectly still!" my captor called out.

One of my enormous kitchen knives pointed at my chest. Frank reached for his holstered side arm very slowly.

"Enough of that." The man holding the weapon waved it at Frank.

"Oh shit," I whispered slowly. It was Scott

I could smell his foul breath, he reeked of alcohol and sweat.

"You are a stupid bitch. You didn't pay me for the wonderful pictures I took of you." He laughed viciously and pointed the knife at me again, this time I could feel the tip against my skin. "You had a good time that night. I loved every minute of it. I even got off on you."

My skin crawled with the thought of it.

Michael stepped toward him, "Com'on Binder. Put the knife down. Nothing can be solved by this. You're outnumbered. You're not going to get out of here."

"Shut the fuck up Michael. You know I never liked you. Always so holier than thou. Always better than the rest of us, saving your little animals. Shit, eat a cow occasionally and grow some balls. If you step any closer, I'm going to slice up your sister before any of you can get to me. She'll be an ugly, bloody, and dead mess."

Everyone was frozen in fear. I felt a small trickle of blood go down my chest inside my sweater. I twisted in Scott's arms, and he pressed the knife firmly against me.

"Stay still you bitch. I'm warning you, or you're going to fucking die," he growled.

"What do you want, you bastard? What is it that you want?" I shouted.

"I sent your fucking lawyer an email about ten minutes ago. The email has a foreign bank account number, and I want him to wire transfer the five million dollars into the account," he instructed.

"This isn't a movie, you idiot, it's not as simple as that. How do you think you're going to get away from here?" I was angry and shaking. He dug the knife into my skin, and it hurt.

"Shut the fuck up. Stupid bitch! I know what I'm doing. I'll get out of here because you are my fucking hostage!" He pointed the blade at Robert again, "Do it!"

Robert reached for his cell phone and called up his email. He started to tap on the face in rapid succession.

"Don't think you're going to get away with anything," Scott yelled. I want you to slide your phone over to me when you're done. I want to see the acknowledgment of the transfer." He looked at Frank, "Take your gun out of your holster with two fingers and slide it over to me, very slowly. I swear if any of you do anything, she will be gone quickly."

Frank did as he was instructed. When he straightened up, I saw a glint in Frank's eyes. What? There was a message there.

Scott bent over slowly to pick up the gun from the floor. His movement stirred the air slightly, and I smelled a very familiar scent. Lavender!

As he slowly came up, I twisted, and with all the force I had in me, my heel came down hard on his instep. Thank goodness for four-inch stilettos! Scott let out a furious howl, and he grabbed me tightly just as Kian tackled him from behind. Scott was a big man, but Kian was larger. All three of us went down hard on the floor with me on the bottom.

The flurry of activity surrounding us was quick. The gun skidded away, and I could roll away as Kian somehow lifted Scott off me. They grappled for the knife that Scott still clung to.

I wanted to bury my face. I didn't want to see Kian get hurt, but it was clear Kian had the upper hand and punched the shit out of Scott. The knife clattered to the floor just as Frank picked up the gun. All three men, Michael, Don, and Robert, pulled Scott away from the pummeling he was receiving from Kian.

Don pulled Kian back, "Enough. We have him!"

Kian almost shook him off and went for Scott again, but he caught the look on my face and quickly kneeled next to me. "*A grá*, are you okay? He didn't hurt you. Oh, sweet Jesus, where is the blood coming from?" His hands were on the front of my sweater, patting at me.

I took his hands in mine. "I'm okay. Are you alright?"

He pulled me to my feet and enfolded me in his big strong arms. "*A grá*," he whispered. Kian turned his head to glare at Scott. "You don't touch my woman. Ever."

Frank handcuffed Scott and read him his rights. Annie had already called a squad car, and Frank led Scott outside.

Siobhan put her arm around me. "You don't lead a boring life do you?"

I smiled weakly. "Not of my choosing."

David approached the two of us, "This is going to make quite a story Christina. You helped take down your blackmailer."

Siobhan looked at David as if noticing him for the first time. An odd expression passed between them both.

"I need to sit down. I need a drink. Robert, please tell me you didn't wire five million dollars to his off-shore bank account." I said as Kian pulled up a chair for me.

Robert laughed heartily, "I would say quite the opposite." He showed me his phone. I laughed too when I saw he had been texting the FBI agents.

"Where are the dogs?" I suddenly realized there were no dogs.

Everyone looked blankly except Kian. "Scott locked them in the garage," he said.

"They didn't bark?" I asked. "Not even Koa?"

"He had what looked like a bunch of steaks with him, I saw Styrofoam wrappers all over the garage floor when I came in. The dogs went after the food. That's how I knew something was wrong. He was probably hiding in that room you call a pantry."

Frank came back into the house. "We had him in the squad car for three minutes, and he started singing like a canary. He has already implicated Busch and wants a deal. Coward."

Michael came in from the kitchen carrying several bottles of Krug Clos du Mesnil Champagne. "Did you want to use the 2000 tonight Christina for the toast?"

I nodded, "Thank you, Michael, will you pour?"

He grinned, "I'd be delighted. It's not every day I get to drink a one-thousand-dollar bottle of champagne."

Annie clapped her hands, "What a treat! I'm looking forward to this!"

Michael poured champagne for everyone, except Elizabeth and Tammy, who had to settle for apple cider. We were ready for Annie's blessing.

Annie lifted her glass, "Christina and Kian, you have already found passion and love, may this house give you peace and joy. I hope your days here are filled with light and that you make good memories. May there always be bread on your table and wine in your cup. Bless this house!"

Everyone, in turn, raised their glass in a toast and drank.

Kian lifted his glass as he recited an old Irish blessing,

"May there always be work for your hands to do,

May your purse always hold a coin or two.

May the sun always shine warm on your windowpane,

May a rainbow be certain to follow each rain.

May the hand of a friend always be near you,

And may God fill your heart with gladness to cheer you."

I raised my glass in gratitude. "Thank you, my family." I sipped on the champagne. "Mmmm… quite tasty."

My new family didn't allow the violent intrusion to mar the evening. We celebrated the new house and our friendships on this special night.

CHAPTER 46

Kian worried me. His nightmares continued. With almost one a week, he would end up leaving the bed and sometimes he would not be able to go back to sleep afterward. It was evident the dream was taking its toll on him.

He confided they had never been quite this bad. Usually he could go several months between the nightmares, but lately, because we could rescue more dogs, they seemed to occur more frequently.

His parents had him in counseling when he was young, but it only brought him so far. Consciously, he understood why the dreams happened, but he couldn't control his subconscious, and they kept reoccurring. I knew he would not be able to go on forever like this. I was almost afraid for his sanity. He would be so ripped apart when he woke from them, and all I could do was hold him in my arms.

One night, several months after we moved into the house, and he had a particularly bad episode, we lay in bed afterward. I didn't know what to say. I didn't know how to soothe him any longer.

"Did any of your therapists have any ideas on how to combat these nightmares?" I asked.

He blew out a big breath. "No not really…" he paused, "except one doctor suggested traveling back to Ireland to confront my uncle."

I sat up, "Did you do that?"

"Yes, sure. We went back to Ireland on a regular basis. I mean, I have family there. My aunts and uncles on my mother's side and my brother are all there."

"Did you see your uncle, the one who beat you?"

"No. I never want to see the bastard again. I'm afraid if I did, I would kill him. I have it in my heart."

I placed my hand on his chest and was comforted by the steady rhythm. "So you never have confronted him."

"No," he said, and the accent became thick again. "I would definitely kill him. And then where would that put me? In prison. I have no wish to be Paddy's new girlfriend."

I giggled. "Kian, you're not killing anyone. Goodness, you wouldn't."

"Yes. Yes, I would. Cut my uncle down where he stands. That's for sure."

"Stop it. I have an idea. Let's go to Ireland. I've never been. You could show me your hometown. I'd love to meet your aunt and get to know the woman who creates the amazing lavender soap. Then you could confront your uncle, beat the shit out of him, leave him for dead and be done with it."

"A nice neat package you're suggesting there, are you? We are not going to Ireland. And I am not confronting the bastard."

I leaned over and kissed his lips, "Please? For me?" I begged a little then proceeded to chew delicately on his bottom lip, just the way he liked it.

"Woman!" He smacked me on the bottom, hard, just the way I liked it. "We are not going to Ireland! That's final!"

"Oh, I think we are." I pulled the covers back and straddled him quickly, and sat firmly on his growing erection. I moved my hips against him slowly.

He pulled my nightgown over my head. "No, we are not."

He palmed both of my breasts, rubbing against my tight nipples. He knew that would be my downfall.

I arched my back in pleasure and threw my head back as he sat up and sucked each nipple in turn. "Oh yes," I cried, "Oh yes," my hands tangled in his hair. "Yes, ..." I let out a whoosh of breath as he lifted my hips with his hands and then firmly seated me on his thick cock, "... you are."

After we had made love, we collapsed together, our legs and arms intertwined, and no one would ever be able to separate us.

As we fell asleep together, I whispered in his ear, "You are going."

He whispered back, "Okay."

CHAPTER 47

The nonstop flight from San Francisco to Dublin took over ten hours. I was amazed I got Kian on the plane. He balked at first, then I pouted, and he came around.

His family lived near Malahide Village located just north of Dublin. He explained that the village and surrounding areas had been an important maritime and agriculture center for centuries. His aunt was so excited to learn we were coming she wanted to pick us up at the airport. We vetoed the idea preferring to rent a car so we could see the countryside.

In the late afternoon, we pulled in front of his aunt's farmhouse in a still rural area on the outskirts of the village.

"I do feel like a fish out of water," Kian remarked. "I don't believe I'm still Irish. I feel like I'm an imposter." His accent was thicker than normal but still understandable.

"At least I can understand you. I haven't been able to recognize what anyone is saying here," I said.

He laughed as he put the car into park and climbed out. The wind was whipping around him. The house was a charming home with rock walls and a lovely garden surrounded by hedgerows in the front. A small arched gate covered with climbing red roses welcomed us.

"A lot of slang I'm not familiar with either," he commented.

His aunt came running out of the house. "Kian!" She flung her arms wide, and he caught her up and swung her around.

"Hello, Aunt Maeve!"

She held him away from her, "Oh my boy, you are a sight for these poor eyes. You're looking so grand too! Come now introduce me to your beautiful lady."

Kian grinned widely, "Aunt Maeve, this is Christina."

I held my hand out to shake hers. She shook her head, "No, my girl. Come here and give your Aunt Maeve a proper greeting." She wrapped her arms around me and squeezed hard.

I hugged her back, perhaps not as hard. I didn't want to break her. She was a small woman, only coming up to Kian's mid-chest. She had a fiery mass of thick red curls, which she pulled back with several clips and combs. I could see she'd have trouble keeping all that hair tamed down. Her face was full of freckles, and while I expected green eyes, her eyes were the exact match of Kian's. Her hands were strong and looked like they had a lifetime of use. It was evident she wasn't afraid of hard work.

A tall man walked out of the house followed by four huge white dogs. The man wore the white collar of the church, and he was almost a duplicate of Kian. Perhaps a bit thinner, but the height was there, and the dark hair accompanied the blue eyes.

"Seamus! How are you? You're looking fit enough! Come let me introduce you to Christina."

They hugged warmly, and he said, "Ah, Kian you are looking well. How is Ma doing? Last I heard she had a bad cold."

"She's in good health enough. I spoke with her just before we left, she said to make sure we take Christina to your parish church."

"Aye, that we will do. And, this must be the fair Christina. I've heard a lot about you and your adventures. It's nice to finally meet you."

I smiled, "Thank you, and I've heard of your adventures too, Father."

He laughed and winked. "And all of them true, I've no doubt. Now there is none of this Father stuff here at the farmhouse. Here I am just Seamus." He gave me a generous hug.

"I have tea all laid out for us. Come let's get out of the wind and go into the house. We had quite the storm last night, which was good because now everything is washed new for you." Maeve said as she wrapped her arms around our waists and led us into the house while the dogs were jumping around.

I bent to pet one. "Are these your famous Irish Wolfhounds?"

She laughed, "I don't know about famous, but they are mine. In a bit we'll go to the back of the house, I have a bitch, Ailbe, who gave birth several weeks ago. She had twelve pups, a record around here. This is her quiet time. I take the pups out to the barn so they can play with the other dogs and give her a bit of a rest."

"Ach, Aunt Maeve don't be so humble," Seamus added. "Her dogs have won awards, and they are especially prized because they are white."

"Now my boy, there's no good coming from bragging." She smiled, "But I do have to admit I'm proud of my hounds."

The house was warm and quaint. Exactly what I would have pictured it to be. There was a fire in the hearth to ward off the late summer chill.

"Seamus, take the dogs to the barn, please. They'll just be underfoot here and start begging for sweets. We can't have our family veterinarian think we give them sweets, now can we?" she said.

"Now Aunt Maeve, I know perfectly well that you spoil your dogs. I'll try to turn a blind eye," Kian winked.

"I don't want Christina to get the wrong idea then. Go help your brother get these beasts out of here." She shooed both men away. "Christina and I will get the tea, I set it to brewing, and it should be ready."

She linked arms with me and led me to a huge kitchen with a large round oak table, which sat in the middle. It was laid out with small tea sandwiches, little finger cakes, fruit, dark bread, cheese, and butter. She put two full teapots on the table. The men joined us a short time later, and after washing up at the sink sat with us at the table.

"It is so good to have two of my sister's boys here with me. Kian, I miss you terribly. I wish you would visit more often," she said as she poured tea for all of us.

We all bowed our heads as Seamus said a short blessing.

As we ate, and they reminisced, I learned more about the family. When the tea was gone, Aunt Maeve called for the Irish whiskey.

Kian fetched it from the pantry and pulled down glasses from the cupboard. "So you're still drinking Killbeggan I see."

"Of course, and only on a Saturday night mind you. I know when and how much I can drink."

He poured shots. After we had toasted to everyone's health several times, Aunt Maeve continued down the road she had been on with her stories.

"My one wish was that my husband Jack and I would have had *leanbh*." She paused to lean over to me and whisper, "babies," then continued in a normal voice. "But it was not meant for us. And now with Jack gone ten years back, I won't even have grandchildren." She looked pointedly at the three of us. "And with the priest here, you know, I'm never going to see any *leanbh* from him."

Seamus laughed, "I hope not Aunt Maeve."

She then turned her attention to the two of us. I knew what was coming. I wanted to roll my eyes badly, but I didn't. Elizabeth would have been so proud.

"So you two. You need to start thinking about children. I can see Christina is older than you Kian, and while I have no problems with that, there is a clock ticking for her. So, you need to get with it! The next time you visit me, you better bring some little ones."

Kian laughed and hugged his aunt. "So you want more than one by then?"

"Don't you be a cheeky monkey, my boy," she said laughing warmly.

We sat into the evening, and when Seamus excused himself to leave, I suddenly felt weary and tired to the bone.

"I expect to see all three of you at mass tomorrow morning," he said, stealing some cookies from the table and slipping them into his jacket pocket. "Don't stay up all evening gabbing."

It rained most of the night, and the wind howled. Kian and I were snuggled in bed together. At first, I thought Aunt Maeve wouldn't take too kindly to us sleeping together, but after Seamus had left, she winked at me broadly and said she was perfectly aware of how babies were made. Yes, I turned beet red when Kian slapped me on the bottom and said we better get up to the room and start baking. And I thought my Greek family was crazy!

Sunday morning brought beautiful blue skies, and by the afternoon, the breeze had turned warm. Kian had been out of sorts most of the day. I knew what was on his mind. His uncle. We had crossed an ocean and flown ten hours, and he still wasn't ready for the confrontation. Even though I was worried he would back out, I wouldn't push him. It was a decision he had to make for himself.

Aunt Maeve had told us there would be Irish stew and rhubarb crumble for Sunday dinner and not to eat too much when we went out for a drive during the afternoon. Kian had been tossing and catching the car keys, and suddenly he seized them and grabbed my hand.

"Let's go. Aunt Maeve," he called out, "we'll be back by six for dinner!"
She called from the kitchen, "Have fun!"

He led the way to the car, and after he had tucked me into the front passenger seat, he went around to the right-hand side of the car. I didn't think I would ever get used to driving in the opposite lane.

"Where are we going?" I asked.

He didn't answer, but somehow I knew and decided to keep my mouth shut. We drove about thirty minutes, and the area became more rural, with homes further apart. Kian finally turned and drove down a long driveway. We stopped in front of a large manor house. Though obviously old, it had been kept up. The gardens around the home were groomed impeccably.

Kian looked over at me as he squeezed my hand. "You can stay here in the car, but I'd really like you to come with me."

I didn't say a word, but only nodded my head in agreement. He looked terrible. I second guessed myself, was this a good idea after all?

We walked up to the massive door. I wondered how large the key would be to fit in the lock.

He pressed the bell ringer, and we could hear a chime behind the door. We waited several moments and saw the door slowly open.

A small gray-haired wiry man appeared behind the door. He peered at us with surprise reading on his face. I was shocked, there was no family resemblance at all. The man didn't even look like the pictures I had seen of Kian's father.

"Master Kian. Is it you? I canna believe this! Wait until I tell the Lord you're here!" He opened the door and ushered us into the huge two-storied entryway.

We heard a rough voice coming from the room next to us. A man stood in the doorway. There was his uncle. There was no mistaking it. He was a large burly man but had Kian's finely chiseled features.

"Who is it?" When he saw us, his eyes narrowed. He sneered, and there was an ugliness about him. "What are you doing here boy? After all these years, are you back for another beating?" Terrible cruelty and malice surrounded him.

Kian stared directly at him. He balled his fists and his entire body tensed. "I came here to kick your ass, you bastard."

His uncle sneered, "You and what army? Yeah, I heard about you. A high and mighty veterinarian are you now. You always were a crybaby. I do whatever I want with my dogs and my land, boy."

I thought it was extremely unwise of this man to bait his nephew like this. His uncle was a big man, but Kian was taller, more muscular, and had the advantage of youth on his side. This man's clock was about to be cleaned by his nephew. Kian's body was primed for a fight, and his uncle was no match for him.

His uncle, after he had postured so grandly, appeared to have thought better of it and stepped back one pace.

Kian didn't say a word. He only looked down at the man who caused him years of pain. Suddenly, I saw his body visibly calm. His face showed immense control, and he relaxed his hands.

"You are such a pathetic little man. Always beating those who are weaker than you. I bet it's the only way you can lord it over everyone. Let me tell you, you're not my superior. You are a shell. There is no life in you, only hate and meanness. All these years I thought you were someone to fight. I was wrong. Very wrong. I can see now that you are not worth the effort. I'll not waste even one drop of my sweat on you."

He took my hand in his and led me outside to the car. He didn't turn back to look at his uncle who now stood on the threshold blustering about something and calling his nephew a coward. The man was wrong, Kian was the strongest man I had ever seen.

He turned the car back toward the highway. He was sweating and shaking. Pulling the car over he drew me into his arms and murmured, "Thank you. Thank you. Thank you, Christina."

"I didn't do anything."

Holding my face in his hands, he kissed me. "You did more for me than you'll ever realize. Thank you for being there with me. *A grá.*"

On the drive back to his aunt's house, the mood and spirit seemed magically to lift. After we had returned, Aunt Maeve told us dinner would be another hour. She suggested we take a walk and enjoy the lavender hillsides behind the barn.

In Ireland, everything was so green and lush. We sat down on the grass and looked out at the acres of lavender fields his aunt cultivated.

Kian picked up my hand and played with my fingers.

"I want to ask you something," he murmured.

"You do?" I said lightly and then saw his serious expression.

He reached into his pocket and pulled out a small velvet box. "I know I'm supposed to get down on one knee to ask you this, but you're not that kind of girl, are you Christina?"

I shook my head slowly and swallowed hard.

"I had this box in my pocket when I arrived in Juneau, but it wasn't the right time. It's the right time now," he whispered

He opened the box and nestled inside was a gold ring with a diamond in the center adjoined by two emeralds on either side. The setting was old-fashioned, one that would have been around in the early twentieth century.

He continued, "This was my grandmother's engagement ring. After I had been beaten, she gave it to my mother to give to me one day. She said that she wanted a hero's woman to have it."

I gasped, "Oh Kian, it's beautiful."

"I was hoping you'd like it because I want it to be yours. Christina, will you marry me? I don't have anything else to offer you. All I have is my heart," he whispered.

Tears ran down my cheeks, "Oh, my champion, that is the one thing I need. Yes, I will marry you."

He cupped my face in his hands, first kissing my tears and then my lips. He slipped the ring on my finger, and I didn't question how it fit. The moment was too magical.

Suddenly, we heard the side barn door slam open and out ran a dozen white puppies! They came rolling and tumbling toward us, and I saw Seamus standing by the door.

"Did ya ask her?" he shouted.

"She said yes!" Kian yelled back.

Seamus called for his aunt, "Maeve, you better get out here, we have a new member of the family!"

Puppies surrounded us now, climbing over us and clamoring for attention. I realized I had known all along Kian was my dream come true.

EPILOGUE

Harry's Hounds became a world-class animal rescue organization. Kian didn't want to worry about the administration, and so, the Foundation took care of the business aspect, hiring additional part-time veterinarians and front office help. All the donations we received went directly to the care of the animals. With Michael and Elizabeth's assistance, we could broaden our scope to include animal conservation efforts.

Former Mayor Busch was apprehended in San Diego after Scott turned as a witness for the prosecution of the dog fight ring, so Scott received a lesser sentence for his part in that crime. It didn't help him much, though. For the blackmail, extortion, arson, rape, and attempted murder charges, he received a full sentence that ensured he'd be behind bars the rest of his life.

I was now an experienced wedding planner. With Aunt Maeve's prompting, Kian and I agreed, Ireland was the perfect place for a wedding. We decided to have the wedding celebration the following summer and fly everyone to Dublin. It was my big fat Irish, Greek, Cajun, German, wedding. We filled all the local hotels, and it was the biggest event to hit the village in years.

Putting it out for a year didn't bother us, because sometimes it is fortunate to have a priest in the family, especially a progressive thinking one. Right after Kian proposed to me, unbeknownst to the entire family back at home, Seamus married us there in the middle of the lavender fields, with Aunt Maeve and a neighbor as witnesses. We never told a soul, and no one was any the wiser when a year later, Kian's brother again pronounced us husband and wife, this time at the parish church.

We made Aunt Maeve euphoric too when we arrived back in Ireland for the nuptials because I was three months pregnant with twins! Kian had conveniently forgotten to tell me twins ran on his mother's side of the family.

Our second marriage ceremony was beautiful, but nothing mattered to me more than the man who stood next to me. Kian finally kissed me, Koa, who sat by our feet, barked loudly. This created hoots and yells inside the tiny church. There was nothing sacred with our family.

The reception was held on Aunt Maeve's property right next to the blooming lavender fields. The summer night was warm and the air fragrant. Kian and I slipped away after the party was well underway and walked up to

the hill behind the barn. We sat looking down at the lights and listened to the Celtic and Cajun music playing, which sounded a lot alike.

"We have a lot of relatives," I said as I leaned back against Kian's chest.

"That we do, but it's all about family, isn't it?" He wrapped me snuggly in his arms.

I nodded.

"How are you feeling? Any more nausea?"

"No. I think I was just nervous this morning. I really haven't had any morning sickness yet."

"I know, but it can start at any time. I don't know what you were nervous about," he laughed, "we've been married for almost a year."

"It has been an excellent year. I love being married to you."

He brushed my neck with his lips, "*A grá*. You are my queen. You are my path. My navigation. We did not come together by accident. There are no coincidences. Everything happens for a reason."

I turned in his arms, "Is that what navigation means on your tattoo? Destiny?"

Kian smiled, "Aye. Our destiny. I believe we were meant to be together. You are the day to my night. I have a surprise for you." He unbuttoned his shirt. "I had it done for you a couple of days ago when we arrived."

I sat back while he opened his shirt. He revealed a large red rose tattoo on his left chest. I hadn't seen it because we were staying in separate rooms at the hotel. Above the rose, I could just make out the written script.

"*Christina, thabharfainn fuil mo chroí duit.*" I read quietly. "You marked your body for me."

"Just as you have marked your body for me." He placed his hands on my stomach. "Our babies will forever celebrate our destiny in the most beautiful way. The love I have for you knows no bounds, Christina."

"*A grá*," I whispered and kissed him.

Koa barked and ran up to us.

"Where did you come from?" Kian laughed petting him. "You're killing my timing here."

Seamus came into view, "They're over here."

Michael followed him, "Just as I thought. Making out again. Kian already has his shirt off," he laughed and squatted in front of us. "People have been missing you!"

"Com'on Michael, give me a break. She's my wife now," Kian laughed.

Michael stood and helped us to our feet. "Don't give me that, you've been married all along!"

Surprised, I asked, "What? How did you know?"

Seamus grinned, "Now lass, you'll learn, there are no secrets among the Irish. Aunt Maeve told Ma, who blabbed it to Siobhan, and she gossiped it to Elizabeth. Good news gets around!"

"And everyone kept it a secret?" I said flustered.

Michael chuckled, "Only from you and Kian. We were all afraid if you knew we knew, you'd cancel the free trip to Ireland. Come back to the party." He slapped Kian on the back, "Take good care of my sister."

I watched Seamus and Michael amble down the hill while Kian buttoned his shirt.

Kian took my hand in his, "Ready?" With Koa under our feet, he pulled me against him and gave me one of his kisses that always made me melt.

"As long as I have you."

The End.

ABOUT THE AUTHOR

C. J. Corbin writes sizzling contemporary romances, which leave you breathless!

She lives in Southern California with her cocker spaniels, Cooper and Isabella. An avid wildlife conservationist, she donates a percentage of her book sales to animal conservancy projects. C. J. relaxes by always being SASSY, and by blasting alternative rock music through her headset, while shopping online to feed a shameless addiction to Coach bags.

The latest news on her books can be found on her website CJCorbin.com

Made in the USA
Monee, IL
21 May 2021